To James,
I hope you love these — go dive sometime!

The Cavern Kings

The Cavern Kings
Jeff Bauer
Copyright Jeff Bauer 2012
Version 2/10/2014
Cover photograph by Michael Browning

Also by Jeff Bauer

Wakulla Bones
Sadie Sapiens

DEDICATION

This book is dedicated to every diver that ever became entranced with the underwater world of cave diving, those still living and those who lost their lives pioneering, pursing and improving the sport.

ACKNOWLEDGMENTS

This book could not have been written without the loving support of my wife, the critical eye of my cave diving instructors, the patience of my dive buddies and the beauty of underwater caves.

Chapter 1

Josh looked across the faces of the six students as Kathy began her final dive briefing on the bow of the fifty-foot dive boat *Minerva*. The weather was typical for midday of midsummer in North Florida—clear bright blue sky offshore with distant thunderheads building along the shoreline. The boat gently rocked against the mild surface current from the attachment point of the anchor line at the tip of the bow. Josh could smell the heavy perfume of salt air.

Kathy was in her mid-forties, attractive and stocky with shoulder-length brown hair done up in a business ponytail, grey eyes and the look of a woman in her element. She wore the bottom half of a lightweight full body neoprene wet suit, black with vertical yellow stripes from her waist down to her black matching dive booties. The arms to the top half of her wet suit were tied at her waist, revealing the top of a one piece blue bathing suit.

"OK, guys, this is your final dive required to earn your scuba certification." said Kathy. "You've already dove this shipwreck once so it should feel familiar. Think of this dive as your final weaning from Josh and me. We are looking for the complete package on this dive – can you, as a group, correctly execute the dive without relying on us. We will be merely observers unless we have to intervene to keep you on task." she said, nodding towards Josh. Josh admired how Kathy always included him by using "we," even though she was the instructor and him merely her assistant.

Kathy continued. "We've covered the parameters of the dive. Like before, I will jump in first, then each of you will enter as buddy pairs and Josh will be in the back.

"This time, though, I expect each of *you* to keep track of your buddy, time and depth and decide when it's time to come back up. If Josh or I has to remind you it's time to leave or that you are too deep then you aren't ready to dive without an instructor just yet – this dive will test if you have the awareness to become a certified diver."

Josh studied the expressions of the six students as they listened to Kathy, lined up and standing against the bow railing. Jason, about his age, stood tall and slender with short sandy brown hair, tan skin, deep brown eyes and an easy smile. Next to him stood Kyle, his dive buddy and friend. Kyle was shorter, thin and fair skinned with black unruly hair, and a lopsided grin on his face.

Josh knew both were very comfortable in the water and easily mastered all of the scuba skills. His job was to keep an eye on the class and these two looked like the overconfident type that might wander off and not stay a part of the group. He'd have to keep an eye on them.

Next were Max and Cynthia, a father and teenage daughter buddy team. Max was about Kathy's age, well-tanned, fit with a receding blonde hairline and crystal blue eyes. Cynthia was the young female expression of her father's physique, with the same skin and eye color. Her long blonde hair was secured in a hair bungee.

Josh recalled Cynthia having trouble putting her diving mask back on underwater during the pool sessions until Kathy had suggested she pull back her hair and keep it away from her face. Josh had the least to worry about with these two; both were strong and confident swimmers and the father hadn't tried to play scuba instructor to his daughter. They would follow instructions and do just fine.

The last buddy team was Jane and Stan Cooper, a married couple in their mid-thirties. Stan was short, slightly overweight with skin splotchy from exposure to sun, eyes that squinted in the sun and a bald head sporting a bright red sunburned scalp. His wife, Jane, was also a bit on the heavy side with short straight black hair streaked with premature grey. She clung to the side of her husband and Josh knew he had to keep an eye on these two.

All during the class Stan had been a know-it-all, confusing his wife and straining Kathy's considerable diplomatic skills. Josh judged the husband overconfident and the wife under confident about their ability to scuba dive. This was the group he'd really have to stay near and keep an eye out. So far, though, they had done all the tasks Kathy had asked them.

This usually was the easiest of the dives during a scuba certification class since everybody knew what to expect but he had assisted in enough classes to know to look for potential problems in students before they ever entered the water. He looked back at Kathy as she neared the end of her briefing.

"So, what's our max depth and max time to dive according to the tables?" quizzed Kathy.

Max nudged his daughter, Cynthia, who squeaked "Er, sixty feet and no more than twenty minutes?"

Kathy nodded. "And what is the minimum PSI?"

"Start to leave from the bottom with no less than 1,000 PSI in our tank," said Kyle.

"Correct. Don't forget our safety stop at fifteen to twenty feet for three minutes." Satisfied her questions were answered correctly she dismissed the class and sent them to the back of the boat so they could prepare for the dive.

"Well, what do you think, Josh?" said Kathy, a slight smile on her face.

"Think I'll need to keep an eye on Jane and Stan. I still think she's a bit scared of being out in the open ocean," said Josh.

"True; be sure to hang behind and above as usual so you can spot the problems before they develop," advised Kathy.

"You bet – the usual drill," finished Josh as they turned to walk towards the stern using the walkways that flanked the superstructure of the dive boat.

Josh glanced over at Elise, his girlfriend, stretched out on the upper deck bench sunbathing in a yellow bikini, her golden skin radiant as she stretched languorously on her red and white beach towel.

Elise was a slender, petite, beautiful woman with spectacular green eyes and short black hair. She sensed his eyes on him and opened her eyes to watch Josh pass by.

She reached down and gave him a slow motion high five, the sensation of her hand rubbing his sent a tingle down his spine as he passed by.

Ten minutes later Josh splashed into the warm Gulf of Mexico water feet first and fins wide, hands holding mask and weight belt buckle, spine straight.

Always want to look good for the students thought Josh as he surfaced and touched his fist to his head, indicating he was OK to the boat divemaster. The six foot drop from the dive boat into the inviting warm blue water was always fun. He could tell the deep blue and purple of the water on the surface meant that the water was clear and the visibility would be excellent.

He grabbed the bright yellow nylon line floating alongside the boat and began to pull himself up towards the bow, to the anchor line. He placed his face in the water and the visibility was as promised, more than sixty feet, good enough for him to make out all six students at various locations along the anchor line, their exhaust bubbles trailing upward.

He could make out Stan waiting patiently by Jane as she carefully descended the line, equalizing her ears due to the increasing water pressure slowly and deliberately every few feet.

Excellent so far – Stan's waiting for her like he should.

A school of palm-sized triangular-shaped Atlantic spade fish swam by, sun sparkling off of their white, grey, silver and black colored scales. A four foot long barracuda had taken residence underneath the boat, swimming stationary as it faced into the current looking for prey.

The other four divers were standing on the top of the wheelhouse of the shipwreck, forty five feet below, where the anchor line was chained to a large cleat. The wreck sat upright on the sandy bottom, bathed in blue-green light and covered in schools of bait fish. The one hundred eighty five foot former supply ship sat intact upright in the sand covered with a rich patina of purple, yellow, green and grey soft corals, the colors muted due to the depth of the water.

Josh saw Kathy hovering nearby, positioned so she could watch the cluster of four near her and the Coopers slowly descend to the bow.

Josh felt a sharp tug on his left fin and a sharper pull on the regulator hose, which ripped the regulator out of his mouth. Frank and Jon, his best friends and diving buddies, rocketed past him on the anchor line. Frank deliberately kicked Josh's mask with his fin as a final insult. The two friends descended to the wreck and disappeared over the bow, heading to the sandy bottom.

Josh just smiled, retrieved his regulator, popped it into his mouth and looked back towards the Coopers as they reached Kathy and the other divers. His friends often joined him on checkout dives so they could taunt him while he worked and enjoy the wholesale dive boat fee Josh arranged for them.

It would be fun to just poke around the wreck with those guys but, hey, I'm getting paid to do what I love, he thought.

Josh hovered ten feet above the group as Kathy herded them towards the wheelhouse of the boat. The class hung together in buddy pairs, loosely swimming in the same direction. At this depth the dominant color was green. Green of every shade and nuance rippling with the light filtered by depth and the wave action above cast hues across humans, shipwreck, wildlife and the dark green gloom in the distance.

It was interesting how new divers always hung close together when they learned the buddy system. Josh looked for the occasional glance by the students at their depth and time gauges.

Good sign.

Kathy slowed her pace and allowed the three pairs to swim past her. Her arms were relaxed and she kicked just enough to counteract the mild current. The students, by comparison, had much more leg and arm motion and the extra bubbles escaping from their regulators demonstrated to Josh the difference between an experienced, relaxed and confident diver and diving newcomers.

He knew over time they would also learn to slow down and be more economical in their motions as the key to a great scuba experience was to be relaxed and breathe slowly. Josh marveled at Kathy's form, despite her being fifteen years his senior. He knew she would use less air than either him or the students.

I'll get better the more I do this, too.

His attention turned back to the Coopers, who had drifted towards the wheelhouse of the wreck.

The wheelhouse was a popular place for divers. All of the doors and windows had been removed so it was easy and safe to swim in and out of the small room where once the captain had piloted the vessel.

Stan poked his head into the portside entrance to the wheelhouse, clearly curious about the view from the inside. He swam through the wheelhouse door space and Jane followed in behind. Josh exhaled slightly, using his decreased buoyancy to sink and propel him closer to the wheelhouse as Stan and Jane disappeared beneath the roof.

A blast of excess air angrily rolled out from under the wheelhouse roof and rocketed towards the surface. Josh caught a glimpse of an arm frantically moving through one of the window holes. He kicked hard and entered the wheelhouse through the nearest window.

Jane's first stage regulator attached to the top of her scuba tank on her back was caught on a loose electrical cable hanging from the ceiling. Stan was trying to grab Jane's arms as she thrashed about, moving erratically and randomly. Josh swam quickly behind Jane, reached her first stage near the back of her neck and pulled Jane backward and down to put slack on the cable. He grabbed the cable and unwrapped it from the regulator, freeing Jane from the ceiling. Jane, sensing freedom, bolted out the starboard hatch.

Josh grabbed the side of the wheelhouse to push off and felt a sharp pain as he punctured his left hand on a black sea urchin nestled in the dark edge between the window and the structure. He kicked hard to follow Jane, who had cleared the wheelhouse ceiling and turned to ascend.

Ouch! Damn, that hurts!

Josh knew if she swam quickly to the surface and held her breath she risked an air embolism and serious injury or death as the bubbles in her body expanded at a faster rate than she could breathe them out.

Reaching out he caught the edge of her right fin and pulled her leg down far enough to grab her ankle. Jane was in full escape mode, legs pumping and arms stroking as she tried to race to the surface. He scuttled up her back, reaching her shoulders. He could feel their ascent rate increase as the air in their buoyancy compensator jackets expanded.

Josh reached over Jane's left shoulder, grabbed her power inflator and dumped the excess air from her BC. Keeping his right hand on her tank valve he quickly dumped air from his own BC, slowing their ascent. He swam down with her until they stopped rising. Their ascent rate arrested, the next thing he knew to do was to make sure she was breathing OK.

Josh looked over Jane's right shoulder and saw she still had her regulator in her mouth and the rapid burst of bubbles from her reg's exhaust valve meant she was still getting air.

Jane was still struggling and trying to reach the surface with no rational behavior. His arms were beginning to ache with the effort of holding her down.

Josh saw the anchor line off to his left and swam her toward the line. He grabbed the line, wrapped his legs around it, keeping a firm grip on her tank valve. Jane's flight reflexes slowed briefly, fatigued by her effort to reach the surface, allowing Josh to check his depth gauge.

OK, got her stable, at twenty feet, on the anchor line and her breathing rate is returning to normal. That was a close one!

Josh looked down and saw that Kathy had Stan by the arm, slowly ascending up the anchor line towards them. The other four students had started their ascent below her. All eyes were turned up toward Josh and Jane. The combined exhaust bubbles from the divers below rumbled over Josh and Jane in a wash of air.

Josh took another look at Jane, who now grimly held onto the anchor line. Luckily she no longer seemed to be in a big hurry to reach the surface so Josh attempted an OK hand signal, looking directly into her eyes for support. Jane gave a tentative OK back, her eyes wide and magnified through her mask. Josh OK'ed Kathy and the rest of the group, reached over and looked at Jane's pressure gauge, which read 400 PSI.

She should make it to the boat no problem.

Josh looked at his left hand, where a broken black piece of sea urchin spine was embedded in his palm. He clamped down on his regulator, as if biting a bullet to endure the pain, and quickly pulled the spine from his palm.

Green blood streamed out from the puncture point, due to the filtering of light at this depth.

I'm bleeding like a stuck Vulcan pig.

He dropped the spine piece, watching it swirl away in the current. He knew the tiny hole left in his palm would sting later but heal quickly.

Josh gave Jane the "thumbs up" hand signal and slowly rose up the line with Jane. He moved her hand from the anchor line to the yellow nylon line at ten feet and gave her a gentle push along the line that would take her back to the ladders on the stern. He swam along her within arm's reach. Before them the twin ladders swayed gently with the mild current. They surfaced together and Josh looked up to see the boat's divemaster and captain looking curiously at them.

"She'll need some help getting back on the boat," said Josh to the DM, who was reaching down to grab Jane's upstretched hand.

Josh dipped below the water line and slipped off her fins so she could climb the ladder. He handed the fins to the waiting captain while the divemaster helped Jane up the ladder and onto the boat deck. Blood from his palm dripped on the deck.

"She OK?" asked the Captain, mild concern etched across his sun weathered face.

"Not sure; she came up pretty fast but I don't think she came up fast enough to hurt herself. We should check her over though," replied Josh.

"What about you? You're bleeding all over my boat!"

"Oh, nothing serious, just a sea urchin spine."

The Captain mumbled something that sounded suspiciously like "damn students" and reached down to take Josh's fins, which Josh had removed and held up.

Josh quickly scrambled up the ladder and walked over to the portside bench, where the divemaster was helping Jane sit down. The stern of the boat was lined with steel benches on both sides that provided storage for dive gear and easy access to donning and removing the scuba equipment.

"She's my student; I got it," said Josh, moving to Jane's right side, releasing her weight belt and assisting her right arm out of the BC. Slightly shaking, she removed her left arm from the BC and put her hands to her face, leaning forward on the bench, salt water gently dripping from her tousled hair.

"I thought I was trapped down there...I didn't want to follow Stan but I couldn't leave him behind; we are buddies...thought I was going to drown", the words forced out from her as if under pressure.

"Relax, you're OK, we made it back safe."

She looked up at Josh, slowly realizing how he had helped her.

"You..saved..me; er, thank you," she said awkwardly, reaching out her hand. Josh wiped the blood off his palm onto his wet suit, grabbed her hand, shook it and nodded.

The Captain stood next to Josh, watching Jane and Josh. The divemaster had returned to ladder duty, grabbing a pair of fins as they appeared from the ladders and helping each diver up.

Stan and the other four students walked carefully back to their bench locations, slightly hunched with a wide stance to keep the tank steady on their backs. Stan sat awkwardly on the bench, slipped out of his BC and unstrapped his weight belt, which fell to the deck with a clunk. His tank slipped on its side as he released the BC and started towards Jane.

Kathy nodded to the divemaster, who handed her back her fins at the top of the ladder and she strode briskly next to Jane, shucking her gear and placing it on the boat deck in one fluid motion.

Josh looked at Kathy with mixed feelings of pride having saved Jane and apprehension that a problem had occurred in the first place. This was his first actual underwater rescue and was much scarier than the simulated ones he had done with Kathy in scuba rescue class.

Kathy, her lips pursed, said "You feeling OK, Jane?" Jane nodded miserably and looked up at Stan, who now stood next to Kathy. Josh reached over to his dive bag, rummaged around and removed a towel from a small dry bag, which he pressed into his palm to staunch the bleeding from the sea urchin spine puncture. His trail of blood on the boat deck and the group huddled around Jane added to the curiosity of the other divers on the boat.

"Well let's go belowdecks and have a chat, shall we?" she said crisply, waving to Josh and Stan to join her as she turned to midships and descended the short stairs to the cabin. Josh knew she wanted to save Jane some embarrassment from other divers on the boat rubbernecking.

"Jane, sit on this bench and let's see how you are doing," said Kathy. The four of them sat on the plastic benches around a table affixed to the deck, Stan helping his wife as she sat down with a sigh.

"Josh, what happened?" said Kathy.

Josh explained the chain of events from the point of seeing the excess bubbles coming from the wheelhouse to the point where Jane reached the ladder at the back of the boat. He tried to stick to just describing the events without judgment or opinions as he had learned in Kathy's scuba rescue class. Kathy nodded.

"Did Jane ever hold her breath?" Kathy asked.

"No, I'm pretty sure, especially while we were ascending, that she kept exhaling," answered Josh.

Stan exclaimed, the salt water still dripping from his hair, "Sweetie, I am so sorry! Things happened so fast when I looked behind me and you were trying to get loose from that cable".

"I didn't know what to do. I just got really scared and all I could think of was to get to the surface. I couldn't help myself," sobbed

Jane. Stan hugged his wife, trying to reassure her.

Kathy looked closer at Jane, paused for a few seconds while she studied Jane and, seemingly satisfied, stated "Well, you don't appear to have any barotrauma injuries, which is lucky. You weren't deep enough or down long enough to be at risk at decompression sickness either. Still, I want to put you on precautionary oxygen – they carry some on board. Josh, please help them back to the deck so they can get out of their wet suits and dry off while I hunt down the Captain".

She rose and walked towards the bow, where a smaller stairway led to the wheelhouse. She disappeared up the stairs.

Josh knew it wasn't his place and this probably wasn't the best time to lecture the scared couple even though he was bursting with advice and opinions on what went wrong and how best to prevent it in the future. Jane's hair was in disarray and her face still had an oval imprint from her mask.

Josh waved to the couple, who slowly got up and followed him up the stairs. He worked on breaking down their scuba equipment while the couple sat down on the bench and removed their dive booties and peeled off their wet suits.

Satisfied he had their gear disconnected properly and returned to their dive bags he went back belowdecks and grabbed two towels, handing each one. They gratefully accepted the towels, Jane shivering despite the June heat. Josh also handed over bottles of cold water to hydrate them and rinse their mouths of salt water.

Josh looked up at Elise, Jon and Frank, who had walked over to the bench, a curious expression on their faces. Josh shook his head gently that they needed to give these guys their space and Elise smiled ruefully, returning to midships and her sun bathing towel. Jon and Frank turned and busied themselves with their own equipment, stowing it for the trip back to the dock. Kathy reappeared from the wheelhouse with the divemaster and an oxygen delivery kit in a large red waterproof Pelican case.

"OK, Jane, let's get you back down below so you can get comfy and breathe this," she said, indicating the O_2 kit. Jane and Stan meekly followed them down the stairs. Josh, figuring his part in the drama was over, walked over to the midship deck where Elise, Jon and Frank were waiting for him in the bright Florida sun.

"Geez, what happened? We were the last ones on the boat and everybody's buzzing about you," said Frank. Frank was a few inches taller than Josh, thin and wiry with an athletic grace. His striking light green eyes were visible beneath a swath of damp dirty blonde hair covering his forehead.

Josh sat down next to Elise. She held up a band aid, cotton swab and some rubbing alcohol.

Josh wiped off his palm as best he could and held it out to her. She expertly swabbed the tiny puncture wound with the swab and placed the band aid across the palm.

Good thing I'm dating a nurse, thought Josh, smiling.

She squeezed his arm and leaned into him. Josh realized he was still pretty jacked up by the event and was grateful for the quick triage work and simple gesture of affection. He calmed down slightly and spoke.

"I entered the water last, as usual with a class, and saw everybody doing fine as they descended to the superstructure of the wreck. Everybody seemed to be doing what they were supposed to do. I noticed that Stan swam into the wheelhouse..." started Josh.

Jon interrupted, "Don't you guys tell students to stay out of any structures?" Jon was Josh's height, weight and body build yet drawn with a darker stroke – black short curly hair, dark eyebrows and an overall swarthy look.

"Yes," continued Josh, "but you guys know how that wheelhouse is on this wreck – it's a pretty minor overhead environment and we usually don't mind if students poke their heads in on the last dive as sort of a treat. Heck, we all dove this same shipwreck three years ago on our checkout dives and went inside the wheelhouse. Never had anybody get stuck and panic, though," he mused before continuing, "It happened so fast. I managed to get into the wheelhouse and saw her first stage stuck on one of those old cables hanging from the ceiling.

"She was trying to swim and get free but her efforts just kept her more trapped. Poor Stan was in front, trying to pull her towards the door as well. I think they just wanted to get out of the wheelhouse and back to open water without thinking about what was trapping her."

Josh paused a moment to recall the next series of events.

"I managed to free her but wow, she took off quickly and I almost lost her. I was sure she was going to bolt to the surface in an uncontrolled free ascent and pop a lung or something. I had to wrestle her a bit and was worried that I was going to be pulled up to the surface by her but luckily I was able to dump her BC and mine and snag the anchor line."

Jon and Frank nodded knowingly. Elise looked alarmed.

"Josh, were you ever in danger? You know how I worry about you while you are diving," she asked, worry furrowing her brow.

Josh knew Elise wasn't a big fan of scuba diving but that she enjoyed the downtime from her busy nursing schedule to take in an afternoon on a boat, soaking up the rays.

"Naw, not Josh; he's pretty cool under pressure," exclaimed Frank. Jon nodded in agreement.

"Aw, you guys, I was just lucky," said Josh, feeling slightly embarrassed. The rescue was still a blur and he wasn't sure if the situation arose again that he would be able to do the right thing at the right time. He certainly felt lucky.

Through the railing that separated the midships from the stern he could see Kathy in a semicircle talking to Jason, Kyle, Cynthia and Max. He knew she was probably discussing how their last dive went. He checked his dive watch on his left wrist and confirmed that despite the dive being cut short the group had stayed down long enough for it to count as their last certification dive. He was happy for those four. They were now certified scuba divers.

Kathy strode up the staircase that joined the midships to the stern area. She looked at Josh and said "Jane's doing fine; breathing the O_2 just in case. I don't think we need to have her go to a hospital, thankfully. I don't see any signs or symptoms of any type of dive injury, except maybe bad judgment. I did give them a bit of a hard time about going into the wheelhouse but I think the event scared them enough to make them think twice about it in the future.

"I told them we'd dive them with another class in the near future before I certified them just to give them time to think about whether they want to continue and to get more diving under their weight belts."

"The captain thinks we're being a bit over cautious but I don't think he wants to risk losing business so he agreed to let her breathe the oxygen. Not like it costs that much to get it refilled," Kathy finished, rolling her eyes.

Deep in the bowels of the *Minerva* the twin diesel engines came to life as the Captain and divemaster prepared to unhook the anchor line from the wreck and start the thirty minute journey back to shore. Josh watched twin puffs of black smoke issue from the stern and the water churn from the spinning props. The sulfur scent of combusted diesel drifted over the boat.

Kathy placed her hand on Josh's shoulder and said, "Hey, I just wanted you to know that you really did a great job literally under pressure down there. If you hadn't stopped her it sure looked like she was going to do a rapid ascent and probably hurt herself. That's the kind of quick thinking it takes to be a scuba instructor. I'm proud of you, Josh."

Josh turned slightly red under his well-tanned complexion. Kathy was an "old school" type of instructor and dive shop owner and praise was rare. He still didn't think he was ready to teach scuba diving but this sure boosted his confidence about becoming a dive leader.

"Heck, Kathy, I was just doing what we did in rescue class while handling a 'panicking' diver during the simulation drills," Josh said.

Kathy released her hand from his shoulder, looked at the others and said, "Still, there's a big difference between rescuing somebody who's faking and an actual diver who is in panic. Well, I'm going to go keep an eye on Jane." She turned and headed back to the lower deck.

"Well, Josh, I still worry about you down there. I see too much injury and death in the hospital," said Elise.

This was a familiar theme between Josh and Elise. Josh found himself automatically replying, "Statistically you are in greater danger driving to and from a dive than from the actual dive."

"Yeah, I know; I've heard you say that before," she said. "It's just that most divers aren't doing daring rescues that put them at greater risk".

"Aw, come on! Give me a break! I just saved a woman's life; shouldn't that count for something?" exclaimed Josh.

Jon and Frank looked back and forth between the couple. Arguing about diving was one of their favorite past times.

Elise backed down, eyes downcast, "I'm sorry; I am proud that you did rescue her. I just naturally worry."

Josh feeling slightly admonished, hugged her and said "it's OK, Elise; I don't want to get hurt being the hero either." and flashed his best boyfriend smile.

She smiled back and returned the hug, the argument settled for now.

"Well now that you two are done I think I'll snag us some waters for the ride back," said Frank.

"I'll help", chimed in Jon. They both headed towards the coolers mounted to the floor in the middle of the stern deck. The divemaster passed them by, anchor line coiled up in his arms as the Captain swung the dive boat back towards shore.

Chapter 2

Josh downshifted into second gear as he turned onto Manatee Lane, his 1992 Ford F-150 blue pickup truck bouncing slightly on the transition from asphalt to the hard shell-covered road. *Semi Charmed Life* by Third Eye Blind blasted from the door speakers, a new hit broadcast from the local university radio station.

Josh drummed his fingers along the top of the steering wheel and hummed as he headed south along the road, both door windows open to stir the early morning humid air.

To his right stood dark green scrub pines and olive colored live oak trees, while to his left he caught the occasional glimpse of the Wakulla River, the rising sun catching the water in golden spots of light filtered through tall cypress trees draped in Spanish moss.

The road followed the contour of the river as it snaked from the Wakulla Springs headwaters to the confluence of the Wakulla and St. Marks rivers, some eleven miles apart. Josh considered it lucky he worked on one of the prettiest rivers in Florida that was still pristine and wild.

The road and river converged and Josh now had an unlimited view of the river. This section of the river front had been cleared by a land developer in the nineteen seventies with high hopes of building expensive river front homes. Three modest homes with docks on the river had been built before the developer ran out of money and patience and the homes had sat idle for years.

The mixture of remoteness, natural beauty and cheap land had attracted an eclectic community of individuals who repurposed the homes for their business and artistic pursuits. The end result was an oddball mixture of businesses sequestered deep within the Wakulla wilderness, twenty miles from the nearest city of Tallahassee.

Josh looked over at the first home, converted into an artist's showroom and residence called the unimaginative name of *River Art*. The front yard was strewn with various pieces of creative sculpture done in wood and scrap metal.

Two magnolia trees framed the side of the front yard and a large likeness of a manatee carved from cypress stood in the center of the yard. The walls of the building facing the road were painted in various shades of green, blue and yellow conveying a likeness of watery abstractness and the flow of the river behind the establishment.

The single front door was closed and each of the jalousie windows flanking the door had their curtains drawn. Josh knew the artists usually stayed up late and stirred around noon. At this hour the owners, Emilio and Cameron, slept in the small back bedroom.

The second house had the same structure as the first and third, built at the same time by the same builder, but Mike and Sue Hawthorne, the owners and purveyors of southern food and spirits, had chosen to remove the two jalousie windows of the original house plan and extend the front rooms into a larger restaurant space, enclosed in a screen porch.

Continuing with the obvious nomenclature of the neighborhood an unlit neon sign hanging over the left corner of the building spelled *The Watering Hole* in glass tube script. Josh smiled with fond memories of relaxing at the *Hole* after days working in the dive shop next door. He would see his friends there later tonight.

In front of the third building two wooden poles three feet high held a rectangle of pine planks in the shape of a scuba dive flag, painted red with a white stripe bisecting the rectangle from the upper left to the bottom right. Horizontally in the center was the word "Wakulla" carved out of the wood and painted blue.

The word "Skuba" stood out in bas relief in vertical writing, a single raised blue "k" in the center of the sign providing the shared consonant between the two words. Josh always thought the obvious spelling alliteration a bit silly but in this setting it felt right. Besides, the art work had been done by Cameron and was top notch.

Josh passed the *Wakulla Skuba* sign and parked next to Kathy's travel-worn red faded 1990 Jeep Cherokee. On the side of the Cherokee was painted the same shop logo, complete with the words intersecting at their "k's" and the phone number of the shop. He turned off the truck and the engine shuddered to a stop.

The silence was soon filled by the rapid click of cicadas in the trees and gentle strains of classical music drifting from the open jalousie windows of the dive shop. The smell of fresh coffee drifted to Josh's nose from the early morning river breeze. Josh opened his door, jumped down, his flip flops hitting the ground with a gentle slapping sound, and entered the front door of the shop, the antique nautical themed entry bell announcing his arrival with a gentle tinkle.

A medium-sized short haired black Chihuahua named Bear ran up to him, curly tail wagging, and nudged his leg. Josh leaned down and gave Bear a rub behind the ears. Bear, having been raised as a puppy around dive shop customers, didn't share the typical yappy small breed penchant for aggressive barking whenever something new entered his environment. Josh enjoyed having the little feller share his work day at the shop.

To Josh's left was the dive shop display area, filled with the usual array of diving products for sale, including scuba cylinders along the wall, tree hanger displays of buoyancy compensator vests, dive skins and wet suits and a glass display of the more expensive items, such as regulators and dive computers.

To the right, formerly the dining room, the classroom contained a long table with chairs that led to a white board on the far wall. The walls were covered in a variety of scuba product posters and oversized dive decompression charts. A small door on the far side of the classroom led to the tiny workshop where Kathy and her staff repaired and tested diving equipment.

Kathy walked in from the center hallway. A window-mounted air conditioner in the front shop area kept both the occupants and inventory in relative comfort and low humidity. She wore her usual business uniform of khaki Bermuda shorts and a blue short sleeved rugby shirt with the dive shop logo embroidered on her chest.

"Good morning, Josh. Coffee's ready in the kitchen. I need you to unload the dive gear from the Jeep and rinse it in the back. Fill the tanks too, please," she said.

Josh replied, "Good morning, Kathy. No problem; I'll get right on it".

It was just like Kathy to not dwell on yesterday's near disaster and to get down to business. Josh didn't mind since he thought plenty had been said already. He enjoyed working at her shop even for barely-above minimum wage. It still felt like an honor to get paid doing what he loved.

Josh walked down the center hallway, passed the small bathroom/changing room on the left and turned right into the small kitchen area that doubled as a break room. Kathy's office and small living space occupied the back left corner of the property.

After pouring himself a cup of coffee from the coffee maker, Josh exited the kitchen back screen door and walked onto the large raised porch that ran the length of the back of the building. Bear hopped through the tiny plastic dog door to follow Josh; all the doors contained a dog door flap that allowed Bear free rein of the property.

The porch was covered with a tin roof and screened in to keep the insects out during the warm months, which at this latitude was most of the year. Two large fans mounted on each end of the house pointed to the porch area, providing moving air to dry wet gear as well providing some relief from the heat. Two ceiling fans equally spaced along the porch hung from the tin roof, lazily pushing air downwards.

Alongside the back of the house sat two one hundred gallon plastic cattle troughs with matching water hoses neatly coiled to the side of each. Josh set his coffee cup down on a plastic table sandwiched between the troughs and checked each rinse trough to make sure they were empty and that the drain cocks at the bottom were closed.

In turn he uncoiled the nearby hoses, stuck the end into each trough and started filling them with clean, fresh water. Bear watched the rinse troughs intently, fascinated by the sound and sight of running water. Breaking from his breed's tendency yet again, Bear was an avid water dog and strong swimmer. Josh smiled at the small dog's intensity.

A third trough sat in the far right end of the porch. Above it stood a panel with a complex set of dials and knobs. Behind the panel, silver lines of thin steel tubing snaked downward and led into a series of holes in the side of a wooden shack attached to the building.

Four larger diameter flexible steel whips fed from the bottom of the panel and ended in small adapters that fit onto the valves of scuba tanks. The adapters were hung on Y-shaped hooks mounted below the panel and above the troughs. Josh looked at the dials on the panel, noting that the storage banks were full enough to fill tanks.

Connected to the back of the porch facing the river was a screen door that led out onto a boat dock. A common walkway connected the docks of the dive shop, *Hole* and *River Art*. A string of lights, currently unlit, hung from small poles set at regular intervals along the walkway connecting the three docks of the three businesses.

Josh stopped, gazed out at the river water as it moved slowly from his left to his right on its way to the Gulf, picked back up his mug and sipped his coffee.

The river bank flourished with cypress, live oak and cabbage palmettos. On the far bank a long-necked anhinga perched on a partially submerged cypress log, its wings spread to dry by catching the morning warmth of the sun. A line of black-shelled yellow-bellied slider turtles balanced on a log that stretched from the far shore into the water. The occasional water lettuce drifted past the edge of the dock and Josh could make out bright silver schools of mullet racing upstream in the clear water.

So peaceful and beautiful, thought Josh as he set down his coffee mug back on the plastic table.

Whistling snatches of *Semi Charmed Life* Josh exited the screen door at the right end of the porch, propped open the door and walked down the small flight of steps to the oyster shell path alongside the dive shop. To his right stood the wooden shack attached to the house, containing the air compressor, filtration system and bank of large storage tanks they used to fill scuba tanks.

Kathy was meticulous about the air compressor being properly maintained and had taken great steps to sound proof the shack's walls, so the neighborhood wasn't filled with the loud sound of air being violently compressed and filtered through the four stage system.

Josh walked the oyster shell path between the air shack, his feet crunching on the rough surface, past a small tin-roofed shed containing plastic kayaks lying across wooden beams mounted horizontally. Orange life vests and aluminum kayak paddles hung on hooks along the ceiling of the shed.

Kathy supplemented her dive shop business by renting kayaks to the growing group of eco tourists who enjoyed plying the waters of the river. Josh enjoyed the occasional weekend kayak trip with Elise along the local rivers on the rare weekend days she wasn't working a twelve hour shift at the hospital.

Reaching Kathy's Jeep, Josh opened up the back hatch and started unloading the dive gear. He shuttled the equipment from the back of the Jeep to the screened-in porch.

The Jeep was loaded from the bottom up with scuba tanks, arrayed in a home built lattice of wooden cradles to keep them stationary. Stacked on top of the tanks were weight belts and weights, wet suits of various sizes and genders, BCs, and plastic boxes crammed with regulators.

The BCs he rinsed inside and out and hung on large plastic hangers on the porch, alongside the wet suits which also enjoyed a rinsing and hanging. The weight belts were rinsed, the weights removed from the pouches in the belts and dropped into bins sorted by their weight poundage.

Josh hung the empty weight belts on poles mounted above the weight bins. He inspected the first stage of each regulator, making sure the dust caps were firmly in place before submerging the regulators in the rinse troughs, having turned off the water after they filled up.

Best to let them soak for a while to get rid of all the salt water.

Finally, Josh rinsed each tank, rubbing the sides to free up the salts encrusted from the ocean dives and placed them next to the filling station troughs. Sixteen aluminum tanks, each affixed with a red sticker bearing the *Wakulla Skuba* logo stood lined up on the porch, ready to be topped off. He went back to the Jeep, the back now empty, and closed the hatch, Bear still at his heels.

Josh placed four of the tanks in the filling troughs and connected a high pressure fill whip to each of the tanks, turning on each tank once the whip was connected so the air pressure forced the O-ring seals to hold with a short hiss.

Each turn of the tank valve and whip valve resulted in a sharp sound of air equalization, the tanks with lower pressures and higher pressures resulting in longer hissing. Bear, accustomed to the sound, simply watched Josh perform this ritual. He eventually had all four whips connected, each to its own tank and all equalized to each other. He looked at the largest dial, which indicated the pressure in PSI – Pounds per Square Inch – of the fill whips and the tanks.

Ideally he preferred to fill the tanks slowly, since adding air to a tank meant the tank temperature would rise.

He twisted the large needle valve knob on the fill panel that opened up the fill whips to the large storage bank. The air rushed from the higher pressure storage bank into each of the four tanks, all at a lower pressure.

Like water flowing down hill; the secret to this panel is realizing where the high pressure air is at and knowing it wants to flow into the lower pressure tanks, thought Josh.

He knew accidents at scuba fill stations were extremely rare but usually quite dramatic due to the high pressures involved. Kathy had trained him to respect what each dial measured and each valve controlled.

The tanks were rated to contain the equivalent of eighty cubic feet of air when pressurized to 3,000 PSI. An "Aluminum 80", as it were, was the most common size and shape of scuba tanks used around the world and it had enough air for the average diver to do a single dive within the typical dive parameters of depth and time for recreational use.

Josh looked away from the fill station out at the river. His eyes caught a two person kayak paddling by with a middle-aged couple gently moving up river. Both wore wide-rim paddler's hats to protect themselves from the morning's rising sun. Josh waved to the pair, who waved back.

The Wakulla River enjoyed the silent running of kayaks and canoes more frequently than the loud *brraaap* of the occasional powerboat. People who traversed the river were never in a hurry and luckily the loud jet ski crowd stuck to the larger lakes nearby.

Chapter 3

Josh looked at the clock on the wall in the classroom. The clock was another piece of practical art by Cameron from *River Art*. It was a foot-wide turtle shell, found unoccupied some years ago and transformed into a clock by the addition of a battery-powered mechanism, long thin clock hands and a minimalist clock face composed of lengths of cypress wood attached to the shell and extending flush with the clock hands in the twelve, three, six and nine o'clock positions. The time read six thirty. Josh put the half-opened cardboard box of scuba masks on the training table and walked back to Kathy's office, poking his head into the doorway.

"It's quitting time – want me to close up?" asked Josh.

Kathy looked up from the paperwork on her desk. "No, you go ahead – I've got it," Kathy answered.

"Cool, thanks; going next door to grab a bite and meet my friends," Josh said.

"OK, see you tomorrow, usual time," returned Kathy.

"'Night, Kathy," completed Josh.

Josh walked out the back door to the porch, through the screen door and headed towards the dock. The lights along the walkway to *The Watering Hole* were on and dimly glowing. Vines of jasmine curled around the strands of light and extended along all three river homes, adding a pleasant scent to his walk.

This time of year the sun was still in the sky but the tree line along the river meant darkness fell sooner than sunset. To the north, heat lightning flickered between distant thunderclouds.

Another summer rain shower was wandering across the region. Bear burst out of the dog door and followed Josh, his tiny claws clattering along the treated pine walkway.

He approached the eating establishment. The *Hole,* like the dive shop, enjoyed a large screened-in porch area connected to the dock and walkway. The porch was adorned with tables and alongside the back a section of the wall from the original house had been removed and an embedded bar built in its place. Country music floated from the speakers mounted in the ceiling alongside the house and a string of festive lights decorated the perimeter of the dining porch.

Josh walked into the screen door on his side of the walkway and waved to Mike, the co-owner of the *Hole,* behind the bar. Mike was in his fifties, tall with a thick head of short salt and pepper hair, a moustache and burly shoulders.

Mike waved back and pulled down a beer glass from the overhead rack and filled it from a tap behind the bar. Josh walked over to the bar.

"'Evening Josh. How's things over at the dive shop?" asked Mike genially.

"Not bad, for a Monday. We had a pretty busy weekend with checkout dives," answered Josh.

"Yeah, heard you had a bit of excitement yesterday on the boat," said Mike, handing Josh the beer.

News did travel fast in a tiny community like this, thought Josh.

"Yeah, some woman freaked out but nobody was hurt," downplayed Josh.

"Well, that's good," said Mike continuing, "You hungry?"

"Going to meet my friends; I'll just wait for them to eat," responded Josh.

"Suit yourself," said Mike good naturedly, waving towards the tables.

Josh nodded and sat down at the table nearest the water's edge, his favorite spot. He sank into the deeply padded chair, one of four nestled around a cypress topped table.

Bear jumped into the chair to his left, sat down on his haunches and watched Josh, dark brown eyes glittering with the reflection of the lights adorning the porch. The *Hole* was dog friendly and a wily dog knew to be quiet and patient.

Ah, this feels nice, thought Josh. *Seems that I hadn't really had much time to just relax since this weekend's dives.*

He reminisced back to yesterday; when the *Minerva* returned to the dock he was busy unloading gear and helping the students load their equipment into their personal vehicles. Elise had left in her own car to get some sleep before her twelve hour shift started at 7 AM today. Even Jon and Frank left without hanging around; both had to work early the next morning as well.

Josh had driven back to the shop with Kathy, where they both decided to wait until this morning to unload her Jeep. He had just gone home to his tiny apartment in Woodville, grabbed a quick bite and went to an early bed, exhausted after the day's events.

Frank and Jon bounded into the porch area through the central hallway leading from the front door of the establishment and plunked down into the other two chairs. Bear gave a soft "chuff" greeting to the two.

"Hey, Josh, how's it going?" said Frank, rubbing behind Bear's ears. His curly tail blurred in response.

"Not bad, how about you two?" replied Josh.

Jon answered, "Busy day for me but it feels great to kick back.

Our new computer system is being installed this summer and it's pretty complex." Jon was a computer programmer for a state agency in Tallahassee and loved the technical challenges of his job.

"You and your boring state job," teased Frank, "I couldn't stand to be chained to a computer eight hours a day". Frank was a sales associate at a popular Tallahassee-based retail outlet. "Gotta be on my feet."

Josh caught Mike's eye and held up two fingers; Mike nodded in understanding and reached up to the overhead rack for two glasses.

"Yeah, well, we all can't have the super-adventure jobs like Josh," teased Jon, smiling at Josh. Josh returned the smile, rose from his chair and walked over to the bar to retrieve the two beers. He returned to the table and set down Jon and Frank's beers.

"Yeah, I'm really getting rich with all this super adventure," retorted Josh, sitting back in his chair and reaching for his half-finished beer.

"Speaking of adventures, guys, I'm not going to be able to get any vacation time this summer because of work," announced Jon.

The smiles disappeared from Frank and Josh. Since earning their scuba certifications three years ago they synchronized their vacations with dive trips to the Florida Keys in August, when Florida spiny lobster season opened. Their dive trips were the highlight event of the year.

"Aw, geez, Jon, really? You can't swing a trip anytime this summer?" implored Frank.

"No, guys, believe me I tried. This new software system installation is going to take months and I'm going to be lucky to even have off weekends," explained Jon, downcast.

"Damn, Jon, we can't go without you!" exclaimed Frank, leaning forward. Bear's ears perked up at the raised voices.

Thunder rumbled from the rain clouds, sounding slightly closer. The ceiling fans slowly redistributed the sluggish, humid summer evening air.

"I agree, Jon, it wouldn't be the same without the dynamic dive trio," chimed in Josh. Josh had already cleared that week in August, even though it was a busy time for *Wakulla Skuba*. He felt disappointed.

"Well you guys can still go play in the Keys. You'll have a great time," said Jon, shifting in his chair.

Frank looked over at Josh, an inquiring look on his face. Josh grimaced, and looked at Jon.

"Jon, we really can't go without you. Heck, except for a couple of checkout dives when I work with Kathy we've always done our dives together, going all the way back to our original dives when we got certified. We can just reschedule later in the year. Besides, we can dive the Keys year-round," said Josh, eyeing Frank carefully.

Frank sighed. "OK, I suppose we can skip the best part of lobster season for you, Jon," he said, voice laden with sarcasm.

Josh glared at Frank, raising his eyebrows. Jon hid his discomfort behind a large guzzle from his beer.

"Come on, Frank, you know it wouldn't be the same without Jon," implored Josh.

"Oh, all right," muttered Frank, his face clouded.

Josh knew that would have to do for now. Frank was always quick to anger and sometimes selfish. Still they had shared many good times despite their differences and he knew Frank would come around eventually. His stomach grumbled.

"Let's get something to eat, guys," Josh said.

By now the sky had darkened and nearby tables started to fill as the locals arrived. Josh waved to Emilio and Cameron, the owners of *River Art,* who had joined Kathy at a nearby table. Their chocolate lab, Chestnut, lay curled at their feet. She sniffed towards Bear, who sniffed back. They were both veterans in the mooching game and knew how to play their owners for treats.

Sue, co-owner of the *Hole,* walked up with menus. Sue was also in her fifties and the years had been kind to her, as evidenced by her blue jeans covering her waspish waist and her tight-fitting cream-colored V-neck shirt. She leaned over, placed the menus on the table, reached in her apron pocket for a butane lighter and lit the candle in the glass holder at the center of the table. The warm flickering candle glow reflected off the beer glasses.

"Hi guys, what'll you have?" she said, handing out the paper menus with a smile. Sue was tall and slender with stylish black curly medium length hair and hazel eyes.

"We'll have the usual," said Frank.

"Three smoked mullet dinners with hush puppies and cole slaw," said Sue, retracting the menus. She smiled again and turned to the next table.

Josh marveled at how well she memorized all of the drink and food orders from customers; he had never seen her actually write any orders down.

Frank took a long pull from his beer and started, "You know guys, we can still get in a bunch of dives this summer, even if we have to resort to short weekend trips..."

Jon asked, "What do you have in mind?"

"Well, there's a group of guys that come into the store now and then and I usually chat them up about diving. You gotta build rapport with customers; it encourages trust and loosens their wallets," said Frank. He paused, taking another drink. Josh and Jon looked at Frank questioningly.

"These guys say there are a bunch of fresh water springs from Pensacola to Jacksonville down to Ocala in the north part of Florida – hundreds of them. We should check them out – they are no more than an hour or two drive from Tallahassee and I don't think they cost much to dive," said Frank.

"But we aren't supposed to dive inside caves. You remember Kathy's scare lecture during class?" said Jon.

Josh did recall the lecture. Kathy was very adamant that their new license to scuba dive didn't mean they could just go out and dive anywhere there was water. They had limits they were to follow – don't go too deep and don't stay too long.

She stressed especially not swimming into anywhere where there was something over their heads that would prevent them from surfacing, such as deep in the bowels of a shipwreck or inside a natural underwater cave. Josh shuddered at the memory her lecture invoked of being trapped inside of a wreck with no way out while his air slowly drained away...

"Yeah, no overhead," affirmed Josh.

Sue walked up, three plastic plates balanced in her arms. The three leaned back in their chairs as she slid a plate in front of each. The smell of freshly-smoked mullet combined with the soothing scent of the hush puppies. Josh's mouth watered. Bear shifted in his seat, his shiny black eyes flitting from person to person.

Josh looked at his empty glass and asked, "I'd like a tea, please; half sweet and half unsweet."

Sue nodded and raised her eyebrows to Jon and Frank. Both shook their heads, pointing to their beers.

"Enjoy, boys," Sue said in parting.

All three dug into their meals heartily, conversation momentarily paused by unspoken decree. The candle flickered as the breeze from the approaching rain shower blew across the porch.

The sound of gentle rain landing on the porch roof muted the sounds of a popular LeAnn Rimes' tune pouring out from the speakers. Josh looked out to the river, where spotlights from the *Hole's* dock revealed a curtain of diamond-like drops striking the river's surface. The darkened sky and light rain shower enhanced the secluded and cozy feel of the *Hole*.

Sue stopped momentarily at their table to deliver his tea, her other arm loaded with plates for other tables. She continued, sashaying to the next table.

"If you recall we did dive Morrison Springs during our checkout dives," said Josh, picking up the conversational thread.

"Yeah, it was OK, but not as much fun as diving in salt water. The salt water south of us is warmer than the springs this time of year and there's a lot more sea life," opined Jon. "Besides, it was kinda boring – we only got to, like thirty feet of depth over the head spring? Kathy wouldn't let us get any closer to the spring entrance."

Frank countered, "True, but just think of the sheer numbers. We can do a lot of dives in a lot of cool springs without the expense and time involved in driving to the shore, loading our gear into a dive boat, traveling an hour off shore and basically being told how long to dive in order to keep the boat on schedule."

Josh picked off a piece of mullet and pitched it at Bear, who snapped it up in a single quick motion.

"Do you know where all these 'cheap' springs are at? Are they really dive able? Any of them deeper than Morrison?" quizzed Josh. They were used to dive sites in the fifty to eighty foot depth and diving anything shallower just seemed so lame.

Frank pulled out a piece of folded paper from his pocket, unfolded it and smoothed it out.

"Ginnie Springs, fifty feet to one hundred feet, twenty five dollars to dive; Orange Grove supposedly gets to one hundred feet, five bucks to dive, Little River is free...the list I got from these guys goes on," he said.

Josh was not surprised he hadn't heard of these places before. The patrons of *Wakulla Skuba* were all recreational salt water divers and spear fishermen. Kathy's equipment and training catered to that crowd. He had heard that Florida had many springs. There were quite a few within thirty miles of the shop but none were open for scuba diving. The local knowledge was these places were either closed to diving (like nearby Wakulla Springs) or on private land. This was just not a style of diving he had really ever considered seriously before.

Morrison Springs and nearby Vortex Springs were great for the first set of checkout dives since the calm clear cold water was an easy step up from a pool. Students could get a taste of what it's like to be on scuba in the open water before jumping off of a boat, miles from shore.

Morrison is where Kathy's last class did their first checkout dives before boarding the *Minerva* for their final day of diving.

Too bad I didn't pay closer attention to Stan and Jane at Morrison's; might have prevented the near disaster on the Minerva, he mused.

Frank pushed his point, "So, why don't we check out one of these springs this weekend?"

Jon popped a succulent hush puppy in his mouth and still chewing said simply, "Sure, I suppose."

Josh couldn't think of any reason to say no either. They always had a great time scuba diving and he felt confident in their ability to maximize fun and minimize trouble.

"OK, let's do it. What spring did you have in mind?" Josh said.

Frank looked at his list again, finger moving down the page. He stopped at one of the names and announced, "Let's try Blue Springs in Marianna. It's less than an hour away and is supposed to be beautiful."

Chapter 4

Early Saturday morning the three piled out of Josh's blue truck in the parking area of Jackson Blue Spring. They had met at *Wakulla Skuba* in the dim dawn light and transferred all of the scuba gear to the back of Josh's truck and squeezed into the front cab. Josh had driving duties, Frank had shotgun and as was tradition Jon sat in the middle. The talk had been animated; they were always excited to dive a new location.

"Wow, this place is pretty," said Jon, looking around the park.

It was the first time any of them had visited this particular park. They walked up to the edge of the water. The water basin was lined with an aging, slightly crooked two foot high concrete block wall that defined the semicircular shape of the swimming area.

The shallow water around the edges ranged from crystal clear to a light green, shading to a blue in the depths near the center. At one end a triangular deep section pointed to the mouth of the spring where a large concrete block boasted a diving board flanked by green-painted hand rails.

Josh could tell it was a spring by the gentle ripples of water current present at the surface directly in front of the diving board, indicating the water flow was from out of the ground and into the swimming basin.

He judged the depth directly below the diving board to be around fifteen to twenty feet, although he knew the high water clarity could sometimes play with perceptions and make the water look shallower than it actually was.

To the right of the diving platform a white sandy beach graced the edge of the swimming area, clearly man-made. Behind the beach a dilapidated wood roofed pavilion sat attached to a small cinder block bathhouse. Wooden picnic tables, grey with age, sat underneath the pavilion. The land from the beach across to the other side of the swimming area sloped upwards, in some places so steep that small concrete stairs had been constructed into the grass-covered hillside.

Among the deep summer green lawn grass Josh could see the occasional white limestone rock erupt from the ground, revealing the true bones of Florida. At the far end of the swim area a white nylon rope adorned with plastic bullet-shaped blue and white floats marked the end of the swimming zone and the beginning of the river that stretched on for miles to the south.

Oak varieties, cypress, sweet gum, and various species of pine trees lined the river and the grassy hill that created a natural amphitheater to the flat liquid stage of the clear spring water. The rising morning sun struck the right side of the river, lighting up the greens, yellows and browns of the foliage and creating a wispy mist across the surface of the water.

Josh marveled at the peaceful sight and the color counterpoint between the variations of blue painted across the sky and the green shades of the water and ground below. This river shared the same clear water as the Wakulla but he noticed how each spring-fed river has its own color personality, its own unique thumbprint found in the variations of water color, vegetation and surrounding land.

Frank walked over to the diving platform and up to the edge, looking down into the water. Josh and Jon followed.

"This is an amazing looking spring," commented Frank. "Glad we came early before the swimmers arrived. It would suck having them jump on top of us".

Josh looked out from the diving board and confirmed that it was placed to make sure the swimmers jumped in over the deepest part of the mouth of the spring.

"I bet it's deeper than it looks. Even if swimmers did show up we could probably stay safe below them," observed Josh.

Jon nodded in agreement.

"Doesn't look like much to dive in the swimming area. Sure is pretty though."

"Yeah, looks like it doesn't get deep until we actually enter inside of the cavern below the diving platform," said Frank.

Josh frowned. "Think it's safe? Wonder how far back and deep it gets?"

Frank grinned. "It'll be good; you've got your flashlight, Jon, and as long as we don't go in too far we'll still see the sunlight." He motioned. "Besides, that water is super clear coming right of the ground like that. It's bound to be even better inside, right?"

Josh nodded in reluctant agreement, looking worriedly at Jon. Jon was his sounding board and risk governor whenever it came to Frank. He trusted the team mentality whenever it came to decisions about diving since they had had so many wonderful shared experiences underwater. He was torn between the excitement of diving such a beautiful place, like kissing a new date for the first time and being reckless. It was sweet anticipation blending the thrill of the unknown with the familiarity of the process.

Jon looked to Josh and back to Frank before speaking.

"I think we'll be OK. We've been in worse visibility during those night dives in the Keys we did last year and still had a blast."

Josh relaxed. Jon was right; they had started many a dive in worse conditions. This did look like a cake walk; no salt water, pitching boat nor rough seas. The spring looked as benign and inviting as a swimming pool.

"Well, let's get this party started," urged Frank, starting back towards the parking lot.

Thirty minutes later, Josh looked over at Jon, fumbling to turn on his flashlight, then to Frank, poised with his left hand upright, his thumb ready to press the deflate button on his power inflator and descend into the mouth of the cavern.

"Come on, Jon," said Frank. "I'm ready to do this."

"Hang on, I want to make sure my light works." mumbled Jon.

Josh felt a familiar tug of sympathy for Jon and mild irritation at Frank's insistence.

"Frank, give him a second to get ready."

Jon activated the light and the beam, barely visible in the morning bright sun, shone on Frank's face. Frank blinked and held up his right hand to block the light. He turned away from Jon and towards the cavern entrance, his regulator firmly clenched in his mouth while the air escaped from his power inflator. His head soon disappeared under the surface of the cool clear spring water.

"Well, guess it's time to go", said Josh with a slight smile to Jon. They nodded at each other, placed their regulators in their mouths simultaneously and slipped below the surface while air bubbled out of their power inflator dump valves.

Josh sank to the white sand in the waist-deep water and touched the bottom with his right hand. A small cloud of sand temporarily covered his hand before the mild current coming from the cavern swept the water clear. A curious crowd of six inch-sized bluegill fish picked at the sandy disturbance, looking for food.

He looked over at Jon who was swimming towards the deeper water at the cavern entrance. The mouth to the cavern was a jagged football shaped gash in the earth fifty feet across and twenty feet high with a large white limestone boulder perched against the cavern wall on the left side like a giant's couch.

In the center the white walls narrowed down to a smaller dark opening. Josh equalized his ears as he descended towards Frank. He looked to his left and could see a number of juvenile freshwater spotted bass hovering above the limestone, facing into the current and eyeing them warily.

The beam of Jon's light flashed erratically as Jon worked his way into the cavern, Frank swimming at his side. Josh caught up to the two of them and they all collectively stopped, as if by design, to catch their breath and adjust their buoyancy with quick squirts of air into their buoyancy compensators.

They glanced at each other, slight grins barely visible behind the plastic and metal of their regulators. Josh realized they hadn't discussed who should be where during the dive but figured since Jon had the flashlight it made sense for him to go first and light the way. Josh motioned Jon forward.

Jon swam towards the back of the cavern where the smaller entrance beckoned, Frank behind him and Josh in the rear.

Josh felt the current pick up as the spring water flowed through the smaller opening and he dumped air from his BC, figuring it would be easier to crawl through the higher flow of water than to try and swim.

Frank, ahead of him, reached the same conclusion and he sank to the rocky bottom, moving forward slowly by pulling along the small limestone boulders littering the floor.

Jon hit the higher flow and began to rise like a kite hit by a gusty breeze. He floundered, dropping the flashlight which landed near Frank's left hand. Frank picked up the flashlight and proceeded through the smaller entrance.

Josh rose up to help Jon. He reached up and grabbed Jon's lower leg, pulling him down. Josh reached behind Jon's left shoulder and dumped air from his power inflator, settling Jon onto the bottom. Jon glanced back at Josh, gave a quick OK hand signal and they both followed Frank deeper into the cavern.

The cavern opened up into a larger room with a shallow rounded ceiling and a tumble of large limestone boulders on the floor. His eyes adjusted to the lower light levels. Josh was surprised how well he could now see in this room with the ambient light from outside. He looked at the stark beauty of the walls and at the haphazard and uneven structure of the floor.

The beam of Frank's light moved around the large room, temporarily lighting up the features surrounding the team. They swam slowly forward, all three bumping on the rocky floor and grabbing the outcroppings of limestone as they appeared, pulling themselves along against the current. This reminded Josh of climbing a rock wall, except it was horizontal and wet.

Bubbles from his buddies' regulators drifted back towards him and over his head, pushed towards the mouth of the cavern by the current.

Josh checked his depth and time gauge, which read a current depth of forty feet at ten minutes into the dive and his pressure gauge.

He had used up 800 PSI of his initial 3,000 PSI.

Plenty of air and time.

He idly wondered how much air Jon and Frank had left in their tanks. Frank was usually the guy who got low on air first, while Jon and Josh usually breathed their tanks down at the same rate.

Even so, Frank should be fine; he's not that much of an air hog.

Frank's light weaved and bobbed near the ceiling, reflecting off of an undulating mirror-like surface and bouncing the light deeper into the passageway, which continued beyond the reach of the light. Josh was momentarily puzzled at the waving mirror on the ceiling until he realized it was air trapped from the exhaust of divers. He watched as bubbles from Frank's exhaust streamed towards the ceiling and rolled towards the mirror, eventually joining the larger silver air bubble and increasing the size of the ceiling mirror.

Wow, that sure is pretty – almost like a seventies style disco ball strobe effect.

As the team swam and clawed their way deeper into the cavern Josh noticed the outside light get dimmer while the contribution of the single flashlight was stronger. Looking backward, Josh could see the entrance restriction illuminated in the shape and color of a large blue hole that grew deeper in blue and harder to see as they moved forward.

Turning towards Jon and Frank, Josh could now only see the area pointed to by the flashlight. The tunnel continued its subway-like appearance and he felt as if they were crawling along the roof of a stationary subway car, the tunnel sloping off on both sides.

Frank stopped and looked back at his two buddies, shining his light in their direction. Josh saw Jon give Frank an OK signal and he followed suit. Frank, seemingly satisfied that the team was doing fine, continued even deeper into the tunnel. Josh looked back again feeling a slight stab of concern as the entrance light was barely visible.

Hmm...think I better call this dive; we've gone far enough.

He checked his gauges and his depth was now forty five feet, time was twenty minutes and he was down to 1,800 PSI.

Josh swam towards Jon and Frank to get their attention but before he could reach them Frank veered off to the left and disappeared down the side of the large boulder field they had been traversing.

Jon dutifully followed the light and Josh had no choice but to follow Jon. The flow of the water now hit him on the right side, moving him gently back out of the tunnel and towards the ceiling.

The curvature of the floor and ceiling gently started to meet and Josh realized that this part of the tunnel was squeezing down. He looked to his left and through a dim milkish blue haze could still make out the exit.

Josh turned back to reach out for Jon and instead of clear water he was met by an angry cloud of swirling brown dirt, like an underwater tornado.

One of Jon's fins momentarily thrashed out of the cloud before returning to the gloom. Josh could see the growing cloud of muddy water start to move towards the entrance.

He realized that he had a choice – he could abandon his friends and swim towards the slowly disappearing blue hole of light and safety or swim into the now black cloud and try to find his friends. His heart raced and his breathing rate increased as the conflicting emotions swarmed through his mind.

A flicker of rational thought from his open water class came back to him – *think, breathe, act.* He stopped, settled down on the white limestone and slowed his breathing down. His divemaster training didn't include handling this extreme of a problem but he had to try.

Josh reached down to look and could barely make out 800 PSI remaining on the pressure gauge from the now-dimming luminescent material recently charged by the sun.

Geez, I've breathed down a ton in a short time!

He started to swim slowly towards the growing cloud of zero visibility, sliding down the side of the boulder towards the cavern wall, right hand stretched out in front as a protective shield and touch sensor.

Soon he was in total blackness, the sound of his exhaust rippling to his ears.

He knew he was descending as the pressure in his ears required the occasional equalization. He felt the water movement before actually touching one of Jon's fins, which was still attempting to swim forward. Josh grabbed Jon's ankle and pressed hard.

I sure hope he feels my squeeze and calms down.

Jon's leg motion subsided slightly and Josh was able to wiggle to Jon's left side. He felt his tank scrape on the ceiling above and his belly on the rock below and knew the passageway was very narrow, even though he couldn't see anything. Josh grabbed Jon's left arm and again squeezed reassuringly. Josh was close enough to hear Jon's high breathing rate and was glad to hear it slow down slightly. They were both in total absolute pitch black darkness.

Working slowly, Josh backed up the slope, gently pulling Jon with him. Josh continued the backwards crab crawl until he reached the top of the boulder and made out the merest hint of milkish blue light to his left. An intense wave of relief flooded through him. They may still get out before running out of air.

He pulled Jon towards the dim light and felt the current shift to behind him, giving him and Jon a grateful gentle push towards the exit. Slowly the ambient light increased enough to where Josh could look into Jon's mask. Jon's eyes were wide and unfocused and when Josh gave Jon an OK hand signal, Jon did not respond.

Crap, at least he's still breathing; I can see and feel his breaths.

Josh read 500 PSI on his pressure gauge and reached over to Jon's, which read 100 PSI.

He fumbled for his backup regulator and found the regulator dragging behind him, occasionally spitting out air as the reg bounced on the limestone floor.

No wonder I've lost so much air. That's not good, he thought as he pulled in the reg and put it in his right hand, ready to give to Jon should he need it.

By now they had half drifted and half swam to the restriction at the entrance. Josh now had enough light to see that he and Jon were covered in a patina of fine silt. Streamers of mud drifted from the sides of his wet suit and joined the thinning cloud of dust floating towards the exit.

Jon's eyes were fixated on the exit and the bright sunlight streaming down over the cavern mouth. Josh worried that as they ascended they would shoot up into the cavern and be spat out of the mouth of the cavern, possibly popping a lung. He hoped that Jon wouldn't turn into another panicked diver, like Jane had the previous weekend.

He dumped the air out of his BC and did the same for Jon. They both gently settled to the floor of the cavern mouth. Sun light filtered through the clear water in front of them, painful in its brightness.

Josh took his backup reg and moved it towards Jon's face, waving Jon to take the reg. Jon continued to stare quietly at the surface of the water only twenty feet away and did not respond. Josh gently pried Jon's regulator out of his mouth and immediately popped in his backup reg.

Jon took to the new reg as a baby would to a bottle switch, not missing a breath. Jon's eyes slowly looked around, as if waking from a nap, and his eyes settled on Josh. He gave a feeble OK sign, lifting his hand in what appeared to be great effort.

Josh exhaled deeply, a feeling of relief finally flooding through his mind. He checked Jon's pressure gauge and it now read zero. His gauge read 200 PSI, which should be enough for both of them to surface from only twenty feet.

Josh pulled Jon forward as he had done while deep in the cave and Jon compliantly followed. They rose slowly up the underwater sand hill outside of the cavern and ascended to the waist deep clear water where this dive had started only forty minutes ago but that now felt like an eternity.

Josh slowly inflated Jon's BC and with the extra buoyancy assisting, stood Jon upright in the water. He removed the reg and mask from Jon's face and removed his own.

Standing nearby was Frank, his eyes wild and wet suit also covered in mud. Around them the peaceful blue sky and quiet green hill contrasted with Josh's feelings.

"What the hell happened, Frank? You almost got us killed!" yelled Josh.

Frank instinctively backed up, his fins causing him to stumble slightly. "Hey, it's not my fault Jon freaked out. He tried to swim through rock!" Frank said.

Josh, too angry to continue talking, reached down to remove his fins. He placed his fins on the concrete wall surrounding the swim area and looked over to Jon, ready to help.

Jon had followed Josh's lead and removed his fins, placing them on the top of the wall next to Josh's fins. They both removed their weight belts and placed them, dripping, on the wall. Frank watched them for a second, shrugged and proceeded to remove his fins and weight belt.

Josh shot Frank a dark look and led Jon to the shallow water next to the wall where the height was perfect for sitting down. He gently turned Jon and pushed him into a sitting position. He started to undo the BC straps for Jon, who had started to shiver partially from the cold water and partially from shock.

"Let's get you out of the BC so you can take off that cold wet suit and warm you up in the sun, Jon," said Josh.

Jon nodded his head slowly and pulled his arms out of the BC. He allowed Josh to pull the BC and tank off his back and set it down on the grass next to the wall. Jon stood up, stripped off his wet suit and walked over to the picnic tables.

Chapter 5

An hour later Josh pulled the truck from the fast food drive-in lane, sipping his cold soft drink. Frank and Jon started on their hamburgers and fries, shoveling food into their mouths. All three of them were very hungry from the cold water exposure, exertion and stress of the dive. In the bed of the truck their dive equipment jostled. They had spoken very little since leaving the spring.

Josh drove in silence while the three finished their meals. His thoughts seemed to churn in sync with his stomach and he barely tasted the food. It was simply nutrition and fuel required to stay alive and not enjoyable. Finally he finished the burger, fries and soft drink and wadded up the trash in the serving bag, tossing it in the back behind the bench seat.

"You know guys," started Josh in a thoughtful tone staring straight ahead, "we've been diving together for a good while. We probably have shared more than one hundred dives."

Jon and Frank looked over at Josh, both wiping off the remains of their frenzied feast with paper napkins. They also wrapped up their debris into their paper bags and pushed them behind the bench seat.

"What happened back there, in the spring, was very dangerous and we were lucky that nobody got hurt or killed," he continued.

"But..." started Frank; Josh stopped him with a quick stabbing stare and returned his eyes to the road.

"I think we've reached a fork in the road with our diving," mused Josh, "Every dive before this one we never had any really big problems nor any giant issues that we had to come to terms with as a group. This dive, though, is different – very different.

"We need to either come clean about what happened and discuss it as friends or never dive together again," he finished.

That last pronouncement echoed through the cab as the tension between the friends grew. Frank and Jon looked at each other and back to Josh. Josh turned left onto the I-10 ramp and started heading east back towards Tallahassee.

Frank spoke first, sounding contrite. "Yeah, OK. We do need to talk about it."

Jon started in too, on the tail end of Frank's statement, "I was so scared, guys...you have no idea..."

As if a dam was released all three of them started to talk at once. Josh held up his hands and said loudly, "Hey, stop talking!"

They all fell silent, only the noise of the tires on the road and the sound of the warm summer wind whistling through the top of the cracked truck windows filled the cabin.

"OK, Frank, please explain what happened during *your* dive," said Josh. He held back his swirling emotions, genuinely curious to know what had gone on in Frank's mind during the dive.

"Well, we all dropped down and swam to the cavern, right? Then Jon dropped his flashlight so I picked it up, made sure you guys were OK, then kept going in," started Frank.

"What do you mean, made sure we were OK?" burst out Jon, "You didn't look back at all, but kept going!"

"Hang on, Jon," said Josh. "Give him a chance to explain."

Frank frowned and continued. "I did think you guys were OK at that point so I continued swimming into the cavern. Boy, it really got bigger inside once we got through that smaller opening. It was so beautiful. I couldn't see the end of the passage. It felt like true exploration."

Josh remembered feeling the same sense of wonder and excitement at finding the large underwater space, totally unexpected given the relatively small football-shaped entrance.

"I did finally stop and look back and saw Jon give me an OK that he then gave to you and that you returned so I kept going," said Frank slightly defensively. "I could also see the entrance behind both of you and saw that I had 1,500 PSI left so I turned to leave. I really thought you guys were behind me, following me out. I figured since I had the flashlight you guys could easily see and follow me."

"I turned to the left to head out and saw light on the bottom of the floor on a sand bed and swam towards it. I think I must have found another way out because it didn't look like where we came in. I started swimming towards the lighted area and when I looked back for you guys all I could see is a huge cloud of silt and it was heading for me."

Jon interjected, "I tried to follow you but when you started to go down that other pathway you kicked up the bottom. It was muddy there, not like the white boulders we crawled in on. Before I knew it I was surrounded in that silt cloud and it got pitch black."

Frank looked at Jon, a horrified expression on his face. "Oh my God, Jon, I didn't know you were in the cloud. I thought you and Josh had seen me disappear down that passage and just decided to turn around and head back down the big passage way."

"I swam down to the sand bed and was planning on meeting you guys back at the smaller entrance. When I didn't see you I thought maybe you had already left so I surfaced. I was about to go back and look for you two when you popped up next to me."

An eighteen wheeler passed in the left lane, temporarily rocking their vehicle in its wake.

Jon continued relating his experience. "I tried to swim after you but it was so dark I couldn't see anything. I could feel the ceiling and walls getting narrower and narrower. I thought I was trapped. I felt somebody grab my leg and squeeze..."

"That was me," said Josh. "I saw Frank turn to the left and head towards the side of the passage. Before I could reach you that same silt cloud covered you up. I could still see daylight behind me but swam into the cloud to find you. Luckily I found your leg and managed to pull you out of there."

Jon gave Josh a grateful look and said, "I'm not sure what was really going through my mind at that point. I just sort of froze up and let you drag me out of the crack and escort me back to the exit. I remember feeling strangely disjointed and unable to make any decisions. Not a great feeling, let me tell you!"

Josh remarked, "I was praying that you wouldn't panic like that lady did last weekend and get both of us in trouble. You had used up almost all of your air so I gave you my backup reg. You didn't respond so I had to gamble that you'd be OK when I swapped 'em."

Jon nodded, "Yes, I do recall you doing that... a small part of me knew what you were doing. I think I was just going on instinct at that point. I knew all I had to do was to trust you."

"Yeah, I think what saved us is all the diving we've done in the past. You must have been on some sort of mental auto pilot," commented Josh.

"Guys, I am so sorry that I put you in so much trouble. I really didn't know what was going on," said Frank in a rare contrite tone. Jon looked at Frank and gave him a friendly poke.

"Yeah, well, next time keep a better eye on your buddies," scolded Jon in a forgiving tone.

"I'm just glad we are talking about it from each other's viewpoint. It really helps me understand what went down," explained Josh, a feeling of relief and camaraderie washing over him.

"Sure wish, though, that we'd had more flashlights. No more cavern diving for us, eh?" He glanced over at Jon in the middle, expecting to see a hearty head nod in the affirmative.

"No, I want to try it again," said Jon quietly after a few seconds of contemplation, his eyes half closed in thought, staring out the windshield.

"What? Are you crazy? After I almost got you killed?" exclaimed Frank, looking over at Jon.

Jon answered, "Don't get me wrong, I definitely don't want to repeat *that* dive. No way. Scared the crap out of me. It just got me really thinking. I really don't like being frozen with fear, unable to move.

"I want to know how to solve problems, *any* problems. It's what I do really well with computers and up until now we've solved every underwater challenge presented to us."

"There must be a way to safely dive in caverns. Remember that large bubble of trapped air that we found deep inside the cavern?" Both friends nodded. "Well, I'm willing to bet that's from other divers' exhaust – lots of other divers who regularly dive in that cave. They must have the right training and gear to go in there and get out safely. And boy, it's so beautiful inside there!"

Josh blinked and concentrated on the bridge as they crossed over the Apalachicola River and crossed into the Eastern time zone from the Central time zone. He was surprised at Jon's decision and realized that he agreed with his sentiment.

He was always interested in furthering his diving skills and experiences. Becoming a divemaster and eventually a scuba instructor satisfied his desire to become more advanced in this sport. He also knew that he was attracted to the stark underwater beauty of the cavern.

He recalled the feeling of being an explorer as the tunnel revealed its dark secrets one fin kick at a time. He looked over at Frank and could see the wheels in his head turning as well. Frank was never one to back down from a challenge. They all three grinned at each other.

"Cool. So we'll look around for somebody to train us in cavern diving, all right?" said Josh. They all nodded, the team reformed and the decision made.

Chapter 6

That night Josh drove to Elise's apartment. He knocked on her door and she opened it with a smile. Josh admired her tight fitting jeans and frilly short sleeve cranberry colored top. They kissed lightly on the lips and he escorted her to the truck, opening her door.

"How was your day?" asked Josh, as he started up the truck.

"Not too bad; it was busy in the E.R. in the morning but slowed down before the end of my shift. How did your diving go?"

"We had a good time," replied Josh. He wasn't ready to tell her what really happened during the dive.

"Good," she replied. Elise went on to describe her day and the antics in the E.R., which usually revolved around a strange combination of office politics set to a backdrop of life and death medical battles being waged.

He knew she liked to discuss her day as a way of releasing the stress of the job and he enjoyed hearing her voice and her passion for her work.

She was relaying a particularly gruesome description of a medical procedure involving the removal of a kitchen knife from a chest when he pulled up to their favorite Italian restaurant, *Casa Di Calabria*.

He parked, walked to her side and opened her door, her hand in his as they walked to the door of the restaurant. They usually ate at the bar since the service was faster than waiting for a table and the bartenders were always friendly and entertaining. They took adjoining chairs at the bar and the bartender took their drink orders.

"That's enough hospital talk; tell me about your day, Josh" said Elise, smiling up at him. Josh idly moved a cocktail napkin on the bar, deciding what he wanted to tell her.

"We had a bit of a scare in the water today, Elise," he said, looking at her.

"What kind of a scare?"

"Nothing really serious, we just got split up for a bit and had some trouble finding each other."

"What do you mean? You told me the spring area was pretty shallow and easy to navigate, like being in a giant pool full of sand and fish."

"Well, we poked our heads into the cavern just a bit, to check it out," said Josh, thankful that their beers had just arrived so he wouldn't have to meet Elise's curious gaze.

"You went inside the cavern? Isn't that dangerous? How far?"

"Um, not...not too far, just enough for Frank to wander off so Jon and I couldn't see him."

"See him? Was it dark? Did you have lights?"

"We had one light that Frank carried around but you could see the outside light from pretty much anywhere in there anyway. We did eventually find him back near the beach area," finished Josh lamely.

Elise looked closely at Josh, her green eyes searching his intently. He knew she was constantly worrying about him diving and he didn't want to alarm her too much but she knew when he was holding back.

"I see...and that's it? End of story?"

"Yeah, for the most part. We did have a nice chat about it on the way back home and agreed we wouldn't do that sort of thing again." He knew how he phrased his answers was crucial. He really didn't want to tell her about their decision to get cavern training and have it possibly spoil their evening.

"So, you going to mention this to Kathy? I know you value her opinion on all things scuba."

Before he could think he responded, "Yes, I'll certainly talk to her. I do trust her judgment and she's been my dive mentor for years."

He hadn't actually thought this far in the future and would rather avoid having a serious discussion about breaking the very diving rules that Kathy instilled in him and his friends. Now, though, he was on the hook to mention it to her. He may avoid telling the entire truth but he wasn't a liar.

His answer seemed to satisfy Elise, who continued on with her earlier story about kitchen knives and cauterizing wounds. Josh had heard enough blood and guts stories before to not be fazed by them as they enjoyed their dinners (a wonderfully tasty medium rare steak heavily doused in Marsala sauce and mushrooms for him and chicken cacciatore for her, the chicken breast covered in vegetables, herbs and a wine sauce).

They finished the evening attending a late showing of *Con Air*, a movie that Josh particularly enjoyed for the hard core prison characters and, as always, Nicholas Cage's so cool to be a bad guy and good guy routine. He fell asleep in Elise's arms at her apartment, after a dessert of love making.

Chapter 7

The next morning Josh parked his pickup truck next to Kathy's Cherokee at *Wakulla Skuba* and walked into the shop through the front door. Bear strutted up, his curly tail wagging with pleasure to see him. He scooped up the small dog and walked back to the workshop, where the sounds of compressed air told him where he'd find Kathy.

"Good morning, Kathy," said Josh, rubbing the short soft black fur on Bear's head.

"Hi Josh," replied Kathy, looking over at him. She sat on a work stool in front of a work bench built into the wall. On the wall above the work bench shelves held hundreds of small plastic drawers, each precisely labeled with the name of the part contained inside.

Most of the tiny parts were used to rebuild scuba regulators. Alongside the shelf peg board mounted on the wall contained a well-organized smorgasbord of tools.

Kathy had taught him how to repair a number of first and second stage regulators from the various vendors she sold and serviced. Josh was still amazed at the large number of tiny parts that had to be installed in the right order in order for the regulators to deliver air at the proper pressure, no matter how deep the diver dived.

He considered scuba equipment, especially regulators, to be life support gear, no less important than the expensive medical gear used at Elise's hospital to keep patients alive.

Josh sat in the work stool next to Kathy and placed Bear on his lap while Kathy returned to the orderly pile of pieces from a first stage sitting in front of her on a clean white towel.

He was torn telling Kathy about the weekend's dive. He didn't want to get a lecture but he respected her opinion about all things related to diving and she had always been his sounding board. Plus he had sort of promised Elise he would.

"Hey, we had ah, problem this weekend during a dive," he started.

Kathy looked at Josh inquiringly, a small regulator spring in one hand and a partially-assembled first stage in the other.

"We, um, went to Jackson Blue Spring in Marianna and tried to do a dive in the cavern. It ended up badly. Jon and I lost Frank in some kicked-up silt and I had to help Jon out. Frank made it out, too," his voice trailed off. He knew his description sounded flat.

"You did WHAT? Went into a CAVERN?" Kathy raised her voice in alarm. She set down the two pieces she had been working on.

"Josh, you've heard me give that lecture for many a class, including yours. No going into *any* structure, be it cave or shipwreck underwater – period. It's just too dangerous. I can see Jon or Frank wandering into a cave without thinking, especially Frank, but I am disappointed in you. I thought you had better judgment."

Josh felt as if Kathy had slapped him, hard. His face flushed red and he placed Bear, who was squirming, on the floor. Kathy's grey eyes flashed in anger. Bear hid under the training table, watching the two, his tail uncharacteristically uncurled and tucked.

"Well, gee, I thought it would be OK, the water was so clear and it's pretty shallow. I thought we could handle it," he managed, eyes downcast.

"You thought...well, it doesn't sound like you did much thinking at all." Kathy let out a huge sigh, as if to shake off her anger somewhat. Her lips pursed.

"OK, I want to hear what happened – every moment you can recall."

Josh retold Kathy the story that he and his friends had relived during the drive home. The start of the dive, Frank taking the lead, the team going far back in the cavern, Frank turning the wrong way and unknowingly losing himself and Jon and his rescue of Jon. He made sure to include the perspective of all three divers, so Kathy could get the whole picture.

"Well, I can't begin to name all of the cavern diving rules that you guys managed to break all in one dive. It's amazing you made it out at all," she said, shaking her head.

"On the drive back I gave my friends an ultimatum that we needed to talk about what happened in an honest manner and come clean with it or I'd never dive with them again," admitted Josh, "We did finally talk about what happened, when things happened and what was going on in each of our minds. We agreed that we would never dive in a cavern like that again."

"Well, let that be a tough life lesson, Josh. This is definitely one of those 'what doesn't kill you makes you stronger' moments. I hope you and your buddies are scared enough to stay out of the overhead environment from now on."

Josh looked straight at Kathy and said, "Just the opposite. We all agreed that we want to get trained on how to dive in a cavern, safely."

Kathy gave Josh a fierce expression, shaking her head, "No, no no...not you! I've lost too many friends in caves; I don't want to go through that again. Cave diving is a part of my life that is in the past."

Josh perked up; Kathy had never mentioned anything about cavern or cave diving. In fact she always went out of her way to pointedly discourage all of her diving students to stay far, far away from underwater caves.

"You used to dive in caves?"

Kathy put down the regulator parts that she had been holding for the past few minutes. Her expression looked inward momentarily.

"Yes, Josh, I used to be a cave diver over a decade ago. I don't do it anymore, though."

Josh got the impression she didn't want to talk about her cave diving past any more, at least not now. A thought occurred to him, though, that she probably still had experience and knowledge she might be willing to share.

"Can you recommend somebody to teach us how to dive in a cavern?"

Kathy looked hard at Josh, clearly thinking how she wanted to respond.

"Are you dead set on this?"

Josh nodded.

"The training is difficult. Very few scuba divers ever even attempt to learn this level of training. Most people just don't like the idea of being underneath something, under water, especially when it's pitch black. Are you sure you are ready for this sort of class?

"It's usually the hardest type of dive training outside of the military and commercial industries and some would argue cavern and cave diving can even give those guys a run for their money. Most people just aren't mentally and physically built to handle themselves properly underwater, underground."

Josh thought a moment then replied in a quiet tone, "I was terrified when I realized that I had to choose between saving Jon or swimming to safety. I honestly can't tell you why I chose to swim into that total blackness and try to rescue him. Maybe it was all of the divemaster training you've given me.

"Maybe it felt a bit like saving a student in the open water with a minor or major problem, like Jane a few weeks ago, and I was just acting on instinct; a conditioned response to a trained behavior. All I know is that I felt compelled to help Jon."

"You do realize you could have easily gotten both yourself and Jon killed, don't you?" said Kathy, quietly.

"I do now, thinking back on it. But at the time it seemed my only clear choice."

Kathy mused, "Actually that is the sort of attitude that is a requirement for cavern and cave diving. You can't just decide the dive is over and surface. You can't let somebody else think for you either. You've got to solve any problems that come up right then and there; there is no do-over or time-out.

"Problem is, I don't know if you were just lucky that you didn't panic yourself, or Jon panic. I still question the giant lapse in judgment that put you and your team in that dangerous position in the first place."

Josh felt her coming around to his viewpoint and pushed his advantage.

"That's why we want more training. I feel that we just stumbled into a place that we had no business in. I want to know *how* to know what is safe and what is not safe."

Kathy smiled ruefully.

"I see you haven't lost your ability to sell. It's one of the traits that makes you a good employee."

Kathy stood and walked through the classroom to her office. Josh and Bear followed, his tail returned to its usual curly self. She opened up a small side drawer on her desk and pulled it all the way out. In the back sat a pile of business cards in disarray. She picked up the cards, thumbing through them carefully. She selected one, a simple white card smudged from years of handling which read:

Drew Thompson - Cave Instructor - Fort White Cave Diving

Below the text was a strange triangular arrow symbol with slits drawn into the sides of the arrow. Below that was a phone number.

"I don't know if Drew is still running his shop in Fort White, much less teaching, but give him a call and find out," said Kathy, handing Josh the card.

"If you guys are determined to continue trying to dive in caverns I'd rather you learned from one of the best first."

Josh felt amazed and honored.

"Wow, thank you; I don't know what to say. I really thought you'd try to talk me out of any more cavern diving."

"The cave community is tight knit and doesn't really advertise their type of training. It's sort of an unwritten code that when people want to learn how to dive in underwater caves they seek out and find the cave community, not the other way around.

"Frankly I'm not sure I'd trust that you guys would never dive in a cavern again, even if you swore it to me right now. There's certainly lots of temptation all around us. I'd rather have you try to learn the proper way and either get it out of your system or master the techniques the right way. You are less likely to become a cave drowning statistic.

"Don't get me wrong, this training is a lot different than what you've done so far. It's more expensive, more physically demanding and certainly requires a much higher level of awareness. You may pass or fail but you certainly will learn to appreciate the dangers of that environment either way."

Josh's elation was tempered by the impression Kathy was making her point by simultaneously offering him a path to enlightenment and a harsh life lesson. He pocketed the card.

"I'll make you proud, I promise," he said, smiling.

Kathy grabbed his arm and raised her voice. "Do *not* do his for me or to try and please me. Let me make it perfectly clear that I am against you learning this style of diving. It is full of ups and downs and some of the downs may change your life for the worse. Do this for *you*."

Josh felt a chill down his spine and he backed up a step, surprised by the vehemence of Kathy's words. Just then the front door bell tinkled, announcing the arrival of patrons to the shop.

Kathy switched expressions, as if the entire cavern discussion had never happened, and said, "Oh, that'd be our kayak rental reservation group. Josh, please go sign them in and issue them their equipment."

Chapter 8

Later that night Josh met Frank and Jon at the *Hole*, sitting in their usual comfy chairs along the river side of the porch. The night was clear and warm with a slight breeze coming off the river. The air was filled with the sounds of frogs and crickets competing with the western music. The scent of jasmine floated from the walkway connecting the three businesses.

Sue took their drink and food orders and returned to the bar. Josh pulled the card that Kathy had given him out of his pocket and announced simultaneously, "Hey, I have us a cavern instructor."

Frank picked up the card and read, "Fort White Cave Diving...hmm, never heard of the place."

"I think Fort White is east of here, right?" piped up Jon.

"Yeah, it's almost all the way to Gainesville, just northwest of that town," answered Josh. He had checked the Florida map sitting in the glove compartment of his truck before dinner.

"So, I called the guy, his name is Drew, and turns out he still does teach cavern diving. He works out of his dive shop which is just south of Fort White along the Santa Fe river off of state road 47. He called it 'smack dab in the middle of cave country'."

"Does he have a web site?" asked Jon.

"No, I asked; I'm not even sure he knew what the Internet was, much less a web site. He also doesn't have an email address. I'm thinking this 'cave country' is pretty third-world."

Frank chuckled and handed the card over to Jon. Sue arrived with their beers. She set them down, smiled and walked away. Josh nodded in thanks.

"OK, so here's how this class works," said Josh, pulling out a small piece of paper he had taken notes on.

"It costs five hundred dollars per person just for tuition, plus we have to pay for any dive fees and extra equipment we may need. The class requires at least two weekends of diving and we have to also buy a manual," explained Josh.

"Ouch! That's a lot of money for a class; lots more than what we paid for our original scuba class," said Frank.

"Yeah, well I got the impression from Kathy that we should be paying more for a higher level of instruction."

Jon frowned, putting down his beer, "You talked to Kathy about our dive?"

"Yes, I, uh, sort of promised Elise I would..."

"You told Elise, too?" broke in Frank. Frank was adept at picking up girls but never found the time or inclination to actually date them for any length of time. Josh suspected that Frank never let himself be attached enough to a woman that he wanted to share his life experiences.

Jon had broken up with his girlfriend a month ago and wasn't ready to reenter the market place, content to work and hang with his dive buddies. Josh was the one with the relatively long term relationship.

"Not exactly, I just told her we had a fun dive with a few minor problems. I didn't want to freak her out and just told her I'd talk to Kathy about it to placate her," said Josh.

"So, how much did you tell Kathy and what did she think about our dive?" asked Jon. Josh knew that Kathy's words and opinions held weight with all three of them, not just himself.

Sue arrived with their meals. She set down a steaming broiled red snapper filet in front of Josh, complete with a side of cauliflower and broccoli and the ever-present luscious hush puppies. Jon dipped his left shoulder to allow Sue room for his plate; a fried grouper sandwich with French fries and cole slaw. Sue set a hamburger and French fries plate in front of Frank.

"Thanks, Sue," they chimed, as they reached for their silverware.

Sue laughed and said, "You boys eat up; I have a nice key lime pie for dessert if there's room." She walked away.

Josh preferred to preserve as much of the natural fish flavor as possible so he squeezed a touch of lemon juice from a half lemon sitting on a side dish. He took his fork, knifed off a section of the tender meat, and ate it; an "um" of pleasure escaping from his lips.

"I pretty much told her the entire story, from all three of our viewpoints," continued Josh, washing down the bite with his beer.

"She was very unhappy that we had broken the rules and it took some coercing but I was able to get this card from her. I never knew it but it turns out she used to go cave diving. I got the impression there's something to that but didn't feel it was any of my business.

"In any rate I think she'd rather have us get some real training than just pay her lip service and continuing trying to dive in caverns without any more training."

Josh didn't mention that he felt that he had come pretty close to getting fired and worse, having Kathy lose her respect for him.

"That's funny, that's pretty much where we are all at anyway," said Frank, biting into his hamburger.

"Can we all afford the class?" asked Jon.

Josh grimaced. This was the delicate part of the conversation. He knew that Jon and Frank could probably swing the $500 but that was a lot of money on his divemaster pay.

He didn't want to borrow money from his friends but he also didn't want to be the one left behind. He had an idea, though.

"I'll need some time to scrape up the money, but I should be good," said Josh.

"You sure?" questioned Frank.

"Yep; I can do it," stated Josh.

"Cool! Why don't we drive over to Drew's dive shop next Saturday morning, check it out and sign up? We have to leave a hundred dollar deposit to lock in the dates," said Josh.

"Sure" and "OK" said both Frank and Jon.

Chapter 9

On Friday night Josh pulled into his parent's driveway. They lived in an upper middle class neighborhood north of Tallahassee, where he had been raised. The home was a two story split-level ranch house made of brick back in the nineteen seventies. The house and yard had been well maintained over the years, as had most of the surrounding homes. Josh was proud of his roots.

"Hi, Josh," said his mother, Jacki, as he entered the house. She gave him a hug and a cheek peck and beckoned him to the dining room. His mother was a middle aged petite blonde woman, thin and still beautiful after raising her only son. She was dressed in a plum colored long sleeve fitted shirt and blue jeans accessorized with a spangly gold necklace and bracelets on both wrists.

The scent of one of his mother's favorite recipes, chicken curry with broccoli, floated up from the table where the elements of the meal were arrayed. His father entered the dining room from the kitchen and shook Josh's hand.

"Good to see you, son. Have a seat." Josh favored his father – medium height, sturdy build, hair a mixture of light and brown that gently curled as it grew, dark brown eyes and rounded facial features. He was dressed in casual tan slacks and a long-sleeve white dress shirt with a button-down collar.

His father, Bill, was a successful executive in the local banking scene. He imagined one day his hair would have noble streaks of grey as did his father's.

Josh sat in his usual chair and waited to serve himself until his parents had taken their seats and said a quick prayer.

He listened to his parents discuss their business lives over his meal. His father liked to talk about the next big happening in town and how his commercial loan department was in the middle of financing all the big deals. His mother was active in their church and in the local women's club.

He loved his parents deeply but hoped he'd never find pride in embedding himself so deeply into the materialistic and social sides of society. The diving business seemed more honest, more pure and certainly more focused on a singular goal.

"So, Josh, how goes the dive business?" asked his father, setting down his fork on the plate containing the remains of his meal.

Josh knew his father wasn't impressed with his decision to drop out of college and start working for Kathy at *Wakulla Skuba* and he liked to remind Josh about it often.

"Business is good. This is the height of our diving season."

"Well, good to hear. You just let me know when you are ready for a real job. I can get you an internship at the bank in a moment's notice."

His father snapped his fingers to drive home his point.

"That's OK, Dad. Actually I want to keep pursuing my diving career. Kathy says I should be ready to test for scuba instructor before the next diving season."

"What kind of money does a scuba instructor pull in?"

"Well, as the expression goes, 'How do you make a million dollars in the scuba business? Start with two million!'."

His father frowned, the joke lost on him. His mother smiled.

"You really should get serious about your life and career goals. You can't just keep playing at a dive shop the rest of your life."

"Dad, it's what I love to do and I make enough to pay my bills. I'm not interested in making a lot of money. I'm interested in getting better at what I already know."

His mother's soothing tone of voice, as usual, gently imposed itself into the conversation. She reached over and touched her husband's hand.

"Josh, we're proud that you are pursuing your dream. We're happy that you're happy, right Bill?"

She looked at her husband. He frowned but backed down as he typically did out of love and respect for his wife.

"Yes, we're proud. It's just I want more for my son."

"Well, Dad, I am interested in taking a higher level scuba class and I could use your help."

Josh knew his father looked at the world as a banker would; a swirl of debits, credits, loans and loan applications. He also knew his best approach to asking for money to pay for his cavern class was to ask for it straight out.

"You want money?" His father's face was momentarily nonplussed. Josh rarely asked for any kind of help from his parents. In addition to his physical features he had inherited his father's pride. "How much?"

"Five hundred dollars," said Josh.

"That's a lot of money. What type of scuba class is it?"

"Like I said, an advanced scuba class. It'll make me a better diver and dive leader. Sort of like a prerequisite to becoming a dive instructor and a better paid dive professional."

His father looked at him closely. He returned the gaze, trying to look as calm as possible, holding steady on his request. His father grimaced.

"Well, the banker in me doesn't mind giving you an unsecured signature loan based on your word, especially if it helps your career. The Dad in me is worried about investing in a dead end job."

"Bill, I think it would be wise to invest in Josh's happiness, too," said Jacki, smiling at her son. Josh smiled back. His mother had been doting on him since birth and he was old enough now to appreciate the unadulterated love and valued it deeply.

"Well, OK, then. The Board has spoken," his father grinned, "I'll write you up a check after dinner. We'll also draw up a zero interest loan document with the repayment details. Might was well get you introduced to specifics of my world, one where a young man can make a decent living."

"Thanks, Dad." Josh was willing to accept these conditions and knew it wasn't smart to rise to the bait about his current job.

His mother reached for the pecan pie, which sat next to her, cooling and releasing the sweet smell of pecans and corn syrup throughout the meal.

"Who wants dessert?" asked his mother. Josh smiled, happy to be at home with family and comforting food and happy that he would be able to afford the cavern class.

Chapter 10

Jon looked up from the tattered map of Florida and announced, "OK, we should be coming up to a bridge that takes this road over the Santa Fe River. The dive shop should be on the other side."

Josh drove the truck farther down state road 47, southbound. Wildflowers grew on the side of the road and fields of cotton surrounded both sides of the two-lane hard top road. He could tell a river was coming up by the tree line bisecting the road up ahead. Soon a bridge came into view and he slowed as they reached the edge of the river.

A green sign posted at the entrance to the bridge proclaimed "SANTA FE RIVER – ENTERING GILCHRIST COUNTY" in white reflective letters. A smaller white sign in black letters warned "NO DIVING FROM BRIDGE" next to it.

"Kind of ironic to be in the heart of cave diving country and see a 'no diving' sign," commented Frank.

Jon and Josh laughed as the truck started the bridge traverse. Jon looked at his cell phone and added, "You can add 'no cell signal' to the list."

Josh noticed the water under the bridge, unlike the clear water of the Wakulla River, was a dark brown tea color.

"OK, slow down, Josh; the turn should be on your left," said Jon.

Josh slowed down as they crossed the bridge, looking left. He saw a small brown sign with faded yellow letters stating "THE SANTA FE RIVER PARK" next to a dirt road.

"I don't see any sign of a dive shop," commented Josh.

"Turn in here anyway," said Jon. "I think it's down a ways from this park."

Josh turned and followed the road. They passed by a series of dirt roads woven around a line of live oak trees that lead to a concrete boat ramp on the water. A number of trucks were parked nearby, empty boat trailers attached to their tow ball hitch.

Josh caught a glimpse of an elderly couple slowly pushing a canoe out onto the river on the boat ramp. A white egret soared across the river in search of food.

The dirt road continued onward until it opened up into a clearing that spread all the way to the river's edge. A wooden sign painted green attached to two posts announced "Fort White Cave Diving" in yellow letters. The clearing turned out to be a makeshift parking lot with a few vehicles scattered around. Along the river's edge to their left sat four structures.

The first was a single story cinder block building painted a dingy white with a single door and a window on each side with black security bars covering them. A tin corrugated overhang sloped downwards from the building with square white wooden posts holding up the extension.

Two picnic benches and a white plastic table surrounded by white plastic chairs stood on the cement porch underneath the roof overhang. A long wooden green painted sign hanging from the tin roof on the left side of the porch stated "Dive & Repair Shop" in the same bright yellow lettering.

To the right of the dive and repair shop stood what looked like a three car garage. The roof was held up by three concrete walls painted in the same dingy white color as the dive shop. The structure reminded Josh of a loading dock without the raised floor and one vehicle was backed up to the building, reinforcing the impression.

Behind the vehicle stood a number of black plastic cattle troughs and above the troughs was a large array of dials, gauges and valves. Josh realized he was looking at a drive-up super fill station.

To the right of the fill station stood a cluster of very large storage tanks, looking like giant upturned black sausages mounted on steel frames. Dozens of thin small steel tubes intertwined between the cylinders. The lines routed to the back of the fill station, where Josh suspected at least one, if not more, compressors must be located.

Wow, look at the size of the storage tanks. They must bank a LOT of air, thought Josh.

The wooden green sign with yellow lettering on this building read "Air – Nitrox – O_2 – Trimix".

Hmm..looks like some pretty exotic types of gas they supply here.

Next to the storage tanks stood another white cinder block building with the same dimensions and color as the dive shop. Another long wooden green sign read "Classroom & Bathrooms" in yellow letters. Next to the last building stood a white doublewide trailer, complete with skirting.

A smaller wooden green sign warned "Private Residence" in the same yellow letters. The windows and door frame were trimmed in green.

Josh pulled up to the dive shop on the left and parked, shutting off the engine. The three of them stared, drinking in the sight.

"Wow, can you believe this? It's like a little scuba city," remarked Frank.

"Yeah, pretty sweet having everything you need in one convenient place," commented Jon.

Josh said, "Looks to me like they are set up for handling serious volumes of divers. Look at the size of the storage tanks near that fill station. And it looks like you can just back up, get your tanks topped off, then go without having to even take the tanks out of your vehicle. Sweet is right."

Frank opened his door and said, "Well, let's go check this place out and see if we can find Drew."

Josh reached the dive shop door first and held it open for his friends and followed them inside. They were met with a welcome blast of cold air. The door closed behind them.

The retail floor space of the shop looked like a supermarket for diving gear – parallel rows of shelving reached six feet into the air and all of the wall space was occupied by equipment hanging from more shelves and hooks.

Josh saw every conceivable type of scuba equipment he knew about represented and some he did not recognize. One wall displayed nothing but a large variety of low and high pressure hoses in various lengths and colors.

A glass display case to his right contained a huge inventory of different high tech diving gadgets, mostly wrist-mount dive computers, regulator kits and a number of different sized pressure gauges.

The back half of the room held a large selection of wet suits, neoprene gloves, dive hoods and dive booties. Next to the wet suit racks were some unusual diving suits that Josh had seen in diving magazines, but never in person.

Those must be dry suits! Imagine being able to be fully submerged in water and only have your head and hands get wet. Amazing, thought Josh.

He walked up to the dry suit rack and casually looked at the price tag on an impressive-looking black dry suit with red trim - $2,199.

Yikes, guess I'll be using my wet suit for the foreseeable future.

Along the right wall a series of scuba tanks stood either free standing or propped up against the wall. Josh saw the familiar aluminum 80 sized tanks that Kathy sold in *Wakulla Skuba* but in this shop they were a minority.

Before him stood small tanks that ranged from one the size of a thermos up to sets of light grey double tanks connected with shiny silver stainless steel bands that easily weighed over one hundred pounds.

Next to the tanks was a bookshelf containing a number of magazines and books related to diving. Jon and Frank walked over to the shelf and started picking up various diving books and thumbing through them.

Josh walked up to the cash register at the corner of the glass cases and nodded at the employee standing behind the case. Jon and Frank joined him a few seconds later. The worker, a wiry tall man in his late twenties, wore shorts, flip flops and a well-worn green t-shirt with *FWCD* screen printed on the left breast and below it a nametag with the name *Roland* printed on it.

"Hi, we're looking for Drew Thompson," said Josh.

"He's in the classroom, teaching. He should be done in about," Roland looked at his watch, "Fifteen minutes. Something I can do for you in the meantime?" Roland's English had a slightly German accent.

"We're here to sign up for a cavern class. I've already called Drew about it and he said to come by to schedule the dates and to leave a deposit," explained Josh.

Roland nodded, "Yes, Drew told me there would be three guys stopping by. I can take care of scheduling your class and take your deposits." Roland reached behind the counter and picked up a well-worn faux black leather appointment calendar. He flipped open the pages and traced the dates with his finger, eventually finding the current month and day.

"So, what days you guys thinking about?" asked Roland, looking up.

Frank stated, "We can only do weekends; when's the next available one?"

Roland looked down, "Um, looks like the first available weekend Drew has is two months from today."

Josh felt mildly disappointed; now that he had his mind set on the training he was raring to go. He glanced over at Jon, who wore the same slightly disappointed look.

"Nothing earlier?" asked Josh.

Roland replied, "Drew is a very popular cave instructor. He's booked up solid for the next two months, even during the week days. Drew teaches almost every day." He looked again at the calendar.

"Ah, wait. There's a notation on today's class. It's a cavern class of four but three of the students canceled at the last minute. There's room for you guys if you can start today. Class starts in," Roland looked at the dive shop clock with a dive flag background on the wall, "half an hour."

"That's great! Yes, sign us up," said Josh.

Roland made a notation on the appointment calendar and handed each of them a form to fill out and motioned to a can of pens. The three dutifully filled out the forms, signed them and handed them back to Roland, who placed them in a file folder. He handed each of them a one-page handout entitled "Cavern Diving Class Prerequisites".

Josh scanned the handout; it listed the minimum scuba requirements needed to sign up for the class and the materials needed.

"Says here we need to buy the *Cavern Diver Training Manual*," remarked Josh, looking up at Roland.

"Yes, you will find those over in the book section," said Roland, waving his hand towards the tanks and books. Jon walked over to the books, grabbed three of the manuals and walked back to the counter, handing one each to Frank and Josh.

Josh flipped through the manual. It contained chapters on gear configuration, the cavern environment, cavern diving techniques and emergency procedures. The writing style was straightforward and the drawings done sparsely yet expertly by hand. The binding, paper and lack of color or photographs indicated the work had been developed and printed locally. It was price at twenty dollars.

Josh opened his wallet to pay for his manual and a thought occurred to him. "Hey, Roland, can you recommend a place to stay that's nearby and cheap? We are on a budget."

Roland looked up at Josh and said crisply, "Continue down the dirt road that follows the river and you'll find an inexpensive place called the 'Santa Fe River Enclave' that is friendly to cave divers."

Chapter 11

Josh entered the classroom door, books in hand. Cool air greeted the trio as they closed the door and looked around the room. In the center of the room three tables were lined up in parallel with chairs arranged on one side of each table, facing the far end of the room, where a large whiteboard occupied the wall.

To the left of the whiteboard was another door, leading to the outside.

On each side of the classroom the walls were covered with large white sheets of paper with black and blue scrawls seemingly randomly applied. In the back of the room signs on the doors indicated the rest rooms.

Josh walked up to one of the sheets and saw that it was a map of a cave system, with tiny lines irregularly drawn over the sheet. Various symbols and numbers marked segments of the lines and occasionally a segment contained a name, such as "Pothole Sink". The legend in the lower right corner of this particular map read "Peacock Springs".

Below the legend was a long list of contributors to the map. Josh marveled at the complexity of the drawing. It looked like a map of a river system or a human circulatory system with large arteries leading off into smaller segments and rejoining back into larger passageways.

"We won't be using those maps for this course," a voice stated. Josh turned and saw a tall wiry man looking at him from the front of the classroom. His hair was short and curly, eyes brown and he looked to be in his late forties. He wore a green short sleeved rugby shirt and jeans and held a dry erase marker in his hand.

Embroidered on the shirt breast pocket was "Fort White Cave Diving" in yellow thread. Behind him, on the whiteboard, he had written "Cavern Class" and below that, "Instructor: Drew Thompson".

Josh looked at Frank and Jon, who had set down their books at the far left chairs on the middle table. He set down his books at the third chair and walked up to the front of the classroom, extending his hand.

"Hi, I'm Josh Jensen," said Josh.

The instructor shook his hand and said, "Drew Thompson."

"These are my buddies, Frank Lasky and Jon Shiloh," continued Josh, waving his hands towards his friends, who rose and walked towards Drew. They took turns shaking Drew's hand.

"Welcome to Fort White Cave Diving, gentlemen," said Drew. "Welcome to the cavern class. Glad you could fill in at the last minute for the students who backed out. I'll be your instructor for the next two weekends. Have a seat and get comfortable; we're waiting for one more student before we begin."

Right on cue the door to the classroom opened and a woman entered, books tucked in her arm. Josh and his friends stared openly. The young woman was petite, with a slim yet athletic build, short blonde hair and crystal blue eyes. She wore a blue tank top under a white fleece jacket worn open, beige shorts and flip flops. She met the gaze of her fellow classmates with an even stare that was neither belligerent nor friendly.

"Ah, Ms Asrid Uhlgren, I presume. Please have a seat," said Drew, motioning her towards the tables. She nodded and sat down at the front table in the middle seat, her back to Josh and his friends. Drew reached over the table and introduced himself to her, shaking her hand. Josh looked over at Frank and Jon, both of whom smiled and winked. It was a pleasant surprise to have another student in the class, especially one so pretty.

"OK, let's get started. I am Drew and will be your instructor for this course. Today we will be in the classroom doing lectures.

"Tomorrow we will meet at Ginnie Springs, right down the road, for land drills and an open water evaluation. Before we start, though, I would like us to get to know each other a bit better," said Drew, standing at the front of the classroom.

"Frank, you start. Just tell us a bit about your diving history and why you are taking this class," said Drew.

Frank looked at Asrid, who had turned in her seat to watch, and stood, giving her a wolfish grin. She looked directly back at him, her face remaining impassive.

He shrugged and said, "Hi, my name is Frank Lasky. I've been diving since I was a kid; my Dad was a scuba diver and he taught me informally. I got 'legal' a few years ago when I took my open water class with my buddies," he nodded towards Jon and Josh, "and we've been diving up a storm ever since. We live in Florida and have done a lot of salt water diving, especially in the Keys but just figured it's about time to learn how to dive in all of these cool springs." He sat down and Jon stood.

"Hi, I'm Jon Shiloh and, like Frank said, I've been diving for a few years. I like the technical challenges of scuba diving and really enjoy being with my friends.

"We've had some amazing underwater adventures the past few years and I'd like to learn how to safely dive in the many caverns of Florida." Jon looked at Drew and his eyes flicked shyly to Asrid. Finally he sat down.

Josh stood as Jon sat and started, "My name is Josh Jensen. As you've already heard from my friends we are a team that enjoys diving and learning together. I am also a divemaster at *Wakulla Skuba*, a dive shop south of Tallahassee and would like one day to become a scuba instructor. I also want to master cavern diving." Josh sat back down.

Drew nodded at Josh and looked inquiringly at Asrid, who stood. She smoothed her short blonde hair, a slight curl springing up. Her deep blue eyes sparkled.

"Hello, my name is Asrid Uhlgren. I am from Goteberg, Sweden," said Asrid. Her English was excellent, with a trace of what Josh figured had to be a Swedish accent. It felt quite exotic and mysterious to Josh.

"I have been diving for five years. The last two years I have been doing technical diving in Sweden and Europe. In my country the caverns and caves of North Florida are known as *the* place to go for overhead scuba training." She sat down.

Drew spoke next. "Thank you. You will all get to know each other more as the class goes on." He cleared his throat and his speech pattern changed slightly as he began a lecture that he had clearly given many times before.

"You have all chosen to pursue cavern diving. Cavern diving is the first level of what we call training for the overhead environment. Basically this means that you will be underwater and underground where you won't have direct access to the surface, like you do in open water.

"It's also dark and cold. Because of this simple fact and because of the nature of the cavern itself this training will be as unforgiving as the environment.

"Some of you may have difficulty mastering the techniques that have been developed over the past thirty years. I will have to break you of open water habits that you were trained to do but that are not appropriate for the overhead environment. This is a rigorous and demanding class, both physically and mentally. You are not guaranteed to pass. If you follow my advice, however, and pay attention to the skills I teach you might succeed. Overhead training has developed by learning from the fatal and near fatal mistakes made by others in a very harsh environment."

Josh squirmed in his chair, slightly nervous. Drew's teaching style was not like Kathy's. Kathy had a knack for making her open water classes a lot of fun for students, even those that were initially tentative about learning how to breathe underwater with a mask on their face.

She used a combination of a disarming easy-going style and in-water games to relax her students as they mastered the basic scuba skills in the pool and open water. Rarely did students fail in her class.

He wasn't sure what Drew had in mind for their training. He looked over at Frank and Jon; Frank was rapt with attention. Josh knew he loved Drew's challenging talk. Jon appeared as worried as Josh felt.

"Please open your cavern diver training manual. We will skim through each chapter and I will hit the highlights that I want you to know cold. There will be a written exam at the end of the class that you must pass with an 80% or higher," continued Drew.

The room filled with the sound of rustling books as the four students opened their textbooks. Drew continued lecturing, using the whiteboard to illustrate various topics and Josh found himself immersed in the details of how caves were formed through years of erosion by underground rivers and how the limestone composition of the Floridan Aquifer made conditions perfect for the formation of these systems around the state. Drew's lecture style was somewhat dry but thorough and he occasionally slung out a challenge question to the class.

"Frank, what is a stygobite?" drilled Drew, towards the end of the morning session.

Frank looked up, startled. Jon reached over and discreetly pointed to the definition in Frank's textbook.

"Um, a stygobite is a creature that lives exclusively in an underwater cave," read Frank.

"And, Asrid, what is an example of a stygobite that you may find in our caverns and caves?" continued Drew.

Asrid replied crisply, "Blind crayfish." She flicked her eyes back at Frank and Josh, raised an eyebrow and returned them to the front.

The class continued in this fashion until Drew declared a break for lunch. "See you guys promptly at one PM back here in the classroom," he said, leaving the room through the door next to the whiteboard.

"Wow, guys, this is pretty intense," said Frank, "Sounds like we have our work cut out for us."

"Yeah, not sure if this guys' trying to psych us out early on or not," said Jon.

Josh said, "I'll take him at his word that we have to step up our game to dive safely. We all know how bad things can get in the cavern."

Asrid, having closed her textbook and notes, glanced back at the three with a slightly curious gaze.

"Um, hi Asrid. Nice to meet you," said Josh, holding out his hand. She reached over and shook his hand; it felt slightly cool and smooth to his touch. She shook the hands of Jon and Frank in turn.

"Hello. Have you guys already been diving in caverns?" she said.

"Well, sort of," said Frank. "We have dabbled into the caverns around here..." his voice trailing off.

Josh didn't want to get into the whole Jackson Blue dive fiasco with Asrid. It didn't seem like a good way to start off with their new classmate.

"Yeah, we've done some cavern diving; no big deal. Just thought it was time to get some training," Josh said, trying to keep his voice low key. Before Frank or Jon could try and impress her with their near death story Josh said, "So, tell us about your diving experience."

Asrid settled back in her chair and answered, "I've never been in a cavern or a cave but have experience in shipwrecks and in cold water diving."

"Sounds exciting, shipwrecks and cold water," said Frank, leering slightly, his green eyes twinkling.

Asrid replied coolly, "I assure you I try to limit the excitement by following the rules and getting the proper training."

"Can you dive year around or only during the summer months?" asked Jon.

Asrid replied, "There are both salt and fresh water sites in Sweden that you can dive year around. The visibility is usually not that good, though, and we all dive in dry suits."

"Are you going to be diving in a dry suit for this class?" asked Josh, curious.

"Yes, I will, even though I hear the water temperature is around twenty one," Asrid answered.

"Oh, yeah, that's around seventy degrees Fahrenheit," said Jon. "We're all diving in wet suits."

"Yeah, we're used to diving in Florida springs with wet suits," said Frank.

"Well, if you guys will excuse me I will eat my lunch now," said Asrid, rising and heading towards the door.

"You want to join us?" said Frank, "We're going to go pick up some subs."

Asrid shook her head. "No, I brought my lunch; I'll just eat out on one of the picnic tables."

They all walked towards the door, following her.

"OK, we'll see you when we get back," said Josh. She waved and headed for her car.

Chapter 12

By the time they returned from Fort White, armed with sandwiches and soft drinks, Asrid has disappeared from the picnic tables in front of the dive shop. The three of them sat around the picnic table and began to eat their sandwiches. A group of divers, hair damp from a morning's dive, sat at the table next to theirs, a laminated map of a cave system unrolled before them on the table.

The divers were all engrossed in discussing the map, clearly planning their next dive. At the corner of the porch an older man sat in a wheelchair, staring out at the sand parking lot. Josh looked closer. The man had an unkempt and slightly disheveled look. His hair was long and in need of a haircut. A baggy t-shirt hung on his thin frame and grubby grey shorts with sandals completed his attire.

The wheelchair was a standard style that was worn from use. A number of stickers from dive companies and dive shops were affixed to the sides and back. Most of the stickers were scuffed up and peeling. The man felt Josh's eyes on him and turned to his right, looking over at Josh. Josh saw a scruffy grey beard and a sad tired face before he quickly looked back at his sandwich.

"Man, that Asrid is hot! I've not come across any hard core beautiful female divers before," exclaimed Frank.

Josh commented, "Yeah, Frank, I know you want to chase her but how about you hold off on this one until *after* the class?"

Jon snickered, "Yeah, we have to work with her. Last thing we need is you pissing her off and making the class tougher. I don't think Drew is going to tolerate those sort of antics in his class."

"I'll try, guys, but you know how it is; once a hunter, always a hunter...," smiled Frank.

Roland walked up to the porch, about to enter the dive shop when Josh waved to him. Roland walked over to their table.

"Hi guys. How did the morning lecture go?" asked Roland.

"Pretty thick lecture; there's a lot of details about the cavern environment that he laid on pretty heavily. Not sure how relevant it is in the long run though. We aren't geology majors," Frank stated.

"Oh, it is all important, believe me. It is about more than just passing the written exam. You really need to learn everything you can about the environment that you will be diving in," said Roland.

Josh spoke quietly, leaning towards Roland and nodding slightly, "Hey, who's that guy over in the wheelchair?"

Roland looked and turned back to Josh. "Oh, that is just Allen. He hangs around here all the time. I guess he has nowhere else to go."

"Um, does he dive?" asked Josh, who had heard of programs for disabled divers from Kathy.

"No, I do not think so. He has been around here for years; before I started working here even. The rumor is he used to be big into cave diving before he got hurt and had to give it up. He pretty much keeps to himself and does not like to talk to anybody. Drew barely tolerates him. I think they used to be buddies back in the day but Drew does not like talking about Allen so I would not ask about him. They avoid each other like the plague." said Roland.

Jon looked at his watch and said, "It's almost one PM; we better be getting back to the classroom."

"Yes, Drew is very punctual. You guys enjoy the rest of the class," said Roland, who turned and walked into the dive shop. Josh drank the rest of his soft drink and got up, throwing the remains of his meal into the plastic-lined trash bin at the edge of the porch. He nodded to Allen as he walked past. Allen appeared to look right through him and did not respond.

The three of them returned to the classroom to find Drew and Asrid engaged in conversation. Josh caught bits of diving terminology before Drew noticed them return and motioned them to sit down.

"Welcome back. I hope you enjoyed your lunch break. I will pick up where we left off before lunch," said Drew. He continued discussing the cave environment before moving on to scuba equipment appropriate for the overhead environment. Drew had an arrangement of diving gear set up on the table in front of the class.

"Now since this is only the cavern level of overhead training you are allowed to dive in your standard open water gear," said Drew, looking around the classroom. "The only required modification I want to make is to swap out your standard length second stage hose with a seven foot hose. We call it the 'long hose' and it allows two divers to share air while swimming single file. You'll see when we start to do the cavern drills how important and natural this technique will feel.

"Tomorrow morning I'll have each of you set up your gear as you normally would so we can see how the rest of your equipment looks. Between now and then if you don't have a long hose please purchase one. I sell them for thirty dollars in the shop." Drew held up a first stage regulator with a long black hose connecting the second stage to the first.

Josh looked over at Jon and Frank. He had read about the long hose in the textbook over lunch but wasn't sure they needed to get one. Looks like they needed them now.

"You'll also need two lights per person. Most divers have a large light they use as a primary light and a small backup light that you can stow somewhere so it's out of the way until needed."

He pointed to his display of a variety of scuba lights of different sizes. "Cave divers prefer to use a canister light, where the light bulb is separated from the canister containing the batteries. The battery canister can then be mounted either on your tank or your waist strap, making it much easier to carry the light source in your hand with a strap."

He demonstrated by turning on a switch at the top of a round canister about the size of an oatmeal container. A thick cable snaked out of the top of the container to a round light fixture that began to glow dimly at first, then brighter and brighter. Drew slipped the light attachment over his wrist with a metal handle and made a half fist, pointing the light towards the class. By now the light shown very brightly, as if a car headlamp was pointed their way.

"The advantage of separating the battery compartment from the light head makes it possible to carry the light head on your wrist, like so. Now your hands are free to manipulate other objects, such as a cavern or cave reel," commented Drew, moving the light back and forth with his hands.

Josh marveled at the output of the canister light and the ease of use. It was much brighter than the lights they had. Too bad the price tag for the canister lights started at $1,000 in the next door dive shop. The largest and brightest light that Kathy carried at *Wakulla Skuba* was the eight D-cell heavy beasts they currently had in their dive bags.

Those flashlights had lanyards that they slipped around their wrists while diving so they wouldn't drop them.

Guess we'll just have to get by with our lights, thought Josh.

"Make sure you have two lights and a long hose for tomorrow. Does everybody have this equipment?" asked Drew, looking around. He turned off the canister light.

Asrid answered first, "Yes, I have a canister light and two backup lights bungeed to my diving harness. I dive a set of double 85s."

Frank covered up a smile and poked Jon, who looked away slightly embarrassed. Josh answered for himself and his friends, "We have hand-held eight D-cell lights for our primaries and some three C-cell lights for backups. Um, we'll have to get some long hoses. We're diving single aluminum 80s in, um, standard open water configuration."

Drew said, "Good, that will work. See me if you need any help figuring out how to replace your standard length breathing hoses with the long hoses. I'm glad you brought up the issue of tank sizes as well.

We need to learn next how important gas management is to cavern and cave divers. Turn to the next chapter on Gas Management and we'll jump into that discussion. I warn you there's some math involved."

Drew proceeded to discuss the various sizes, shapes and materials of scuba tanks and the different missions for each type.

"As cavern divers you are permitted to dive with either a single tank or with a set of double tanks. Usually open water divers use a single tank with a buoyancy compensator designed for open water diving. Cavern and cave divers use a back plate, harness and wing configuration, which better balances the weight of the double tanks across your back and makes it much easier to stay horizontal in the water column." Drew lifted up a set of doubles, complete with a back plate, harness and wings attached.

Frank leered at Asrid when Drew said "horizontal" and Josh shot him a quick glare. Josh wished that Frank would behave, especially during this part of the class. Josh has always been a scuba gear fanatic and this was all new and welcome territory for him.

"So it looks like Asrid and I will be diving doubles with back plate, harness and wings while you three in the back will be diving singles with BCs, right?" asked Drew.

Asrid nodded, followed by Josh, Jon and Frank.

"Great – this won't present any problem since you will all dive as a team and even if you are carrying different amounts of air on your back you will make a team adjustment to account for the smallest amount of gas in use by any one diver," Drew said. He picked up a dry erase marker and started writing on the white board.

"We dive what we call the *rule of thirds* in cavern and cave diving. Who can tell me what that means?"

Jon and Asrid's hands shot up.

"Yes, Jon?"

"You breathe one third of your starting gas for entering the cavern, use one third for exiting the cavern and save the last third as a reserve," said Jon, who had also skimmed the textbook during lunch.

"Exactly!" exclaimed Drew, continuing, "So you should consider one third of the gas in your tanks to belong to your buddy and not to you. It's there in case there's a problem with their air supply and you both have to get out of the cavern or cave with just a single working system."

The class, even Frank, was rapt with attention now. Discussions involving life saving measures had a way of drawing in an audience.

"So, if Asrid is diving two tanks and you guys are diving a single tank how do we account for the difference in volumes? Let's pretend that it's just two of you diving in a cavern—Asrid and Frank."

Frank perked up and smirked at the back of Asrid's head. Drew frowned and continued.

"Let's say worst case scenario is that you are both far back into the cavern and Frank has used up his first one third of his tank. It's time to leave, right?"

The class nodded.

"Frank gives Asrid the 'thumbs up' sign, which is the universal sign in cavern and cave diving that it's time to turn around and exit," Drew held up his thumb, pointing it towards the ceiling repeatedly.

"OK, so what if Asrid has a catastrophic loss of gas from a blown manifold O ring and within seconds she has no air left? She will have lost *all* of the gas in her set of 85s. She must rely on the remaining air supply in Frank's tank, his itty bitty aluminum 80, to get both of them out of the cavern. So Frank will breathe his second third and Asrid will breathe the last third. Assuming they don't have any delays and remain calm they should just barely make it out." Drew paused, letting the point sink in.

"So even the rule of thirds is optimistic and assumes that you breathe air on the way out at the same rate you did coming in. My experience is that people tend to breathe more under stress and can even panic if not mentally and physically conditioned to share air properly on exit. My job is to over train you so that you will survive this worst case scenario."

Josh was riveted. This was the core of the message from the class for him - how to deal with any problem that occurs under water, underground, and under stress and survive. He could definitely relate to using more gas under stress; their Jackson Blue dive had proven that.

By the time Drew was done with this chapter Josh had pages of hand-scrawled equations and a slight headache. Frank looked slightly lost with all of the numbers but thankfully Jon and Asrid appeared to track the discussion perfectly. At least somebody on their team understood all of the "gas math".

Drew wrapped up the afternoon with a discussion of the various emergency procedures they would be learning and mastering as well as the special light signals they would use in the darkness.

"Don't worry if you don't quite get what I mean by a 'touch contact zero viz air share' drill. We'll simulate it tomorrow on land and practice in the open water before we ever try it in a cavern. The water skills you are to learn and master are presented in a progressive style that builds up from the earlier skills," said Drew as the afternoon session neared the end.

Drew went on and reviewed some of the medical aspects of diving and more on the new diving techniques that the cavern environment required. Josh felt exhausted from both the fire hose effect of all the new material plus the heightened stress of realizing he will soon be facing new challenges underwater.

Finally, Drew looked at his watch and stopped. He looked over the class and a slight smile crossed his face. Josh thought it looked predatory and slightly menacing.

"OK, well that's the end of the lecture portion of the class. Tomorrow we put all of this theory to practice and see if you can apply this knowledge to actual diving." He paused and looked slowly around the room, catching the eye of every student one by one. Josh felt uncomfortable when his stare reached him but held his return gaze without outward emotion.

"We'll meet at Ginnie Springs promptly at nine AM, out front. If there aren't any questions I'll see you then. Don't forget that the dive shop is open for another two hours if you need to pick up any more equipment." Drew turned and picked up a dry eraser, clearing the board.

Chapter 13

The truck hit a buried root and lurched, jostling the occupants and the gear in the back. A gentle clank floated from the rear of the truck as the scuba tanks momentarily touched.

"Slow down, Josh," cautioned Jon.

Josh let off the gas pedal and steered carefully down the dirt road, trying to avoid any other bumps. After a quick dinner in a sub shop downtown they were looking for the lodging that Roland had recommended. Ten minutes down the road from FWCD they were still searching for any signs of civilization other than the dirt road overhung with live oak tree branches laded with grey Spanish moss.

The Santa Fe River snaked to their left as they followed the white dirt road. Gloom settled over the live oaks, palmettos and cypress trees as late afternoon transitioned into early evening. Josh turned on his head lights with a pull of a button and the road illuminated with the erratic beams from the swaying truck.

A family of deer looked up curiously near the side of the road, their eyes glowing a bright yellow, and returned to dining on bushes that lined the road. Josh noticed they certainly didn't look caught in the headlights. On the contrary the deer seemed perfectly content to share the evening with the interlopers in the truck.

"Um, maybe it's not here?" said Jon, "It sure looks like we are going nowhere. Sort of like a scene from *Deliverance* or something. Maybe we should just head back to High Springs and I-75 and find a hotel."

"Oh, come on, Jon, where's your sense of adventure?" prodded Frank, "What's more fun than wandering down a river road late at night after a busy day, getting thoroughly lost?"

Josh grinned and kept threading his way around the exposed roots on the road. Across the river a light from a home on the other side flickered momentarily through the trees.

"See guys? There still is civilization out here," commented Josh, pointing to his left. The night had deepened enough to attract clouds of insects swarming around each head lamp.

A bit farther down the road they could see a glow alongside the river. The left side of the road opened up into a clearing. A line of cinderblock buildings on the right side of the road were arranged in an arc that matched the concave bend in the river. The single story buildings each contained two motel rooms with a numbered door and window.

Festive white lights hung across the border of the roofs gave the scene a relaxed cozy feel. Vehicles occupied positions in front of most of the doors. Across the dirt road and sandy parking lot a small dock extended out onto the tannic water river, lit by a pair of blue and green colored spotlights mounted at the base of the dock. A number of lawn chairs sat around the dock, some occupied by tenants enjoying the coolness of the night.

Josh could see the glow of a cigarette floating above one of the chairs. On both sides of the dock permanent black cooking grills mounted on black poles sprouted next to wooden picnic tables. An orange flickering glow accompanied by a tantalizing scent of cooking meat from one of the grills indicated it was being used.

Josh spotted a bright burnt orange "Office" sign in neon script sticking out from the central building and parked in front of it. A poster inside the window proclaimed "Santa Fe River Enclave" by the light of a lamp.

"This must be the place," said Frank, unnecessarily. They piled out of the truck and walked up to the door of the office.

They stepped inside of a tiny lobby, with barely enough room for the three of them to stand. Overhead a dual neon strip buzzed out harsh white light. Josh tapped on a silver office bell sitting on the tall counter. A display of aged leaflets advertised the amazing wonders of Florida tourist attractions. A short middle-aged man of Indian heritage walked into the room from behind a cloth curtain, from which they could hear the sounds and see the flickers of a television set.

"Hi, we would like a room for three for one night, please," said Josh, smiling. The manager pushed across a small registration card and said "Forty five dollars. Fill this out," in a Hindi-accented monotone.

They all three looked at each other and shrugged. Josh completed the card and they each pulled out fifteen dollars and laid it on the counter. The night manager swept up the money, reached underneath the counter for a few seconds and produced a hotel room key attached to a large green plastic diamond shaped tag with the number "15" stamped in gold, faintly visible from years of wear. He slid it over to Josh, along with a battered TV remote and returned to his retreat behind the cloth curtain.

A few minutes later Jon held open the screen door while Josh opened the inner door to room # 15 and flicked on the overhead lights, which turned out to be more ceiling mounted long tube harsh white neon. The room was sparse but large with three beds arranged in a row, two wooden chairs with worn seat cushions and a door leading to what appeared to be a small bathroom.

Near the bathroom stood a full sized white refrigerator with chipped enamel, it's compressor motor buzzing. Two metal poles mounted horizontally near the ceiling next to the refrigerator provided the illusion of closet space, complete with a few plastic hangers. A small TV sat perched atop a long simple wooden dresser along the left wall. Between the beds sat two night stands, each with a single-bulb lamp perched on top. Above the middle bed a narrow high mounted window contained an AC unit. Josh walked over to it and turned it on to high cool. The unit fan whirred to life, blowing out stale smelling warm air.

Within a few seconds the air began to blow cool. Frank walked over to the bed nearest the bathroom and plopped his bag on it, clearly claiming it. He turned on the lamp beside the bed. Jon threw his bag on the bed in the middle and Josh took the far bed, nearest the dresser and TV. Jon clicked on the second lamp. Both lamp shades were stained with yellowed burn marks from years of incandescent bulbs.

Josh turned off the overhead light near the door and the room transformed from an over lit dingy tired room to a peaceful place to rest among the comforting yellow light and mild shadows.

Jon went to the bathroom door, opened it and peered inside curiously. He looked back to his friends and shrugged.

"This'll do," said Frank.

"Let's go grab a beer and check out the river," said Josh. They followed him back to the truck, which Josh had parked directly in front of their room. Josh pulled out a six pack of beer from the truck bed and walked across the parking lot towards the chairs near the dock.

The chairs were now empty yet Josh could still smell lingering cigarette smoke and grilled meat scent from the previous occupants. Across the lot TV lights flickered in the windows of the rooms where vehicles waited at their doors. An occasional moth passed in front of the lights outlining the buildings, casting giant winged shadows across the dock.

They each took a chair and a bottle of beer, twisting off the tops and settling back, watching the river. Moonlight traced the flow of the black water as it passed them, small slivers of silver alighting on the ripples of current. Josh felt himself relaxing as the sounds of the cicadas, crickets, frogs and other night creatures combined with the gentle burble of the river and the taste of the lukewarm beer.

"So, what'd you guys think about today?" asked Jon.

"That Drew's a ball buster," started Frank, "and boy did he fill our heads with lots of stuff today. I still don't get how to calculate our turn pressures. Jon, you're gonna have to do that for the team."

Josh smiled and waded into the discussion. "Well, we should all know how to figure out the gas math, I'd think. Don't worry, we'll get it. I'm sure Drew will help us more as the class goes along."

"Not sure about that, he sure makes us feel that we aren't worthy of his instruction and doesn't seem as helpful as, say, Kathy," opined Frank. He took a healthy swig from his bottle.

"I think it's partially his style and partially just the way you have to teach divers who go underground," offered Jon, rubbing his chin while he stared out at the river, "I'd think that we should all appreciate just how dangerous this sort of diving can be IF we don't pay attention to the rules and procedures."

"Yeah, I agree," said Josh, "It feels like we are learning from the mistakes of those who dove in the overhead before us."

"Well, I can't wait until we get to do the actual DIVING finally," said Frank, pointing his beer to the sky, "So I can master this type of diving too."

Jon punched Frank in the arm, "Boy, you are always so full of yourself. It's amazing there's any room left for anything else."

Frank punched back good naturedly, "Yeah, well, we are a great team and we've mastered every diving class we've taken so far – all of us."

Josh leaned his head back and looked up at the ribbon of sky visible above the river, trees framing the view.

This far away from any city lights the night sky glowed with background light and he could easily make out the Milky Way scattered across the sky like loose diamonds spilled on the ground as they dribbled out of a black felt bag. Bright stars competed with moonlight to fill the darkness.

Frank was right. Tomorrow they would be tested underwater as they had been many times before. He felt confident that all three of them would flourish and add the cavern rating to their growing list of scuba accomplishments.

"Besides we have to look good in front of Asrid. She's way hot and all techie diver and stuff," commented Frank.

"Not that again, Frank," said Jon, exasperated. "We already warned you not to screw up our class with your woman antics." Josh nodded and clinked bottles with Jon. Both took a swig from their bottles.

"I know, guys, I know – I'll leave her be. I'm just saying that it certainly spices up the class having her in it. I certainly plan on enjoying that."

Josh grudgingly had to agree but didn't want to voice his opinion. He didn't need to fuel any possible fires between himself and Elise with buddy crosstalk.

"She is easy on the eyes, I'll grant you that. I'm thinking, though, that we can learn a lot from her besides just enjoying the eye candy. She is diving doubles and already has some technical training. Heck, she may out-dive us all," offered Jon.

He set down his empty and reached to grab another beer. The other two accepted their seconds from Jon as well. The splish sound of twist off beer bottle tops momentarily overwhelmed the steady watery background sound of the river.

"Well, I'm glad we decided to do this guys. I love the challenge that Drew is giving us and can't wait to dive in a cavern," said Josh, "Here's to a successful class!"

They all clinked bottles and drank.

Chapter 14

Early the next morning Josh parked his truck in the Ginnie Springs sandy parking lot, next to Asrid's late model white rental sedan and Drew's white van. The day was clear and sunny. They climbed out of the cab, the early morning humidity and still air already drawing sweat. The three friends opened the truck door and walked over to Drew and Asrid standing in front of Drew's white van.

"Good morning guys," said Drew, turning to greet the rest of his class. Asrid turned as well. Today she wore a white t-shirt with a black silhouette image of a diver and blue writing, cut-off blue jean shorts and flip flops. Josh figured the writing was in Swedish and was probably related to her dive shop back home. Drew wore the same rugby-style light green short sleeved shirt with "FWCD" embroidered in yellow thread above his left breast, light brown shorts with pockets and flip flops. Josh loved the informality of the scuba instructor dress code.

"Good morning," said Frank waving at Drew and Asrid. Josh and Jon just nodded in hello. Asrid nodded back to Josh and flashed him a quick smile, her blue eyes briefly capturing his.

"Follow me, guys," said Drew.

The class followed Drew down a dirt path towards a copse of trees arranged around a clearing. Josh could see a hint of clear water through the trees in the middle of the clearing. Buttressing the tree line was a large wrap-around wooden porch with built-in benching. Drew stepped onto the wooden porch and stopped near a set of wooden stairs that led down into the water.

The porch was populated with swimmers, many carrying inner tubes and inflatable floats down to the spring. The occasional diver or snorkeler made their way down to sets of wooden stairs that lead into the spring.

Josh looked at the spring itself and was surprised at the beauty in front of him. The trees formed a circular ring around the basin of water that was constantly being filled by the spring. The excess water drifted lazily down a spring run that lead to the tea-colored Santa Fe River. The water was crystal clear with a variety of tints of blues and greens, darker hued in the deeper water. He could clearly make out white limestone rocks and a sunken tree trunk on the bottom of the spring basin.

The water on the Wakulla River was clear as well but this spring water, fresh from being filtered underground, was the clearest he had ever seen. He could see a few scuba divers swimming casually near the sandy bottom of the basin, their exhaust bubbles occasionally breaking the surface.

Drew stopped along a line of wooden benches built into the porch and turned back to face the class, the spring as his backdrop. The four students gathered around him in a semicircle.

"Welcome to Ginnie Spring. It is one of a number of springs on the property. What are the tell-tale signs that this is a spring, Jon?"

Jon looked at Drew and answered, "The water is coming out of the ground and to the surface. You can tell by the clarity of the water and by the direction and presence of flow."

"That's right; notice near the center of the spring basin there is a slight ripple of water, indicating flow. We call this a boil. Of course it's not really hot water; you'll be thrilled to know the water temperature is a steady sixty eight to seventy two degrees, year 'round," stated Drew, a slight smile on his face.

"The cavern zone starts right over there," continued Drew, pointing to a submerged limestone ledge, "where the entrance starts at around twenty feet in depth. The cavern opens up into a small alcove that leads into a larger room we call the Ginnie Ballroom. About two hundred feet back into the cavern there is a steel grate made from steel rebar that prevents divers from going deeper into the cave."

Josh watched as the group of divers disappeared into the cavern, their fins slipping under the limestone ledge.

Absolutely beautiful; I can't wait to dive here.

He looked at Frank and Jon. All three shared the same excited grin. He looked at Asrid and the sides of her mouth were slightly upturned in an apparent understated expression of excitement.

"Max depth at the back is no greater than sixty feet. We will be doing our initial cavern dives here. It's one of the few 'safe' cavern zones in the state where divers, even those without cavern training, are allowed to enter with lights. I still want you to respect the overhead environment though; you will still be underwater with thirty feet of solid limestone between you and the surface when you get two hundred feet back," intoned Drew.

Josh felt his excitement ebb slightly and was reminded that he was still in class and even though he would get to dive here soon it would be working in a class setting.

"OK, well, that's where we will be diving later today. First, though, we will be doing land drills," said Drew. He walked away from the spring and they all followed. Josh was curious what land drills entailed. The textbook never explained this particular part of the class.

Drew walked over to a stand of young oak trees near the parking lot, each tree trunk a foot or less in diameter. He reached to his waist and unclipped a blue spool hanging from a belt loop on his shorts. He took the spool and twisted a small knob on the side of the spool, releasing white line.

Grasping the free end Drew wrapped it around a tree trunk at shoulder height and proceeded to unspool the string from tree trunk to tree trunk, wrapping each trunk so that the line was taut. He wrapped the string around the last tree, reeled in the excess string and locked down the spool by tightening the knob on the side. He stepped to the side of his creation, clearly satisfied with the result. To Josh it looked like the initial strands of webbing from a giant spider.

"I have just set up a line that we will use to simulate the in-water drills. Recall from yesterday we discussed that a cavern dive must always have a way to exit back to open water and the surface by using a line," said Drew. A slight breeze rustled through the trees, providing temporary relief from the heat.

"This is one of the major differences between an open water dive and a cavern dive. You will always be within an arm's length of this line. The line will be installed by the team and removed by the team on every dive. It is literally your life line and if you lose all visibility this will be your way home."

They spent the rest of the time before lunch practicing following the line around the tree trunks. At first Drew had them each walk alongside the line separately. Next he had them try following the line with their eyes closed, their arms out in front to ward off colliding with wood or each other.

He kept adding more and more variations until they could easily navigate the line, pretending to share air, handling line entanglements and position switches.

Finally they took turns running the line as a group, each of the four occupying all possible team positions. They each also took turns being the 'reel man', which had the responsibility of tying off the line, running it around the tree trunks and reeling it back in when the 'dive' was over. Josh, on his turn, thought that the reel was fairly easy to use and he had little trouble handling the task.

"OK, that's good," said Drew, after a particularly complex route that went around a few trees, under some branches and beside a picnic bench. "Just know, though, that you won't be able to communicate by talking when you are underwater. You will have to rely on hand signals, light signals and eventually touch contact when you aren't able to see. The next round of drills will simulate swimming in zero visibility water."

"My underwater hand signal for you to close your eyes is this," said Drew. He passed his open hand in front of his eyes, palm towards his face, in a slow gesture, like a magician casting a spell. "Keep your eyes closed until I tap you on the head; that means that the drill is over and your vision is restored. Don't open your eyes during the drill or you won't get the whole point of practicing with the lights out. If you open your eyes you are only cheating yourself. The point is to simulate total darkness and see if you can handle tasks without the benefit of being able to see."

Josh thought about what Drew had just said. He nodded inwardly. He thought it actually sounded pretty cool, if a bit scary, to purposefully close your eyes underwater and perform tasks. He recalled that during his divemaster training there were many times when Kathy drilled him in some sort of underwater skill that involved removing his mask and swimming around. Vision was so impaired underwater without the benefit of a mask capturing an air pocket in front of your eyes you might as well be blind. He also recalled having to pull Jon out of Jackson Blue in total darkness and a slight shiver went down his spine, despite the warm summer day.

"If I do see any of you peeking, though, I'll just make you do the drill again," smirked Drew. Asrid smiled briefly.

"OK, line up along the line – Jon, Frank, Asrid then Josh," directed Drew, motioning them towards a straight segment of line between two tree trunks. The four students obediently walked next to the line and stood in single file, facing Drew, the line to their left.

"Put your hand on the line like this."

Drew made the classic scuba diver "OK" sign, an exaggerated "O" with his thumb and forefinger, with the line placed inside the "O".

"We call this 'OK'ing the line'. This not only gives you tactile reference to the line but encourages a light touch. You only use the line as a guide to the way out of the cavern. You do not want to grab it and pull yourself out. It's too frail for that.

"The line won't break but you'll pull it off of anything that you placed it around on the way in. If the line comes loose you will be in danger of getting entangled in it and possibly never finding your way out. Now, everybody 'OK' the line," Drew said.

Josh watched the three students in front of him reach their left arms out, shoulder height, and circle the line with their thumb and forefinger 'OK' signs. He did the same. The nylon line felt smooth in his fingers, the line stretched firmly across the insides of his "OK".

"OK, now, grab the person in front of you. The best place that most closely simulates one of the positions you would use in the water is to hold them above the elbow on the same arm that they are using to follow the line, like this."

Drew stepped between Jon and Frank, put his 'OK' on the line with his left hand and placed his right hand on Jon's left elbow, above the joint. He lowered his head and match Jon's posture, as if drafting in a race.

"I want to take advantage of the fact that the person in front of me will follow the line and lead me out. I don't want to totally trust them, so I have my hand on the line to validate their direction. But it's to my advantage and his to stay tucked in beside him, out of the way of his fins and body and follow him."

Drew continued, explaining the hand signals for "stop", "go", "back up" and "problem"; all that might be needed while swimming behind or in front of somebody in the dark and cold.

Josh followed the demonstration, fascinated by this more intimate style of underwater communication. Divers learned hand gestures early on in their training but this was taking it to another level by combing hand gestures with touch.

"OK, let's try it as a team. Grab the person in front of you again and close your eyes when I give you the signal. Then only react based on what you feel, not what you hear."

Josh watched the team re-establish contact with the line and touch contact. He saw Frank look back and grin when Asrid grabbed his left elbow. He reached out and grabbed her left elbow in turn. Drew gave the "lights out" sign and he closed his eyes. Being at the end of the train he knew he had to start the ball rolling as Drew had mentioned so he gave Asrid a gentle nudge.

A few seconds went by and she started moving forward, slowly. Josh followed, keeping his left hand on the line and his right hand on her elbow, his head tucked down towards her shoulder. They moved forward as a group, still slowly. At one point Josh walked into the back of Asrid; he quickly stepped back and muttered a soft "sorry". He paused a few seconds, giving the rest of the team time to figure out what obstacle was in their way and after ten seconds went by he gave her a nudge again, indicating that he was ready to continue. After a few seconds he felt her move and followed.

Josh felt this was a slow process and wasn't too sure that it would work in the real underwater world, where time was measured in breaths. Finally Asrid stopped and he felt a tap on his head. He opened his eyes and saw that the team had reached the literal end of the line, back to the imaginary open water part of the dive.

"Very well. So, what do you think of touch contact?" asked Drew. Josh dropped his hand from Asrid's shoulder, realizing that the others had disconnected as well and he didn't want to seem too forward. Asrid looked back and gave him a smile. They all turned to face Drew, hands at their sides.

Josh commented, "It sure feels like it takes a long time to do touch contact. I'm not sure we'd ever really make it out if it takes longer to swim back than it did to swim in; we'd run out of air."

Drew smiled, "Great observation, Josh. Yes, you need to keep in mind what your personal and team limits are for any dive parameters, including your comfort level with having to navigate as a team in zero visibility. In real life, luckily, you are rarely in touch contact for very long.

"Actual silt outs tend to be localized within a small area of a cavern or cave. There are the rare occasions, especially for new caves, where you only have visibility on the way in and zero viz on the way out. Experienced dive teams know to adjust their dive planning to leave before the standard one third rule so they won't worry about having enough gas to exit."

Frank asked, "How am I supposed to monitor my air supply with my eyes closed?" He swatted a gnat from his face.

"Ah, another great point – dealing with loss of vision while cavern or cave diving is mostly mental. If you start to obsess and worry about things like how much air you have left or the speed of the exit you may start to forget your technique and slide down the path to panic. Let me tell you, having been there, that you should take the mindset of not worrying about your air. Don't worry about not being able to read your gauge. Tell yourself that you turned the dive to exit with plenty of air and since you are moving slowly and calmly you aren't going to use it any faster than normal. Just thinking about being more relaxed and not worrying about things you really can't control will increase your chances of survival," instructed Drew.

"But what if you do run out of air or lose contact with your buddy?" asked Asrid.

"Wonderful – I see you guys are thinking about the possibilities! That's the type of thinking that I want to encourage, especially when you are actually underwater in the cavern," exclaimed Drew. "Let's go through the steps of what to do to get air from your buddy while in zero viz touch contact and what the rules are for finding your buddy in the dark."

Drew proceeded to show the team the various methods to deal with sharing air and finding your buddy in the dark and he lead them through a number of drills on the line, each taking turns being "lost" and "out of air".

Josh found the drills challenging as he had to remember the steps for each scenario. He also enjoyed the interaction with his class mates as they learned to work together to handle the obstacles thrown at them by Drew.

Eventually Drew stopped the drills and looked at his watch.

"OK, that's enough – it's lunch time. Let's meet back here in an hour. Jon, please retrieve the reel," said Drew. Jon walked over to the end of the line, where the reel was clipped to the line. He unclipped the end, unlocked the spool and started to reel in the line. Josh walked in front, helping to keep the slack minimal and assisted in unwrapping the line from the tree trunks. Jon handed the reel to Drew, who turned to go back to his van.

Frank said, "So let's go up to the deli to get some lunch, OK?"

"Sure, Frank," said Jon.

"Asrid, do you want to join us?" asked Josh, looking at her.

"Sure, give me a minute to get my lunch," said Asrid, walking towards the dirt parking lot.

They followed her to her car, a modest white rental sedan and watched her retrieve a small cooler from the back seat. A group of raucous college-aged students passed by, clutching oversized floats and cans of beer.

"So, what do you think of the class so far?" asked Josh, walking next to Asrid as they trudged towards the main building. Frank and Jon fell in step to their left and right.

Asrid responded, "I like it. Some of this feels like the technical training I had in Sweden but there's a lot more to learn and worry about."

"Yeah," said Jon, "He sure threw a lot of stuff at us in a short time. I just hope I can remember all that while we are underwater."

"I'm sure that he'll cut us some slack if we forget up front," said Josh, "My experience with scuba students is you can tell them and show them things but they usually don't get it until you have them do the skill underwater multiple times."

"Not too sure that Drew will be as understanding as you or Kathy," said Frank.

They lined up single file on the right side of the dirt road as a truck full of tubers lumbered past, the back overloaded with grinning children happy and adults holding onto their inner-tube sized floats.

"Who is Kathy?" asked Asrid.

"She's my boss and our scuba instructor. She taught us open

water. She's a great teacher; I've learned everything I know about diving from her," said Josh.

"Yeah, Kathy's great," said Jon and Frank nodded. They neared the main building and approached the attached deli on the far end.

"I'll wait here for you guys," said Asrid, sitting down at a park bench underneath an overhang near the deli where other patrons were enjoying their lunches.

"Do you need anything from the deli, like a drink?" asked Jon.

"No, I'm fine; I have everything I need here," said Asrid as she opened her cooler and started to pull out a sandwich and a water bottle.

"OK, see you in a bit," said Frank.

A few minutes later the three returned and sat around Asrid at the bench. Fans overhead combined with the shade to make their lunch repast enjoyable.

Between bites of his turkey and cheese sub sandwich Josh asked, "So, Asrid, tell us about your technical training."

"The technical diving class I took taught me how to dive in the dry suit, how to dive with doubles and mostly importantly how to dive horizontally," she said.

"Horizontally?" asked Jon.

"Yes, just like Drew was talking about yesterday. We learned to do all of our scuba skills with our body position parallel to the bottom, sort of like a sky diver. You have your knees bent and the bottom part of your legs pointed up so that nothing breaks an imaginary plane from your shoulders to your knees. The idea is to keep your body still while you manipulate only your arms and your lower legs to propel yourself and to handle tasks, such as sharing air," explained Asrid, sipping from her water bottle.

"Sounds easy to me," said Frank. He took a bite from his roast beef sub and grabbed a handful of chips from the bag in front of him.

"Well, it wasn't easy for me to master. Took me weeks to finally get my buoyancy and trim just right so I didn't break the plane. It's not too hard to position yourself horizontally once you have your weight and balance right. The hard part is mastering movement and doing things with your hands while maintaining that body position," explained Asrid.

Josh recalled the body position lecture Drew gave yesterday and he had read and re-read the section on diving techniques in the textbook, even to the point of memorizing the hand-drawn illustrations. This was the most intriguing part of the class to him.

"I would imagine Drew will work on our body position first thing this afternoon in the water," said Jon, musingly.

"Still doesn't sound all that difficult," said Frank. Josh felt a familiar irritation. Frank had an annoying habit of bragging about being able to master new physical challenges and even more exasperating he usually managed to do so.

"Well, thanks, Asrid. We'll see how it goes later," said Josh, trying to squelch any more of Frank's bragging.

"Do you have a boyfriend or husband, Asrid?" asked Frank.

"Um, no, I don't," said Asrid, slightly affronted by the sudden direct and personal question.

"Well, Josh here has a steady girlfriend but Jon and I are single," said Frank. Jon blushed slightly and Josh opened his mouth to try and smooth things over when Asrid looked quizzically at Josh and addressed Frank.

"I assure you, Frank, that I am not looking for romance. I am here for a month, diving and touring Florida before I return home. I don't have time to get involved with anyone, especially a fellow student in class," she said, looking directly at Frank with a straight face.

Frank just smiled and said, "Well, if you change your mind I'm right here."

"Sorry, Asrid, Frank fashions himself as a bit of a ladies' man. We already advised him not to bug you in class," said Josh, glaring at Frank. Frank just smiled back.

"I'm not offended, Josh. I am pleased to be sharing the class with you guys anyway; you seem like a tight-knit group of friends that would help each other out no matter what. Good trait for a diving class," said Asrid. Josh admired her ability to steer the conversation away from being uncomfortable.

"Tell me more about the cavern diving you guys have been doing," said Asrid.

Jon, Frank and Josh looked at each other, deciding what to say. Finally Josh turned and said,

"Well, we actually had a really bad experience in a cavern that scared the crap out of us, at least me. It's the main reason we decided to take the class," said Josh.

The three of them retold the story of the Jackson Blue silt out, complete with the buddy separation and small air share at the end.

Asrid nodded at the right times and held her hand to her mouth in surprise during the dramatic moments.

"Wow, that sounds scary! You guys were lucky. Did you notice that you broke many of the rules that we are learning about cavern diving?" she said.

Jon nodded, "Yes, we've been told. We just didn't know any better. I pride myself in seeking knowledge and that dive really guided me to this class. I nearly panicked and lost it during that dive. I really want to know what we did wrong and more importantly how to do it right in the future."

Asrid looked at Josh, "Sounds like you were quite the hero as well, Josh."

"Um, not really. I actually wasn't really thinking too well. I just sort of went after Jon because he's my friend. Believe me I've thought about that dive and I get more scared thinking about it than I was during the dive," said Josh, turning slightly red.

Frank slapped Josh on the back, "Ah, he's being shy! He was a hero. I wish I had thought of going back for Jon myself."

"If you hadn't lost me in the first place maybe we wouldn't have gotten lost," said Jon.

Josh squirmed slightly on the wooden bench. He looked around and noticed that they had all finished their lunches. He stood up, wrapped up the remains of his meal, and walked over to the nearby plastic-lined trash can.

"OK, guys, that's enough. Let's go back and get our gear ready."

The remaining three stood to leave. Jon took Frank and Asrid's lunch trash and discarded them. Asrid closed her cooler lid and they all began the short walk back to the spring.

"Well, it's still an exciting story and definitely a learning moment for you guys. It should help with this class," said Asrid, as they reached the dirt road. To their right a line of swimmers stood in line as an employee handed out floats and inner tubes.

Chapter 15

Half an hour later they met Drew at a picnic table near the spring porch. Their scuba equipment was set up on the table and each student stood near their gear, finishing up their last minute configurations. A slight breeze kept the heat bearable; the sky was partly cloudy with the occasional white fluffy low altitude cloud drifting by. Drew motioned the class over to the back of his van, where his scuba gear was set up.

"My gear is suitable for cave diving. Notice I have two tanks with a manifold and extra valves that I can use to isolate the tanks. That gives me two separate sources of air, should one fail," said Drew, pointing to the tanks and the isolator valve that connected the valves of the two tanks.

"Continuing the theme of redundancy each tank has a separate first and second stage so I have two different breathing supplies if need be. Normally the isolator valve is open, allowing the two tanks to share pressure equally. Notice that the right post, or right tank valve, has my long hose attached to it."

Drew uncoiled the seven foot hose connected to the right valve, pointing to the second stage at the end.

"The other regulator is connected to the left post and it uses a standard sized regulator hose. The second stage regulator is on a bungee necklace." He pulled the left regulator away from his rig. A piece of black thin bungee material was attached around the mouthpiece of the regulator. The bungee was arranged in a circle that would easily fit around a person's neck.

"Having the backup reg on a necklace means that I always know where it is, even in zero visibility. So if my buddy needs air I just hand them the primary regulator on the long hose that I am breathing and switch to my backup reg. Better to give a stressed out-of-air diver a working regulator than to hand them one that may or may not be working properly due to a malfunction or dirt build up. Even though I will be temporarily out of air I get to control the events. This is how you will do your air shares."

Drew went on to point out other features of his equipment, centered around the theme of having backup devices – backup lights, knives and other diving equipment.

After about an hour of explaining each piece of gear in meticulous detail Drew announced it was time to go look at their gear.

Drew walked from his van to the picnic table with their gear and walked around the table, inspecting and commenting on each person's piece of gear.

"Asrid, this must be your gear; a set of low pressure 85s with tank bands and a manifold. I see you have a long hose and a necklace for your backup reg. Were you trained to breathe the long or short hose?" he asked.

"I was taught to breathe the short hose and to stow the long hose on the side of my right tank, like you see there," she said, pointing to the hose attached to her right tank with bungee cords.

"What was your instructor's reasoning for breathing the short hose?" asked Drew, eyebrows raised as he looked at Asrid.

"He said that it's safer to hand over the hose you weren't using so that you don't have two people out of air at the same time," explained Asrid.

"Ah, yes; there is a school of thought that runs along those lines. I prefer to donate the hose I am breathing so I know my buddy is going to get a reliable air source. Plus you don't know if your long hose reg is working until you actually give it to your out of air buddy. Hmm...I'll give you a choice on how you want to dive it in this class, since there's merits for both views and as long as you give air to your buddy one way or another it shouldn't affect the ability for you to help out your buddies."

"I'd prefer to deliver air the way I was trained," said Asrid.

"Agreed," said Drew. "You are more likely to revert to that behavior anyway since it's ingrained from your earlier training."

Drew turned to the other three scuba systems, where Josh, Frank and Jon stood awaiting their turn.

"I see all three of you are diving with standard BCs and a single tank with a single first stage. Hmm, identical long hoses too and you even put bungee necklaces on your backup regs. That's good. Have any of you dove with a long hose before?"

They shook their heads, all at the same time. Josh thought it probably looked comical and saw Asrid's lips twitch slightly.

"OK, then, I will teach you how to breathe and donate the long hose. It is the most common technique used in the cavern and cave diving community," said Drew.

Josh watched as Drew continued the review of their gear, making constructive comments as he found items configured in a way he didn't agree with. Drew also asked them whether they had two light sources (they showed him their large eight D-cell primary lights and their small three C-cell backup lights) and they used some spare bungee material to secure them to the BC straps.

"You want to work on not having anything dangling below your horizontal body position. If anything drags behind you or beneath you it may cause a silt out or at a minimum leave annoying drag marks on the cavern floor.

"Securing your backup lights with a clip at one end and a piece of bungee at the other will keep it snug against your chest until you need it and it won't hang down," said Drew, patting Frank's backup light that he had just clipped and tucked into place.

Josh thought all of the gear modifications were pretty cool and it made him feel like a cavern diver already. He remembered during the Jackson Blue Spring fiasco dive his buddy regulator had dragged around on the bottom, dumping precious air and risking entanglement. He fingered the new stainless steel spring loaded boat clip that Drew had attached onto his primary light and looked over at Asrid's expensive kit, hoping someday to be able to dive with all that type of equipment.

Drew moved over to an empty picnic table and laid a large beach towel across the surface. He laid on the towel, belly first, and spent a few minutes explaining the proper body position for cavern diving. It looked like an advanced yoga pose to Josh, one guaranteed to pull muscles, pinch nerves and tear cartilage.

Each of the students took turns hopping up on the table and demonstrating the horizontal position. Josh tried not to stare as Asrid stretched out on the table, her back arched and cleavage visible beneath the white t-shirt. Frank clearly enjoyed her time on the table. Josh climbed on the table when his turn came, a bit apprehensive about the experience. He wasn't used to having to dive this way.

"Make sure to arch your back more, Josh," said Drew, as he placed his hand in the small of Josh's back, pressing gently.

"Keep your knees and elbows bent; the lowest point of your body should be the imaginary plane created by your shoulders and hips."

Josh arched his back more, a slight twinge of pain hitting his lower back. As if reading his mind Drew commented.

"Until you get used to this position it will feel awkward and it'll be slightly uncomfortable. Do it enough and it will become second nature. It'll minimize the chances of you pointing your fins towards the ground, which is the most common way untrained divers stir up the bottom."

Josh thought back momentarily to his ill-fated cavern dive at Jackson Blue and sure enough he recalled seeing all three of them kick up silt from the bottom as they kicked merrily around the cavern, none the wiser. Josh jumped up from the table and handed the towel to Drew.

"A well trained cavern diver can swim along the bottom, no

matter how low and silty, and propel themselves forwards without stirring up silt or clay," said Drew, folding up the towel.

"OK, that's enough dry stuff. It's time to get in the water. Get your gear on and I'll meet you down at the stairs at the spring," announced Drew, who turned and walked over to his white van.

Josh grinned at his classmates. They all grinned back, even Asrid. About time they got into the water.

Chapter 16

Josh walked down the stairs carefully, fins and mask in hand. Before him a group of teenagers were walking in the chest high clear water, the occasional gasp as they reacted to the cold water. Josh walked down into the water, his wet suit slowly filling up with the chilly fluid.

He braced himself for the initial shock as the water worked its way up to his chest but he knew as his body heated up the small layer of water trapped inside his suit he would begin to feel relatively warm. He pressed the power inflator with his left hand; the matching hiss of air filling his BC. He reached out to steady himself on one of the many cypress tree knobs growing around the edge of the spring.

"I never get used to this," grumbled Frank, coming down the stairs alongside Josh.

"The cold water is bracing, especially on a hot day," said Josh, placing one of his fins on the top of the tree roots. He reached down with the other fin and slipped it on his right foot, securing the strap.

"Yeah, well, it still sucks initially," commented Frank as he duplicated Josh's fin motions. By that time Jon had descended to the bottom of the stairs, slid into the water and plopped one of his fins on a nearby root shelf.

Just as all three of them completed putting on their fins Asrid walked down the stairs. Josh looked at her curiously; he could barely make out the lovely young woman beneath her gear. She wore an all-black dry suit that covered all but her head and hands.

Twin scuba cylinders jutted out from her back, looking like a rocket jet pack. The tanks were held in place with a harness made of black straps and Josh could just make out the leathery-looking wings sandwiched between her back and the tanks. He knew this was her method for buoyancy control and he admired the efficiency of a design that placed the air bladder along the length of the tanks. It made sense to balance the things that made you sink with the things that made you float across your body at your center of gravity.

The right side of her waist held one of the oatmeal-container sized battery packs for her primary light. A black thick wire snaked from the top of the battery pack to a series of silver stainless steel D-shaped rings placed at shoulder height on her black harness, the light head clipped off and swaying gently with her motion. On her left side a short black hose lead from behind her neck to a pressure gauge clipped to another D-ring on her waist.

Her long hose, also black, disappeared behind her wing. Around her neck Josh could just make out the black bungee attached to her backup reg, where another black hose disappeared around her right shoulder. Josh knew that hose lead to the first stage on her left tank, providing independent air sources should the need arise. He felt a momentary pang of jealousy that quickly passed.

"Impressive rig," said Frank, looking up at Asrid, his face wearing the usual leering smile.

Asrid lumbered down to the water, ignoring Frank. She added a bit of air to her wing by pressing the power inflator on her left side, twisted a knob on her left shoulder attached to her dry suit and entered the water.

Josh watched as the air in her dry suit worked its way up, pushed by the water. It escaped through the valve she had just opened on her left shoulder, hissing gently.

"Does that thing really keep you dry?" asked Jon, who was also watching Asrid's descent.

"Yes, for the most part," said Asrid, as she reached the limestone bottom. She moved towards the left side of the stairs and placed her fins and mask on roots.

"Sometimes I get a bit of water in my arms through the wrist seals," she said, holding out her right hand and pulling back the latex seal around her right wrist with her left hand to demonstrate, "and sometimes from the neck, especially if I twist my head suddenly," she said, pointing to the latex seal surrounding her neck.

"Does the neck seal feel uncomfortable?" asked Josh.

"You trim it when you first get it to fit your neck. It's a little uncomfortable at first but eventually the latex relaxes and you hardly notice it," she said, fingering the seal around her neck.

Josh blanched at the thought of being choked to death by ill-fitting dive gear.

"But, believe me, it's worth it when it's all set up right. I can feel the spring water through the dry suit and my undergarment but it's just like a cool breeze, comfortable," she said, smiling.

"Yeah, well, if nature calls we can just go in our wet suits," exclaimed Frank with a touch of bravado.

"Oh, I wear adult diapers if I am going to dive for a long time," said Asrid in a matter of fact tone, "but not today," she finished.

Josh was relieved to see Drew plod down the stairs just before the conversation strayed too far into inappropriateness. His equipment resembled Asrid's in general, although it showed more wear and tear and items were attached in a more minimalist and streamlined fashion. He also had his long hose wrapped around his neck, instead of bungeed to the side of the tank, like Asrid. Even the light cord from his hip battery pack to the light head attached on his right chest D ring was tucked neatly in his waist strap. The light head did not move as he gingerly walked from the stairs and into the water.

"OK, guys, I'll keep you moving. You wet suit guys are more time limited on your exposure to cold water than those of us wearing dry suits," He slipped on his fins, pulled a dive hood over his head and rinsed out his mask in a few short efficient motions. Josh was impressed; clearly Drew was in his element now. Asrid also wore a dive hood; she was only recognizable by the feminine oval of her face and her bright blue eyes. Neither Josh nor his friends wore dive hoods. Josh was starting to wonder if that was a mistake.

Drew motioned the class away from the stairs as a particularly loud and boisterous group of college students in bathing suits splashed past them, jumping on to their inner tubes for a leisurely float down the spring run into the river. The class positioned themselves around Drew in a semicircle, water up to their shoulders.

"OK, I want to see how your technique looks before we start diving. I'll demonstrate the horizontal swimming technique that I want you to attempt and eventually master. As we discussed in class and simulated on the picnic table I'll be using a modified frog kick. You don't want to use the flutter kick since the up and down motion can stir up the bottom."

Josh was a bit worried about his frog kick. Kathy had taught them the typical kicking methods used in open water scuba diving but for the most part everybody used the flutter kick; it was the most natural and easiest for new students to master and one that any swimmer could easily identify. The frog kick was the same leg motion used in the breast stroke which usually only people who had had swimming lessons knew how to do.

"So, just drop down here on this shallow limestone shelf and watch me swim around a bit," said Drew.

Drew placed his mask on his face, put his primary regulator in his mouth, took a few test breaths and dropped down to the bottom. Josh and the others did the same. They settled to the bottom, watching Drew.

Drew proceeded to swim down to the middle of the basin, ducking underneath a group of floating tube riders. He swam perfectly parallel to the gentle slope of the basin floor, his knees bent and his arms held out in front of him, elbows bent, head craned back to see forward like a turtle out of its shell.

He effortlessly moved around the basin floor, the only motion from his ankles, feet and fins. Josh marveled at the efficiency of his movement and he could tell by the slow exhale of bubbles that Drew wasn't working hard to move around.

Drew circled a few more times, gave the team an "OK" hand signal and gave the thumbs up. They all surfaced and inflated their BCs. Drew swam back to the group on his back, facing away from the group with the occasional look over his shoulder to guide him. He turned and stood.

"OK, that's what you want to work towards – slow steady movement using just the bottom part of your legs. You can move forward, turn and even swim backwards all by modifying how you pull and push the water with your fins. It's like having a boat with two independent motors," said Drew, his eyes moving from student to student.

"Any questions?" The class stood quietly in the spring water.

"OK, let me see how you look. Who wants to try it first?"

Asrid said, "I'll go."

Drew nodded and gave her the "thumbs down" signal. She put on her mask, cleared her reg and descended. Josh, his friends and Drew dropped down to watch underwater.

Asrid sank slowly and settled on the bottom. She added a bit of air to her wing and she waited for the change in her buoyancy to stabilize. She slowly rose off of the bottom, knees up and body in a nice horizontal position. She began her frog kick, moving forward slowly. Josh thought she looked pretty impressive. She turned to the left, using her right hand to paddle slightly in the turn and her hands returned to a neutral spot in front of her, arms out and elbows bent. After a few minutes she looked over at Drew, who gave her an "OK" and a "surface" sign. They all ascended.

After Asrid swam back to the group Drew spoke, "Nice job; you have a clean frog kick and your body position stayed parallel with the ground. I did notice, however, that you tend to cheat a bit with your hands on your turns. Your hands should never be used as a method of propulsion or assisting in a turn. Work on minimizing your hand motions by only using your fins to turn."

Asrid nodded, her mask off and clutched in her hand, water dripping from her hood.

"OK, who's next?"

Josh raised his hand. "Me," he said.

"OK, Josh, let's see what you got," said Drew.

Josh donned his mask, cleared his reg, dumped the air out of his BC and fell forward, slowly settling to the bottom. The cold water wrapped around his face and head. He felt the eyes of the others on him and decided to not rush it. He reached the bottom and touched it with his outstretched right hand, arresting his slow descent.

He pressed the power inflator button for a little over a second, judging from experience how much air he needed to add to become neutrally buoyant. He felt his descent slow and stop and lifted his feet off the bottom, neck craned back and knees bent, like he had down on the towel. The position felt very awkward. He tried a few tentative frog kick strokes with his feet and started moving slowly forward, towards the bottom.

Oops, can't crash into the bottom; gotta add some air, he thought, giving a quick shot of air to his BC. He turned towards the deeper middle of the basin and sank slowly to the bottom, equalizing his ears automatically as the pressure increased. Bare feet and legs from a group of tubers hung down in the crystal clear water, the occasional hand reaching into the water from the tubes to gently propel themselves down river.

He added a touch more air as he approached the maximum depth of the spring basin, around twenty feet. He felt his thigh muscles start to twitch at the effort of holding up his calves above his bent knees.

Reaching the bottom he had to stop by placing his hand onto the bottom, which had changed from limestone worn white from years of people walking over it to a white bottom of coarse sand.

Well, that sucks. Can't control my buoyancy worth a hoot.

He pushed off the bottom and tried to turn right by sculling to the left with his fins. The effort caused his right shoulder to lean and he reached out, fanning with his right hand to counteract the motion. Too late, his legs flipped upwards and he stood there, hands on the bottom, legs waving erratically above him in a crude scuba parody of a handstand.

Crap!

He tucked himself into a ball and allowed his body to settle back to a normal position. He extended his legs slowly and swam slowly off of the bottom using a slight flutter kick, his knees slightly bent.

Well, it ain't pretty but at least I'm not plowing into the bottom anymore.

This method of propelling felt more natural and he swam a lap around the rim of the basin at ten feet, his hands still at his side, his modified flutter kick gently moving him in a slow circle. As he passed by Drew he saw the "thumbs up" signal and returned it, rising to the surface.

"Well, I don't see any frog kick there," said Drew, a frown on his face, "You can do a modified flutter kick, which will have to do for now. Just realize that to go farther with your training you have got to learn and master the modified frog kick. OK, Jon, your turn."

Josh felt crushed; here he was supposed to be the professional diver and he couldn't even master the most basic method used by cavern and cave divers. He shuffle-walked over to Frank in the waist deep water, eyes downcast, and removed his mask.

"Wow, that was pretty freaking funny, Josh. What a show - a handstand on the bottom," whispered Frank in a voice loud enough for Asrid to hear.

Josh just looked straight ahead, his lips pursed, fury boiling inside. He was angrier with himself more than Frank; they didn't cut each other much slack usually.

Asrid reached over and touched Josh's shoulder lightly; she looked like she wanted to say something but her hand dropped instead, creating a slight splashing sound. Josh's face burned red.

"OK, guys, let's drop down and watch Jon," said Drew, who had ignored the jibe.

Josh placed his mask back on his face, popped the reg in his mouth and dropped down, grateful for the attention shift. He watched as Jon started the same way he had – settling to the bottom to get the air balanced in his BC before he started swimming.

Jon proceeded to swim tentatively forward, his knees bent and his ankles swishing from side to side. His body moved forwards, towards the basin bottom. Josh noticed that Jon was able to keep his shoulders and hips balanced like Drew and Asrid could do.

The only difference was Jon had to occasionally use his hands to assist in turns and his knees dropped slightly on each frog kick stroke. Josh watched with a touch of jealously tempered with pride as Jon lumbered around the edge of the basin, sustaining a passable horizontal position.

"Not bad for a first time, Jon," said Drew as Jon surfaced, "You do tend to drop your knees on the downward part of the frog kick, though, and it's making your knees dip below your hips. I suggest you bend your hips more to force your legs up higher. Look between your legs as you go through the stroke and if you can see your knees you know they are dipping."

"Also I want you and Asrid to put your hands somewhere where you won't be tempted to use them to help with propulsion. I usually tell students to either put both thumbs in your waist strap or weight belt or hold them out in front of you as a balance so you'll be less tempted to swim with them." He looked around. "That's good advice for all of you."

"OK, Frank, last but hopefully not least," finished Drew.

The class placed their masks on their faces and stuck their regs in their mouths and as a unit dipped below the surface. Josh watched Frank settle down on the bottom, his right hand reaching out to his power inflator on his left shoulder. Frank adjusted his buoyancy, lifted his legs off of the bottom, craned his neck back to almost a 90 degree angle from his body and proceeded to swim forward.

He glided down to the basin floor, his hips and shoulders in parallel with the bottom. His fins moved rhythmically from side to side in unison and his hands were stable, held out in a V shape in front of him, the plane of the V in line with the plane of his shoulders and hips. He swam slowly around the edge, glancing occasionally at the rest of the class gazing at him from the ledge, lying in a belly prone position on the limestone shallow shelf.

Josh felt the familiar twinge of jealously but it quickly was staunched by a mixture of awe and pride.

Man, that Frank always manages to master physical skills sooner than the rest of us.

Drew looked at Frank as he surfaced, a bemused expression on his face.

"Have you had any overhead or technical training before?"

"Nope," answered Frank, a smug expression on his face.

"Well, you have good technique. Let's see if you can sustain that as I throw drills at you later," said Drew. He turned his attention back to the class.

"OK, well, now that you've all gotten your feet wet as it were I'd like you to take some time to practice your modified frog kick."

"Aren't we going to do a cavern dive today?" implored Frank.

"No, as a class your technique needs more improvement before we go into the overhead environment," said Drew, looking briefly at Josh, "You need more practice." Josh felt the eyes of the class on him and he burned with embarrassment.

Drew droned on, providing tips on how to improve their swimming technique. Josh only half-heard; his ego felt crushed. He was the worst student in the class! All of them, even Jon, looked tons better than he had. Maybe cavern diving wasn't such a good idea.

They spent another two hours in the water, just practicing their swimming techniques. They swam around the spring basin in loose formation, each working on their frog kick with the occasional tip from Drew at the surface. Josh would try the modified frog kick once in a while but stuck to the flutter kick since it was the only reliable way for him to swim around. Every time he tried to move his fins side by side instead of up and down he would start to list head first towards the bottom. Eventually Drew thumbed them all to the surface.

Josh looked around - Jon's lips were blue and Frank had started to shiver while Drew and Asrid looked comfortable in their dry suits. Josh felt the cold as well. This was a lot longer in a spring than he was used to doing. Kathy limited her spring checkout dives for new scuba students to no more than an hour because of the risk of hypothermia.

"OK, that's it for today. You guys look pretty cold. We'll debrief back at the dive shop. See you there," said Drew, as he pulled off his fins and headed for the wooden stairs.

Josh waddled over to the roots along the edge of the spring, dodging some children swimming past, screaming with laughter at the brisk cold water. He braced himself against the cypress roots and reached underneath the water, pulling off one of his fins. He felt tired, cold and dejected.

Chapter 17

The class sat outside the dive shop, a cool breeze in the early evening bringing a respite from the day's heat and humidity. Drew had just finished giving his debrief of the activities and had retired to his trailer. For Josh the debrief had just sunk him deeper into a blue funk because of his lousy performance. Asrid, Jon, Frank and Josh occupied both sides of a picnic table, sipping soft drinks. The parking lot was mostly empty. Roland walked out of the dive shop, closing the door and locking it for the night.

"How did your cavern class go?" asked Roland.

"We survived," said Frank, smiling up to meet Roland's gaze. Josh noticed Allen in his wheelchair at the edge of the porch, clearly within earshot. He was staring across the parking lot as usual.

"Ah, yes, the first couple of times in the water are grueling; he usually has to break all of your open water diving habits and rebuild your skills," commented Roland, walking past the group.

"Yeah, some of us are more broke than others," cracked Frank. Josh just glared at him.

"Good luck and see you next weekend."

"Bye, Roland," said Asrid.

"It felt good to finally get in the water," said Frank, turning his attention back to his fellow students.

"Yeah, although he sure worked us over," responded Jon, "I was hoping to actually do a cavern dive."

"We need to work on our technique as a team before we venture into a cavern," offered Asrid.

"Yeah, some of us REALLY need to get better," said Frank, smirking at Josh.

Josh responded hotly, "Yeah, I know; I suck. I just can't get the modified frog kick down. I see that you guys can do it with some degree of success. I'm pretty frustrated," he finished. He wasn't used to admitting weakness, especially among his friends but Asrid's presence somehow opened him up a bit more than usual.

"Josh, you shouldn't beat yourself up too much," offered Asrid, looking his way. She sat next to Josh and across from Jon. Josh felt she was trying to avoid too close of contact with Frank. He didn't blame her.

"Yeah, that's easy for you to say; your technique looks flawless," said Jon.

"Thanks, but it's not perfect. I thought that my technique would be great for cavern but watching and listening to Drew I know that I still can get better. To be able to glide real close to the bottom and not kick up a single bit of dirt is quite impressive.

"We didn't worry about such tight tolerances in the wreck dives of Sweden where I learned the modified frog kick," explained Asrid.

"Well, Jon, you and Frank looked pretty good. Kathy would be proud," said Josh.

He noticed Allen's head bent slightly in their direction, eavesdropping.

"I did look pretty darn good," said Frank, "It must be in the genes or something. Always picked up physical skills quickly."

Jon turned to Josh, "You about ready to head out? I have to get up early tomorrow for work."

"Yeah, OK; let's head on out, guys," said Josh, standing up. "See you next weekend, Asrid." He held out his hand to shake her hand; she returned the gesture.

"Good night, gentlemen. Have a safe trip back and I'll see you next Saturday," she said. Frank and Jon shook her hand as well and began to walk towards Josh's truck. Josh sighed, watching his friends and Asrid walk across the hard shell lot, still animatedly discussing the class. The sun was setting to his right, orange light blazing off the tops of the trees. He turned to go when Allen wheeled in his direction.

"Hey," said Allen, motioning to Josh. His voice was gravely with a distinct southern accent.

"Er, hello," said Josh.

Allen handed Josh a small piece of crumpled paper and muttered, "I can help you with your technique. Give me a call sometime."

Before Josh could offer a thank you Allen spun on his wheels and headed across the lot, towards a beat-up light blue bottom and white topped rusty VW van parked at the far edge of the open area, near the tree line.

Josh looked at the paper; a phone number was written on it in loose wobbly handwriting. He placed it in his pocket and looked to where Jon and Frank were talking to Asrid next to his truck. He thought they hadn't seen the exchange between him and Allen. He shrugged and shook it off, wanting to just get home and forget about the day. He walked over to his truck.

Chapter 18

Later that night, after dropping off Jon and Frank, Josh knocked on Elise's door. He was tired and it was late but he enjoyed his time with her and could use some sympathy. She opened the door, having already changed from her nurse's uniform into comfortable yellow shorts and a light blue tank top. Her black hair was slightly damp and hung loose, evidence of a recent shower. Josh knew she liked to relax by reading on her couch as a way of unwinding after a long shift. He also knew she liked to unwind in other ways, especially with him.

"Hi Josh," she said, reaching out to pull him inside her apartment and into her embrace. He enjoyed the feeling of her lithe warm body against his and the small kiss she planted on his lips. He tasted the tartness of white wine.

"How was your cavern class?" She held his hand and walked him over to the couch, where they both sat facing each other. A hardbound book lay on the coffee table, opened up to the page she had been reading. Light classical music floated out from a small stereo system on the other side of the room. A half full glass of white wine stood next to the book.

"Well, it was challenging, that's for sure," started Josh, settling back into the couch.

"On Saturday we did a lecture and Drew, our instructor, went over the scuba gear with a fine-tooth comb. I had to buy some more gear to be compliant."

"I thought you had all of the dive gear you needed from Kathy's; why did you have to buy more?" asked Elise, moving her legs under her hips to get more comfortable. She knew he had a tight budget.

"There's some things I needed to get, like a long hose, that Kathy doesn't sell. I hated paying full retail, though." Josh thought for a moment how fortunate he was to get the employee discount at *Wakulla Skuba*. "I also realize that my gear really isn't what I eventually need to dive in a cave."

"But I thought you said you weren't going to go farther and actually dive into a cave," said Elise, her back arching slightly forward. Josh recognized she was slightly irritated.

"I said I'd see how it goes. It's just that, well –"

"Josh, you know I am not too thrilled about you doing cavern diving, much less actually going into a cave where you can't see the outside. I am really concerned for your safety!"

Elise reached over to the coffee table and grabbed her wine glass, taking a quick drink.

"Well, my safety is the least of my problems," said Josh, looking down.

"What do you mean?"

"Turns out that I suck at the swimming techniques. I made a fool of myself in front of the guys and Asrid."

"Who's Asrid?" said Elise, her green eyes flashing at him.

"Oh, just another student in the class. I just really had problems doing the modified frog kick. Turns out it's the most important kick you need for cavern diving and I just can't do it," Josh squirmed in his seat, slightly uncomfortable admitting fault even to this girlfriend.

"Tell me more about Asrid," persisted Elise.

Josh looked at Elise, something in her tone setting off a small alarm in his head.

"She's a diver from Sweden who is taking the cavern class. And before you ask, yes she is pretty and yes Frank tried to hit on her multiple times which embarrassed us all and no I am not interested in her," he reached out his hand and rubbed her shoulder, looking into her eyes, "You are the only woman I'm interested in."

She looked down and smiled slightly and looked back up, the smile still on her face. He knew she was insecure sometimes about their relationship but he had always been a one-woman-at-a-time sort of guy and he had no problem reassuring her now and then. He didn't even think of Asrid as a threat to their relationship, frankly.

"Yeah, well, Asrid's way ahead of the rest of us. She dives real technical equipment – dry suit, doubles, back plate, wings and a canister light. Easily five thousand dollars in gear or more. Drew also has a nice tech rig that he dives. You could just tell that both of them have a big advantage because of the gear, or at least that's how it seemed to me. There's no way I can even think about affording that type of gear, even if I did want to dive in a cavern, much less a cave. I'm not sure fancy gear would help though…"

Josh hesitated for a second, not sure how to continue and the words tumbled out.

"Elise, today we got into the water and I was so bad. I couldn't frog kick to save my life. Frank, as usual, had no problem picking it up. Even Jon looked pretty good once he got the hang of it. Drew and Asrid looked like they were born swimming that way. I was the only one who failed that part of the class miserably. Drew didn't come out and say that I wouldn't pass but I got the strong impression that if I don't learn the modified frog kick I'll never get my cavern diving rating."

Josh was surprised at how much he wanted to talk about this, once the flood gates had been opened. He had kept them closed during the long drive back to town.

"Aw, Josh, you shouldn't beat yourself up too much. Maybe all you need is more practice. Did the instructor take the time to try and help you out as an individual? I know how you and Kathy pride yourselves on tailoring your scuba instruction to each student," said Elise.

She reached over to touch Josh's knee as a supporting gesture. Her soft hands felt warm and inviting on his knee.

"Yeah, Drew did take some time to give me some pointers. We even tried to shift the weight distribution around a bit but it didn't help. I could tell he was getting frustrated at my frustration and lack of progress. I've just always had no problems mastering scuba skills," he said morosely.

"What about Kathy? Didn't you say that she used to cave dive? Maybe you can ask her for help," offered Elise.

Josh thought for a moment. "Yeah, that did occur to me on the drive back. Problem is I'm not sure she will. She reacted pretty badly when I first brought up the issue of cavern diving –"

"And I think she's right –"

"—yeah, I know you don't like it but it's something that I want to do, at least I thought I did..." Josh trailed off.

"Well, you should ask her for help anyway. Maybe she'll help or maybe she'll just talk you out of pursuing cavern diving all together," said Elise. Josh could tell she would love nothing more than to have him quit the class. He looked over at her carefully, trying to judge whether she was being helpful or duplicitous. Elise was a sophisticated intelligent woman who was too polite to directly criticize him but he had felt her gentle but firm persuasions before.

"Yeah, I'll ask her tomorrow. Enough about me; let's concentrate on you," said Josh.

He slid down the couch, closer to her and reached out to take her in his arms. She responded by unwinding her legs from underneath her, reclining slightly and pulling him down to her. Despite the long disappointing day or maybe because of it he wanted to spend the rest of the evening wrapped up in delicious passion.

Chapter 19

The next morning started off busy for Josh. He and Kathy unloaded cardboard boxes full of snorkeling equipment, dive flags on floats and mesh goody bags for the upcoming scallop season. The waters along the shore of the Gulf of Mexico to their south teemed with scallops for hundreds of miles along the coastline and soon their shop would be filled with weekenders looking to gear up hunting for the delicious bivalves.

"OK, let's open these boxes and set up the gear. I want folks to come in and see a snorkeling package right next to the dive flag and goody bags. We'll price them cheaper that way; folks usually end up buying more than they need," said Kathy, opening up the first box of dive mask/fins/snorkel kits.

"Assemble the dive flags and let's attach the mask/fin/snorkel combo packages to the dive flags. We'll drape the goody bags on the flag poles so our customers can see what they'd be getting."

Josh responded, "You bet," and started to unload the Styrofoam balls and assemble the flags to the balls using a yellow fiberglass rod that ran through the ball.

At the bottom he attached a large lead weight that would hold the flag up in the water at the top of the float.

Bear sniffed around the packaging as they worked, his curly tail wagging in a slow tempo while he inspected the merchandise. Kathy reached down and rubbed between his ears, which pointed up in twin triangular furry arches above his head, not unlike a bat's ears. Josh could tell Bear loved the attention and the feeling of just being with the pack.

"So, how did your weekend go?" asked Kathy as she started to distribute the snorkeling kits around the display area on the left side of the front door.

"Oh, I guess it went OK," said Josh, propping a completed dive flag behind the first snorkeling kit, "We spent the first day in the classroom and going over gear and yesterday in the water."

"Do you like Drew? Is he doing a good job of teaching?" Kathy pulled out one of the bright green goody bags, tugged back the drawstring that closed the bag and fed the white nylon drawstring around the dive flag. She arranged the bag, snorkel kit and dive flag until she was satisfied with the display.

"Well, he doesn't teach like you do, that's for sure. Seems like cavern diving requires a heavier hand. I wouldn't exactly call him mean to his students but he didn't cut us much slack and didn't offer much encouragement like you do," said Josh. He moved on to the next dive flag, keeping pace with Kathy as she continued to set up the next snorkel kit and goody bag.

"Well, that's to be expected; the overhead environment is a lot more unforgiving than open water. He needs to be tough on you now before you get yourself in any more trouble."

She pursed her lips.

Josh didn't need to be reminded of the Jackson Blue fiasco. He wanted to ask her about help with his frog kick but didn't want her to know the depth of his despair in being unable to master the skill. Having her rub his face in past underwater snafus didn't help.

"I could use your help with a part of the class, though, Kathy," he started. She looked up from the growing array of kits and paused, waiting for him to continue.

"My frog kick isn't so good and Drew wasn't able to help me get it working any better. Could you help me?"

Kathy put down the snorkel kit in her hand and rubbed her chin. Bear sniffed at the Styrofoam balls lined up along the wall. Thinking idly and not trying to obsess over Kathy's answer, Josh knew a lesser-trained dog would see those as chew toys. He looked back at Kathy, waiting for her response.

"You know, Josh, I really enjoy having you as an employee and as a budding dive leader. You've shown me time and time again that you have great judgment both out of and in the water. I think you have a great future ahead of you as a scuba instructor.

"I've also helped you develop all of your scuba skills and I know you have a great arsenal of kicks suitable for open water diving, like the flutter, frog and dolphin kicks. I'm sure you'll master the variations of these kicks that you need for cavern diving, eventually.

"The thing of it though is I still don't like the idea of you learning how to dive in the overhead environment but I respect you enough to stay out of your way and be neutral; you have to take your life's journey where ever it may take you to. I'm sorry but I can't help you. I don't want to either promote your overhead training or stop you from doing it."

Josh's face turned red; he was both angry at her and grateful at the same time. She had allowed him to take off the next few weekends during the height of the scuba training season because she knew he wanted to pursue overhead training.

He had thought, though, that Kathy would mentor him in all aspects of diving, not just what she did these days. He knew, though, that he had to honor her decision not so much because he wanted to keep his job but that a part of him understood and respected her position, even if he didn't agree with it.

"Besides, I haven't been cave diving in years and never taught cavern or cave diving; I'm not sure I could help you anyway," she finished, turning back to setting up the next snorkeling display.

Josh felt the topic come to a close and continued to help set up the displays. Once they had a row of kits ready for sale along the wall Kathy went back with brightly-colored price tags and attached one to each of the packages.

"OK, that looks great. We'll just replace them as we sell them. Let's go ahead and put the rest of the gear in the back," said Kathy with a satisfied look on her face, "and then we need to rinse out the gear I used on last weekend's checkout dives."

Josh worked through the rest of the day, the occasional amicable conversation between her and Kathy filling in the dull moments between helping customers with their questions and sales. Neither one brought up his cavern class.

He ate his packed lunch with Bear out on the dock, enjoying the Wakulla River flowing by and felt the stress of the weekend leach out of him as the natural habitat acted as a salve on his soul. He reached in his pocket and felt the crumpled piece of paper that Allen had given him and stared at it.

Should he reach out in desperation to a crazy old guy who more than likely would be nothing but a giant waste of time? Or would Allen provide just the right corrections to his technique? He just wasn't sure what to do. He sighed and pushed the paper back in his pocket.

Chapter 20

Josh waited for Elise outside of the *Hole*. She had the day off, which gave her time to drive down south of Tallahassee and join Josh and his friends for dinner.

Night had started to settle over the neighborhood; fireflies sparkled occasionally in the dirt parking lot and the sound of crickets permeated the humid air. A pair of headlights moved down Manatee Lane and passed by *River Art* before turning into the *Hole's* parking lot.

Josh recognized Elise's late model garnet Camry and walked forward as she pulled into an available spot near the entrance. Behind him were the sounds and smells of guests enjoying themselves on the screened-in front porch of the *Hole*. Mouth-watering and tantalizing sea food scents competed with the jasmine and magnolia blooms on the nearby trees.

"Hi, sweetie," said Josh, opening her door and reaching out his hand to help her out of her car.

"Hi, Josh," said Elise, pecking him on the cheek. She wore cut off blue jeans and a crop top tank top, black with the lettering "Obey the Nurse" stamped in white across her chest. Her light perfume intertwined with the smell from the flowers as she passed by him. He placed his hand on the small of her back, guiding her towards the screen door of the *Hole*.

"The guys are already inside," offered Josh as he reached around Elise to open the screen door. Sue, the co-owner of the *Hole*, waved at the couple as they walked down the central hallway of the restaurant and headed towards the back porch. The *Hole*, having the same basic floor plan as the other two shops along this part of the river, maximized patron space with the addition of the screened-in front porch and the conversion of the two front rooms into dining spaces.

The kitchen resided in the back right side of the building and shared an open space with the porch bar, where Mike tended.

Josh led Elise to their usual table on the back wall of the screen porch, closest to the water, where sat Frank and Jon, nursing beers. Caribbean beach music drifted from the speakers and light twinkled from the glass-enclosed candles on the tables and the string of lights along the ceiling. The candles flickered from the downward gentle push of air by the slow moving ceiling fans. Most of the tables were full of locals enjoying their meals and drinks. On the river a small boat drifted past on low power, green and red running lights glowing in the dusk.

"Hi Elise," said Frank, standing to greet her with a slight hug. She returned the hug and turned to hug Jon before sitting in the chair that Josh had pulled back for her.

"Hi guys, great to see you. I hear you had a tough weekend," she said, reaching for her bottle of beer that Josh had pre-ordered.

"Naw, it wasn't too bad. We got through it," said Frank easily. He motioned to Sue as she walked by, arms full of plates for another table. Sue nodded and smiled, continuing on.

"Well, he did stuff a lot of things in our head in a short time," offered Jon, "That has to be the most information I've ever had to learn in so short a time for a scuba class. We'll have to study hard to pass the cavern exam; I bet it's going to be hard."

"Ah, Jon, you always worry about that kind of stuff; I say it'll come naturally because we're experiencing the very things that he'll more than likely test us on," countered Frank.

Josh smiled slightly as his friends continued debating the academics of the cavern class. He enjoyed the mild banter of the two and for the first time in days a feeling of gentle contentment settled over him. He reached over and squeezed Elise's hand to reinforce the good feeling. She smiled, squeezed back and looked up at Sue, who had just walked up to take their order.

"Hi guys. Hi Elise, cute tank top; does the message work?" said Sue.

"Hi Sue," said Elise, giggling, "No, but usually a needle brings an unruly patient in line and they obey just fine."

"Maybe we should use sharp objects in scuba to make our students obey," offered Josh dryly. Frank and Jon grinned and looked up at Sue.

"OK, what'll you guys have?" said Sue. She took their food orders, beamed a nice smile and disappeared back into the restaurant.

"I can't wait for next weekend's class. We'll get to actually go into a cavern," said Frank.

"Yeah, I feel like he drilled the hell out of us in the open water; seems like he spent a LOT of time just having us practice our swimming techniques," said Jon.

Josh pursed his lips. The elusive feeling of contentment evaporated. He really didn't want to rehash his lack of cavern ability yet again but knew the conversation was heading that way.

He decided to go ahead and plow through it, like pulling off a band aid in one quick motion.

"Yeah, clearly that's an area where I need work," said Josh, in a small brave voice.

"Aw, don't worry about it, Josh. You can always just swim using the modified flutter kick. It's acceptable, I think," offered Jon.

"Well, I got the distinct impression that Drew really wants all of us to have a decent modified frog kick since it's the least likely way to stir up the bottom," countered Frank, looking at Josh.

"Guess the test will be the cavern, right?" said Josh, slightly defensively, "If I can swim into a cavern that has silt on the bottom, no matter what kind of kick, and not stir it up then it's all good."

Jon came to his defense, "Yeah, I think that should be acceptable. Shouldn't matter how you swim, as long as your technique is clean." Josh gave Jon a grateful smile.

"Guys, I'm not so sure," Frank said slowly, "I would think that the flutter kick is basically a flawed technique for a cavern or cave because it's an up and down motion. You'd really have to work hard to get the fins up high enough all the time to not have the downward thrust hit the floor."

"Maybe it's too dangerous to swim into a cavern without the right kick?" said Elise helpfully.

Josh looked at her, slightly miffed at her response. He could read concern with no malice in her green eyes.

"I don't think you know enough to judge, Elise," he said hotly, without thinking. They glared at each other in a stalemate, neither willing to back down or continue throwing verbal barbs.

"Well, guys, no use getting worked up about it now," said Jon, squirming slightly, "Besides, it'll be totally safe when Drew takes us into a cavern no matter how good or bad we are. You should know best, Josh; the instructor would never put a class in real danger. It's his job to make sure that we learn the correct way to do this sort of diving or fail us."

Josh slunk in his chair. Jon had meant to make him feel better but now the growing truth that he wasn't worthy of being a cavern diver came back to him in full force. Elise reached over and touched his arm; she could read his concern.

"I'm sorry, Josh, I just don't want you to get hurt. I worry about you when you dive."

"Elise, he's a great diver and safe – I'd dive into a cavern with him anytime," said Frank with bravado.

"Oh, yeah? And how safe was that cavern dive in Jackson Blue where you guys almost drowned?" said Elise, her voice raised and shaking slightly.

"Hey, that not the same, this is a class we're taking because of how badly that dive went," argued Frank.

Josh stretched out his hands towards Elise and Frank, palms out and fingers up and said, "Stop, guys, that's enough. Let it go. Besides, our food's here."

Josh could see Sue heading their way, plates balanced in her arms. She hesitated, catching Josh's eye and sensing a private conversation was in play. Josh waved her over and forced a smile on his face. Sue was always considerate of her guests and sensitive to the mood of a table.

"Here's your food, guys," Sue said cheerfully, setting down each plate in front of the correct person. Josh leaned over to give her room as she placed his plate in front of him. The broiled grouper filet still sizzled from the grill. Steam rose from the plate and he could smell the delicious blend of butter, lemon and seasonings enter his nose. The tantalizing smell of the grouper competed with the fresh baked corn scent of the hush puppies and the slight earthy odor of the wild rice.

"Thanks, Sue," Josh said, grateful for both the food and the disruption. She nodded, took the drink refresh order and departed.

Chapter 21

Later that night, in his bedroom at his apartment, Josh contemplated the dinner discussion. Elise had politely declined his desire to stop by her apartment; he asked more out of obligation than necessity although her rebuff still stung. They both needed private time. His friends had said their goodbyes and skedaddled back to their apartment in town.

Josh looked over at his clock, which read 10:35. He walked over to the dresser and picked up the crumpled piece of paper from Allen. What if Elise was right? What if he was leading himself and his buddies into danger? What if he was blowing this diving technique thing way out of proportion?

Seemed that he needed somebody else's advice, no matter how strange the messenger might be.

Shrugging, he sat down on his bed and reached for the cordless phone. He dialed the number and placed the phone to his head, waiting for Allen to answer.

"Hello? Who is this?" said a voice in a slightly annoyed tone. Josh recognized the gravely southern accent.

"Hi Allen. This is Josh."

"Josh who? It's kinda late..."

"Josh, the cavern student from last weekend. You gave me your number at Fort White Cave Diving on Sunday afternoon," said Josh. The words came out in a rush since he was afraid Allen may hang up at any minute.

Maybe this wasn't the best idea after all.

The line fell silent in the way only a phone line at night can while waiting for a response, full of imagined crackling noises and anticipation.

"Oh, yeah, I remember you, kid," said Allen.

"You offered to help me with my cavern diving technique," prompted Josh.

Josh heard a sigh come over the line and another long pause. This time he actually heard a slight crackle in the long distance line.

"I reckon I might be able to help you," said Allen grudgingly, "Meet me at Ginnie Springs Wednesday morning at ten AM." Josh heard the click as Allen hung up.

Josh considered calling him back to try and arrange a different day and time but it occurred to him that Allen probably wouldn't have the common courtesy to work out a time arrangement and might even call the whole thing off.

Josh felt a thrill of anticipation shoot through him, tempered by concern over how he was going to pull this off. He had to work Wednesday and didn't want anybody knowing what he was doing. He didn't need the extra flak from Kathy, Elise or his dive buddies, especially if this turned out to be a horrible waste of time.

Chapter 22

Josh woke up early Wednesday morning at 7:28 AM. He reached over and disabled the alarm, before it tried to wake him up in the next few minutes. He got up, relieved himself, washed up and changed into a t-shirt and bathing suit. He hesitated for a moment, picked up the phone and dialed the number for *Wakulla Skuba*. It rang three times before the answering machine in Kathy's office picked up.

"Hi Kathy. I'm not feeling well today and won't be coming into work. I hope this thing will pass and I'll be at work tomorrow. I'll let you know later."

He hung up, feeling slightly ashamed. He had never done that before and felt bad leaving Kathy in the lurch at the last moment.

Too late to back out now.

Five minutes later he was eastward bound towards Ginnie Springs in his truck, dive gear in the back. Fifteen minutes later he was munching on a fast food breakfast and drinking coffee from a paper travel cup, fueling up for the day.

Two hours later he pulled into the parking lot at Ginnie, looking for Allen's old blue and white trim VW van. There was no sign of it. Discouraged, Josh went inside, signed up for diving, paid his fees and drove deeper into the property. Perhaps Allen was already down by the spring.

Josh spotted Allen's VW van. He was parked in the Handicapped spot nearest the boardwalk that lead down to the spring. The day was bright, sunny and hot. The dirt lot was only partially filled, mostly with the vehicles of campers who were milling about lazily in the morning. Children romped in the playground tucked under a copse of oak trees near the spring.

A few thick-skinned souls were already drifting down the spring run, enjoying the difference between the ninety five degree heat and the seventy degree spring water. Compared to last weekend the place was quiet and peaceful.

Josh parked next to Allen's van and hopped out. The right side door was slid back. Allen was wrestling with a scuba cylinder, pulling it out of the van and onto the arms of his wheel chair. The tank had a first stage attached to the tank valve.

Various hoses snaked from the first stage and were held in place against the tank with a large flat piece of what appeared to be black inner tubing from a large truck tire. Josh could see a second stage regulator and an SPG poking out from the side of the inner tubing. Allen had one hand near the tank neck and the other grasped what looked like a large mountain climber's carabineer, attached near the bottom of the tank to a large hose clamp that encircled the entire tank.

"Hi Allen. Thanks again for doing this. Do you need any help?" started Josh.

Allen turned to Josh and wheeled the chair towards the wooden boardwalk. He started moving towards the spring.

"Don't need help. If I did I'd ask for it. Get your gear ready and come on down to the spring. We're going diving," said Allen, continuing down the boardwalk.

"Uh, sure," said Josh. He followed Allen anyway, curious as to how he was going to get his gear into the water, much less go diving from a wheelchair.

Allen wheeled up the ramp to the wooden porch that wrapped partially around the spring. Bathers moved out of his way, curiosity in their eyes. Allen ignored them and expertly spun his chair near the edge of the stairs leading down to the water, engaging the brake. He strong armed the tank from the chair hand rails using the carabineer and the tank neck and placed it gently down on the top stair. He placed his arms on the hand rails and lifted himself off of the chair and placed his legs gingerly down on the wooden porch.

Josh stood awkwardly by, wanting to help but not daring to offer. He realized that Allen did have some movement in his legs as he watched him half shuffle half drag the scuba tank down to the water.

With a grunt Allen rolled the tank into the water and, using a small piece of thick nylon attached to the rigging at the top of the tank, clipped the cylinder to a sister piece of nylon wrapped around one of the wooden vertical beams at the bottom of the ladder.

The tank sank into the water, joining another cylinder already placed there earlier. Josh followed as Allen shuffled back up the stairs, plunked into his chair and wheeled back towards his van. Allen returned to the open side door of his van, intent on the next step of preparing to dive, ignoring Josh.

"Did you enjoy the show?" asked Allen, his expression pinched. Stunned, Josh shook his head and walked over to his truck.

Josh opened the tailgate of his truck and slid his gear towards the back. He attached the BC to his tank, connected his first stage to the tank valve and completed the rig by attaching the low pressure hose to the power inflator. He glanced over at Allen, who was wrestling into an old bleached-blue wet suit with patches and scuff marks.

Josh pulled out his full body wet suit from a large plastic bin he kept in the truck bed and hopped up on the tailgate. He slipped an old plastic grocery bag on his left foot and used the slippery device to guide the wet suit on his leg. He switched the bag onto his right foot and repeated the procedure for his right leg. Finally he stood, pulling the wet suit up the rest of the way and slipped in his arms, one at a time. He reached behind him and grabbed the length of the draw cord that attached to the zipper head at the bottom of the wet suit on his back.

He pulled the cord up and felt the wet suit fabric envelope him in the back as the zipper worked its way to his neck. Satisfied that it felt fully closed he reached behind him and tucked the cord underneath a small flap of neoprene using the Velcro attachment conveniently placed there by the wet suit manufacturer.

He sat back on the tailgate, reached into his plastic bin, pulled out his dive booties and slipped them on his feet. Next he extracted his mask and squirted some defogging juice in the mask, smearing the inside lenses. He lugged his weight belt from the back of the bed and placed it around his waist, securing the buckle in front. He stood and turned back to the truck bed, pulling his scuba rig into an upright position.

He turned, half sitting on the tailgate for support and slipped each arm into the BC, as if putting on a coat. He pressed the two sides of the Velcro cummerbund around his waist, just above the weight belt and finished by connecting the two halves of the BC's plastic clip at chest level.

Josh rested momentarily, looking over at Allen. Allen looked ready for the water but his gear was unlike anything Josh had seen before. Instead of a BC attached to a single tank or a back plate and wings with double tanks Allen wore what looked like a vest with a wing stuffed underneath it, upside down in the back. The battery canister of a light hung from two attachment points on the bottom of the rig, forcing Allen to sit halfway out of his chair.

A cable lead from the canister to a light head attached to a D-ring on the right side of the vest. Allen's lap held his fins, dive hood and mask.

How was this dive-able? thought Josh.

Allen looked over at Josh and said, "OK, let's go, kid."

Josh stood up, turned around and grabbed his fins, dive hood and mask and followed behind Allen, his tank gently bumping against his rump as he walked. A group of eager swimmers, inner tubes in hand ready to float down the spring, parted way as Allen wheeled up to the stairs. Josh could see mild irritation on some of the faces but nobody dared to raise the specter of complaining to a disabled person.

Allen repeated the early series of moves; he wheeled his chair next to the top of the stairs, locked the wheels, muscled himself out of the chair and worked down the stairs using mostly his arms on the wooden rails with the occasional assist from his damaged legs. Finally he slid into the water near his tanks, relief to be in a near-zero-G environment written on his face.

Josh walked down the stairs and set up shop on the other side of the stairs, allowing the tubers to enter the spring. Between the swimmers whoops and hollers as they hit the cold water Josh could make out Allen reaching for each of the scuba tanks he had placed there earlier. Josh quickly pulled his fins on, pulled the hood over his face, placed his mask on his forehead and shuffled over to Allen in the waist-deep crystal clear water. He wanted a closer look at Allen's equipment.

"What kind of a rig is that?" he asked.

Allen clipped the carabineer at the bottom of one of the tanks to a matching large D-ring strategically placed at his waist and pulled a thick cord of stretchy rubber material from his shoulder to the top of the tank. The tank hung in place on his right side, parallel to his body.

"This is a side mount rig. If you haven't figured it out by now my legs aren't strong enough to walk around with a single tank on my back, much less a set of doubles," said Allen.

He reached for the second tank and repeated the connection process from top to bottom. He pulled out a low pressure hose from the bundle of hoses held in place with a large inner tube on the tank and attached it to an inflator hose that was bungeed to his vest.

"This way I can put the tank on in the water and avoid having to carry them," continued Allen. He pressed the power inflator button and Josh heard the hiss of compressed air fill the wing sandwiched on Allen's back. Allen pulled on his dive hood, slipped on his fins, one at a time, using the roots as a perch and slid neck-level down into the water.

"Ah, that's better," said Allen, "OK, let's see what your problem is, kid. Go swim around in the basin and I'll take a look." Allen motioned towards the center of the spring basin, the darker blue water indicating an increase in depth.

Josh nodded, rinsed his mask with spring water, secured it to his head and sank below the surface. Surprisingly he didn't feel anywhere as nervous as with the class; he figured he had nothing to lose since he couldn't do a frog kick anyway.

He added a touch of air to his BC and swam forward, towards the deeper water. He swam to the middle of the basin and descended to the bottom at twenty feet of depth, using the modified flutter kick.

Might as well show him what I can do half decently.

Josh turned and looked for Allen. Allen swam towards him, gliding with minimal effort through the water. The transformation was amazing to Josh; on the surface Allen required wheelchair assistance for most things and struggled to get around, albeit admirably. In the water, with the advantage of neutral buoyancy Allen looked more alive and happy, at least as best Josh could tell given the restricted view of his face with a mask on it.

Allen was a picture of minimalist grace in motion and at rest in the water, even more so than Drew. The side mounted tanks snugged up against his left and right side, balanced perfectly. One of the regs was in Allen's mouth while the other lay tucked between the other tank and his vest, within easy reach and eye sight. Two short high pressure hoses lead to pressure gauges bungeed to his vest, also within easy sight. Josh admired this adaptation to Allen's disability that not only allowed him to dive but possibly enhanced his safety. It seemed having all of the moving and pressurized parts right up front where they could be viewed and worked on was a better idea than having them behind your back, like his was.

Allen settled near the bottom, hovering with no motion or effort a few feet above the sand. He motioned to Josh, ordering him to swim around some more with a back and forth gesture of his fingers.

Josh did a slow lap along the basin edge, using his best modified flutter kick and turned to look back at Allen. Allen gave him the "watch me" sign (two fingers to his eyes, then he pointed to himself) and did a slow lap along the edge using the modified frog kick. Josh could see just the tiniest of muscle contractions in Allen's legs that transferred down the fulcrum of his legs to his large black stiff fins, which imparted enough energy to propel him through the water cleanly and with little effort. Allen stopped and looked at Josh, waiting.

Josh sighed, an extra flurry of bubbles floating to the surface and started his dance of disaster. He bent his knees and tried to touch his heels together in frog kick style, as Drew had tried to get him to do time and time again. He felt the familiar face down list start and tried to counteract by dog paddling. Eventually he ended up nearly vertical, as usual, and had to recover by relaxing his legs, straightening out his body and waiting until he slowly drifted to the bottom. This was getting to become a habit, a bad one at that.

Allen swam closer, appearing to study Josh closely. He gave Josh the "do it again" sign (spinning circle with his index finger). Josh started again and before he could bend his knees he felt Allen's hands on his legs.

He relaxed, figuring that Allen was trying to help him place his legs where he thought they should be. He allowed Allen to position his thigh, calves and ankles where he wanted, trying to remain pliant as he was manipulated.

He felt Allen let go with a slight push and tried to sustain the last leg position. Allen came into view, hovering off to his left. He felt his head start to sink and Allen darted back, adjusting his lower leg to counteract the off balance body position. Josh closed his eyes momentarily, trying to read where Allen had placed his legs and attempted to keep them there.

He found his lower back felt crunched as he strained to maintain horizontal balance. He opened his eyes and Allen swam back into view and gave him the "hold" sign, indicating that Josh shouldn't try to swim.

Josh just hung there, waiting to see what would happen to his balance. He strained to keep his legs bent at the hips and his knees bent at the correct angle. He found that by adjusting his joints just a tiny bit - either the hips or the knees - he could feel his body begin to either fall forward or backward, slightly. It was only through extreme effort that he could hold a horizontal position at all. He looked at Allen, hoping he would stop the drill before his lower back cramped.

Allen gave him the "start swimming" sign and Josh tried a tentative frog kick, concentrating on keeping his hips and knees in the same position.

Slowly he started forward and he continued kicking, remembering to bend his knees and hips to adjust for any unwanted vertical motion. Eventually he managed a lap around the edge of the basin; his body porpoising and undulating with his leg strokes.

Finally Allen gave him the "thumbs up" to surface and Josh gratefully stretched out his legs, relieving the burning muscle buried at the base of his spine. He and Allen swam towards the waist deep water near the stairs and their heads broke the surface at the same time.

Allen removed his mask and turned his head, snorting the excess mucus out of his nose and wiping it with his hand. Josh understood these things; diving often involved gross things like pee in wet suits and nose goobers at the surface. You just learned to accept it as a part of the sport.

"Well, you do have a terrible frog kick," said Allen, swishing his hand to clean it in the water and turning back to face Josh. He stayed mostly submerged in the water, to avoid the weight of the tanks.

"Wow, that was cool! I actually did a frog kick for a bit there," gushed Josh, pleased at any progress. He pulled the neoprene dive hood away from his right ear, to break the water seal and hear better on the surface.

"Hold on there, kid; your frog kick is still nowhere near good enough to go underground. The majority of your problem is in the uneven weight distribution of your scuba system. That tank on your back is a major source of negative buoyancy, as is your weight belt.

"Plus that BC air bladder isn't designed to keep you balanced. It's designed to keep your head up out of the water on the surface. All of the force vectors are off."

Josh nodded. Allen seemed more animated now that they were actually in the water and doing what he clearly still loved.

"Drew noticed that too and we tried to adjust the weight on my weight belt so I could be better balanced. It just never seemed to work with the frog kick," commented Josh.

"Drew's a good instructor but he missed the slight back and forth motion of your lower leg as you go through the frog kick. That, coupled with your equipment unbalance, resulted in a tiny window of body position where you could get away with moving your legs while maintaining a nice horizontal body posture. You basically fell flat on your face and quickly got past the point of no return by bending your knees too much, bringing the added weight of your feet and fins over your center of gravity."

Josh revised his initial impression of Allen. He had looked and acted like a burned out diver with only a shred of intelligence remaining in his broken body. Clearly, though, Allen was a true master of the art of diving, at least when it came to body positioning and equipment balance.

"It really is a tiny window. My lower back was all knotted up with me trying to hold my legs in the right position. I'm not sure how much longer I could have held that. So, what should I do about it?" asked Josh.

Allen paused, watching a four person float drift by packed with bikini-clad college age women, all laughing and screaming at their initial exposure to the cold spring water.

They both watched, temporarily distracted, until the float passed by. Allen turned his attention back to Josh, a grin on his face.

"Let's get out and work on your equipment," said Allen.

Josh felt a pang of disappointment. He had finally gotten a taste of a real frog kick and he wanted to work out the kinks, especially the one developing in his lower back. He remained silent, though, and reached down to slip off his fins. Allen repeated his earlier steps in reverse, eventually shedding his tanks, fins and dive hood.

He clipped the tanks back onto the line attached to the stairs, stuffed his hood in one fin pocket and his mask in the other and set the fins up on the roots near the stairs. Josh copied his move; leaving his fins, mask and dive hood sitting next to Allen's.

Sure hope nobody steals them, thought Josh.

Josh stood next to Allen a few minutes later as he slid open the side door to his van. Josh had walked to his truck, lowered the tailgate and deposited his scuba system into the truck bed.

Not knowing how long Allen would be on the surface or even if they'd dive again he pulled the top of the wet suit down and tied the arms into a knot around his waist. The noon air beat down on his cool wet upper torso, providing warm relief after exposure to the spring's cool waters.

Allen moved some equipment around inside the van. Josh's eyes wandered around the van; it was filled with scuba gear – tanks, boxes of regulators, a number of canister lights, reels, spools of line, a large toolbox, various wet suits and fins. Allen shoved some of the tanks around from his wheelchair, digging towards the far side of the van.

"There they are – reach in there and pull out those tanks, Josh," said Allen, pointing.

Josh reached back and pulled out a set of grey double tanks, held together by a set of dual thin steel bands. The top of the tanks were connected with a manifold system, somewhat like Drew's and Asrid's but thinner and older looking. In the middle of the manifold a valve pointed upward. Josh grabbed the tanks and slid them out, curious.

"OK, put those over on the picnic table."

Josh hugged the tanks and lifted; they felt very heavy and bulky. He lumbered over to the nearest picnic table and set the tanks down on the rounded bottoms first and gently laid them the rest of the way. Behind him Allen wheeled up, a harness, back plate and wing in his lap. An old army green canvas bag of additional equipment swung on the side of his chair. Josh assumed it held regulators for the doubles.

"OK, let's see if this still works. I haven't dove this rig in a really long time. Heck, I can't dive it any more anyway since my accident. Been meaning to sell it but just couldn't part with it. Lots of great dives on this rig," mused Allen. He handed the harness system to Josh.

"OK, you might as well learn how to assemble this rig if you are going to dive it."

Josh couldn't believe his ears – he was going to get to dive doubles? How awesome was this? He could never afford to rent such equipment, much less own them.

"Er, I can't afford to rent these," said Josh lamely, looking down, "Are you sure? In fact I'm not even sure I can pay whatever it is you are charging for this lesson..."

Allen laughed, the first time Josh had heard him utter any sound of joy or delight.

"Naw, kid, don't worry about it. I won't charge you for the class or the doubles, at least not now," Allen grinned, wheeled closer to the table and sat back in his chair, clearly enjoying himself.

Josh pushed the problem out of his mind for now, excited to learn about this new equipment. Well, at least it was new to him. He noticed the visual sticker on the tank read 1985 and the last hydrostatic date on the tank necks were from 1982 so he knew the tanks were out of spec and couldn't legally be filled with more air. Hopefully they were still safe.

Allen spent the next hour showing Josh how to put together the doubles. He also learned how to adjust the single piece of one inch webbing that wove through the back plate so that it fit his frame perfectly. Josh tried the harness on over his wet suit top and was surprised how snug and securely the system felt once the straps were adjusted correctly.

The wide strap secured the back plate firmly to his back much better than the jacket-style BC he usually wore. Most interesting was the crotch strap that connected from the bottom of the back plate, through his legs and into the belt loop at his waist. It felt weird.

"The harness has to hold the hundred pounds of tanks on your back and you definitely don't want it sliding around no matter what your body position," explained Allen as he taught Josh the specifics of the harness.

They connected the back plate to the tanks with the wing sandwiched in between and screwed down with two wing nuts.

Josh reached into the army surplus canvas bag and pulled out two sets of regulators, complete with hoses, second stages, a pressure gauge and extra low pressure hoses. He inspected the hoses, which showed slight wear and tear, especially near the attachment points. The second stages were of an older design made primarily of chrome plated steel components. Josh read the name etched in a circular pattern around the purge valve in the front: *BreathMaster 250*.

'Wow, these look like antiques! My buddy has one of these he got from his Dad. He loves how it breathes. We joke that the 250 is how deep you can dive them."

Allen retorted, "Well, those have been to 400 feet in Mexico so I doubt that's what it stands for."

Josh connected the two independent regulator systems to the tanks and learned how to route the hoses. Like Drew and Asrid's rigs the hoses were designed to be just the right length and to avoid sticking out.

Finally the rig was fully assembled.

"OK, Josh, let's see if you can handle these doubles," announced Allen.

Josh pulled his wet suit top back on again and zipped up the back. He pulled the doubles up and followed Allen's instructions as he explained the steps of putting on the doubles, securing and testing the regulators. Josh sat at the end of the bench in the harness while Allen went through helping him memorize by touch the location of all of the pieces of equipment.

Josh whispered to himself as they repeated each piece of gear, its location and purpose. This was definitely more complex than the open water scuba gear he was used to.

Allen, noticing the sweat beading on Josh's forehead, commented, "I think it's time to get in the water before you pass out from hyperthermia. One more thing, though."

Allen reached inside the bag hanging on his chair and pulled out a battery canister attached to a light head. The canister looked battered, the cord had clearly been repaired a number of times and the light head housing looked well beaten. To Josh, though, this was the icing on the cake. A canister light!

Josh held up his hands while Allen wheeled around him, undoing the belt, pulling back the webbing and sliding the canister onto his right hip. He clipped the light head onto Josh's right D-ring and showed him where the embedded on/off switch was located on the top of the battery canister. Josh felt the tug of the canister on his right hip. He hoped it wouldn't affect his balance in the water.

"No, the canister is actually only slightly negative in the water and compared to the weight vectors for your tanks and wings it's minimal. You'll hardly know it's there. OK, stand up and let's see if you can handle the weight," finished Allen, wheeling backwards to give Josh room.

Josh bent forward, bringing the full weight of the doubles against his back and straightened out his legs, standing mostly erect. The extra weight required him to lean forward slightly, else risk falling over like an upside down turtle.

"Doubles are very awkward on land and you have to be very careful of your footing. Just wait, though; you'll love how they dive," said Allen, motioning Josh towards the water.

Josh took one tentative step, getting the feeling of the weight. *This must be how an astronaut feels in their suits. Too bad we're not diving on the moon with its lower gravity*, mused Josh in thought.

He proceeded to walk. The weight was manageable, even tolerable, as long as he hunched forward slightly to keep balanced. Allen kept pace behind him, keeping a careful eye on him.

Josh reached the wooden porch and stepped up, placing a hand on his bent knee to steady his leg. He walked slowly over to the stairs and took them one at a time, holding tightly to the wooden rail. He was thankful for the outdoor carpet tacked onto each of the stairs, ensuring a solid grip by his dive boots.

"Put the long hose reg in your mouth and add some air in the wing; you don't want to sink and drown on your first doubles dive," remarked Allen as he parked his chair and started down the stairs.

Josh took the long hose reg, wrapped around his neck, and placed it in his mouth. He added a blast of air to the wing and felt it pushing against the sides of his body.

He stepped into the water and bent his knees, allowing the weight to transfer from his legs to the wing. The equipment felt more *there* than a single tank; things felt more *solid* as well. Gone was the feeling of the BC and tank sliding around and he sure didn't miss his weight belt. He usually had to adjust the weight belt during a dive as it shifted around or loosened. Not so with the harness and back plate; things just *stayed* where they should.

He picked up his fins and moved out of Allen's way. In a few moments they both had their gear fully on.

Allen looked at the pressure gauges on his twin side tanks and looked to Josh. "Check to see how much air you have in your doubles."

Josh knew Allen was testing him, to make sure he knew where the pressure gauge was located. He reached his left hand down to his waist and felt for the D-ring attached on the webbing. Attached to the D-ring was the gauge, secured with a bolt snap. He thumbed the bolt snap and pulled the bolt back, freeing the hook from the D-ring. He pulled the gauge towards his chest and read the display.

"I have 2,000 PSI," said Josh.

"Plenty of gas. Remember you are reading the combined pressure of two tanks that hold one hundred thirty cubic feet when pressurized to 2,400 PSI. That means you've got about three aluminum 80's worth of air on your back. Not bad, eh?" stated Allen, grinning. Josh grinned back and secured the gauge back in place, using the snap bolt.

"OK, let's try this again. Drop down, breathe for a second to let your system decide where the buoyancy wants to be and then add enough air to the wing to hover neutrally. Remember it'll take more air to counteract the extra weight of the tanks. Don't rush your buoyancy adjustments," instructed Allen.

Josh stuck the long hose in his mouth and fell forward into the water. He slid downward in slow motion, transitioning from air to water smoothly. He settled to the bottom and waited, taking stock in how things felt. He certainly felt more secure in the gear and idly thought how more difficult it would be to get out of the harness if he had to in an emergency.

He waited for things to settle and added a bit of air to the wing. Allen floated into view directly in front of him, intently watching. Josh admired the clean line of Allen's torso and tanks. Above them two yellow kayaks glided past, paddles dipping in the water. Sunshine filtered brightly through the water, the sun slightly off center from overhead as the day aged beyond noon.

Josh rose slightly, bending his hips and knees to the desired position. His body felt balanced and he found it much easier to maintain a horizontal posture with the doubles and wing. Allen swam behind him and he felt him do the same leg adjustments as before, only the final position was much easier to hold. He still felt his lower back bent like a pretzel but it was not as severe.

Allen swam past him, motioning for him to follow. Josh, keeping his knees up, frog kicked to follow and soon found himself gliding smoothly over the sandy bottom behind Allen. They sank down to the bottom of the basin and Josh practiced keeping horizontal as he adjusted his depth to match the ground. Josh was giddy with the difference in how easy this was compared to his earlier attempts. He watched Allen watching him, seemingly satisfied with the results.

Allen swam up to Josh and gave him the "stop" sign. Josh rested, hovering easily six inches off of the bottom. Allen reached up, unclipped the light head from Josh's right chest D-ring and slipped it on Josh's right hand. He signaled for Josh to turn on the light.

Josh reached down, found the buckle and followed the webbing around his right side until he reached the canister.

He fumbled around the top of the canister for the recessed switch and found it; flicking it on. He moved his right hand, looking inside of the light head and could see a growing tiny yellow glow. Soon he had to turn the light head away, as the beam was too bright to look at directly.

Allen had placed his light on his hand and turned his on as well.

The beam of his wrist-mounted light head competed with the sun's brilliance. He motioned for Josh to follow.

Josh swam behind Allen, curious as to his intentions. Allen swam straight towards the mount of the cavern, into the current.

Cool, we get to go in the cavern!

Allen paused, near the entrance and hovered next to an outcropping of white limestone jutting out from the edge of the basin. He reached near his belt and unclipped one of the small reels he kept there. He unlocked the reel, looped the end around the watermelon-sized outcropping and pulled it snug, the white nylon line taut.

Allen looked back at Josh and gave him the "thumbs down" sign. Josh, understanding he wanted to start the dive into the cavern, returned the sign.

Allen pushed off from the wall of the basin and turned back into the flow of the cavern. A large boulder in the middle of the entrance split the entrance into two sides, either of which was tall and wide enough to fit a diver with plenty of room to spare.

Allen chose the left side entrance and swam slowly, spooling out the line as he went. They both slid underneath the rocky ceiling and into the cavern. Occasionally Allen would pause and wrap the line around a rock, always keeping the line low and tight. Josh swam next to the line, shining his light at Allen's hands, careful not to blind him.

He found himself in a small room. The room was low but long; approximately five feet high and twenty feet wide. The left side of the room pinched into a small alcove and ended in a wall of pure white stone. The right side was littered with a number of garbage can-sized boulders above which a large rectangular picture frame shaped entrance dropped down into another chamber, mostly hidden in the dark.

Josh pointed his light momentarily down the right side and could see the ceiling of a larger room below them, enticing them to visit. The current was steady but not strong; Josh mimicked Allen's movements with the occasional gentle frog kick coupled with slow pulls on rock outcroppings. Josh looked down and saw that the floor of the cavern was mostly sand and coarse grains of limestone, some the size of peas. He hand fanned the floor and debris swirled and quickly settled back down.

Doesn't look like anybody could kick this up too much.

Allen threaded his way around a number of smaller boulders, heading towards the passage in the back right of the room. He pulled himself up to the edge of the drop off and stopped, looking back at Josh. Allen pointed his light to the right wall and drew a large circle, slowly, with his light beam.

Josh remembered that in the dark this was the cavern "OK" signal, since it was easier to spot than a person's encircled forefinger and thumb in the dark.

He returned the "OK" using his light, circling the same patch of wall. Allen turned and plunged down the drop off, his fins flicking a final frog kick stroke before disappearing. Josh caught up and looked over the ledge. A large room came into view, lit by the powerful beam from both his and Allen's lights. It was easily three times larger than the first room. The room was shaped like a rough tear drop, pinched off on the left into a pile of boulders, expanding in the middle and terminating in a rounded wall on the far right end.

Josh could make out black thick lines of some material crisscrossing the passage as it shrank down and continued at its deepest point at the bottom right of the room. He slowly moved his light from one end to the other, drinking in the view of the stark white walls, ceiling and floor. A large white nylon rope, tattered from years of use, bisected the room from the top of the drop off to the back. Thousands of years of constant erosion had created a room of broken beauty, the crumbly limestone carved into a variety of strange shapes and sizes.

Man, this is so pretty and I can't believe how clear the water is. Guess my eyes have adjusted to the light better and these lights are way brighter than anything I've ever used before. Really makes a difference.

Allen worked his way down to the deepest point, continuing to run the guideline along the floor and scattered boulders, following the current to its source in the far right corner. As he swam closer he realized the black crisscross pattern was actually metal rebar put in place to prevent divers from going any farther into the passage.

He swam up to the grate and grabbed on, again following Allen's lead. They shone their lights deeper into the passage. Here the current was at its strongest; small grains of sand dancing in liquid dust devils on the undulating floor. The tunnel was much lower, too low for a diver with a tank on their back. Josh thought, though, that Allen's side mount tanks could probably still continue onward, if the way hadn't been blocked.

Wonder why it's blocked off?

He looked behind him, keeping his light forward and noticed the large room was dark, with the only light coming from the cavern entrance some hundred feet back and fifty feet up. The color of the twin entrances was a deeper blue, a true aquamarine created by the distance the light had to travel through water to reach his eyes. Josh felt a quiet peace come over him, at awe with the beauty of this place. The current buffeted the side of his face as he watched the exhalation bubbles from their regulators mix and float towards the surface, like a bunch of helium-filled silver balloons released all at once on a windy day.

Allen flashed his light slowly, back and forth and Josh turned reluctantly from the sight. He pointed to the pressure gauge on his right tank and pointed to Josh.

Josh paused momentarily, trying to remember where his pressure gauge was located. Allen pointed to his left side at the same moment Josh remember that the gauge was clipped off on his left waist D-ring. He reached his left hand to his waist, found the high pressure hose and followed it to the gauge. He pulled the gauge up to his face, the ambient light providing enough light to see that he still had 1,900 PSI in his set of twin tanks.

Geez, I have so much gas left; this is wonderful!

He swiveled the gauge towards Allen, who quickly read the pressure and gave him an "OK". Allen wrapped the line around a piece of rebar and continued the dive, following the back wall.

Josh turned and the current pushed him into Allen; he reached out with his right hand to stop his forward motion. Allen dropped lower to avoid more of a collision.

Oops, this thing on my back acts like a sail with the current when I turn away from it. Gonna have to remember that!

Allen continued, eventually arriving at the other end of the room where a confusion of boulders filled the back, looking as if the ceiling had collapsed in some hopefully distant past. Josh could see small catfish fingerlings swimming in rapid circles on shelves of white limestone along the tops of the largest boulder, stirring up small trails of sand.

Eventually they ended up back near the entrance, where Allen turned and gave Josh the "thumbs up" signal to end the dive. He began to reel in the line slowly, coming towards Josh.

Josh looked behind him, noticing for the first time that they had made a breadcrumb trail of thin white nylon line leading back along the wall, to the grate and back up the other side of the drop off.

We should go back the way we came in.

He swam back along the line as Allen continued reeling it in, the line pulsing with the motions of the reeling. As Allen reached one of his tie off points he would deftly unwrap it and continue reeling, in a single fluid motion, never having to stop nor allowing slack in the line. Josh just tried to give him enough room to detach the line from the various boulders as they exited.

They swam back to the grate where Josh, reaching it first, gingerly released the line from the piece of errant rebar. He held on to the line to avoid slack and released it when Allen tugged gently.

They worked their way up the drop off, both releasing air from their wings to maintain neutral buoyancy as their depth decreased. Josh was surprised at how much brighter the first room now appeared as they entered it.

Guess my eyes have adapted to the darkness down there.

Allen flashed Josh right at the cavern exit and gave Josh the hand sign for "safety stop". Josh, so enamored with the cavern, totally forgot the need for a safety stop. It was harder to judge depth with a rock ceiling.

Josh nodded to Allen and relaxed, one hand holding steady on a rock. His body slowly rotated with the current until he was pointing back into the cavern, head first.

Like a flag in the wind.

After a few minutes Allen again gave him the thumbs up and they glided out of the cavern and into the sunlit basin. A group of open water divers milled about in the basin, their bodies vertical and their flutter kicks sending puffs of white sand from the bottom. Josh already felt far removed from that type of diver, totally unaware of how their body position and fin kicks affected visibility.

He watched them swim into the cavern using the other entrance as Allen unwrapped his line from his initial tie-off, locked it and re-clipped it back on his waist. He followed Allen as he swam slowly up and ascended near the wooden stairs, surfacing in the waist-deep water.

"So, kid, how did you like that?" asked Allen after the usual post-dive nasal purge.

"Man, I love these doubles! SO much easier to dive! And that cavern, wow – it's so beautiful, especially with these big lights!" gushed Josh.

Allen smiled, "Yeah, the right equipment can sure make the difference between an OK dive and a great dive. Speaking of lights, go ahead and turn yours off. The light head is designed to work only while in the water; it can overheat in air."

Josh noticed Allen's light head had already been extinguished and stowed back on his left chest D-ring. He switched off his light, removed the light head from his wrist and clipped it on his right chest D-ring. This time he was able to find the light switch and D-ring slightly easier.

Practice makes perfect, he thought.

"So how come you let me go into the cavern? And what about that group of open water divers that went in after us? They didn't even have lights," asked Josh.

"This is one of the few caverns that is safe enough for open water divers to dive. Technically they are in the overhead but there have been very few accidents in the Ballroom over the years," said Allen, "You noticed the grate at the end. That was put in there years ago to keep divers from going farther. Plus they put in that large rope for any idiots that may have trouble finding their way out," explained Allen.

"Your body position and frog kick looked good enough for a cavern diver so I decided on the spur of the moment to take you on a tour dive. You'll do more of that in Drew's class, of course. But before I allow you to continue we need to work on your familiarity with your new rig."

Allen proceeded to walk Josh through the different types of procedures he now had to memorize wearing the back plate, wings and doubles. He would explain the workings of a particular piece, like the isolator valve now located behind Josh's neck and he showed Josh how to open and close the valve and when it was important to do so. This continued on the surface until Josh had an appreciation for the extra complexity of the rig.

Allen repeated the drills underwater, using hand signals until he was satisfied that Josh could swap regs, check his pressure gauge, turn on and off all three valves across the top of the tanks and even get totally out and back into the rig while under water.

Josh, his confidence back, found the tasks easy to master and enjoyed doing the drills. Allen's last drill involved Josh swimming around, maintaining his horizontal posture at all times while performing skills in a rapid fire manner, including sharing air, removing his mask and repeating all of the valve drills. Finally, Allen gave him the "thumbs up" and they surfaced.

"OK, kid, I'm done about as much as I can do with you. It's important that you perform as you just did, keeping your head and body level, no matter what happens. That matters deep within a cave or cavern where a silty bottom can make the difference between an easy exit or a difficult one," said Allen, removing his fins.

Josh nodded and copied Allen, removing his fins, mask and dive hood. "Yeah, I can see that. It sure helps practicing it in the open water." He suppressed a shiver from the cold water.

"You'll want to practice these skills a lot more than the typical open water skills, that's for sure. How many times do you think open water students actually practice an air share after they get certified?"

Josh thought and answered, "Um, probably never? Kinda embarrassed to say that except for helping Kathy in class, me and my buddies never practice our skills. Guess we figure we'll know them when we need them."

Allen's eyes widened momentarily at the mention of Kathy's name, which intrigued Josh, but he decided not to ask about it, as the expression disappeared as quickly as it had appeared. No reason to possibly upset Allen and end this impromptu class prematurely.

"Yeah, well, the overhead environment is a lot more unforgiving than open water. You never have immediate access to the surface underground. In a real emergency you will perform the emergency procedures only as well as you've practiced it. If it's been months or even years you probably will freeze up or panic and never do the correct procedure. Believe me, I've done enough body recoveries to know," intoned Allen, clipping off his second tank to the nylon loop on the stairs.

Before Josh could ask more questions Allen loped up the stairs, dragging one of his tanks to his waiting wheelchair. Josh started to grab his second tank and thought twice; afraid to offend Allen and also not too sure if he could handle the extra weight with the doubles on his back.

Later, after all of the gear had been packed up in their respective vehicles and both had changed into dry clothes, Josh approached Allen at the side of his VW van. The afternoon heat lay hard over the land, subduing all but the hardiest swimmers in the spring. To Josh it felt like siesta time in the camping site.

"Well, Allen, again, I really appreciate this class. Where do you want me to load these doubles and the canister light?" asked Josh, pointing to Allen's gear sitting on the edge of his tailgate.

Allen wheeled around, faced Josh and simply said, "Go ahead and borrow them for now," and turned back to packing his equipment.

"Gee, thanks again. I really don't know what to say..." Josh trailed off. When Allen didn't respond Josh finally shrugged, feeling dismissed.

"OK, well, I'm going back home now; see you around." It seemed to Josh that Allen's personality changed back to grumpy when it was back on dry land, out of the water; his true element.

Allen waved his hand casually behind his back, clearly his way of returning the farewell. Josh pushed the doubles back into his truck, closed the tailgate and hopped into the cab. He looked in the rear view mirror as he exited the parking lot and saw Allen still tinkering in the side of his van, engrossed in his work.

Chapter 23

As Josh exited Ginnie and reached the hard top his mind started replaying the day's events. It had gone a lot better than he thought. Now he could continue with the cavern class, confident that he could handle the rest of the training. Allen was a bit of a mystery, though. Josh admired that he had found a way to continue diving despite his initial outer appearance of being beaten and withdrawn from life. He was totally a different person while in the water, seemingly normal and a pleasure to interact with.

Was he that bitter about his disability? What was his disability and had he always had it? Perhaps he got injured in a car wreck and was bitter about life's little twists of fate? Maybe it was an old diving injury. It would be difficult to reconcile that the very thing you love to do, that defined you also harmed you and almost took the ability away.

Josh turned westward, back towards Tallahassee, the sun low on the horizon. He stopped at a fast food store in Branford and grabbed a quick bite, realizing how all of the time in the cold spring water had made him hungry. Continuing his drive he wondered what he should say to Kathy about his "sick day". Hmm, what about Elise and his friends? The guys would definitely know next weekend that something had changed. It's not like he could just hide the doubles and there was no way he was going to dive his open water gear in a cavern anymore. He crossed the Suwanee River, thoughts still whirling around in his head when behind him he heard the "whoop" of a sheriff's tan patrol car accompanied by the familiar flash of red and blue.

Crap, he thought, *sure hope he's stopping somebody else.*

He looked forward and saw no traffic and looked down at his speedometer. He was going eight miles per hour over the posted speed limit. He slowed slightly, hoping it would help.

Really?

The patrol car edged up directly behind him, making the target clear. Josh sighed and slowly decelerated, looking for a safe place to pull over. He pulled off the two-lane road and onto the wide grassy shoulder. He stopped, shut off the vehicle and waited.

The engine tick tick noises competed with the sounds of summer birds punctuated with the occasional swoosh of passing traffic. Clearly the officer wasn't in a big hurry as Josh could see his silhouette in the patrol car.

They always make you stew.

Finally the officer exited his vehicle and sauntered over to his truck, dark green uniform matching his flat brimmed Stetson hat. The setting sun reflected off his dark sunglasses, making it impossible to read his emotions. He was taller than Josh with a muscular build on his middle aged body. Josh could see the light blonde sideburns of a severe crew cut projecting out from underneath the Stetson.

"License and registration, son," drawled the officer in a thick southern accent. His left chest was adorned with a five point star and on his right a thin gold plated badge spelled "J. McDonald" in black.

Josh pulled his driver's license out of his wallet and retrieved the vehicle registration from his glove compartment, reaching slowly across the truck's cabin. His heart was pounding yet he did not want to appear rushed or nervous. Being stopped for speeding was thankfully a rare event in his life and he never got used to the feeling of one moment being a law-abiding citizen to the next a potential criminal, at least in the eyes of the lawman watching his moves. Josh knew his best bet was to play it cool and polite. He had been, after all, slightly speeding although he wasn't going to admit it first.

"Here you go Officer McDonald. Is there some sort of a problem, sir?" asked Josh, who wanted to get this over with.

This wasn't the first time he regretted the lack of air conditioning in his truck. The secret to staying cool in Florida in an unconditioned vehicle was to keep the windows open and the truck moving.

"You wait here and stay in your truck. I'll be right back," said the officer, who turned and walked back to his clearly air conditioned cruiser. Josh fumed and stayed put, watching the officer in his rear view mirror. The officer paused at the end of his truck and looked at his array of dive gear laid out on the bottom of the truck.

Sure hope he doesn't think those are bombs, though Josh idly, sweat beading on his forehead and rolling down his arm pits.

The officer continued back to his cruiser and sat back inside, probably discovering every crime and misdemeanor that Josh had ever done or contemplated since birth.

Ten hot minutes later Officer McDonald returned to the driver's side of the truck. He held a small ticket-sized silver metal container that no doubt spelled trouble in the form of an expensive speeding ticket.

"Do you know the speed limit along this road?" challenged the officer. Josh swallowed dryly and decided honesty was the best policy at this point.

"Um, yes sir, sixty miles per hour. I think I was a bit over, but not by much," he said meekly.

"I clocked you at seventy miles per hour," said the officer, his face impassive. Josh felt a tiny twinge of anger; why did their radars always read greater than speedometers?

"Um, sorry, Officer; guess I didn't realize I was over the limit...," said Josh, eyes downcast.

Officer McDonald removed his sunglasses and looked closer at Josh.

"Are you a cave diver?" he asked.

Josh, taken aback by the sudden change in the conversation, stammered out a response, "Um, I am training to be one."

Josh noticed the officer's eyes were a kindly hazel and a small smile flickered on the officer's face.

"Yeah, I'm a diver myself; member of the Sheriff's Dive Team too. I've worked with you guys before in the past, although never on a happy occasion."

Josh simply sat and waited, not sure where this was going.

"Tell you what, son. I'll let you go with a warning this time." He opened up the silver metal clipboard and handed over a piece of paper.

"Just watch your speed limit on this road and dive safe."

Officer McDonald slipped his glasses back on, transforming back into the inscrutable arm of the law and tugged at his hat.

"Th...thank you, Officer," said Josh, smiling weakly. He watched and waited as the officer returned to his vehicle, turned off the bubble gum lights and accelerated smartly past Josh's truck, west bound.

Josh looked at the violation ticket and confirmed that it was indeed just a warning.

Talk about your close calls.

He wiped the sweat from his brow, started the truck and pulled slowly off the shoulder, taking care to watch for traffic. The moving air felt wonderful as he accelerated up to the speed limit and made his way home.

Chapter 24

The next morning Josh pulled into the parking lot of *Wakulla Skuba*, his mind tense. He still wasn't sure what he was going to tell Kathy about yesterday. He had never pulled the fake sick day trick with her and despite his newfound success with diving the double tanks he dreaded Kathy finding it out. He parked, grabbed his sack lunch and opened the door to the truck.

Kathy opened the front door to the shop, moving out the displays of snorkeling equipment onto the front porch. Bear squeezed out the door and ran up to Josh, curly tail vibrating with pleasure. Josh picked up the dog and nudged his head to the dogs, the soft fur tickling his nose.

Bear chuffed softly and sniffed the sack lunch, curious. He set Bear down and walked up to the porch.

"'Morning Josh. Hope you are feeling better. Would you give me a hand setting out this gear, please?"

"Hi Kathy. I feel fine this morning – good to go," responded Josh, setting down his lunch bag and helping her place the snorkeling kits they had made up for scallop season.

He hesitated, thinking he should tell her what really happened yesterday and suddenly decided to not tell her, remembering that she wasn't thrilled with his cavern class anyway. Why poke at it?

They settled into the typical morning routine of a Florida dive shop in the height of the warm months. Josh did all of the chores – filling tanks, fixing regulators, answering phone calls and dealing one on one with customers. In mid-morning a young couple stopped by to look at buying their own dive gear. Josh remembered them from a scuba class they had taken through the shop in spring and was glad to see them back. Many people took the initial scuba class, did the checkout dives and never bothered to dive again. He was always glad to see those return who truly enjoyed the sport.

"So, Josh, what type of BC do you recommend? Weight integrated or go with a weight belt?" asked the male member of the couple. They were standing near the display of buoyancy compensators. Kathy sold a wide variety of BC models from different manufacturers so there were many variations to choose from.

Josh found himself wondering why anybody would even bother with an open water BC when it was clear to him that the back plate, wings and harness was superior but he mentally shook that off before replying.

"It depends on what you prefer. If you remember from class we had you guys use weight belts. Some people prefer to keep their weight system separate from the BC so if you have to get rid of one thing you still have the other. Others like the convenience of having the weights in the BC so it's one less thing to worry about," said Josh, pointing to the different types of BCs, "it's been my experience that it boils down to whether or not you like the extra weight to be in the BC on the surface."

Josh proceeded to demonstrate how the weight system worked differently between a weight integrated BC and a BC that required a weight belt. He even attached a tank to both types of BCs and had the prospective buyers try each one out with weights so he could get a feel for how different they behaved on land.

Kathy walked up to Josh later as he opened the door for the couple, their newly purchased BCs and regulators stowed in their new wheeled dive bag. He waved goodbye to them.

"Nice sales job, Josh. That's how you get repeat customers, by taking the time to listen to what they say they want and then demonstrating the alternatives. Everybody leaves happy," said Kathy, checking the register.

Josh beamed, "Thanks, I just went with my instincts on what I thought they needed."

"You notice I never tell you to sell a particular brand that might have a larger profit margin; I prefer to keep your selling honest. It comes through to our customers," she continued, sitting down behind the counter. Bear jumped into her lap and she absentmindedly scratched behind his ears.

"That's good; I don't want to try and juggle what will make you the most money with what the customer really needs. I'm just not that devious," commented Josh.

"You let me worry about what makes me the most money," Kathy said, and then she smiled.

"Go ahead and take your lunch break now; I'll cover the store."

"Thanks, Kathy," said Josh. He walked to the back of the shop, grabbed his sack lunch and filled a plastic cup with water and headed out to the back porch. Bear padded along silently, his step light and bouncy. He set down his meal on a wicker end table and pulled a wicker chair around to face the river and plopped down, grateful for the comfort of the plush outdoor cushions.

A slight breeze off the river combined with the ceiling fans moderated the mid-day summer heat to a bearable level. He reached into his bag and pulled out a sandwich, some chips and an apple. Bear sat at his feet and stared directly at Josh, waiting for tidbits. To his left Josh could see the *Hole* serving up a lunch crowd on the back porch, the sounds of mild conversation mingling with the smell of freshly fried foods.

Josh ate his meal slowly, savoring the peaceful visage of the river community. He occasionally broke off a small piece of his bologna sandwich and tossed it to Bear, who snapped it out of midair with minimal neck movement.

The back door to the shop swung open behind Josh, the familiar sound punctuating his meal downtime.

"Hey, Josh," said Kathy, a slight edge to her voice. Josh turned as Kathy came up to him, curious.

"Where did you get those doubles sitting in the bed of your truck?" asked Kathy, hands on hips, squared off, facing him. Josh quickly placed the remainder of his meal down on the wicker table. Bear disappeared into the shop through the dog door flap.

"Um, a friend loaned them to me," said Josh. His heart rate doubled.

"Were you really sick yesterday?" Kathy frowned.

"No, I wasn't; I am so sorry but I didn't have a choice…" started Josh, his hands spread.

"What? What do you mean by didn't have a choice? Choice doing what? Coming to work to get paid or blowing off your responsibilities?" Kathy stepped closer, clearly angry now.

Josh stood, uncomfortable with her towering over him.

"Well, you remember how badly my cavern class went last weekend," he started hesitantly.

She waited, a stern expression on her face, her arms still planted on her hips.

"This guy offered to tutor me but yesterday was the only time and he did help me and he loaned me his doubles and I offered to pay but he wouldn't accept any money which is good because I'm broke anyway," rushed Josh, the words all jumbling together.

"Josh, stop; you are mumbling and hard to follow," said Kathy, her voice still stern. She pulled up another wicker chair.

"Let's both sit down and talk about this. I want to understand what would make you do such a thing."

Josh sighed heavily and sat back down.

"OK, start over," ordered Kathy. She sat back in her chair, re-crossing her arms. Josh sat perched on the edge of his chair and started.

"Well, last weekend after the diving this guy in a wheelchair named Allen approached me after class –"

"Allen Walborsky?" asked Kathy, sharply.

"Um, I don't know his last name," said Josh. He went on to describe Allen, his vehicle, the conversation over the phone on Tuesday night and the day of training at Ginnie Springs on Wednesday. Kathy merely listened, arms firmly crossed, as Josh told her everything.

"So you decided to just lie to me about not working yesterday instead of just telling me the truth?" Kathy remarked quietly, after Josh had finished. Bear had returned from inside the shop and jumped into Kathy's lap. She uncrossed her arms and slowly petted her dog.

"I'm sorry; I know how much you hate me learning to cavern dive. I figured that you'd be even more upset if you knew I went off to meet with Allen," said Josh, hands down at his side, face downcast.

"Josh, like I said before I am not thrilled about his new fascination you have with the overhead environment but that I wouldn't support nor deter you from it," said Kathy, her voice softening slightly for a moment before hardening again. "I really don't appreciate you blowing off work like that and if you ever do it again I'll fire you," she said in a matter-of-fact tone. That scared Josh more than her anger.

"I understand completely, Kathy. It won't happen again. I swear. I was just so desperate," said Josh.

"Hmm...yes, well desperation can be dangerous," said Kathy. She sat back, relaxed slightly and appeared to have reached a decision.

"I'm going to tell you the story, Josh, about why I quit cave diving. It involves Allen and another cave diver named David Delaney," she started. Josh listened, attentive and curious. Bear looked up at his owner.

"David, Allen and I were inseparable; we did everything together. Sort of like you, Jon and Frank. We learned to dive together, took our cave diving lessons together from Sheck Exley, considered the best cave diver of all time, and dove many a cave as a team. In fact we got so good that we started exploring new cave systems, mapping them.

"There's nothing quite like being the first human being to swim into a new cave passage; being the first to view sights that have formed underground for thousands of years in total darkness. Nothing like it at all.

"We were all in love with each other as friends and with the intoxication of discovery and the thrill of being the first to 'lay line' in virgin cave. The bond that develops while cave diving is strong; you literally learn to rely on each other to save your life. We thought we were invincible.

"David had heard of some caves in northern Mexico that

promised to be deeper and longer than any other cave systems known at the time. This was in the late eighties and many of the caves in Florida had been found, if not totally mapped out. Mexico was the new frontier, the new underwater Wild West.

"Seems that each month we heard about some new amazing system being discovered in the back yard of a Mayan farmer. The Yucatan Peninsula is probably still full of undiscovered underwater caves.

"One day we met David at Fort White Cave Diving and he told us of a sinkhole in the Mexican state of Tamaulipas named El Verde Profundo that he had a lead on. We knew that Sheck and his team were diving similar deep holes in the same region and thought we had the guts, equipment and time to dive with the big boys. The rumor is that the sinkhole went down to 500 feet.

"So, young and impetuous that we were, we proceeded to train for deep cave diving. We even asked Sheck for help; he was a mathematician by trade and had access to Trimix dive tables, which were still secret and mysterious outside of the military and commercial diving realms.

"Competition for exploration in cave diving is generally a genial sport. Sheck and his team encouraged us to dive safely and explained their techniques for being able to dive that deep and return to tell about it. We lapped up every word of wisdom they had to offer.

"We figured out how to blend the correct gas mixes to get to 500 feet, calculated the decompression stops and practiced in the relatively shallow hundred foot caves in Florida. There are some plus two hundred footers in the middle of the state. Sheck even got us permission to dive those systems so we could get some actual Trimix decompression under our belts.

"We were heady with success in our training and thought we were destined for exploration greatness. I was personally hoping to break the women's world record for deep diving by completing a 500 foot dive.

"After months of training on the weekends, hitting up our friends and family for money and saving as much as we could, we were ready. We drove to Northern Mexico along the Gulf coast, taking two vehicles full of dive gear; most of it tanks and regulators that were either donated or borrowed.

"We each had six different mixes of gas in our back gas and in our stage tanks and were planning for three hours of decompression for a two minute stop at 500 feet. We actually did two simulation dives at Ginnie Springs using the same decompression profile to make sure that we could handle the time in the water physically and mentally.

"We made it to the state of Tamaulipas and set up camp in a small nearby town named Azufrosa. Luckily David was fluent in Spanish and he helped us find the right landowner that would give us permission to dive El Verde Profundo.

"We struck a deal for access to the sinkhole that didn't break our bank but that must have seemed like a lot of money to them. Seems like half the village came out to help lug our gear around and see what these crazy gringos Americanos were up to.

"The day came that we had picked to do the dive. David and I were to dive together and try to reach 500 feet. Allen's job was to dive with us down to 250 and help us with the extra tanks we needed to reach 500, sort of like a dive sherpa. He would wait at 250 feet for fifteen minutes then start his long decompression schedule. Even Allen's smaller dive was challenging.

"Things went as planned for the first 200 feet; these sort of dives aren't like a typical dive. You aren't enjoying the sights, there's no time for it in the schedule.

"Luckily the sinkhole was pretty much a straight shot down. If there had been a lot of twisty passages to negotiate we wouldn't have been able to go as deep as quickly. The visibility was poor on the surface; a green layer of algae reduced visibility to less than 10 feet. Below 50 feet, though, the water was clearer and colder.

"We left Allen at 250 feet as we had planned. He gave us a huge 'OK' with his dive light and we returned it, proceeding down. David and I faced each other as we descended, checking both ourselves and each other to make sure we were using the correct gas at the correct depth.

"We also took turns with the spools of line. We had to make sure that we always had a line to the surface since we couldn't rely on being able to see throughout the entire dive.

"At 326 feet David's regulator started to free flow. We stopped our descent and tried to shut down the reg, as we had trained. We knew we had less than a minute to fix the problem and continue or we would have to abort the record attempt.

"Unfortunately the tank valve froze open and we couldn't stop the bubbles. The sinkhole had doglegged above us and the stream of constant bubbles hitting the ceiling started a rain of limestone particles. Within just a few minutes we were in a grey-white cloud of suspended particles with no visibility. I figured the record attempt was over and we should just leave.

"Problem is I had to tell David. I had the reel in my hand and had locked it off and clipped it to one of my D-rings on my harness. I knew David would lose reference to the line if I didn't find him and place him on the line.

"I covered my light and looked around, trying to find David's light source. Even in bad visibility sometimes you can see a distance glow, even if the person is only a foot away. Simultaneously I felt a double tug on the line from above and saw a dim light below me. I knew the tug had to be Allen above us, wondering what was going on.

"I'm sure he saw the massive blast of bubbles float past him on the way up to the surface and he probably had a bird's eye view of the blow out in visibility where the line disappeared into the cloud we had created.

"I ignored Allen's signal and decided instead to go get David, below me. I unclipped the spool and started descending, reeling out line. I found David some seventy feet below me, not breathing and slowly drifting deeper. The water had cleared somewhat. I clipped the line to him and stopped his fall.

"I was pretty shook up by now but tried to get him to breathe again by trying to blast air in his mouth with the purge valve on his reg. The free flow had emptied the tank quickly at that depth. Not believing he was gone yet I grabbed one of my stage bottles that I knew to be safe to breathe at this depth and shoved that in his mouth instead.

"I even tried pushing on his chest but that's difficult to do underwater, being practically weightless. At that point I knew the mission to rescue David had turned into a recovery operation and I had to worry about getting myself out of there alive.

"About that time Allen arrived through the milky cloud that hovered above us. He swam up to David and assessed the situation. When he tried to resuscitate him as I had just tried, I stopped him and gave him the 'thumbs up'. Allen understood and together we started the long journey back to the surface. The mission had changed from breaking records and exploring virgin cave to a grim body recovery of our best friend.

"I still don't know how we made it all the way back sane. We just stuck to the decompression schedule that we had developed for the 500 foot profile. We took turns hauling David up, having to dump air out of his BC and dry suit at the appropriate moments so he didn't become too buoyant and shoot up like a helium balloon.

"Allen had to borrow the decompression tanks from David, which was horrible but necessary. The worse was watching his dead eyes and once, when the excess air in his lungs came out his mouth and nose, I thought I was going to lose it.

"The longer stops are nearer the surface and the hours of required decompression seemed like days. Allen and I exchanged notes on our dive slates, trying to understand what had happened and trying not to think too much about the loss of our friend. Finally we surfaced and after inflating our wings and making sure David wasn't going to sink back we took off our masks and cried like babies.

"Eventually we swam David to shore. I got out of my dive gear and collapsed on the small beach, too mentally and physically exhausted to continue. Allen, with the aid of locals, helped get David out of his dive gear and lugged all of the tanks from the water onto land. The worst part was when the local authorities and press arrived. They treated the event like a side show circus. Photos of David's dead body even showed up in the front page of the next day's paper. It was horrifying.

"To top it off within a few hours of surfacing Allen showed signs and symptoms of decompression sickness. The most we could do is to just get him on pure oxygen from our own supplies; the nearest chamber was across the U.S. border in Brownsville, a six hour drive.

"Allen's legs became slowly paralyzed as we started the long trek back home. We spent a week at the hospital in Brownsville. Allen did a number of chamber rides which helped but when he was released he was in a wheelchair. I drove him back to Florida and dropped him off at his trailer in the woods. We never really talked about what happened, even with all that time in Texas and the trip back home. I guess neither one of us were ready to deal with the tragedy of David's loss and the death of our team.

"Somehow we managed to get David's body released to come back to the United States with the help of the U.S. Consulate. Soon after David's funeral, which was attended by most of the cave diving community, Allen and I went our separate ways. I sold all my gear and never went into a cave again. I used the money to buy this house and start *Wakulla Skuba*."

Kathy paused, tears clearly visible in her eyes. Josh handed her a clean napkin, she accepted it and dabbed her eyes. Bear's ears were pinned down. He licked Kathy's arm.

Kathy took a deep purging breath, ruffled Bear's ears, straightened her back and regained her composure.

"So, you see, Josh, why I don't want you cave diving, even cavern diving?"

Josh sat, still stunned from the story, his head reeling. It was a lot of information to absorb in a short time. Kathy, a world-record cave diver?

Dealing with the accidental death of a dear buddy in a foreign country? He wasn't ready to answer her question, though. Instead he had one of his own.

"So why did David die? Didn't he have other scuba tanks to breathe from when he descended below you?" he asked.

Kathy's face flickered in a painful grimace for a split second and she answered, looking out at the river flowing peacefully by.

"We recovered all of the tanks that were used that day by clipping them off to the line as we ascended and we pulled them up later, after David's body had been taken away by the authorities. When we got back to the States we analyzed the tanks and found that one of them, the one I think I handed off to David, had the wrong mix in them.

"Each tank was clearly marked with the percentage of oxygen, nitrogen and helium and the maximum depth that it could be safely breathed. One, though, was labeled for 400 feet and we found out that the percentage of oxygen was too high for that depth. The tank had been mixed and tested by David; he must have just made a mistake. If only myself or Allen had double-checked that tank he would still be alive..."

Her voice trailed away softly. Bear looked up at her and whined. For a few moments the only sound was the occasional tinkle of glassware and gentle sounds of laughter from the restaurant next door floating through the soft summer breeze that rippled the surface of the clear green river.

Kathy visibly pulled herself together and looked up at Josh, her tears already drying.

"Listen, Josh, I care about you as a colleague and a friend. David wasn't the only friend of mine to die in a cave. There's a sinkhole near El Verde Profundo named El Zacaton that also has a mixed past. Ann Kristovich dove to over 500 feet there in 1993, setting the women's deep dive record years after my attempt.

"The men's record was broken by Jim Bowden; he almost made it to 1,000 feet. Unfortunately on that same day Sheck Exley died at around 900 feet also trying to break the record. Cave diving lost its foremost pioneer that day. I don't want you to die needlessly either."

Josh frowned and said carefully, "Sounds like they didn't die needlessly. Sounds like they died doing what they loved doing on the cutting edge of exploration. They died as heroes."

Kathy gave him a rueful smile, "You're not the first one to make that observation."

He continued, "Besides, I don't know if I have what it takes to be a super cave diver; all I know is that I am finding this level of dive training extremely challenging and rewarding, more than any other scuba training I've had. I'm not content to just stay an open water diver."

Kathy broadened her smile and looked at Josh directly, a maternal look in her eye.

"Well, I do understand and remember that passion. Just Be Careful. Remember this story. Learn everything you can from your teachers about how to be safe. Don't take unnecessary risks."

Josh nodded, relieved that at least for now Kathy seemed to accept his desire to continue with his training. Kathy sat back in her chair, a look of relief on her face. Josh figured the catharsis of telling her story was long overdue.

"So, tell me more about Allen. How did he look? How is he able to dive? Last time I saw him he was paralyzed from the waist down," said Kathy curiously.

Josh proceeded to tell her about how Allen was able to half walk, half crawl from his wheelchair to the water and how his scuba system used tanks mounted on his side. She seemed especially curious about this unique adaptation and Josh spent more time explaining how the rig was assembled and worked.

"You know, Kathy, Allen has a bit of a split personality. There's his land persona, which is tired, sarcastic and pretty much a burn out. Then there's his water side. He is truly happier in the water and even sounds way more intelligent, patient and understanding when he's debriefing me on the surface. It's like night and day."

"Yes, the Allen I remember, before David's death, was like your water Allen – he was the smart one of the team; the one who did the major thinking for the dives. We couldn't have done what we did without him," said Kathy, the reminiscing look back on her face.

She shook it off and placed Bear on the patio.

"Well, enough heavy talk. Let's get back to work. After yesterday you owe me some extra time and hard work."

Josh knew she meant it but also could sense that she felt somewhat unburdened by retelling her amazing story of tragedy in Mexico. He felt honored that she shared her story with him, even if it was to prove a point.

Chapter 25

Later that night he heard the door open as he toweled himself dry in his apartment's small bathroom. He had worked extra hours and extra hard to make up for missing a day of work. He had also taken the time to pull apart the doubles, clean the inside of the tanks, perform a hydrostatic test and completed the ritual with a visual inspection.

Finally he had put the doubles back together under Kathy's tutelage with the tank bands and filled them with air to 3,000 PSI. Satisfied that they were now "legal" and clean he had stowed them back in his truck for the coming weekend's cavern class. He had finished the day in the equipment room; taking apart, cleaning and reassembling the regulators that Allen had loaned him.

He had left work under the cover of darkness, his truck passing *The Hole* with a parking lot full of patrons.

Elise poked her head into his bathroom and wolf whistled, waving a bag of Chinese takeout food in front of her. Josh grinned and wrapped the towel around his waist, following her into the apartment's common room. They sat down at the small table.

"Hey, Elise, great to see you. Thanks for picking up dinner," he said as he reached out to help unload the white bags.

"I missed you, Josh; haven't seen you in days," said Elise, her green eyes large, black hair held back in a bun. Josh watched her gather her food, her dainty features attractive even late at night after a busy work day. She wore white jean shorts with a simple plum-colored t-shirt.

"I missed you too, Elise," he said, scarfing down an egg roll. Lunch time was way in the past. For a few moments they simply ate, occasionally looking at each other. The conversation started light, mostly about the details of just another day at their respective jobs. Finally Josh sat back in his chair, his meal complete and stretched his legs under the table, his bare feet brushing against her sandaled ones. She returned the stroke with her other foot, a light smile on her face.

"I'm sorry about Tuesday night, Josh. I'm just really having trouble wrapping my head around your desire to go underground and underwater. It just seems like it's too risky. If something goes wrong you might get stuck down there and..." her voice trailed off.

Josh stood and walked behind her, kneading her shoulders with his hands. He could feel her muscles begin to relax.

"I know it sounds super dangerous, Elise, but the training is really rigorous. They think of every possible danger and try to figure out a way to make it safer. In fact that's what really fascinates me about this class. It's really taking my diving to a whole new level; much more demanding and difficult to master," said Josh, moving to her neck muscles.

She sighed and shifted her head from left to right, exposing the muscles to his kneading fingers.

"I thought you were really discouraged from the weekend's class, though. Now you sound like you've almost passed the class already. Why the sudden change? I don't get it."

Josh stopped the massage, realizing that he better come clean with yesterday's impromptu class as he had with Kathy. Besides he was happy with the results and there was no reason to hide it from her. He wanted to share his successes too.

"I took off work yesterday and drove to Ginnie Springs where another instructor taught me how to swim properly. He even loaned me some real cave gear," said Josh enthusiastically. He resumed her neck massage. Elise reached up and touched his hand, stopping the movement and looked up at him. He could see the beginnings of a storm brewing in her emerald green eyes.

"You did what?"

"It's no biggie; some guy on Sunday must have heard me mention Kathy's name and he handed me his phone number to get some help. Turns out he's an old friend of Kathy's."

Josh decided not to retell Kathy's tragic story of David's death. Elise did not need to feed her worst fears about cavern diving.

Elise turned in the chair, facing him, her face screwed up. "Why didn't you tell me about this before?"

"Well, I was too upset with myself to even mention it. I didn't decide to call him until late Tuesday night. I really thought it was going to be a dead end. But Allen, that's his name, really helped me out a lot."

"How much did he charge you?"

"Nothing – and he's letting me borrow his cave gear for the cavern class."

"That sounds kind of fishy; what's his motive?"

Josh thought for a moment.

"I think because he's a friend of Kathy's and probably has some sense of ancient obligation. I didn't sense that he's trying to trick me. He genuinely seemed interested in helping me learn how to dive his gear. It was amazing, Elise. I really had low expectations on what he could do for me. He noticed what I was doing wrong and corrected it. It turned out not to just be my technique but the gear I was using as well. The cave gear he loaned me turns out to be SO much easier to dive."

Josh recalled the feeling of accomplishment as Allen transformed him from a diving embarrassment to a competent cavern diver. He looked at the far wall, reliving the feeling of floating effortless at the bottom of the Ginnie Ballroom, in perfect harmony with the watery environment. Elise's voice cut through his reverie with her sharp tone.

"Josh, I don't want you doing this anymore. It's too dangerous and you keep hiding things about it from me."

Elise stood and turned to Josh, her arms crossed under her breasts and her brow furrowed. Josh tightened his towel around his waist, feeling slightly vulnerable at her hostility.

"Look, Elise, I'm sorry if I haven't been forthcoming with the way this is happening. I'm just trying to protect you..."

"From what?" her voice raised slightly.

"From your fear of me dying, frankly. You seem so worked up, irrational and emotional about this training. It's NOT that dangerous."

Josh could feel the conversation taking a downward slide but he couldn't help himself. She just didn't hear the siren song of the cavern; feel the lure of the underwater labyrinth and the challenge presented by the mastery of the diving required to safely travel there.

"Not dangerous? Are you crazy? It's bad enough that you dive at all, but to knowingly increase your risk by going underground is just asking for trouble."

"I don't think you understand; if only you could see how awesome it is inside a cavern," retorted Josh.

"I don't care how beautiful it is - no cavern or cave is worth dying to see. Period." Her voice trilled off and tears glistened in the corners of her eyes, threatening to flow.

Josh grimaced. He reached out his hand to calm her down. She shook her head and stepped back, sitting once more in her chair, her head bowed. Josh sighed and sat down, pulling his chair closer to her.

"Elise, look at me." Her green eyes looked up at him, swimming in tears that now softly flowed down the smooth skin of her cheeks. "What is it? Why do you really hate the idea of me doing this?" He kept his tone low and gentle and handed her a clean paper napkin from the remains of their meal.

Elise accepted the napkin, sniffed delicately and wiped her eyes. She inhaled deeply and exhaled slowly, still looking at Josh. Her expression was a mixture of anger and sadness.

"My little brother drowned in a pool when I was a little kid," she said quietly.

Josh reached out to her and this time she accepted his hands. They felt damp and warm in his.

"Oh, Elise, I didn't know; I'm so sorry," he offered. His mind filled with a number of reasons why comparing an accidental pool drowning to scuba wasn't a fair comparison but this would definitely not be the time to defend his decision to dive. Better to see if she wanted to talk about it more. After a short pause she began to tell the story.

"Chris was only eighteen months old. I was five. We had a below ground pool in the backyard and we were all enjoying the warm weather one day; Chris, myself and my parents. Chris was in a baby walker, scooting around the pool deck like a little demon. He was so cute and energetic. My parents doted over him and I loved being his big sister. He loved the attention and I loved taking care of him, as best as I could at that age.

"It was just one of those things; the phone rang, my Dad went inside to get it while my Mom and I stayed on the pool deck, keeping an eye on Chris. Chris could zip around on the concrete deck and my parents had strategically placed a number of beach chairs across the deck so Chris couldn't propel himself into the pool.

"My Dad called for my Mom to come talk on the phone. I never did find out what the big deal was about but it was important enough I suppose. My Mom looked at me and said 'Keep an eye on Chris – I'll be right back.' I'll never forget those words. Anyway, she walked into the house and when I turned around Chris was bumping his walker against the beach chairs in a rhythmic way only a baby can constantly do over and over again. He was strong for such a little guy and I blame myself for what happened next. His cute chubby legs were powerful. He kept pushing and pushing on the end of the chair; it was plastic with cloth-covered foam cushions and it must have been fairly lightweight. He managed to nudge the chair aside enough to create an opening towards the deep end of the pool. I just stood there; just STOOD THERE and watched, waiting for my parents to return, totally paralyzed.

"He giggled loudly and took a final big push towards the water. I'm sure the pretty blue color of the pool must have attracted him. He loved being carried into the pool by my parents and splashing around. He rolled into the deep end, still inside his walker. I remember he just slipped underneath the water, quietly and with a very small splash. I ran up to the edge of the pool and started to scream. I could see Chris through the wavy water, on the bottom, his little arms thrashing around. I started screaming and couldn't stop. My parents ran out of the house. I remember my Dad dropped the phone and it fell on the deck, shattering into a million pieces. The battery slid across the deck, spinning, and plopped into the pool at the exact spot where Chris had fallen in. They looked at me and I pointed to the pool and yelled 'Chris!'

"Both of my parents jumped in at the same time and within a few seconds they thrust Chris, still in his walker, on the deck, one on each side. I guess it was the fastest way to get him out of the water. He wasn't breathing. They hopped up out of the water and my Mom pulled him out of the walker. He was all floppy, dripping wet and pale. I'll never forget that scene as they laid him down on a towel, his eyes open and water drooling out of his mouth. My Mom looked at me and screamed 'What did you do, Elise?' while my Dad tried what I later figured out must have been CPR. I ran into the house and into my room and stayed there until much later, after the ambulance arrived and left. My Dad finally entered my room, hours later.

"His clothes were still damp from the pool and his wild eyes matched his wild hair. He hugged me, tears on his face, and told me everything would be OK. I hugged him back and bawled that it was my fault and would he ever forgive me. He just hugged me tighter and cried along with me.

"Eventually my Mom forgave me, at least I think so. They tried their best to get past it and we even visited a family therapist. That was kinda creepy, especially at that age. My parents never had another child and they dutifully saw me through all of life's events – grade school graduations, high school and college and they even had tears of joy in their eyes at my nurse pinning ceremony. I think part of the reason I became a healer was to be sure I knew what to do should anybody ever get hurt again. I suppose it's my tribute to my brother."

Elise stopped, her tears continued but at a slower pace. Josh knew this was much older and deeper pain that she was expressing now. He simply held her hand, allowing her to relive and emote. She blew her nose, wiped her eyes and looked Josh straight in the eyes. Her green eyes flashed with extra intensity and beauty; it almost took Josh's breath away.

"So, Josh, that's my big dark secret. That's why I don't want you anywhere near water, especially in a cavern. I know it's irrational in some ways; you aren't an eighteen month old baby who can't swim being cared for by an inept sister."

Josh squeezed her hand and gave her a brave smile, "You know you can't be held responsible. I'm sure that came out in the therapy."

She smiled briefly, a dark smile, tears still brimming at the bottom of her eyes, "Yes we all worked terribly hard on making sure nobody felt guilt or remorse. It's just I was so young and I think my parents felt they had to take the burden of their own guilt and pile mine on top. They do love me but I still have that nagging feeling of blame; it's as if the ghost of Chris is always hovering around at family get-togethers, reminding all of us that he left too early and that it could have been prevented. The worse is my Mother; she does all the typical Mom things but I always feel as if sometimes she's hiding her resentment and trying extra hard to be loving and caring."

Josh released her hands and sat back. He chose his next words carefully, using a slow tone.

"Elise, I am so, so sorry about Chris. I'm sure you miss him every day and still love him dearly. It sounds like his death was a tragic accident."

She looked up at him, a miserable mixture of pain and remorse still visible on her face.

"But you said it yourself a few minutes ago – your fear of my diving IS irrational. I am not your little brother that you have to protect. I am confident of my skills and know my limits, whether it be driving a car, working in a dive shop or diving in a cavern," her cheeks began to turn red so Josh finished his point quickly, "I will continue my training."

Her face flush deeply and her expression turned to anger.

"Well, you can die in a cavern if you want but it won't be my fault!"

Elise jumped up from the table and started to walk to the door. Josh leapt towards her, grabbing her arm. She stopped and turned, her green eyes now blazing a different color; the color of the deeper green sea water during a descent to the endless bottom.

"Let go of me Josh," her voice steely and even, cheeks full flush now.

Josh begged, "Please, Elise, I didn't mean to upset you. I don't want you to leave; we can talk this out more."

"I'm done talking; I'm done crying and worrying about you." She wrenched her arm out of his grasp, walked briskly to his apartment door, opened it and slammed it behind her. Josh stood there, stunned. His towel slipped to the floor, unnoticed.

Chapter 26

Josh left work late Friday afternoon and headed northbound towards Tallahassee on US 319. He was heading to Frank and Jon's apartment to pick them up for the weekend's class. Strains of the latest Spice Girls tune drifted from his radio as he drove north. Most of the traffic was streaming away from the city heading towards small towns like Woodville and Crawfordville, where one could enjoy a lot of land cheaply. A late afternoon July thunderstorm cell boomed to his left, heading for the airport. To the east the sky was mostly clear.

Typical summer weather pattern, he mused.

Josh hadn't talked to Jon or Frank since last weekend and was excited to relay his story of training with Allen and his new diving equipment. Anything to not think about Elise and his failed attempts to contact her since she stormed out of his apartment. She never answered nor returned his calls.

Twenty minutes later he pulled into the parking lot in front of the apartment building off of Apalachee Parkway, a major artery clogged with yuppie apartment complexes, retail stores and restaurants. He parked his truck and beeped the horn.

Frank and Jon bounded out of their apartment on the first floor, lugging bags full of dive gear. Josh hopped out of the cab and walked over to help. Jon and Frank, although an unlikely personality match, found that they made great roommates.

"Hi guys, ready to roll?" asked Josh, grabbing a bag from Frank.

"You bet," said Frank, striding to the back of the truck. He looked inside and exclaimed "Where did you get these doubles?"

Jon placed his bag on the truck bed, looked down at the tanks and looked up inquiringly at Josh.

"Yeah, pretty cool, huh? I've got a great story to tell you about how I got those tanks and the rest of the gear to dive them. Short answer is that I shouldn't have any more problems with technique in the cavern," Josh answered confidently, "I'll tell you the rest on the way."

"OK, that's gotta be some story; you really sucked last weekend," Frank reminded Josh. Jon just smiled and walked back to grab more gear.

Soon they had their equipment secured; the tanks pinned down by bags and bungee cords to prevent them from sliding around. All three piled into the cab as usual and Josh backed the truck out of the parking lot. The cabin filled with small talk as the three friends caught each other up on their lives during the past week. The setting sun behind them lit up the buildings and pine tree-lined highway before them.

Finally, between Tallahassee and Perry on US 27, Jon asked "So, Josh, tell us the story of how you got those doubles?"

Josh smiled, his right hand balanced on the top of the truck's steering wheel. He sustained a steady sixty four miles per hour for fear of getting stopped again.

"Remember that guy in the wheelchair at FWCD?" he started. Jon and Frank grunted assents.

"Well, his name is Allen and it turns out he used to be a cave explorer with Kathy," he announced.

"What? Our Kathy?" asked Frank incredulously.

"Yep, she, Allen and another guy named David used to be big-time cave divers. She even attempted a world record dive to 500 feet with Allen and David. Unfortunately David died in a cave during the record attempt. Allen got badly bent and ended up paralyzed. Kathy sold her equipment and got out of cave diving." Josh felt odd summarizing Kathy's tragic story in just a few sentences but felt that he didn't need to reveal all of the pain of her story.

"You're kidding! That's amazing," said Jon.

"Nope, all true. Ask Kathy yourself. Be careful, though, I think it's a pretty sensitive topic, even all these years later," cautioned Josh, "So anyway, Allen is the guy in the wheelchair that hangs out on the porch at FWCD. Last Sunday while you guys were walking back to the truck he hands me this piece of paper with his phone number on it and tells me he can help me with my diving technique."

"That sounds fishy as hell," said Frank.

"Yeah, it was odd and I didn't find out about Allen's relationship with Kathy until later in the week. I stewed about it until Tuesday night when I gave him a call after work, late. My technique was so bad last weekend I was ready to try anything at that point. He grudgingly agreed to help me but only if I showed up the next day," continued Josh.

"What did you do, call in work sick or something lame like that?" asked Frank.

Josh looked briefly over to Frank, a grim smile on his face, and returned his eyes back on the road. The setting sun cast longer shadows among the trees lining the road, the green needles of the pine trees illuminated by the golden glow.

"Yeah, I know, pretty lame but I really wanted to check it out so I called in sick and drove to Ginnie. I met Allen in the parking lot where we did our class with Drew. Turns out he DOES still dive, using tanks mounted on his side. It's pretty crazy watching him lug his gear down to the water and wrestle with his wheelchair and the tanks but he somehow makes it work.

"Once he's in the water you'd never know he has very limited ability to use his legs. He's still a natural and has great technique."

"So what about the gear? Why do you have it?" pushed Frank.

"Well, he started off doing the same sort of evaluation of my technique that Drew did. He figured out what was wrong a lot faster though and instead of just being critical of me he told me to try out his old set of doubles. See, he can't dive them anymore anyway because of his legs so he lent them to me, along with the regs and even a canister light. At the time, before Kathy told me his connection to her, I didn't know what to think. I think now, though, that he must have overhead us talking about Kathy at FWCD and this is his odd way of reaching out to her. At least that's my theory. Don't you guys dare bring it up to him or Kathy! I don't want it to screw up my free gear rental."

Frank and Jon chuckled lightly. Josh knew they would respect his request for silence.

"So, anyway, it did turn out that for whatever reason it was a LOT easier for me to do the modified frog kick with doubles, back plate and wings. I had such a blast the rest of the day, swimming around in the basin and getting used to the new gear. We even did an AWESOME cavern dive into the Ginnie Ballroom. It's wonderful and beautiful and I can't wait for you guys to check it out during our class this weekend."

"Wow, Josh, you really did score big time," said Jon.

"Yeah, but things have a way of evening out. You know, one door closes and another opens sort of thing? Well, last night Elise closed a door, actually closed my door, hard. She walked out on me last night; she's very angry that I blew off work and am still continuing with the cavern class. She won't return my calls either," informed Josh.

"That's too bad, Josh. But if she really doesn't get it then maybe this is for the best," said Jon.

"I suppose...sure miss her though," said Josh.

Chapter 27

Josh flipped the burgers on the tiny grill with a cheap plastic-handled metal spatula, beer in hand. The pre-formed patties sizzled as the heat from the glowing charcoal briquettes ignited the dripping juice from the meat, flaring up flames. Josh dribbled a touch of beer into the palm of his left hand and flicked the liquid into the flames, reducing them.

Jon and Frank sat nearby on the picnic table, laying out the store-bought meal components – paper plates, paper napkins, plastic sporks, bottles of beer, cold potato salad in a sealed deli container, bags of chips, hamburger buns and small plastic bags of condiments accumulated from many fast food trips. Jon even provided a couple of bug candles on the table; the lemony smell of citronella competed with the scent of the sizzling burger patties.

They had arrived at the Santa Fe River Enclave shortly before sunset, checking back into room # 15, claiming the same beds and starting the slow process of cooling the room via the underpowered window unit.

The parking lot was half full with vehicles that bore signs of belonging to cave divers, evidenced by the bumper stickers and dive gear piled in the back of pickup trucks and visible through the windows of SUVs.

The river glistened darkly as the dimness of the early summer evening met the sparkle of lights along the edges of the roofs of the motel cinderblock buildings. The dock glowed green and blue from the spotlights mounted at the base of the dock and the permanent grill on the other side of the dock was populated with another group of guests also enjoying outside cooking, the ruddy glow from their charcoal lighting up their faces, too dim to recognize. Laughter echoed across the river from the group; clearly their party was in full swing.

Josh noticed one of the individuals in the group separate and walk towards their table, a female silhouetted by the lights from the buildings. She looked back and waved at her companions, many who returned the wave and turned back towards Josh and his group. Her face became visible as she approached them and Josh recognized Asrid.

"Hi, Asrid," said Frank, who had also noticed the faux interloper.

"Hi guys, great to see you," said Asrid, smiling. She wore a low cut halter neck cotton camisole, bubblegum pink, with white denim shorts and flip flops.

Her short blonde hair reflected the whites, yellows, oranges, blues and greens from the various light sources and her blue eyes sparkled with orange and yellow hues from the coals in their grill and the light from the citronella candles burning on the table. She held a bottle of beer in her right hand.

"I didn't know you were staying here," said Josh, poking gently at the patties. He was surprised at how feminine she appeared in this setting; his recollection from last weekend was of a more severe and serious student of the underwater arts.

"Oh, yes, Roland recommended it," she commented, sitting down at the picnic table nearest Josh. Jon slid the bags of chips and buns away from her spot, a feeble attempt to welcome her.

"Yeah, we stayed here last weekend based on Roland's recommendation and decided that the price and atmosphere was worth a repeat," said Frank, who slid down to sit directly across from her.

"So, how did you spend last week?" inquired Jon, sitting to her right.

"I did the Orlando thing for the first part of the week. You know, playing tourist in the expensive theme parks," said Asrid, her elbows resting comfortably on the table. She took a sip from her beer. Josh noticed the flickering light from the candles played gently across the curve of her breasts.

"The parks are fun; really amazing how they engineer those places to handle that many people and spend that amount of money creating illusions. I love the rides, the food and just the overall ambiance they create," she continued.

"Yeah, I do enjoy going to Orlando once in a while," said Frank.

Jon nodded in agreement and added "EPCOT's my favorite place. I love 'eating and drinking around the world'."

"Yes, EPCOT is pretty fun but I am a sucker for the classic Disney characters at Disney World," Asrid offered. She tilted her head back to drink the last of her beer. Josh felt inadequate discussing Orlando theme parks; he hadn't been since his parents took him as a kid. Funny how growing up in Florida how little of the state he had seen as a tourist. At least this cavern class was exposing him to the little-known springs and beauty of natural parts of the state.

"Want another?" said Josh, "The burgers are ready too; want to eat with us?"

She put down her bottle and said "Yes to the beer but no to the food. I just ate with those guys." She motioned behind her. Jon reached under the table, opened the lid to the cooler and pulled out a bottle of beer. He twisted off the top and handed Asrid the bottle.

She nodded in thanks, tipping the bottle towards him. Jon smiled hugely.

Frank handed Josh a paper plate. Josh slid the burgers one by one onto the plate, holding it gingerly underneath to make sure it didn't collapse as the flimsy paper plate bent to the weight of the burgers.

The heat from the patties seeped through quickly; Josh plopped the plate in the middle of the table, shaking his hand to cool it off.

"There ya go, guys. Dig in."

Josh took the seat next to Frank, catty-corner from Asrid. He tried not to look at her cleavage as he built his plate of food using the ingredients in front of him – burger on bun, squeezing condiments from their plastic containers, spooning potato salad with his spork and pouring chips from a bag onto his plate. Soon all three of them were busy chowing down their meager yet tasty meal.

"So what did you do the rest of the week?" asked Josh, blotting his face with his paper napkin and purposely looking at her eyes instead of her chest.

Asrid smiled and said, "Diving, mostly. Those guys are all cave divers that I met at Ginnie. They offered to do some dives with me. Don't worry; I didn't dive beyond my training," she smiled mischievously, "it was all fresh water open water stuff. Just trying to keep my technique up for the cavern class. They are a group from Ohio that has been cave diving together for years. They are here for a few weeks of vacation, just doing diving.

"They usually spend the first few days down here knocking off the rust by diving in open water with their full cave gear, to get used to the environment and their equipment. I was lucky enough to be able to tag along with them and practice my tech diving skills while they brushed up on their cave diving skills."

"Sure hope that doesn't screw up your cavern training," offered Josh. She frowned at him.

"Um, I mean, you know, if the cave skills they are practicing don't match what your tech diving skills are you may be learning something differently than Drew would teach us," he backpedaled.

She shrugged, sipping her beer.

"I'm not too worried about it. There's a lot of similarities between techniques. They explained how they thought many of the tech diving skills actually evolved from the first set of cave divers and what the environment demanded they do to survive, like swimming horizontally and modifying your kick to not stir up the bottom," she said.

"Besides, the best part about hanging with those guys is hearing stories about their cave dives. They've dove many of the caves in Florida and in the Mexico caves between Cancun and Tulum. Just amazing stuff; such beautiful descriptions. You can tell that cave diving for them is a passion that they all share and revisit each year as a group. I can't wait to get full cave certified."

Josh felt the familiar tug of the underwater; she reminded him of the incredible experience he had with Allen in the Ginnie Ballroom.

"Yeah, I'd like to get full cave certified too one day," he blurted out. Frank and Jon looked over at him, curious.

"Really, Josh? We haven't even finished the cavern class and you want to go all the way to full cave?" said Jon.

Frank added, "Yeah, and even though you got lucky and pulled out a miracle fix after doing so bad last weekend it doesn't mean you are ready. Heck, I'm not even sure I'm ready for that sort of diving and I'm a natural at this stuff."

Josh blushed slightly, hoping the dim shifting light hid his reaction.

"You weren't there, Frank. You don't know what you're talking about. My session with Allen was transformative. I think I get it now; like Drew said cavern diving is mostly mental. It sure helps, though, to have the right gear help you get to the right mental state. If your gear isn't right for the environment you'll be fighting it," he lectured.

"Aw, come on, Josh. Just because you lucked out and got some old crippled guy to dump his ancient doubles on you because he can't use them anyway doesn't automatically make you a cave diver," said Frank.

"Doubles?" said Asrid, her eyebrows arched.

Josh glared at Frank and looked at Asrid to explain.

"Yeah, well, I felt so bad about my technique from last weekend that I accepted an offer from Allen, the guy in the wheelchair who hangs out at FWCD. He offered to help me and we spent a day this week at Ginnie. He loaned me his doubles and he taught me how to dive them. I understand now why you and Drew dive doubles – it's awesome."

"That guy, Allen, he can still dive?" asked Asrid.

"Yes, he dives side mount, you know, with the tanks strapped on the sides of his body instead of his back. He has just enough leg strength left to swim in that configuration. I was pretty amazed too to see him in the water."

"Yeah, well, Josh, we'll see tomorrow if you are as good as you think you are," said Frank, a smirk on his face.

"OK, Frank, I got your point. Maybe I'm not ready for cave but I feel a whole lot better about cavern," said Josh hotly.

"OK, you two, shields down and phasers on stun. We're still a team in this class and this isn't a competition," said Jon. Josh stared at Frank a bit longer, glanced at Asrid and nodded towards Jon.

"Yeah, you're right Jon, we don't need to be bickering," he said. Frank just nodded in response.

"Well, I sure hope you guys are in a better mood tomorrow. Thanks for the beer; it's been a long day for me and I'm going to bed. Good night," said Asrid. She stood up, grabbed her two empty bottles and walked across the sandy parking lot towards the motel building where her white sedan rental car sat.

"Nice, guys," said Jon, who started to pick up the remnants of their meal.

Chapter 28

Josh woke, momentarily unsure where he was. The competing compressor motors of the laboring refrigerator and the vibrating window mounted AC unit reminded him that he was in unit # 15 of the Enclave.

In the bed next to him Jon lay curled up under a fake felt blanket and cotton white bed linens, worn but clean. Frank snored gently in the next bed, nearest the bathroom door, similarly wrapped up. He picked up his wristwatch that he had placed on the nightstand next to the bed and saw 2:14 AM glow dimly from the display. He sighed, got out of bed and walked over to the bay window, pulling back the cheap curtain. The parking lot was dark, the decorative lights along the roof having been extinguished hours earlier.

He could see the green and blue spotlights illuminating the dock at the river's edge. He felt restless and anxious, partially from troubles with Elise and irritation with Frank. Normally he would let Frank's acerbic comments go but the combination of recent events had him on edge. Frank was a friend but a pain in the ass at the same time. It was like trying to argue with a rain storm, though. It was just his nature.

He looked back at his friends, still sleeping, and walked to the door. He slowly unlocked the deadbolt, cracked the door and slid through, slowly closing it behind him. The warm moist summer air enveloped him, along with the late night cadence of cicadas, crickets and frogs. Overhead an occasional low cloud drifted by, blocking the view of twinkling stars.

Josh walked slowly to the river bank and continued out on the dock marked by the blue and green spotlights, the warped wooden planks rough on his bare feet. The planks creaked slightly as he made his way to the end of the dock and sat, feet dangling in the river water.

The dark water swirled around his legs, cool and mysterious. The magic of the late hour slowly started to work on him as his breathing slowed and his anxiety eased. Nothing better than a commune with nature to calm the soul. It almost felt like the Wakulla River at night, the clear water also dark and mysterious and the clarity only visible during the day. He sat quietly, his palms pressing into the edge of the dock, legs slowly moving back and forth as he tried to empty his mind and stop thinking so much. Next to him a frog croaked loudly.

Minutes passed, only detectable by the slight movement in the star patterns, the silent drift of the clouds and the rippling sound of the moving river. Josh felt and heard the creak of a plank on the dock and turned. He saw a slight human shape approach him, lit eerily by the dim blue-green glow of the spotlights, walking slowly in the low light. The nearby frog stopped croaking, on predator alert.

"Asrid?" said Josh.

"Is that you, Josh?" said Asrid, reaching the end of the dock.

"Yes. I couldn't sleep so I decided to come out here to relax and think," said Josh. He touched his t-shirt and hoped that wearing only a pair of boxers wouldn't be too forward.

"Oh, sorry to disturb you then. I couldn't sleep either. I'll leave you alone." She turned to leave.

Josh wiggled to his left, slowly as to not catch hidden splinters and motioned to her.

"No, I don't mind the company if you don't. Have a seat," he said, patting the dock.

She sat down next to him, not too close, and placed her legs into the water as well, a light gurgling sound accompanying the movement. He glanced over and saw she also wore a t-shirt, no bra and a pair of boxers.

"Ooh, that's a bit chilly," she exclaimed.

"Funny coming from a girl from Sweden," commented Josh.

She smiled, her teeth dimly glowing from star light and spotlights. She placed her hands on the wooden planks and swirled her legs, mimicking Josh's posture.

"So, what brings you out so late?" asked Josh, looking back at the river flowing past.

"Oh, nothing really. Our summer nights are much shorter than here since we are closer to the North Pole so I'm used to longer days this time of the year. We have true seasons and I like to enjoy the summer temperatures as long as I can. I'm fascinated by the longer summer nights at this latitude," she said softly, "What about you? What brings you out on such a beautiful night?"

Josh paused a second to think about how much of his troubles he wanted to unburden. The frog, having decided luring a mate was more important than the danger of being eaten, starting croaking loudly again.

"Well, I guess I am a bit angry at Frank," he admitted.

"Is he always that, well, annoying?" she asked.

He reached down, stroked the river and removed his hand, water dripping, the droplets picking up the blend of blue and green from the spotlights behind him.

"He's always saying the wrong thing. I've known him since college and he's always been the one to speak his mind directly. Usually, though, there's a kernel of truth in his sarcasm that I listen to.

It's probably the main reason that we are still such good friends. Plus he really is good at everything he does and I sometimes hope that rubs off on me," he admitted shyly.

"So what's the kernel of truth this time?" she asked, legs moving back and forth slowly in the river.

Josh opened his mouth to respond when she uttered a yelp and pulled her legs out of the water, backing away from the edge of the dock. Josh looked down into the water and saw a brief glimpse of a number of torpedo-shaped silver fish zoom past.

He smiled and looked over at her. Her arms were crossed over her knees, wet legs shining in the light, her face staring at the end of the dock in surprise and shock.

"That was just mullet running. Did they hit your legs?" he asked gently.

She nodded and reached down to her legs, as if to feel for bites or missing toes.

"Wow, that scared me! Thought it might have been an alligator looking for a late night snack," exclaimed Asrid, rubbing her legs in relief upon finding no blood nor missing toes.

Josh slowly pulled his legs out of the water, suddenly worried that an alligator just MIGHT decide to take him under for a taste. He had heard stories along the Wakulla of alligators grabbing deer and dogs drinking by the edge of the river, drowning them and dragging them back to a den to stew under a hot sun for later eating. Asrid noticed his actions and started to laugh. He joined in, both of them laughing out of relief.

Asrid laid back, her legs still bent, and placed her arms behind her head as a pillow. She stared up into the night sky. Josh mimicked her this time. He traced the edge of the Big Dipper's ladle and found the North Star, twinkling above him.

"Yeah, well, you are right; there are alligators in these waters and they do feed at dusk and night. Just taking precautions," he said.

"You are scared now too, yes?" she teased.

"Not of mullet," he retorted.

She pushed gently against his right arm and tucked her left arm back under her head, facing him.

"So, back to your kernel of truth, Josh," she re-inquired.

Josh raced through a variety of thoughts; about how he had lied to Kathy, tried to protect Elise from unnecessary pain and how that had backfired and even his hubris towards his friends about this sudden change of cavern diving fate.

"Well, let's just say I haven't been forthright with people lately. I guess I've been somewhat obsessed with the cavern class, at the expense of some important relationships," he offered tentatively.

"Oh? What relationships have suffered?" she asked quietly.

"Well, for one, my boss and friend Kathy. I lied to her about being sick instead of coming to work so I could blow off the day and learn how to dive with Allen," he admitted.

"Hmm…that does sound a bit obsessive." He looked over at her; her lips held a soft smile.

"Well, I did come clean with her later on and we had a great discussion about my training and about the need to be forthright. Turns out that she even used to be a cave diver back in the day but stopped for personal reasons. In any rate I feel that we are in a good place."

"OK, so you almost screwed up that relationship but you did the right thing. Hardly enough to keep you awake at night," she gently teased.

"Well, there is my girlfriend, Elise…," he started and stopped. Talking about Elise seemed like crossing a boundary with what amounted to pretty much a semi-complete stranger. It's just he felt comfortable around her. He paused a bit more, wondering if she would prompt him to continue. Her continued silence either meant she respected his privacy or was bored by the whole thing and was too polite to just leave. He decided on the former.

"She has not been a fan of my diving ever since we met and started dating. She knows, though, that I am working on my scuba instructor rating and work at a dive shop." He looked over at her to see her level of interest. She looked back, alert, her head propped up on her left arm.

"I told her about the first cavern dive I did; you know, the story where Jon and I lost Frank in Jackson Blue Spring?" – Asrid nodded – "Well, she was very unhappy about that. I think she was more scared than any of us were and she didn't even do the dive.

"It just got worse as things went on. It would be a touchy subject any time I mentioned it but I always wanted to talk about it. You understand, the passion for cavern diving and all." He paused.

She murmured her assent with a low "um, hm" and looked back up at the sky. A small cloud drifted directly overhead, temporarily blotting out the Milky Way.

"After last weekend she was almost overjoyed that I did so bad and encouraged me to just forget the whole thing. I was discouraged alright but I couldn't get her to understand that my lack of technique last weekend just made it harder to quit. When I told her about skipping work, seeing Allen and getting more overhead training she finally just said she'd had enough and left. She hasn't wanted to talk to me since," he finished.

"Do you love her still, despite your differences regarding cavern diving?" asked Asrid. She turned her head towards Josh again, her eyes glittering with star light.

Josh sighed.

"Yes, I still love her. I just don't know if there's any hope left for us. It feels that as long as I pursue cavern diving she'll just be adamantly opposed to it, to the point of not wanting to be with me," said Josh. He swallowed.

"I miss her."

Asrid slowly reached out her arm and gently touched his shoulder. He felt a shock travel through his arm. He knew it was a gesture of friendship and support but his primitive male brain felt differently.

"Josh, you must go with what you feel is right, whatever that is. If you quit now will you be content? Have you really tried everything possible to explain to her how important this is to you? Can you reconcile with her?"

He looked at her, lying down next to her on the dock, both bathed in dim star light. He could feel the thrum of the river flow transferred through the pilings, an almost audible hum of earth energy. He thought about Elise, the unslakable thirst of the training, the bond between his friends; this new budding friendship with Asrid.

"I'm not really sure, Asrid. Maybe not, maybe so," he mused.

She pulled back her arm and sat up, looking out at the river, arms supported on her knees.

"Well, you owe it to you and her to figure it all out," she finally said.

"Thank you for the advice and allowing me to share my issues with you," said Josh, tentatively, "I feel we have the beginnings of a great friendship."

He sat up and looked out at the river, arms on knees as well.

"Yes, I agree," she said, a smile visible on the side of her face he could see.

"So, enough about me. What about you?" said Josh, attempting to switch topics.

"Oh, maybe some other time. I think I am ready to go back to bed. We do have a long day tomorrow," she said, standing and dusting off her hands.

Josh felt a slight pang as he felt the private moment slip away, hoping she really was tired and he didn't screw things up.

"Oh, OK, I understand. Still, thanks for listening," he added. It felt lame to say it. He stood and faced her.

She reached over, gave him a quick hug and said "Goodnight, Josh. See you in the morning."

Josh watched as she spryly traversed the rest of the dock and briskly walked back to her motel room, her door closing quietly behind her. He could still feel the press of her body against his and the dusky scent of the tannic river water on her arms.

Chapter 29

Josh reached for his fins propped on the cypress tree roots that grew on the edge of the spring. Nearby Jon, Asrid and Frank adjusted their equipment as they stood chest height in the clear waters of Ginnie. The day was already hot and the building clouds visible through the trees promised scattered afternoon summer showers.

Throngs of swimmers, tubers and fellow divers surrounded the group; just another busy Saturday morning at Ginnie Springs. He took turns slipping his fins on, crossing his legs in a figure four position to reach his feet. The doubles on his back shifted left and right as he stepped first on one leg and then the other.

"Looking good in those doubles, Josh," commented Frank as he also put his fins on, "Hope you can dive them."

"Don't worry about me; I'll do fine, Frank," said Josh.

Drew was the last to enter the water, stepping gingerly down the plastic carpeted-covered wet wooden stairs, fins and mask in one hand, stair rail in the other. He settled down into the clear cool water, a wet hiss of bubbles accompanying his transition from weight supported by his legs to weight buoyed by his wings. Drew slipped on his fins, spat in his mask, rinsed it in the spring water and motioned to the group to move over to the left of the stairs, out of the way of the steady traffic.

"OK, guys, this is your first cavern dive. I will be the lead diver and run the reel. On the way in, before we turn the dive, your job is simply to follow me and maintain your position in line. Based on what you've learned so far, what should be the diver order?"

Frank looked over at Asrid, the woman again transformed into a ninja diver, her black dry suit, black wings, black hoses, black trimmed mask, black hood and black wires conspiring to hide her female form with sheer bulk.

"Ladies first?" he offered, grinning, as he waved his hand towards Drew in a gallant gesture.

Drew frowned and looked around the class, fishing for a better answer.

Jon answered, "We should put the divers with the lower powered-lights in front of the ones with the brighter lights."

"Correct. And why?"

"So any light signals given by the weaker lights aren't drowned out by the stronger lights," offered Asrid.

"Also correct. OK, so after me will be Jon, then Frank, then Asrid and Josh you'll be the last diver in and the first diver out," ordered Drew.

"On the way out I will simulate failure of your primary lights by passing my hand in front of my light head," he demonstrated, his light head resting on his right hand, "and each of you will turn off your primary, stow it and then deploy a backup light. Right now, with your eyes closed, I want you to find your backup light, pull it out and unclip it and turn it on."

Josh closed his eyes and felt down the left side of his chest, following the inch-wide webbing towards his waist. His fingers first found a D-ring threaded into the webbing and attached to the D-ring was the clip of one of his backup lights.

He felt down the length of the light until he reached the loop of thin bungee material that kept the light snug against the strap and pulled the flashlight up and away. He twisted the end of the light as if to tighten the head of the flashlight, which he knew would activate the light.

He reached over with his right hand, still blind, and unclipped the bolt snap tied to the bottom of the flashlight from the D-ring on his harness. He pointed the light in front of him and drew a circle in the air. He felt a tap on his forehead and opened his eyes to the sight of Drew nodding at him.

Looking around he saw Asrid and Frank with their eyes open, backup lights in their hands, a small glow visible from the head of their backup lights as they competed poorly with the bright sunshine.

Jon's eyes were still closed and Josh felt a pang of empathy as Jon fumbled with his light, dropping it. It splashed into the water and sank to the bottom, rolling slightly before settling next to Jon's left fin.

Jon frowned.

"Keep your eyes closed, Jon. Let's go with this. OK, so you just lost your backup light. It's pitch black and you can't see anything. You don't know where the rest of your team is but they more than likely are nearby. What are your choices?" said Drew.

"Um, I could go to my second backup light?" asked Jon, his eyes still closed. Josh could see the dropped flashlight visible on the bottom, the image rippling with surface waves.

"Yes. What if you didn't have one or it failed?" asked Drew.

"I guess I would stay on the line and have to wait for somebody else to provide light," answered Jon, thinking.

"OK, so time passes by and still no light and no buddies. What next?" pushed Drew.

"Well, I would 'OK' the line and turn around, ready to leave. I would wait a few seconds for my buddy, like we did in the drills, and then start my exit," said Jon.

"Yes, that's correct. OK, open your eyes and get your light; it's next to your left fin," said Drew.

Jon opened his eyes, saw the black light against the white and green limestone, four feet underwater and placed his mask on his face to retrieve the light.

Jon stuck his reg in his mouth and dropped under the surface, returning a few seconds later with the light. He twisted the light head and looked into the lens, satisfied that it was working properly and twisted it back off, pressing down on the lens to make sure the switch didn't accidentally activate underwater under higher pressure. Drew nodded in approval.

"OK, any questions about the dive plan?" asked Drew. "No? OK, then, stow your backup lights and let's do our buddy drills right here. Pick a buddy and go through the steps.

"Remember, practice your air shares as clean as possible; if you practice sloppy in a real emergency you will perform sloppy. Repeat the drill until both of you are satisfied that you did it to the best of your ability."

Asrid turned to Josh and said, "Let's drop down, do our leak checks and take turns sharing air, OK?"

Josh nodded as he tucked his backup light back into the bungee material and re-secured it with the bolt snap. He unclipped the light head from his canister light and slipped it over his right wrist, rotated his mask 180° on his forehead, pulled it over his face, placed the long hose reg in his mouth and sank below the surface. He was a tad nervous, this being the first time he would be diving his new tech rig in front of his classmates and instructor.

Just relax and let the Allen training kick in, he told himself.

Josh descended and leaned forward, allowing the balanced weight of the twin steel tanks to settle him into a horizontal position. He raised his calves and craned his neck so that his body stayed parallel with the limestone floor. He started to sink slightly; a quick squirt of air into his wing arrested the descent and he hovered a foot off the ground and waited, breathing slowly and deeply to settle his nerves. Soon he felt at ease as his body remembered the familiar position.

Asrid dropped down in front of him, her left hand on her power inflator, right hand out in front to balance her positioning. Soon she was facing him, her body a mirror image of his in the crystal clear water.

Asrid gave Josh an "OK", which he returned. She gave him the "look" sign, the "bubbles" sign and pointed over her shoulders. Josh understood she wanted him to check for any air leaks in her tank valves, isolator valve and manifold that connected her two tanks.

He gave her the "turn around" sign and watched as she slowly pirouetted in place, using only her fins in a sculling motion, arms held out front, bent slightly at the elbows and loose. She executed a 180° turn while maintaining a perfectly parallel body position with no hand movement.

She must have been working on that since last weekend. Nice.

As she spun slowly in place he noted her backup lights, her long hose looped and tucked into the tank with bungee material and the general appearance of her kit. He didn't see anything out of place or dangling, which was part of his job during the buddy check.

He looked to his left and saw Jon and Frank facing each other as well, performing their buddy drills. He looked back at Asrid, paying close attention to all of the places on her tanks, manifold and hoses where air could possibly leak. He noticed a small dribble of air bubbles emanating from her left first stage. Asrid continued turning, coming full circle. He gave her the "thumbs up" surface sign and they both stood up, facing each other.

"Hey, I noticed a slow steady stream of bubbles coming off of your left post," said Josh.

"Oh, that's normal for that type of first stage. Good catch, though," she said. He could make out the edges of her smile hidden behind the silicon skirt of her dive mask.

"OK, cool. Shall we continue then?"

She placed her reg back in her mouth, nodded at him, the bobbing regulator exaggerating the motion, and sank below the surface. Josh followed her down and they quickly re-established their mirror image positions hovering above the bottom, facing each other.

Josh started a 360° turn to the right while she watched him for unwanted bubbles. He sculled slowly and carefully, trying to maintain his balance. He had practiced helicopter turns with Allen and felt he was able to spin in place over a common spot on the ground fairly easily.

As he came back around to her he saw her give him the "bubble" sign followed by an "OK", which meant he didn't have any leaks in his system nor any piece of gear obviously out of place. He "OK'ed" her back and motioned for her to start the out of air drill. He glanced over to his right and saw Drew watching them, evaluating their drills.

She gave him the "out of air" sign, which was his signal to start the underwater ballet that is the air share procedure. He took in a deep breath and pulled the reg out of his mouth, swimming towards her and handed her the reg. He reached down and grabbed his backup reg hanging from his bungee necklace and stuck it in his mouth.

She replaced her reg with his and took the long hose in her right hand, tugging gently at it to make sure the full length of the hose was available. His head brushed against a yellow bikini bottom encased in a clear plastic round float; surprised he looked up and noticed that he had ascended near the surface and directly into a line of tubers launching from the wooden stairs.

He could hear a startled cry from the bikini-clad girl above him and watched as hands reached down on each side of the float and quickly paddled away from him.

Oops.

He quickly dumped air from his wing through the pull string located on the back right side and settled back down towards the bottom. Asrid looked up curiously and he thought he could detect a faint grin on her face through her mask.

Argh, gotta watch my buoyancy, especially when switching regs.

He looked into her eyes, a deeper blue than the surrounding spring water, and gave her an "OK" to let her know he was back on track. She languidly returned the "OK" and he swam to her right side, grabbing her elbow. They proceeded to swim side by side toward the middle of the spring basin.

She stopped and spun back to face him, handing him back his reg. A thin line of bubbles trailed from the reg as he accepted it and switched from his backup reg to his primary reg. He re-wrapped the long hose around his neck and stuffed the excess hose back into the webbing at his waist.

Asrid hovered, patiently waiting for him to continue the drill, where he simulated being out of air and she donated her reg. Josh gave her the out of air signal and watched as she quickly grabbed her backup reg from behind her back on the right side of her tank.

She yanked the long hose free and thrust the reg towards him, the hose uncoiling with the effort. He pulled his reg out of his mouth and accepted her reg, purging it by forcing air through the reg before starting to inhale. The mouthpiece felt odd in his mouth and the reg spat out air more loudly and forcibly than his own. It was still breathable though.

Josh returned her "OK" and allowed himself to be guided by her firm grasp on his right elbow as they swam side by side. This time he had been careful not to breathe in too much air when switching between regulators so that he wouldn't float up again and find himself colliding with another swimmer.

He turned and handed Asrid back her regulator and switched

back to his primary regulator, left dangling off his right shoulder. He watched as Asrid coiled up her seven foot long hose and stuffed it back into the bungee loop attached to her right tank.

Satisfied that they had completed the air share drill he gave her a "thumbs up" and they swam back to the shallow limestone shelf near the stairs and surfaced next to Drew, who was still leaning into the water with his mask on, face in the water, watching Jon and Frank.

"That was pretty funny when you bumped into that girl on the tube," said Asrid. She removed her mask, held it in her right hand and gently squeezed her nose.

Josh looked downstream and saw a clump of college students drinking beer and slowly floating out to the Santa Fe River. In the middle of the clump his yellow bikini girl was enjoying the attention of her male companions, no worse the wear from her unexpected underwater encounter with him.

"Yeah, well, at least I have good taste," said Josh, looking back to Asrid and smiling. She smiled back. Jon and Frank surfaced a few feet away and Drew withdrew his head from the water.

"OK, not too bad. I saw some issues with buoyancy during the reg exchanges though. Plus some of you are being stingy with the long hose. Be sure to pull out all of the long hose so if you have to go in single file your out-of-air buddy won't stress over having the reg yanked out of their mouth."

Josh spoke, "Drew, we are going to do ours again; I'm guilty of losing control of my buoyancy during our drill."

Drew nodded and grinned. "Yeah, I saw you molest that poor child. Clearly she looks like she's scarred for life from her encounter with the creature from the black lagoon." He nodded at the group fading from view downstream.

"You also don't look half bad in the doubles, Josh." Josh felt a flush of warmth at the unusual praise. Earlier, when they first met Drew for the day's class, Drew had commented to Josh in front of the rest of the class how it usually was a very bad idea to switch equipment in the middle of class. Josh had taken the advice without comment, hoping the moment would pass quickly.

Josh and Asrid chuckled while Jon and Frank looked on in curiosity. It was unusual to see Drew actually crack a joke.

"But do try to control your position better. Crashing on the bottom, where it's usually silty, can really screw up an air exchange. It's not as bad bumping into the ceiling and it's what I see most students do. Best, though, to not pile on problems while in a cavern by losing visibility. Bad enough that one of you is out of air," said

Drew.

"We should do ours again as well," offered Jon, "I don't think I pulled out the entire length of my long hose to Frank."

Frank remarked snidely, "That's not something I really dream about, Jon."

"OK, switch partners and keep practicing," said Drew.

They spent the next fifteen minutes redoing their air share drills, switching buddies. Josh felt more and more comfortable giving and receiving air from all of the others in the class until it started to feel second nature. He was careful not to inhale too much air before removing a reg and managed not to scare any more swimmers.

They all surfaced, Drew repeated the dive briefing and they all descended, watching as Drew tied off his large cavern reel to an outcropping of limestone next to the Ginnie Ballroom entrance in twenty feet of water. Josh noticed it was the same watermelon-sized white chunk of limestone that Allen had used earlier in the week.

He could see that years of wrapping nylon line around the limestone had created a series of shallow grooves. Drew wrapped his line within a groove and gave the team the "dive" sign. All four of them returned the sign simultaneously.

Drew reached down and turned on his canister light, the beam flickering to life on his right wrist mount. Josh flicked on his own light and watched Asrid do the same. Jon and Frank unclipped their large open water eight D-cell underwater flashlights and flipped them on, the large lights unwieldy in their hands.

One by one Josh watched the team disappear into the left side entrance of the Ginnie Ballroom as they followed Drew. Asrid's fins slowly frog kicked against the flow and he moved in behind her as she glided down into the cavern.

Soon all five divers were inside the cavern, in the first room brightly lit from the two entrance holes. Josh remembered the layout of the room from his dive with Allen and pulled himself along next to the line behind Asrid as Drew, near the top of the entrance to the second room, paused and looked back.

Drew painted a large circle on the left wall with this light and waited until all four divers returned the "OK" light signal. Josh noticed the different brightness, color and sharpness of the different lights. His older canister light threw out a strong yellow beam with a large single point of focus that was easily visible.

Asrid and Drew's lights were even brighter and the light beam a whitish-blue color. Their focal points were smaller spots of lights that lasered the wall. Jon and Frank's meager lights were a dim yellow with a large unfocused area on the wall. Josh found it slightly more difficult to detect the circular motion of his friend's lights.

Drew disappeared down the pile of limestone breakdown that separated the small alcove top room from the bigger bottom room, followed by Jon and Frank. Astrid waited, hovering above the sandy bottom, until Frank's fins frog kicked over the ledge. Josh followed Astrid as she descended into the Ballroom. He pulled himself along the white limestone boulders until he crested the top of the last boulder and looked down.

Below him, strung out along the quivering line Drew spooled out he could see the entire room lit up by the cumulative power of five flashlights. This time he could get a full appreciation for the size and beauty of the room. Drew's beam held steady as he slowly worked his way towards the rebar barrier on the bottom right of the room. Frank and Jon's lights roved around as they took in the view.

Astrid's bright light illuminated the left side of the room as she inspected a small alcove tucked along the upper part of the room. The tattered nylon rope undulated in the spring's current and bisected the room from left to right.

Man, with this much light the room looks absolutely amazing! I can see wall to wall.

He slowly sank downward, now parallel with the ceiling of the Ballroom and enjoyed the dancing beams reflected from the silver mirrors of trapped air pockets. He pointed his light at the air pockets and moved the beam slowly back and forth; the cascading beams of reflected light wobbled into the Ballroom as the air pockets rippled with the current. The effect was a breathtaking panoply of yellow and white light tinted blue in the clear water of the Ballroom.

That's pretty cool. Probably why they call this the Ballroom.

Josh looked and saw Drew stop at the rebar and turn. Drew gave another light "OK" against the back wall of the Ballroom, which was returned by one bright yellow beam, one brighter white beam and two diffuse dim yellow beams in the same spot on the wall. He tied off the line to the rebar, just as Allen had done, and worked his way up the sloping sandy floor to the left side of the room.

Each student took turns grabbing the black metal bars and peering into the lower passageway, which snaked and shrank down to a tight fit, pure white grains of sand and limestone dancing on the floor in the current.

Drew gave one last "OK" and waited for the responses before he next gave the "thumbs up" sign, illuminated by his white-blue light. Josh watched as each student returned the sign, acknowledging it was time to turn around and leave. He gave his "thumbs up" and turned to leave.

He started swimming next to the line, Asrid directly behind him and began the short trek back up to the entrance alcove. Suddenly Drew's bright beam flashed in front of him, moving rapidly. He turned and saw Drew give the "your primary light just failed" sign.

Oh, yeah, we are doing drills now...

He reached down on his right side, found the top of his light canister and flicked the power switch off. Behind him the lights of his team extinguished as well, leaving them in partial darkness, the only light coming from the ragged rectangle of natural blue tinted sunlight above them from the entrance alcove.

Josh switched on his backup light and pulled it out, unclipping it. He turned and could see the smaller lights come on one by one, the masks of his buddies mirroring the blue tinted sunlight from the surface in silvery outlines.

He circled an "OK" with his backup light and was answered by three small beam "OK"s. The Ballroom felt smaller as the cumulative light from the four backup lights barely lit up the immediate space around each diver.

Where's Drew?

He turned to start his exit and noticed Drew hovering above him, near the line. He swam up to Josh and gave him the "close your eyes" hand signal. A shot of adrenaline went down Josh's spine.

OK, he wants us to exit using touch contact. Cool!

Josh turned off his light and reclipped it back on his left chest D-ring. He reached for the line with his left hand and closed his eyes, waiting for Asrid to grab him from behind and nudge him to start the exit. The sounds of the bubbles from his exhaust rumbled past his ears as he waited...and waited.

This is taking a while. Wonder if I should just leave?

He felt a hand touch below his right knee, followed by two deliberate pushes. He started swimming slowly, following the line as it ascended towards the cavern exit.

Gonna take it slow; don't want to break the train.

He worried momentarily about his air supply but reasoned that he had plenty since they had only been in the cavern for a short time and the last time he checked he had only used 200 PSI out of the total starting pressure of 2,900 PSI.

Best not to worry about something I can't really check now anyway. If this was a true silt out I doubt I could read the gauge and hate to take the time to even try. Besides with these doubles I have tons of air left.

His reasoning was sound but he couldn't totally get rid of the nagging doubt about running out of air in the dark.

He felt Asrid squeeze his leg twice, quickly, and her grip disappeared and he was left disconnected, hovering next to the line.

Hmm..something must have happened. I know I'm supposed to just stop and wait it out.

A few minutes later and still no Asrid. He fought the temptation to open just one eye and see what was going on and take a quick peek as his pressure gauge. He felt his exhaust bubbles kiss the side of his face as the bubbles rose to the ceiling.

I have to do SOMETHING.

He decided to go back, blind, and see if he could figure out what was going on with just his sense of touch. What if she was out of air or tangled? What if she somehow got off the line or got disconnected from Jon? She might need his help, drill or not.

Josh turned slowly into the line, switching from his left hand to his right. He bumped into the wall of the cavern. He felt the line descend back towards the bottom of the Ballroom and released a small burp of air from his BC and descended with the line. He reached out with his left hand in front, slowly moving back and forth and in a few feet was rewarded by the feel of short hair on a human head.

That's not Asrid! Must be Jon or Frank.

He couldn't resist any longer and opened his eyes, curious at the turn of events. He saw that he had indeed touched Jon's head. Jon was positioned on the line in the correct posture waiting for Asrid behind him, who was untangling the line from Jon's fin.

Frank waited patiently behind Asrid, in loose contact with her left knee as she worked the entanglement. All three had their eyes closed, dutifully performing the correct procedures. Above them, Drew hovered like some underwater puppeteer, lording over the events. Drew looked over at Josh and immediately shot him the "close your eyes" signal.

Oops, busted!

Josh closed his eyes and reached out to where he last saw Jon's hand on the line. He found Jon's hand and gave it a quick squeeze, to let Jon know he was there, ready to continue the exit. He felt Jon work his way up to his left elbow and grab it firmly.

Josh pivoted towards the exit, knowing he had to keep his body higher so he didn't bump into Jon, and switched back to his left hand on the line. He imagined the team spread out on the line and staggered at different depths, their bodies overlapping like flags on a flag pole.

After a few seconds he felt Jon give him a forward nudge and he started to swim up again. This time the train moved forward without a hitch.

Josh followed the line, being careful to dump air from his wing as he felt his buoyancy increase due to the shallower depths and continued until he felt a tap on his head from Drew.

He opened his eyes to see that they had worked themselves back into the upper alcove right behind the boulder separating the two exits, only ten feet away from the open water.

He watched as the light dimmed slightly as a cloud temporarily covered the direct sun, the sunbeams rippling in the water disappearing. He turned around and watched Drew tap the heads of the rest of the team, eyes opening in his wake. He grinned and waved. Jon gave him an "OK", Frank a "thumbs up" and Asrid nodded. Felt great to have the drill finished and their first cavern dive completed.

Chapter 30

Two hours later the four of them sat at a picnic table outside the deli, eating lunch. Rain pattered loudly on the overhanging tin porch roof, cascading down in sheets of water that pooled at the base of the porch's concrete slab and carved out tiny canyons in the sand road. Through the curtain of water Josh could just make out bathers hunkered down underneath their rubber rafts while others walked barefoot down towards the spring, oblivious to the storm.

A flash of lightning appeared in the sky in the distance, followed three seconds later by the crack of thunder, sending the bathers under the trees in the campground across the street. Tent roofs sagged under the weight of the rain and the tent walls shuddered with the gusts of the winds from the storm. Josh was glad they decided to share a motel room instead of camping out over the weekend.

"That was pretty close," commented Jon. Jon's dark hair was still damp from the morning's dives; he sat across from Josh and next to Asrid.

Asrid's short blonde hair poked out from underneath a light solid blue head wrap and Frank's dirty blonde hair naturally spiked in a rakish style from being wet, a strand hanging over his green eyes.

They had completed the morning dives, stowed their gear and hiked up to the deli just before the clouds released their pent-up moisture. Drew had sent them off for lunch with orders to return in an hour to resume the class.

"Yeah, sure glad we got out of the water," said Frank, sitting to Josh's left. He took another bite out of his turkey sandwich, shredded lettuce, mustard and mayonnaise dripping on his paper plate.

"Wonder if anybody's ever been struck by lightning in a cavern or cave?" asked Asrid, nibbling on her salad of greens, chopped carrots, cucumbers, green peppers and cherry tomatoes lightly drizzled with oil and vinegar.

"Not sure that the electrical energy would travel far underground," said Jon as he finished up the last slice of his BLT.

"It might travel a ways underwater though," said Josh, wiping his mouth after completing his freshly-cooked hamburger.

"I'd imagine if you are way back in a cave and a storm came up you probably wouldn't even know there's thunder and lightning if it was sunny when you started the dive," said Jon, "Imagine if a bolt of lightning could travel that far back and you didn't know what it was when it hit you?"

Josh shuddered inwardly at the thought. Yet another danger of cave diving.

"Actually, there has been a case of cave divers getting struck by lightning," boomed a voice behind Josh.

Josh turned and saw three men standing next to the picnic table, paper plates of food and drinks in their hands. They were all in their late thirties and early forties and all wore wedding bands on their ring fingers.

Asrid smiled and said, "Hi guys, why don't you sit down with us? We can scoot over to make room."

"Sure," said Josh as he shuffled towards Frank who moved to the edge of the bench. On the other side Asrid and Jon did the same. Two of the three men sat on Asrid's side and the other, a muscular black man with a salt and pepper crew cut wearing beige shorts and a black t-shirt with a gold line arrow symbol stitched on the left breast pocket, squeezed next to Josh.

The one sitting next to Asrid was runner-thin and had a long face with coal black eyes that matched his jet black short hair. He wore dark blue running shorts and a tan tank top silk screened with a fading black outline of Yoda. The last guy was pudgy with short grey hair, small brown eyes set close to his round nose, thin lips and wore jean shorts with a black t-shirt wearing the same gold line arrow symbol stitched on his left breast pocket. They dug into their meals.

"Asrid, is this your cavern class?" asked salt and pepper between bites.

"Yes. These are the guys that I dove with last week," explained Asrid. She made introductions around the table, resulting in many nods and the occasional hand shake. The crew cut leader was named Tony, the Yoda aficionado was Steve and Alan sported the grey hair. Josh couldn't shake the feeling of being slightly intimidated by these older, more experienced divers.

Between bites Tony said, "I recognize you guys from the Santa Fe Enclave last night. So how's the cavern class going so far?"

Jon leaned back and answered, "It's going pretty well. Drew's our instructor. He's a bit of a hard ass but we're certainly getting the right experience."

"Drew's a great instructor. He taught me up through my full cave," offered Steve, sipping his drink.

"So what have you guys been doing?" asked Josh, curious as to what these guys did for fun. Except for cave instructors and Kathy, who had retired from cave diving, he'd never actually met any active recreational cave divers.

"We entered in the Eye, jumped back to the main line, jumped over to Hill 400 and followed the main line over to the Bats, then came back out the Ear," said Tony, a slight smile on his face.

Josh had no idea what that meant. Eyes? Bats? Ear? Before he could ask Frank chimed in, "We did the Ginnie Ballroom today, multiple times."

The three older men smiled at each other.

"Yes, that's would I would expect for the cavern class," said Alan, "You should stay within your limits." His deep voice drifted softly across the table.

Frank bristled and crossed his arms, "As should you guys."

Tony looked sidelong at his two friends and back to Frank. They seemed slightly annoyed at Frank's moxie.

"Look, you should really check your ego whenever you dive in the overhead environment. It's not a competition and we all support each other, no matter what level of diver."

Asrid jumped in, "Yes, these guys have been very supportive last week, helping me work on my technique and cavern skills. I am very appreciative that they took the time to dive at my lower level," she added helpfully.

Josh knew Frank loved to compete always, on any field. Sometimes he felt Frank went too far. This was one of those times. He felt slightly embarrassed, especially for Frank. Experience had taught him, though, to either let Frank dig his own way out of these situations or just stay buried.

Tony continued, "We've been coming down here every year for the past decade. We started like you three, at the cavern level. We've progressed through the levels as a team, sharing the good things and the bad. We've learned that for the most part the cave community is full of people who care deeply about making sure nobody gets hurt and that the environment we dive in stays protected.

"We've gotten support from not only our cave instructors but from the community, workers at dive shops in the area and pretty much any other cave diver in the vicinity. The environment will humble you one of these days when something goes wrong. The cave doesn't care about egos. You'll see."

He paused and looked at his two buddies, who were nodding in agreement.

"My advice is to take advantage of any and all resources around you as you start this journey. Follow the rules; they are there for a damn good reason and don't let your emotions rule your diving decisions. If you are competitive, turn that energy in towards yourself. Compete with you to make you a better diver."

Tony paused, letting the words sink in a bit. Josh could see that

Jon and Asrid were rapt with attention while Steve and Alan nodded in agreement as they ate their sandwiches. Frank still looked unconvinced but he had uncrossed his arms and was watching Tony.

Josh decided to turn the conversation back from the brink. It was starting to feel like a lecture and while Frank did deserve to be put down a notch Josh knew there was little use pressing your advantage with him.

"So, tell us about those divers who got shocked by lightning during a cave dive."

Tony's face erupted in a large grin as he turned to Josh.

"Oh, that's a fascinating story. The next best thing to cave diving is telling stories about cave diving, especially ones where something doesn't go right."

The rain had started to let up, the downpour now just a light shower. Already Josh could see the sun peeking out between the clouds, the heat generating small clouds of steam issuing upward from the sandy road.

Whoops of joy echoed from the campsite as a line of bathers started their march down to the spring, tubes in tow. The rumble of distant thunder confirmed that the cell had indeed moved on, leaving a steamy bath of sunny humid air in its wake.

Everybody around the table had finished their meals as Tony started his story.

"A few years ago there was a cave diving couple – it's surprising how many couples cave dive," said Tony, eyeing Asrid, "Anyway, this couple had planned to do pretty much the same dive we just did, here at Ginnie. Basically the plan was to enter the cave system at Devil's Ear and go up the main guide line in the cave system up to the Hill 400 tunnel.

"Look at any cave map of Ginnie and you'll see what I'm talking about. More than likely Drew will take you over to Devil's Ear and Devil's Eye tomorrow; I don't know. Both of them have caverns but they aren't as large as the Ginnie Ballroom.

"So anyway they did the jump up Hill 400. The bottom of the cave at the jump is around ninety to one hundred feet in depth. The tunnel is large enough for a team of divers to swim side-by-side if they didn't mind fighting the current and the snaking passageway.

"So, this couple started up the Hill 400 line which curves off to the right before it climbs up an incline that takes you up to a sixty foot depth. Just as they are at the top, about two thirds the way through their planned dive, they both say they felt bad all of a sudden, like a weird simultaneous feeling of deep dread overcame them, and their air tasted metallic.

"At the time, though, neither of them knew the other had the same exact experience at the same moment. One of them, I forget which, decided to turn the dive, thinking they had a bad air fill or was developing some sort of medical problem. Believe me, you don't want to have a medical issue more than 500 feet back in a cave system!

"They both came out of the cave at the Ear, did their required decompression and felt no more ill effects. They did notice twenty feet above them was one whomping storm; there was nobody else in the water and they could see the sky was dark and the occasional flash of lightning. Pretty scary, seeing as how they were both in the water with steel on their backs."

Tony paused, enjoying the attention of the cavern class students as they looked on with wide eyes.

"Lucky for them the storm had already passed, just like this one here, and they exited the Ear, swam back to the stairs and walked back to one of the picnic tables near Little Devil's, under a large pavilion. There was a bunch of cave divers having a party; we were all there as well. I remember we all wondered what in the world they were doing out in that weather.

"We helped them get their gear off and listen to them describe their dive. We calculated from their dive computers that they had been almost directly underneath a large bolt of lightning that hit the ground across the river from our party. If you look at a map of where the cave is in relation to the land you'll see that they were underground and underwater in the same place near where the bolt hit.

"Once they talked about what each of them was experiencing they realized that it had to have been the surge of electricity through the water in the cave that gave them that bad feeling and made the air taste funny.

"Thankfully both of them were swimming in the middle of the water column, not touching any rocks. If they had been doing so no telling how bad the jolt might have been since the electricity would have had more of a conduit to the ground through them. They considered themselves damn lucky that day."

Steve spoke next, "We make it a point to always check the forecast before any long cave dive, just in case."

Josh, Jon and Asrid chuckled politely. Frank's face stood passive.

"Well, looks like our forecast is looking good for the afternoon's cavern dives," said Josh. Sunlight had returned in full force around them, increasing the heat and humidity, the sky clear blue, the cumulonimbus clouds having retreated to the east.

"You guys ready to head back?" he asked. The two groups said their goodbyes and left the cave divers under the porch, finishing their drinks.

"See you guys around," said Tony, "and good luck with your dives." He waved from his seated position along with Steve and Alan, who turned to watch them leave. Josh felt glad he had made some new friends in the cave diving community.

"You too, guys," returned Asrid as she walked to catch up with Josh, Jon and Frank.

Chapter 31

The rest of the afternoon was spent diving multiple cavern dives in the Ginnie Ballroom with every diver in the class taking turns running the reel, to varying degrees of success. Josh managed to only get the line tangled once, but was able to untangle it with the help of Frank. Asrid proved the most adept with the reel while Jon's reel mishap resulted in the line becoming so hopelessly tangled and jammed that Drew had to intervene to unjam the reel during the dive.

Jon redeemed himself on his next turn with the reel by keeping it taut during the entire dive. By late afternoon the cold and stress of performing drills had taken its toll and Josh found himself getting bored with repeated short dives into the same cavern time and time again.

When Frank complained once about the monotony between dives at the surface, Drew had responded that they weren't ready for a more advanced cavern until they mastered the emergency skills, especially working with the reel and handed Frank the reel for the next dive.

Josh could tell, though, that despite the grind the team was getting more adept at handling all of the emergencies Drew threw at them. They moved more efficiently as a group during touch contact and the response time for air shares shortened.

Josh was beginning to actually enjoy closing his eyes during the "lights out" portions of the drills, telling himself to just forget about vision as a sense and to rely more on touch, including the way the water spoke to him about his surroundings through a slight change in the flow or a ripple felt across his hand.

"Tomorrow we will meet at Peacock Springs State Park. We will be diving Orange Grove sink. Unlike Ginnie, Orange Grove is a low flow system. That means no strong current to erase your mistakes and clear out the water. If you kick it up there it will be more obvious to the team," lectured Drew at the front of the room.

They were in the classroom at FWCD, having finished up at Ginnie and dropped off their tanks next door to get filled. Josh turned and looked across the table. The shared experience of the class had brought them all together as a team, which he could see even in the way they sat together.

Rather than Asrid sitting apart they sat four abreast, side by side, listening to Drew. They all looked tired but filled with the satisfaction of a good day's work. All were dressed in fresh clothes and cleaned from the showers at Ginnie; Asrid's blonde hair was combed straight back in neat rows.

"You guys did well today; I know it was a long day but you can consider the cavern class to be the place where you learn and master the fundamental skills that you will use throughout your cave diving career, if you decide to pursue higher levels of certification."

Drew paused and looked around the room. Josh reveled in the warm words and thought back to the rollercoaster week – from his diving ineptitude a week ago, to the miracle performed by Allen midweek, Kathy's cave diving revelations, the estrangement with Elise and today's successful dives.

"OK, then, if there aren't any questions I'll see you tomorrow morning at 9 AM at Peacock Springs."

Chairs scraped the floor as the students started to leave. Jon and Asrid were chatting about the drills, with Frank in tow, animatedly joining the conversation. The three of them left the classroom.

Josh snapped from his introspection and pushed back in his chair, ready to rise when Drew spoke.

"Hey, Josh, I'm curious about your doubles."

"Yes?"

"Where did you get them from and how did you get up to speed so quickly? It takes most people a lot of dives to transition from single tanks to double tanks."

"Allen taught me. He also loaned me the gear," said Josh, figuring with Drew it made sense to just be straight forward.

Drew's brows knitted together and a frown wrinkled his face.

"Allen? The wheelchair guy that hangs around the shop? For real?"

"Um, yes, he was great, teaching me how to put the gear together and helping me in the water," offered Josh.

"Allen went diving? How did he do that?" Drew's tone was laced with incredulity and hostility, his stare fiercer. Josh instinctively sat farther back in his chair.

"He, he used side mount tanks…"

"Curious; I'd heard that some guys with serious back issues were switching to side mount…had no idea that Allen figured out a way," mused Drew, his hand rubbing his chin.

"Sounds like you aren't a big fan of Allen's…" Josh trailed off.

Drew sighed and sat on the edge of the table, crossing his arms, head cocked, his eyes staring at the ceiling above Josh.

"Yeah, Allen and I go way back. He killed my cousin David years ago." Drew's voice was flat, the tone taut with old anger. Josh stood straighter, putting the pieces together.

I bet that's David Delaney – the diver who died in Mexico that Kathy talked about.

"Who's David?" said Josh quietly. He figured that it would be interesting to get Drew's side of the story rather than explain what he had learned from Kathy.

Drew looked at Josh, a wistful expression on his face.

"David was my diving mentor, my cave instructor. He not only taught me a lot but was worldly, you know? He was fluent in Spanish and was obsessed with deep caves, especially in Northern Mexico. Anyway, David died trying to reach 500 feet deep in a Mexican cave. I blame Allen for it."

"Why was it Allen's fault?" probed Josh.

"You sure ask a lot of questions," Drew glared at Josh, who simply sat and looked passively back.

Drew slapped his hands on his knees and stood.

"Damn it, they never could prove HOW he actually died but I was there when they started planning and training for the dive. I wasn't qualified to dive with them to those depths at the time, though, so couldn't be on the team, even though I desperately wanted to.

"I do know that all of them, Allen, Kathy and David, were meticulous. I watched them mix all of the tanks, label them and analyze them. When Allen and Kathy came back with all their gear I helped them analyze the tanks and discovered the one that killed David because it had the wrong mix. I confronted the two of them and they tried to blame it back on David!"

He started to pace in front of Josh, muttering as he recalled, almost as if he was speaking to himself and had forgotten Josh was there.

"David was the gear nut; he was the one who taught all of us how to mix Nitrox and Trimix. There's no way he could have mislabeled a tank or gotten the gas mixture wrong. No way."

"So why not blame Kathy, too?" probed Josh, afraid that Drew would explode at his insolence. Drew stopped pacing and looked down, his brown eyes slightly covered by a forelock of curly dark hair. The anger seeped out of him, deflating like a punctured inner tube.

"I've never forgiven either one of them, frankly. Allen's just been the easier one to hate because I see him occasionally. He's a visible reminder of that tragic event. We try to avoid each other as much as possible, which isn't easy in our small community."

Drew shook his head slightly, as if awoken from a dream.

"Well, that's enough of that. None of your business, really. Forget about it, it's ancient history anyway. I'll see you tomorrow at Peacock."

He spun on the last words and headed out the back side door, closing it abruptly.

    Josh sat for a moment, a surprised look on his face, thinking. What was the real story of David's death? Why does everybody involved in it feel responsible or place blame? Why such strong feelings almost a decade later? He wondered idly about his own relationship woes, especially with Elise, and mused briefly about how the correlation between extreme diving and extreme relationships.

Chapter 32

Later that night Josh and his friends sat at the picnic tables sipping beer and watching the tannic river water drift by. Asrid had joined them for a hearty meal of steaks at a Gainesville steak house; Jon had ridden with her in her rental car followed by Josh and Frank. The conversation had been genial and centered mostly around the dives of the day, with each regaling the other of lessons learned and skills mastered.

Josh was surprised at her appetite and the appetite of the group in general. He knew a day of diving usually meant a night of eating and the extra energy required to withstand the cold spring water coupled with the pressure of performing in a class setting really used up their internal energy stores. Asrid wolfed through a medium rare steak, baked potato with all of the trimmings and salad with an equal amount of verve as the men.

The group sat in a comfortable silence, the sounds of the water gurgling past accompanied by the twilight tweets and chirps of insects and amphibians.

The picnic table on the other side of the dock was occupied by Tony and his cave diving crew; their voices a low murmur punctuated by the occasional sound of deep throated laughter, their faces painted white by the light of a battery-powered lantern.

The dock was bathed in its typical blue and green light. Illumination from the white lights on the roof's edge enhanced the ambient light. Josh had waved to Tony and his friends after they had parked, grabbed some beers from the room fridge and plunked down wearily onto the picnic benches.

"So how do you think we'll do tomorrow?" asked Jon, hunched over his beer.

"We'll do fine," yawned Frank, "This class hasn't been that difficult after all."

Josh felt the day's fatigue enhanced by the digestion of complex food and stifled a yawn himself.

"I'm not sure about that so much, Frank. It's been the hardest dive class I've ever taken." Josh swigged more of his beer and stifled a belch.

"I know what you mean, Josh. My tech classes in Sweden were as demanding, certainly, but Drew is more demanding of us as a team than I'm used to. Most of the diving we do in my country is with the attitude of you have to save yourself if you get off the wreck and drift," Asrid explained, her legs splayed out on the edge of the bench, feet dangling from the side, her back to Josh.

"Well, I certainly feel that we gelled as a team and can take on any cavern," Frank stated, his eyes half closed with fatigue.

"Yes, we did come together rather nicely. I think we even impressed Drew. He seemed almost like a normal happy person by the end of the day," said Jon.

Josh thought about his private conversation with Drew after the class and decided not to bring up Drew's animosity towards Allen and Kathy. He chose instead to keep the flow of the conversation going.

"Well, let's see if we make him happy tomorrow and finish the class with a passing grade. Don't forget we have to do the remaining dives and then take the written exam." He was worried about the gas math problems, even though Jon had gone through many examples since the initial lecture. Before every dive Drew had also made them calculate their turn pressures on the fly, which was relatively easy since they already knew the difference in volume versus pressure for the tanks they had been diving. No telling what ugly math problems might be on the test, though.

"Yeah, that pesky written exam," said Frank, "Too bad we can't get an answer key or something."

Asrid stood and stretched, all of them watching her back arch and arms raise with feline grace.

"Well, guys, I'm done. See you in the morning."

"G'night Asrid," said Josh, slightly disappointed she was leaving but bone weary himself. He knew he'd soon be asleep as well.

Chapter 33

Josh took one last look at the limestone cliff rising above Orange Grove sink, the occasional sound of bubbles breaking the surface below him. He stood half way up the wooden stairway which snaked in right angles down from the cliff to the sink, stopping directly at the water's edge.

The grey-white cliff was pock marked with hundreds of small holes created from ancient erosion arranged in horizontal lines depicting past water levels. A patina of browns and greens across the Swiss cheese vertical structure revealed the presence of moss, lichen and hardy plants growing on the limestone.

The roughly circular shaped sink was covered with thousands of tiny green floating duckweed plants, spinning lazily in the slight current created by the steady stream of exhaust bubbles from cave divers. The duckweed would separate from the bubbles, provide an enticing glimpse of dark clear water beneath and inexorably drift back together, closing the view beneath the calm spring water and returning the surface of the sink back to soupy green quicksand.

A dragonfly flitted by, momentarily lighting on the top of the wooden stair rail, before buzzing off towards the young oak trees ringing the top of the cliff edge. He took a deep breath, taking in the humid summer air, a hint of chalky limestone flavor evident in his nose and palate.

Josh felt the excitement of the unknown and the draw of the deep pull at him. Unlike flamboyant Ginnie, Orange Grove sink was stingier with its underwater natural beauty; hiding its secrets under a green blanket, unsullied by the steady stream of swimmers and tubers.

The only people who came to this park were cavern and cave divers and the occasional eco tourist interested in the flora and fauna, giving the park an aura of solitude and silence. This reminded him of the peaceful atmosphere along the Wakulla River where few ventured and the general public had yet to discover.

He gazed at the middle of the tallest part of the cliff, where most of the escaped exhaust bubbles from divers surfaced and tried to visualize the world underneath the duckweed, using Drew's dive briefing as a guide. Below the stairs the depth was only twenty feet which steeply funneled down to a cavern zone beneath the cliff at sixty feet, the floor fine silt, jutting rocks and scattered sticks.

The entrance to a cave system started right at the cavern zone, a small tunnel leading back farther under the rock and protected by a fallen tree stripped of leaves. Off to the left side Drew had talked of a small cavern zone with entrances into a larger, deeper cavern zone that reached a max depth of one hundred feet. Their dive would require greater team communication and single-file swimming to traverse the smaller sections.

The biggest point of the lecture had been to stress the importance of not stirring up the bottom since the water flow in this system was much slower than Ginnie. Here there was much more silt, it was finer and if kicked up would hang around longer, meaning the likelihood of losing vision was higher.

The thought of actual zero visibility instead of simulated zero visibility made Josh equal parts excited and nervous. The last time he had been in zero viz he was rescuing Jon, wondering whether or not they would both survive.

"You OK, Josh?"

Josh turned to the voice and saw Asrid at the top of the stairs, looking down at him. Her short blonde hair was swept back and held in place with a blue bandana. She wore a grey Minnie Mouse t-shirt with matching loose-fitting grey shorts and white low cut sneakers, the line of her running socks visible along the top edge of the sneakers.

"Yeah, just imaging what the dive is going to be like," he said, motioning back to the carpet of duckweed.

"Ah, are you visualizing the dive?"

"Yes, a trick Kathy taught me whenever doing a challenging dive. I know it seems kinda hokey but I just want to be ready for anything that happens. This cavern dive will be more challenging than the ones we did yesterday." He walked up the remaining stairs and reached Asrid. They both turned and headed back along the thin dirt trail that lead back to the main dirt road.

"That's a great idea. I should try it sometime."

Josh looked at her and smiled, grateful that she didn't make fun of his pre-dive technique. He had gotten tired of Frank teasing him of "meditating" before diving to the point where before a big dive he would usually just wait for his friends to wander off and take a quiet moment or two to privately run through the dive plan.

"Thanks. I find it really helps calm my nerves and get into the right mindset."

"I've never thought of going through the dive in my mind; I usually just rely on the team's dive briefing. Any special technique you use?"

He shrugged lamely, not really sure how to explain it.

"Not really, I just go over the dive briefing again quietly by myself and try to visualize the actual dive – where I am, where my dive buddies are, what the location looks like…that sort of stuff. What to do if something goes wrong, remind myself to check my air…"

"I understand. Makes sense, especially today where we are bound to have 'problems' that Drew creates," she said, smiling.

They reached the parking lot, a larger clearing of dirt road framed by tall back wooden benches, perfect for setting up scuba tanks. Sunlight filtered through the young oak trees, sugar maples, water hickory and dogwoods creating a lush blend of deep summer greens and yellows. The air was still, warm and moist.

The only sounds came from the mild banter between Jon and Frank muted by the silence pressed on the landscape by the thick vegetation and punctuated by the occasional buzz of a bee or mosquito or cry of a bird. Josh could see Drew working on his dive gear through the open back doors of his white van, preparing for the dive. Drew's van acted as a mobile dive shop and a platform to get into and out of his gear. He would sit on the back bumper, doors wide, and slip into his set of doubles.

Josh admired the efficiency of the operation. The tailgate of his truck bed was too high to sit and safely slip into his diving harness. He preferred to relocate his doubles from the bed of the truck to a picnic table or park bench before donning his gear. Today was no exception; his doubles sat waiting for him next to the single tank setups of Jon and Frank.

Asrid's doubles were also perched against the high back wooden benches installed at the park for cave divers, her hoses coiled cleanly. The rutted white sandy road split around a stand of trees held back by a short brown painted wooden fence and ringed by more tall back wooden benches. Another set of vehicles full of dive gear and surrounded by cave divers preparing their equipment occupied the other split in the road.

The blue plastic of a portable toilet broke up the riot of earth and plant tones dominating the primitive park. Josh could see the other dive team sitting on park benches and slipping on their dive suits, slow of pace with easy laughter and smiles freely exchanged.

Must be nice to just enjoy a dive here. I can't wait until after class when we are certified to dive in caverns and can really enjoy the experience.

"How did your snipe hunting go?" smirked Frank, breaking his contemplation. He turned and looked at his friends. They were both sitting on nearby picnic tables, slipping on their wet suits.

"Ha ha. Just enjoying the scenery, smart guy," Josh responded, reaching into one of his large plastic bins in the back of his truck to retrieve his wet suit. He shook the suit and squeezed the neoprene, gauging the amount of water still trapped in the suit.

"I'd say so," Frank responded, sliding his eyes towards Asrid, who had her head stuck into the back seat of her rental car, retrieving her dry suit. Josh pursed his lips and was grateful that Asrid missed the snide snipe comment. Jon's eyes flicked back and forth between the group, catching the interchange.

"Well, it is a beautiful park. Much more pristine than Ginnie and thank goodness there's not as many people here. I enjoy the peace and solitude." Jon's comments, as usual, were designed to deflect Frank's antagonism, for which Josh was, as usual, grateful. Asrid slapped at her neck suddenly, her dry suit undergarment held in her other hand as she rose out from the side door of her car.

"Well, I don't care for the mosquito population in these woods. I'm getting eaten alive here."

"Do you even have mosquitoes in Sweden?" asked Jon.

"Yes, of course, in the summer but only in certain parts of the country. If you go up to the North or to higher altitudes you can avoid them."

"Well, there's none underwater so let's get moving," said Josh.

Chapter 34

A short time later the group descended underneath the duckweed at Orange Grove sink. Josh led the dive, followed by Frank, Jon and Asrid in the back. Their four lights danced around the open water basin underneath the duckweed ceiling. The tiny floating plants created a green gloom in the clear water, giving the illusion of being inside a cavern.

Above them their exhaust bubbles hit the surface, creating a temporary hole in the mat of floating plants. Unfiltered sunlight blazed shafts of golden light from the openings, lighting up portions of the silty bottom and reducing the visibility of covered areas as their eyes adjusted to the light. Slowly the holes would collapse as they progressed deeper into the open water basin, new holes appearing above as if a spotlight followed them.

Josh hovered over an arm-sized branch attached to a fallen tree, the wood dark with watery age and paused, looking at his dive team.

Frank, Jon and Asrid hovered behind him, dutifully shining their lights on the branch to help him attach the cavern guideline, all three in perfect horizontal cavern position. He looked to the left and up and saw Drew hovering a few feet above the class, watching, his light off.

Today Drew was deliberately transitioning from being the leader and focal point of the dives to more of an observer as he judged their ability to dive into the cavern following the rules and procedures they had been working on so far in class. Josh grimaced as well as he could with a regulator hanging from his mouth, knowing that the team and his actions would decide whether or not they earned the coveted cavern card.

He secured the end of the reel to the black branch and gave it a firm tug before circling the tie off with his light, a signal to the rest of the team that he was ready to start the cavern portion of the dive. He was rewarded with three circles of light, Asrid even having the presence of mind to make sure her brighter circle from her canister light didn't overwhelm the weaker lights of Frank and Jon.

Above him the duckweed parted into a larger circle as their combined bubbles pushed the plants and a large splash of bright sunlight shone on the tie off as if to confirm their right to be here, in this place, ready to start their cavern dive. Josh felt a moment of *right*, knowing that he felt trained, equipped and mentally ready for the adventure of the dive, giddy with the excitement of swimming into a place heretofore unknown to him.

He spun slowly in place, his helicopter turn avoiding any motions that would kick up silt, and faced into the cavern, the light springing from the light head on his right hand to pierce into the darkness. He was rewarded with a view of logs and a wall of pure white limestone. The team moved forward slowly as he worked his way down into the cavern, body parallel to the descending slope of the basin.

He felt no current but knew they had transitioned into the pure aquifer's waters when he felt the drop in temperature and the increase in visibility, which all but crackled as the four beams of artificial light passed around the floor, walls and ceiling of the cavern. Unlike the high flow sandy bottom and smoothed walls of the Ginnie Ballroom here the artistry of years of erosion had created limestone with a more intricate, delicate and curved design.

Huge boulders of white limestone dusted with fine silt were riddled with scallops of sculpted design and fluted end points. The lack of flow and clearer water gave the illusion of there being no water at all until a tiny bubble of air floated upwards and reminded him of where they were.

Josh threaded the cavern line around available objects, including logs and branches as well as helpful outcroppings of natural sculpture. He could tell by the lights behind him that his team was following him closely, allowing him to set the pace and giving him time to secure the line snugly before moving on.

Each time he went to wrap the line around something three beams would stop their lazy meanderings and focus on his workspace before returning to each owner's natural pattern of curiosity. Ahead of him the underwater cliff wall of the sink prevented forward movement. He saw a small tunnel entrance straight ahead that lead into an underwater cave and to his left the cavern dipped and bobbed along the cliff face.

He knew that the cave entrance was off limits as Drew had discussed since it quickly transitioned from the cavern zone into a true cave, with no visible light from the outside. Still he was tempted by the subway tunnel symmetry of the passage and the lack of silt or clay on the tunnel's smooth floor.

Save that for a cave class one day, hopefully.

Bisecting the floor of the cave entrance a single white line lead from the cavern zone into the mouth of the cave; evidence of the other team of divers that he had seen preparing for their cave dive in the parking lot. Their passage was indicated not only by the presence of the line but by a slight trace of suspended silt hovering near the entrance, like a trail of bread crumbs announcing the team's recent passage.

Josh wrapped the line around a rock wedged below the cave tunnel and turned to his left, the line taut in his hands. The cavern sloped down and Josh could just make out the silhouette of Drew hovering inside the cavern zone above them, his outline illuminated by the multi-hued green glow of sunlight filtered through the duckweed that had regained full control of the surface of the sink. The effect was like an underwater aurora borealis of gently shifting greens.

Sure wish I had a camera; what a beautiful picture that'd make.

Josh continued his underwater trek across the side of the cliff wall until he came upon a large area of breakdown, where boulders of limestone lay scattered about the cavern floor, some larger than him and all dusted with a fine layer of grey silt. He gingerly threaded his line within a curved outcropping on the top of the nearest boulder and looked around, hunting for a going passage.

Beneath him and to the right a black hole beckoned, large enough for a diver to pass through in single file. He peered down into the hole and caught a flash of light.

Somebody's already down there?

He looked back at the team and saw Asrid's beam pointing down into a similar hole that he had swam past.

That's Asrid's light I'm seeing - ah, the lower chamber that Drew had mentioned!

He pulled the string on the bottom left side of his wing, burping just enough air out to start a slow descent. He glided into the lower chamber, his light moving back and forth to take in the room's dimensions.

Soon all four of them were inside the chamber, which proved larger and darker than the previous part of the cavern. Josh wrapped his line around a big boulder on the floor and swam into the center of the room, his light slowly panning across.

He covered his light momentarily and was rewarded a few seconds later with the entire team also covering their lights. This way they could easily discover the amount of ambient light that came from the summer day outside.

Twin shafts of dim green light beamed down into the room from the two entrances. Satisfied that they were still within the cavern zone Josh uncovered his light and painted a large circular "OK" on the floor below him. As before, three beams circled the same area, with Asrid's having the brighter and larger diameter.

Josh swam farther into the room, using the combined lights of his team to get a sense for the size and shape of the room. The lower chamber was also a product of some ancient ceiling collapse that resulted in a jumble of large boulders strewn along the floor in a rough rectangular tilted room, where the side nearest the exits was higher than the lower edge in the back.

The room gave Josh the sensation of gently falling down a slope. He stopped, hovering, and checked both his depth and pressure.

Plenty of gas but we are almost at the one hundred foot maximum depth and turn pressure. Better call the dive.

Before he could turn and thumb the dive he saw a rapid waving of light behind him, the brightness of the light clearly Asrid's. He turned and saw only himself, Jon and Asrid on the line.

Both Jon and Asrid's lights were pointing to a trail of bubbles that rose from the jagged mouth of a pit below them.

Damn, Frank, what are you doing?

Suddenly a fifth light ignited above him and descended towards the group. Josh figured it had to be Drew, swooping in to rescue Frank and call the dive. Josh knew he was closer to Frank. He turned and pulled himself into the pit, streams of exhaust bubbles from Frank breaking against his mask.

He could see Frank's fins twenty feet below, stirring up bubbles and silt as he struggled to turn around at a ninety degree downward bend in the narrow shaft. He swam down to free Frank as a wave of dizziness and lassitude swept over him.

Damn! I'm narc'ed!

The exposure to higher concentration of Nitrogen and exertion combined to give him a nice buzz of nitrogen narcosis at a very inconvenient time.

He paused, allowing his heart rate to settle and the narcosis abated slightly. A flash of bright light caught Josh's eye and he looked back up the shaft. Above him Drew's head popped over the mouth of the pit but Josh knew there wasn't enough room for Drew to enter.

The pit was irregular, narrow and wound its way down. He stretched out and nabbed the tip of Frank's fin and gave it two sharp tugs. Frank stopped moving and he could see the outline of Frank's body through small openings in the rocky shaft. He reached down farther, grabbing Frank's calf, and squeezed reassuringly.

He felt Frank relax and began to slowly pull him up through the 90 degree bend. Frank slowly rose up through the mixture of bubbles and silt and rotated his body feet up until eventually they could see each other. Josh looked Frank in the eye and saw a sleepy narcosis-induced form of mild euphoria. He placed the line in Frank's hand, squeezed and gave him the "start" push signal, hoping that Frank's addled brain would revert to the basic behavior recently grooved into his brain in the grind of training.

Frank began to slowly work his way up the line towards the ring of anxious faces partially hidden by masks and a small cloud of suspended silt that awaited him at the mouth of the pit. Josh followed, slowly reeling in the line as all five of them hovered in place above the pit, the silt cloud suspended below them. The ascent had removed all but a small trace of the narcosis from his head. Drew gesticulated emphatically with a deliberate "thumbs up" and the team meekly started their ascent back to the surface.

Drew swam next to Frank, keeping a close eye on his behavior while Josh reeled in the cavern line. The rest of the team had the presence of mind to help remove the line wraps and placements so that Josh had little to do but concentrate on keeping the line taut, reeled in and control his buoyancy during the ascent.

By the time they reached their safety stop at twenty feet they were in the green-roofed open water and Frank had regained his composure, behaving properly to hand signals and helping the team remove the cavern reel.

Drew hovered around like a nervous flying nanny, checking dive computers and firing off hand signals to make sure everybody was OK and understood they had to wait out the required minutes at their safety depth.

Josh was the first to surface. He quickly inflated his wing to stay afloat and swam towards the stairs. The duckweed closed in around him, clinging to his arms, mask, face, equipment and any other part of him exposed to the surface. He heard the pop of exhaust as the other three members of the dive team also surfaced, followed by Drew.

"I..I...I'm so sorry," started Frank, looking towards Drew.

Drew glared, the non-obscured portion of his face beet red underneath his neoprene hood. He drew breath as if to retort hotly and blew it out instead, a violent hiss of air moving water and duckweed in front of his face.

"I'm too angry to speak right now. Get out of the water. We'll meet outside the Luraville Country Store."

Drew reached the stairs before the others, removed his fins in two quick underwater motions, and clambered onto the top of the wooden stairs. He grunted as he pulled himself up to full height, water and duckweed dripping from his dry suit and doubles. Despite the weight of water and tanks he moved deftly up the wooden stairs and disappeared along the dirt trail, never looking back.

"What the hell happened?" asked Josh, turning back to look at Frank.

"I don't know; I guess I got pretty narc'd. I saw that cool hole and wanted to explore. I really can't tell you why I decided to leave the team and swim down into it. I just recall being so thrilled and excited to be in the cavern and then to have a deep hole to explore, well…" sputtered Frank, his mask in his hand.

He waved the duckweed in front of him idly, watching it slowly encroach back.

"It's like you totally lost all rational thought, Frank," said Jon, "I've never seen you behave that way before. I tried to grab you when you decided to dart into that pit but you were too fast. You totally ignored my light signals, too."

"I tell you, I didn't do it deliberately! It's like I was drunk or something," muttered Frank, despair clinging to his words.

Asrid stuffed her mask into one fin pocket and her hood into the other and placed them gently on the bottom wooden stair. She looked over at Frank. "I think you were heavily narc'd. What's the deepest you guys have been before?"

Josh considered the question, recalling his history of dives with his buddies. "Um, I don't think we've been any deeper than about eighty feet."

"Well, that's probably it – you all know there is variance with nitrogen narcosis between individuals" – all three men nodded their heads – "perhaps you, Frank, are just more susceptible to narcosis than the rest of us."

Frank frowned, clearly not happy with the thought of being weaker than everybody else at something.

"I was narc'd when I went into the pit and grabbed you, Frank," admitted Josh, "so it definitely is a real phenomenon. It went away once we got out of that pit into shallower water."

"So, how do I counteract it? Am I doomed to not dive safely beyond one hundred feet?" Frank made the question sound like a challenge to the world, as in how dare the world be a place where he didn't excel at everything.

"That's simple – just reduce the amount of nitrogen in your air supply, especially if you plan on going deeper than eighty feet," said Asrid, as she wiggled out of the water onto the bottom stair.

Frank shivered. Josh, feeling the cold himself, swam over to the edge of the stairs behind Asrid and started his slow slither from the watery world back to the dry world. It felt primeval and difficult as gravity pushed the heavy tanks onto his back.

"Well, let's get out, warm up, and give Drew some time to settle down. He was furious. I sure hope he doesn't kick you out of class,

Frank," gasped Josh as he hoisted himself up the stairs.

Frank was uncharacteristically quiet as he removed his fins and reached for the first stair.

Chapter 35

An hour later the group of four sat huddled together, unusually quiet around a heavily weathered picnic table next to the Luraville Country Store, their stomachs full of lunch yet minds empty of thought. The store, besides having the typical convenience store products, boasted a deli where fresh sandwiches were made.

A large map of the springs of the Suwanee River graced the exterior wall next to the line of picnic tables. The parking lot was half full of the lunch crowd vehicles, most from cave divers enjoying the springs sprinkled along the river as documented on the fading painted wall map.

The parking spot nearest their picnic table was occupied by Asrid's white rental car, which provided the most comfortable way for all four of them to travel together from Peacock Springs a short few miles to the east, a trip that had also been cloaked in contemplative silence.

A mild breeze signaled the transition from the calm of the morning to a summer afternoon that promised slow-moving low altitude cotton ball shaped white clouds and relatively low humidity for this locale and time of year. Despite the doom and gloom of the class Josh was at least grateful for the weather.

"When do you think Drew will speak to us?" asked Jon. Josh, sitting next to Jon and across from Asrid, responded.

"He knows we are out here. He saw us come into and out of the store to pick up our lunches. I imagine he'll come out when he's ready to deliver his verdict about the class."

Frank pushed away his half-eaten lunch and sighed heavily.

"Damn, guys, guess I've finally let you down for once. Gotta admit it's difficult for me to believe it's come down to this." He bunched up the remains of his lunch in the protective wax paper and tossed it into the nearby trash can, the ersatz ball bouncing off of the plastic-lined rim.

"Geez, it's just not my day," said Frank as he stood up, swooped up the lunch remains and slammed it into the trash, a rattling thud of subdued metal echoing up through the top of the can.

"No, it's not."

Josh turned his head to see Drew approaching from the front of the store. His sunglasses hid any sign of emotion as he approached the table. His damp hair was combed straight back, giving the illusion of an angry police officer approaching a miscreant. Frank sat back down next to Asrid, eyes staring at the rental car instead of at Drew.

Asrid shuffled closer to Frank and patted the bench next to her, indicating that Drew could sit by her if he cared to. Josh knew it was bad when Frank didn't rise to the bait as Asrid accidentally bumped against him in her haste to offer Drew a place to sit.

"No, I'll stand." Drew crossed his arms.

Asrid looked quickly at Frank and moved back towards her side of the bench, as if to distance herself from the focus of bad news.

"OK, Frank, convince me why I shouldn't just kick you out of class right now," challenged Drew.

Frank turned to Drew and straightened his back, regaining a semblance of his usual confident self.

"The way we figure it I was pretty narc'd. I was too under the influence of excess Nitrogen to make rational decisions."

Drew rocked back on his heels, his right hand coming up to his chin, a bemused expression on his face.

"Oh, really? That's what you think it was? You sure it had nothing to do with your cowboy style? You've been skating on thin ice since the class began."

Josh interrupted, "Maybe you two should talk in private?"

Drew turned to Josh, his eyes unreadable behind the sunglasses. Light glinted off the lenses as the sun started down towards the west on its daily trip. Behind him a mud-covered pickup truck with monster wheels squealed out onto the two-lane highway, the whoops of bare-chested young southern men matching the volume of sound from the distressed tires.

"No, you all dive as a team. You need to hear everything that makes a team succeed or fail."

"Look, Drew, I know Frank can be a real pain in the ass. Especially when he opens his mouth. But he's always tried to do the right thing when it comes to diving." Josh rose to his friend's defense.

"Lord knows sometimes he's more trouble than he's worth but he's my friend and I believe him when he says he got narc'd and acted irrationally," offered Jon earnestly.

"I can appreciate your allegiance, guys, but are you willing to bet your lives on it? Frank left the line, busted the max depth, ignored his buddies' signals and almost got stuck in a cave restriction. Think of all the rules of cavern and cave diving he broke! That sound like the kind of a buddy you want to dive with?"

Drew leaned forward. "I am not only judging Frank by his actions but all of you in your ability to make proper judgments in and out of a cavern or cave."

Drew removed his sunglasses and looked at each of their faces. "You have to be willing to make rational non-emotional choices about who you choose to dive with and who you choose not to dive with and why. I can't, in good conscience, allow all of you to pass this cavern class if you can't show the ability to even pick dive buddies that have the proper attitude and concern for their own safety as well as that of the team."

He punctuated each sentence with his sunglasses, speaking slowly and deliberately, stabbing at each of them through the air with the glasses, the lenses flashing occasionally with the reflection of the sun.

Frank, who had been openly looking at Drew during his monologue, finally broke contact and looked down at the table, his shoulders slumped. Josh thought he had the look of a man beaten, all but ready to quit the class on his own accord to save his buddies from failure.

"I have an idea," said Asrid quietly, her lips pursed. Drew lowered his sunglass arm and nodded to her.

"I think we should redo that dive but let Frank dive Nitrox instead of air. I think the lower amount of Nitrogen in the Nitrox will keep the narcosis at a minimum so he can still keep himself in control. If he starts to behave irrationally then we can call the dive and exit."

Josh looked across the table – Asrid struck a pose of earnest honesty, trying to find a way out for Frank. Jon and Frank both held a mixed expression of hope and fear on their faces.

"That's a great idea. We are all three Nitrox certified already," offered Josh.

"So why haven't you been diving Nitrox all along?" said Drew, his tone making it clear he still wasn't convinced this was a good idea.

"It's more expensive than air, especially in Tallahassee," said Frank, frowning. Josh knew what he meant; at *Wakulla Skuba* every time he sold a tank of Nitrox it meant dumping all of the air in the tank and filling it from scratch with just the right amount of pure Oxygen and compressed air to reach the desired Nitrox mix. It cost twice as much as an air fill, was labor intensive and not really needed by most of the spearfishers in his area.

"You mean you've never bought Nitrox around here? Most of the caves around here have a one hundred foot profile so all of the cave diving shops, like FWCD, pre-mix 34% Nitrox and charge only by the volume sold," offered Drew.

"Um, you never offered up that information," Josh spoke quietly.

Drew glared at Josh for a second, shifted his weight from foot to foot and twiddled with his sunglasses briefly before answering.

"Well, right you are. I never did mention it during class. Shame, too, seeing as how we sell it right there at FWCD. Guess I figured it's common knowledge. Are you so sure that a lower partial pressure of Nitrogen will reduce Narcosis? Not everybody agrees on that."

Asrid spoke, "It's certainly been my experience in cold deep Swedish waters that I get less narc'd when diving Nitrox over air to the same depth. What's your experience, Drew?"

Drew allowed a small smile to creep onto his lips. "Well, yes, I agree, Asrid; it does reduce narcosis for me as well, despite what some of the books say." Josh sensed that Drew was enjoying this battle of diving wits between himself and his students. Despite his curmudgeonly ways and anger against Allen and Kathy he was an educator first and foremost.

"So," Drew spoke slowly, "you'd all be willing to risk passing the class by doing another dive with Frank? Knowing if it goes badly and I have to intervene that you will all fail the class?"

Frank looked around the table, a pained expression on his face. "Hey, guys, no; it's not worth losing your shot at a cavern rating. Think of all the wasted money and time if I screw up again. Besides, there's no guarantee that diving Nitrox will work. Go dive without me."

Josh looked over at Jon, who gave him a knowing nod. He looked over at Asrid questioningly. She gave him a slight nod graced with a small smile.

"Consider us the underwater musketeers, Drew. All for one and one for all. We'll accept your terms and dive with Frank under those conditions," said Josh.

"Are you guys sure?" Frank responded.

Asrid placed her hand on Frank's arm and looked him in the eye. "Yes, Frank, we are a team united. I have faith in you and in our diving knowledge and experience. We are making the right choice," explained Asrid.

Frank beamed a crooked smile, his self confidence partially restored.

"OK, Frank, tell you what – you get some 34% Nitrox and we'll do that same dive, right back to the mouth of that pit. Just to make it interesting you'll run the reel, too. I want you to constantly be mentally challenged during the dive so even the slightest slip from narcosis will be immediately evident to everybody."

The students all looked at each other, a small smile growing on their lips. They all turned to Drew and nodded vigorously. Drew nodded in return.

"OK, then, see you back at Orange Grove in sixty minutes. You can get Nitrox at that dive shop between here and Peacock Springs."

He jammed his glasses back on his face and spun on his heels, heading back to his white van parked nearby.

"Wow. That was amazing. Nicely done, Asrid," said Jon.

Frank turned to Asrid, momentarily shy and murmured a quick thanks to her as well. She rewarded him with a quick hug which he returned without misbehaving. Josh chuckled at the exchange, his head still dancing with the new chance for redemption.

"Let's go get that Nitrox," he said, rising from the bench.

Chapter 36

Two hours later Josh hovered in the lower chamber, watching Frank work the cavern reel around the room. Drew hovered up higher, near the ceiling, the lord of the dark. Josh was last in line, followed by Asrid, Jon and Frank, who had successfully navigated them back into the cavern zone in less time and effort than had Josh during the first dive.

Frank passed over the top of the pit, giving it a slow, deliberate "OK" circle of light, to show he was in complete control and not suffering from narcosis. They meandered over to the far end of the room before Frank called the dive. Just as they turned to leave Drew descended from the ceiling, flashing a small backup light, and gave the "lights out – get into touch contact and follow the line out" signal.

Josh groaned, knowing it would take longer to work their way out without the advantage of vision. He also, though, had complete confidence that the four of them could successfully navigate over the silty rocks and through the single file restriction with little muss and fuss.

He flicked off his light, clipped the light head to the D-ring on the right side of his harness, turned towards the exit, "OK'd" the line with his thumb and forefinger and closed his eyes, hovering slightly off the line.

A few seconds later he felt the familiar push from Asrid signaling it was time for the human train to start the exit from the cavern zone. The team ascended uneventfully.

His head broke the surface among the thick duckweed, soon followed by his mouth breaking into a smile as his other team members surfaced alongside him. Regulators left mouths and masks left faces as they all tried to talk at once.

"Awesome!"

"We nailed that exit!"

"I didn't see a bit of silt kicked up after we opened our eyes again!"

"Thank God for Nitrox!"

They waited patiently as Drew cleared his nose, duckweed clinging to the tip. He brushed it off absentmindedly and rinsed his hand in the cool spring water.

"OK, guys, that was nicely done. Frank, I do believe breathing Nitrox saved you at the max depth. I must admit that's the first time I've seen Nitrox save an entire class, though." A small smile erupted on Drew's face. Josh felt the warm glow of a job well done permeate the group, almost strong enough to beat back the ever-encroaching duckweed.

"But, we aren't done yet. You still owe me one more cavern dive and then we have the exam to do," finished Drew. The smiles all disappeared as the duckweed closed in inexorably.

Chapter 37

Five hours later the group sat around the familiar weathered bench outside the Luraville Country Store. The sun flickered through the line of pine trees in the west, throwing shades of gold across their exam papers. The mild breeze turned up the edge of the occasional piece of paper, threatening to blow them off the table and onto the grey carpet of loose rocks that formed the parking lot.

Josh removed his watch and placed it on top of his exam to protect it from the wayward wind. He sat at one end of the picnic table, facing out towards the parking lot, where Drew's white van sat next to Asrid's rental sedan.

Josh's own blue pickup truck wore a light coat of white limestone dust from the dirt roads at Peacock Springs; the tires painted a dingy white from the same dust. The windshields of all three vehicles displayed dried-up swaths of clear glass surrounded by white speckled dust in the patterns of windshield wipers, looking like giant happy eyes. Next to Josh sat Asrid and Jon.

Frank sat across and next to Drew, who was busily scribbling on class paperwork. The only sounds came from the gentle rustling of papers, the scratching of Drew's pen and the swoosh of the occasional passing car. All of the students were quiet, lost in their own thoughts as Drew continued with his paperwork.

Josh could feel a growing sense of anticipation. Soon the class would be over and their hard-earned cavern ratings handed over, hopefully. For now, though, they all waited for the final verdict.

His mind slipped back to the excitement of Frank's first Nitrox cavern dive and the feeling of accomplishment as the team had completed another cavern dive, this time with Asrid running the reel. Drew had continually swooped down from above, unseen until betrayed by his backup light. He sprung drill after drill after drill on the team in a frenzy on the last dive.

At one point, eyes closed with Asrid holding on to his knee and tucked beside Jon's elbow he had thought that Drew was purposefully over drilling the team with a vengeance, as if daring them to make a mistake that would cause them to fail or lose their cool.

Thankfully the hours Drew had spent teaching and refining their cavern skills had really paid off and the team brushed off each of the drills as a minor inconvenience, like wiping duckweed from a mask. Frank had behaved like a perfect gentleman above water and dive team member underwater.

Josh looked back down at his graded exam and again felt relief knowing that his 85% was a passing grade. All of the team had passed the exam and had endured Drew reviewing all of the missed answers.

Josh appreciated that while scuba exams tended to be very straight forward and geared towards anybody with at least an eighth grade education it was important that the instructor reviewed every wrong answer and probe the student to make sure that they understood why they got it wrong and the underlying principle that the question was evaluating.

He had assisted Kathy in many an open water class test review and had the answers to her exam pretty much memorized by now, including the justifications for the answers.

The cavern exam, though, mirrored the physical skills they had learned. It wasn't enough to just stick a reg in your mouth and be told not ever hold your breath (the essence of every beginner's scuba class) but to master all of the cavern underwater skills to a higher standard. The written exam was no different and his brain was pretty fried from answering and reviewing the class's missed questions in great detail.

Naturally Jon had scored the highest, followed by Asrid, himself and Frank, who had seen fit to challenge Drew's grading on each question he had gotten wrong, to no avail. At least Drew had demonstrated great patience as he re-explained the underlying theory behind each of Frank's missed questions.

Drew flipped through the pile of official-looking paperwork, double checking his work and, seemingly satisfied, tap shuffled them and set them on the table, hands crossed on top to keep them secure from the breeze. He looked across the anxious faces of his students, a neutral expression on his own face.

"OK, guys, I've reviewed all of your work – the results of the written exam, your individual performance during the dives and your performance as a team."

He looked directly at Frank for a moment before continuing.

"I must admit that this class has been a challenge for me based on today's dives. There comes a point in time during a class where I have to decide whether each of you is not only capable of diving in a cavern but that you are also capable of choosing the right type of dive team members. Frank, the night and day difference between your earlier dive and later dives on Nitrox proved to be most troublesome to me.

"While I admire your moxy to try again after such a disastrous failure of the rules and your team's perhaps misguided loyalty to you I still have concerns."

Drew frowned and waited, letting the words sink in. Josh felt his heart sink along with the words; maybe none of them had passed after all. He didn't dare look at any of his dive mates. Drew raised his fingers as they rested on the table, the two index fingers steepling together as if he was a priest performing last rites over their dead class.

"This class has been designed to test your underwater mettle as an individual and as a team. This may be the last time we speak so I want to make sure to take this last opportunity to impress upon each of you the need to respect the underwater overhead environment. Pay attention to the rules you have had drilled into you.

"You have literally learned how to dive safely in a cavern from rules built on the mistakes of others, some of whom have paid with their lives. You are human. You will make mistakes in the future, sometimes while in a cavern. Just be sure that you've followed all of the rules and procedures you've learned in this class to lessen the risk."

Another pause. Drew looked each of them in the eye for a full second before moving on to the next.

"Answer me now. Do each of you feel that you are trained to safely dive in a cavern?"

Josh waited, not sure if Drew required a response and croaked out a "yes" just to be safe. The others nodded or murmured their assents.

Drew reached underneath the pile of papers and pulled out tiny light yellow envelopes. Josh could see "Asrid" hand scrawled on the outside of the top envelope. Drew handed out the envelopes, dropping one in front of each of them.

"Well, don't just sit there. Open them up," said Drew, his face still passive and inscrutable.

Josh picked up his envelope and slid open the unsealed top. He squeezed the sides of the envelope and looked inside. The edge of a bright red card revealed itself sandwiched inside the envelope. He shook it out and the credit card sized object dropped onto his exam.

He picked it up and examined both sides. On one side he saw his name – Josh Jensen – Rating: Cavern Diver, along with his height, weight, eye color and today's date. On the back was Instructor: Drew Thompson along with the name of the cave diving agency that issued the card.

Josh looked up, a huge grin on his face. He looked around and saw matching smiles on the other's faces, even Drew's.

"Wow! Yes, we passed!" whooped Jon, high fiving Frank across the table. Josh nudged his hip into Asrid, who pushed back and smiled warmly at him. They laughed and slapped open palms around the table.

"Yes, you all passed. Congratulations and don't forget to dive safe," said Drew, "Well, if you don't have any further questions I'll be getting back home."

"Yeah, why is our height, weight and eye color on the card?" inquired Jon, holding up his card.

"Same reason it's usually on your driver's license. It helps with body identification." Drew's response was matter of fact.

Josh's jaw dropped slightly. The four former students looked at each other incredulously.

"Well, that's a bummer. Let's hope it never gets used for that," Frank opined dryly. The group tittered nervously and the moment passed.

Josh stood up with Drew and reached out his hand, grasping Drew's and pumping it enthusiastically.

"Thanks so much, Drew. It was an awesome class. You did a great job," he gushed, releasing Drew's hand.

Each of the others shook Drew's hands as well and offered similar expressions of gratitude. Drew gracefully accepted their thanks, said goodbye, opened up the door on the driver's side of his white van and slowly backed out of the gravel driveway.

He turned to the east, gave two quick horn blasts and trundled off, vortices of limestone dust trailing from the back. The group waved as he departed and dropped their hands as he crossed through the intersection and headed home.

"Well, sort of anticlimactic now, isn't it?" said Frank, gathering up his card and paperwork.

Jon, looking over his card, responded "I'm just glad it's over and that we have the cards. Cavern certified. Sweet!"

Josh felt a swell of pride for himself and the team. "I'm really proud of you guys. It's been a long tough couple of weeks but we did it!" He looked at Asrid and realized this may be the last he'd see of her.

"So, Asrid, you heading back to Sweden soon?"

She looked up at him and he thought he detected a slight wistful look in her face, as if she was also sad the class was over.

"I still have a few weeks left in my holiday," she started.

"Hey, you should come dive with us next weekend!" blurted Jon.

"No, that's not possible. I have commitments to travel with friends down to South Beach and the Keys. Perhaps the week after that?" she offered.

"Sounds good. Here's my number if you head back up this way before you leave the country," said Josh.

Josh wrote down his phone number on a blank corner of his exam and tore it off, handing it to Asrid. She looked at the number, satisfied it was legible and stuck it in the front pocket of her tight blue jean shorts.

"Give me a call when you are free and we'll see if we can coordinate a dive. We are going cavern diving next weekend, right guys?"

"Of course!" said Frank, "Now that we have the license let's use it."

"Well, you guys have fun. I'll be thinking of you. Don't forget to dive safe," said Asrid, reaching out to hug Josh. He embraced her, inhaling the scent of womanly sweat, limestone dust and a whiff of leafy duckweed fragrance. He patted her back heartily, rubbed it gently and pulled back. She whispered in his ear, "Good luck with your girlfriend."

Josh responded out loud, "It was a pleasure diving with you Asrid. I hope we get to dive with you again someday."

The words sounded awkwardly formal but were the best he could manage in the swirl of emotions going through his head. First the near failure of the entire class, followed by a stellar performance by all and the final emotional release when Drew announced they had all passed.

He had gotten used to Asrid's stable presence on the team, her diving acumen and the pleasure of her physical beauty. Perhaps in another time, another place he could have pursued her romantically and had it reciprocated.

Asrid squeezed his hands, tilted her head and offered him a wry smile before releasing his hands and turning to hug Jon and Frank. They chatted as they packed up the rest of their class detritus, sputtered rehashing of the class events swirling through the threads of conversation as the excitement started to wear off.

Soon Asrid was waving goodbye through her open window as her white sedan turned southward at the intersection. The three of them piled into his truck and started their long trek back to Tallahassee, the glow of the sunset below the tree line illuminating the base of the clouds; a beacon towards home.

Chapter 38

Josh tapped nervously on Elise's apartment door, still wondering if this was the right thing to do. She had not answered any of his phone calls over the weekend and since his return. He paused, listening for any movement. Her car sat parked outside the apartment, illuminated in a harsh pool of mercury vapor light from a nearby streetlight so he knew more than likely she had to be home. He had driven straight from Jon and Frank's apartment after unloading their gear, promising to celebrate over dinner at the *Watering Hole* some night during the week.

Elise cracked open the door and glumly looked out at Josh. Her short raven black hair hung loose on her shoulders and she wore a full length pink robe, her sash tightly cinched around her waist and arms secured on the wide lapels.

"What do you want?" Her voice was flat and unemotional.

"Can I come in to talk? Please?"

She frowned and moved out of the way. He walked into the apartment and paused as she brushed past him to close the door. Sensing his uncertainty she waved him towards the couch. Josh sat on one end of the couch and was disappointed when she chose to sit on the other end, slightly facing him.

She tucked her legs under the robe and snugged it tighter, reinforcing the look of being aloof, distant and untouchable. She had removed her makeup, about to take a shower. Josh admired how her clear complexion, rosy lips and natural eye accents still gave her a fresh look even without makeup.

"Elise, I've been trying to reach you for days. Why didn't you answer the phone or return my calls?"

"I've not wanted to talk to you, remember? Since you decided to continue with your dangerous diving class," she said, tone still flat.

Josh's heart sank. Her beauty flickered through her reserved demeanor.

"Yeah, well, I finished my 'dangerous' class and nobody got hurt. Imagine that."

He couldn't help pounding on her lassitude, trying to get more of a reaction out of her. At least that might mean she still cares. She just glared back at him.

"I'm sorry. That was mean. But I did pass the class and was hoping that you would be supportive." Her glare and posture remained unchanged.

"Look, Elise, I love you and want to be with you. Can't we just agree to disagree on my diving?"

Elise inhaled and sighed deeply, a small frown crinkling the skin around her mouth.

"I'm sorry, Josh. It's like I told you before. I'm done worrying about you."

Josh swallowed, a knot growing in his throat. His vision blurred slightly with nascent tears.

"So this is it? We are breaking up?"

"I love you too, Josh. I just can't get over your diving, especially now that you are certified to dive in caverns. I just can't."

Tears started to slowly slide down her smooth cheeks.

"I can't see you anymore, at least not now. If you want to call it a break up, well, that's your choice."

He felt like reaching over and wrapping her in his arms, murmuring that it would be OK and that she would accept him back, sans robe. Instead he stood and looked at her. She looked back from the couch, still in a defensive closed posture.

"I..I..I don't know what to say other than goodbye, Elise. It's frustrating, though. It's like you are breaking up with me but you still have strong feelings for me."

"Let me make it easier, then, Josh. We are no longer a couple. You are free to go dive or date where ever you want with whomever you want. Please leave now."

Her words cut acidly into his ears and straight to his heart. Rebuffed, he stepped back, rocked on his heels slightly and quickly wiped the edges of both eyes. He took one last look at her, devastated by her decision. He had hoped that she would be happy for him, even if she didn't agree with cavern diving. He hoped that their love would withstand their differences and that even if she didn't like it she could learn to respect it.

Without another word he turned, strode to the door of her apartment and left, closing the door softly behind him.

Chapter 39

The back porch of the *Watering Hole* restaurant was bustling with patrons of food and the arts. Emilio and Cameron, the owners of *River Art*, sat at a table near the entrance to the restaurant, chatting excitedly with a throng of art lovers.

At their feet lay Chestnut, her tail thumping gently as she enjoyed the stream of petting from admiring dog lovers. All of the tables on the porch had been pulled towards the center of the room and long tables had been set up along the entire interior perimeter.

Each table held various collections of art work from *River Art*, showcasing local painters and sculptors, including works by Emilio and Cameron.

This was their annual charity art auction and dinner known locally as "Raw Hole" (*River Art at the Watering HOLE*). The porch was packed with people milling around the perimeter, admiring the art and making the occasional auction bid on sheets of paper placed at each table.

Others sat at the exterior tables, enjoying the edible artwork of Mike and Sue. Light strains of classical music could be heard occasionally over the burbling of human voices.

The weather had cooperated, with spring-like temperatures, a soft breeze and low humidity. The ceiling fans were all dialed on low, ensuring that the food stayed warm and the diners cool. Some of the larger displays were illuminated by strategically-placed spotlights while the rest were visible from the usual string of festive lights around the perimeter.

Josh sat at a table near the dock, next to the screen door. Sue had reserved a table for his group out of professional courtesy. She knew that Kathy usually picked up a piece or two of art for *Wakulla Skuba*; the turtle clock in the classroom being an example. Josh admired this year's lineup of art.

The tables depicted the usual collection of paintings inspired by the wild river and estuarine environment. Sunset paintings of the tree-lined Wakulla River dominated the offerings, each reflecting the individual style and method of the artist.

Josh especially enjoyed a painting of Big Dismal Sink, a steep-walled sink hole only a few miles away. The large painting depicted the lush overgrowth hanging into the sink with a variety of greens and yellows while the perfectly round sink hole glowed a brilliant blue, hinting at the promise of refreshing deep clear water beneath.

The artist had enhanced the natural beauty of the dramatic sink hole by combining the realism of the water with impressionistic flora.

The effect drew the viewer's focus into the darkening blue waters.

Around the table Frank, Jon and Kathy enjoyed their beers. Bear sat on Kathy's lap, his attention drawn to the extra sights and smells of the special occasion, evidenced by the constant head swiveling and nose quivering. Kathy absentmindedly stroked his soft triangular ears.

"Congratulations on your cavern certifications, guys. Cheers!" spoke Kathy, raising her glass towards the center of the table, over the glass-enclosed lit candle. Three glasses of beer clinked against hers, followed by simultaneous swallows from four glasses.

"You were right, Kathy, that was the hardest scuba class I've ever taken," said Josh, setting his glass down next to his empty plate.

"Just remember what Drew taught you – be safe," intoned Kathy, leaning forward slightly in her chair for emphasis. Bear sat in the curve of her chest and lap, a tense expression on his face, a canine punctuation mark.

"Yeah, we'll be safe, don't you worry, Kathy," said Frank, waving his hand airily.

Kathy frowned and continued, "Time for me to make the rounds looking for a nice piece of art for the shop. See you guys later."

She slid back her chair and Bear hopped down, timing his leap perfectly to minimize the distance traveled to the ground. He trotted after Kathy as she walked over to Emilio and Cameron's table.

"So, guys, I have a place picked out for Saturday," Frank started, leaning forwarding in a conspiratorial fashion.

"So where?" said Jon.

Frank looked around to see if anybody else was within earshot before announcing triumphantly, "Emerald Sink!"

"Whoa. Emerald? I thought that was off limits?" Jon questioned.

Josh could hear a chorus of oohs and ahhs from the closest table where a recently-purchased wooden sculpture of a manatee was being admired.

Frank grinned. "Turns out one of my regular customers knows a guy that can get us into the sink without any trouble."

"What's the dive profile like for Emerald?" asked Jon.

Josh thought a moment and recalled a discussion he'd had with some local divers in the shop some time ago.

"Emerald is a true sink hole with no obvious water flow. I think it's sort of like Orange Grove where the green surface makes the clear water underneath look emerald-colored," Josh said.

"Supposed to be a youngish sink with steep walls, a large debris cone that rises to sixty feet and a huge cavern zone that has eroded out over many years. There's a cave entrance around sixty feet on one of the walls and a deep cave section that goes down to one hundred sixty feet, maybe deeper," he finished.

"That sounds like it's within our training range, as long as we keep within the limits of natural light and don't go too deep," said Frank, "Kinda sounds like Orange Grove but a heck of a lot larger. My friend says he did a sneak dive in it a few years back and that it was awesome; just huge."

Josh could see the sparkle in Frank's eyes at the thought of diving such a gem. He felt the same tug; diving into what for them was an unknown place of underwater beauty. Still, he felt that they really had to show they understood their limits of their equipment, training and judgment.

"OK, I'm up for it, Frank. We're gonna dive it by the book, though."

Jon nodded in agreement and added, "It's close to town too. I really like that part."

"That sounds like a great idea, Jon. Josh, if Elise isn't working you could invite her to come see how safe cavern diving can be," prodded Frank.

Josh frowned. "We broke up," he said simply.

Jon returned the frown. "Oh, sorry to hear that, Josh, I really liked her."

"Forget about her. She never could get used to your diving. Her loss."

Frank's logic was typically blunt but Josh could appreciate a modicum of the wisdom. He missed her still and needed time to heal from severing that emotional attachment.

Sue walked up and gathered up the remains of their meal.

"Another round, guys?"

"No, thanks, Sue. Gotta get going anyway and after last weekend I'm pretty broke anyway," said Josh. He slung down the last of his beer, set the empty glass on the table and leaned to his right to pull out his wallet.

"Oh, don't worry about your bill, guys. Kathy paid it. She said it was her present to you for passing your class. Congratulations, Cavern Kings." Sue beamed.

Josh looked over at Kathy still talking to Emilio and Cameron. She caught his eye and he waved, mouthing a "thanks". She returned a silent welcome, smiled broadly and returned to her conversation.

"OK, I'll pick you guys up at ten AM on Sunday," said Josh while he stood.

"Yep, see you then," chimed in Jon. Frank nodded and slapped

Josh a high five as he walked away.

Chapter 40

Josh walked to the edge of the sink, looking down. The surface of Emerald sink looked dark and murky with no hint of green, not at all what he had expected. The sink was mostly circular, some fifty feet across and surrounded by a smattering of live oak, sweet gum and loblolly pine trees, all in late summer dark greens.

A large live oak dominated the northwestern corner. A rope swing dangled from a large branch that hung over the water. Six inch blocks of pine two by fours nailed crookedly into the tree trunk every foot led up to a two foot plank of lumber mounted twenty feet up.

A rough steep trail that started in the south east corner of the sink lead from the sandy dirt road down to a white exposed outcropping of limestone that jutted out from the side of the sink.

The water surface was still and cluttered with brown oak leaves, which broke up the brown-tinted reflection of the shrubs and trees. He could see the outline of water-logged branches barely floating on the surface. Damselflies danced and water striders scurried across the surface. The sink was far back enough from the paved road to mask all but the loudest vehicles as they drove by. The air smelled of pine sap, earth and the faintly musky odor of the tannic water. Cicadas burred rhythmically and bird chirps filled the still morning humid air.

"Doesn't look too great," he said.

Frank and Jon stood to each side, peering down.

"Yeah, well, maybe it'll clear up when we descend," said Frank hopefully.

Jon picked up a small limestone rock and threw it into the center of the sink. They watched as the rock fluttered down four feet, changing color from white to beige to dark brown before disappearing, the ripples from its entry into the water distorting the image.

"Hmm, it still doesn't look all that great," repeated Josh.

He thought for a moment about how to safely dive this place. "Let's give it a shot. We can always call the dive if the visibility isn't good enough. I'll run the reel and we'll tie off to a branch or a root along the shore so we'll have a guideline out of the water."

He turned back to his truck parked alongside the sink and began to prepare his dive gear.

Thirty minutes later they picked their way carefully down the south side of the sink, using an old frayed rope tied off to a tree root that swimmers had installed years ago to pull themselves out. Josh moved slowly, finding sandy flat spots among the tangle of roots and pine straw.

His face poured with sweat from the mental and physical exertion of the effort.

Getting pretty warm in this wet suit. Gotta get into that water soon, he thought.

He held his fins in his left hand, mask and dive hood pushed into the fin pockets while his right hand slid down the swimmer's rope.

"Hurry up, slow poke. The mosquitoes are eating me up," said Frank, who scampered behind Josh. His and Jon's single tank systems were much lighter. Josh looked back at Frank and Jon behind him, shaking his head to sling sweat from his eye brows.

"You're killing me, Frank. You know how heavy these tanks are."

Frank swiped his face with his right hand, his fins swaying with the motion.

"Yeah, well, I'm burning up here."

"Me too. Here, hold my fins while I get into the water."

Josh had reached the edge of the water and could see that somebody had built a small three-step stair perched half submerged on a limestone ledge visible through the tea colored tannic water a foot below the surface. He handed his fins to Frank and grunted as he gingerly stepped on the top stair.

The rickety structure wobbled but held his weight. Satisfied that he could continue, he slowly walked down the remaining two stairs onto the limestone ledge. His neoprene dive boots stirred up white-grey clouds of silt as he stepped farther out. The cold water seeped into the top of his dive boots.

"OK, looks like we'll just have to inflate and float out to put our fins on. There's not enough room here to stand and it's not deep enough anyway. Give me my fins back, please."

Frank leaned over and handed Josh his fins while Jon held onto the swimmer's rope with one hand and the top of Frank's tank with the other. Josh pushed his power inflator button with his left hand, firmly grasped his fins in his right and stepped out over the limestone ledge into the sink.

He bobbed slightly underwater, the chill of the water washing off the sweat from his face and providing relief as it flowed within his wet suit, before breaking the surface. He shook the excess water off of his face and kicked slowly back towards the submerged ledge, working his way to the left side so Frank and Jon would have room to enter the sink.

He waited while first Frank and Jon repeated his entry, turning his head away as the splash of their entries washed over his head.

"Man, that feels much better," said Jon as the three of them floated next to the limestone ledge, clutching the bottom of the stair for support. They took turns pulling on their dive fins and masks while the others held their remaining equipment. Soon all three were fully geared and testing their regulators and dive lights; the sounds of hissing regulators filling the pine forest. They quickly did a safety check and air share drills on the surface before calculating their turn pressures.

Josh removed his long hose regulator from his mouth, satisfied it was working properly. The team had drifted towards the center of the sink. Josh swam back over to the limestone ledge, pulled out his cavern reel and attached it to the base of the small ladder.

"OK, me, then Jon and you're in the back, Frank. Looks like we'll have to follow the line for a while." He looked doubtfully down into the water. He could barely make out his fins five feet below in the dark red brown water as he sculled them gently. "If it doesn't clear up I'll just turn around and we'll follow the line back to here."

Jon nodded and Frank acknowledged the plan by turning on his flashlight. Josh adjusted his mask, placed his regulator back in his mouth, purged some air out of his wing and started to sink slowly below the surface, slightly apprehensive. So far this dive was a lot different than any of their training dives.

Josh watched as the vertical limestone ledge slowly disappeared into a reddish brown haze of water until the only reference he had was the white line from his reel angling up towards the surface. The ambient light faded into a dark reddish-brown tint as he descended, a faint flavor of earthy tea-like tannins seeping onto his palate.

He continued downward, occasionally looking back to see a dim spot of moving light that had to be Jon following the line down. He could feel movement on the line as well.

Not much of a dive; if this doesn't clear up I'll just turn around.

He squinted at his depth gauge. Twenty feet and the surface light had all but faded, leaving him in a deep, dark red gloom.

Suddenly he felt the water temperature drop a few degrees and the visibility go from near zero to hundreds of feet below him.

Wow. This is so beautiful!

He stopped his descent, hovering a few feet below the ceiling of the tannic water and decided to wait for the rest of the team. He moved his light head slowly around, pointing down into the cavern zone. Before him he could clearly see a huge mound of silt with a tree trunk standing upright in the center.

The tops of the tree trunk disappeared into the base of the tannic water cloud. At the base of the tree was a jumble of branches, all finely dusted with a layer of black-grey silt.

Josh spun around slowly and turned his head back up to watch as Jon descended through the tannic cloud, curlicues of tea-colored water streaming off of his gear and body.

Josh heard the *gasp* through Jon's regulator as he too took in the natural underwater beauty of the huge cavern zone. He gave Jon an "OK", which Jon returned, and he looked behind as Frank also descended into the clear water. Soon the cavern zone was full of enthusiastic light signals as they all shared in the excitement of discovering such clear water after twenty feet of near-mud conditions.

Josh pointed towards the dead tree perched on the top of the silt mound and glided downward to the base of the tree. He wrapped the line around the eight inch diameter trunk of the tree, which was black from years of being submerged and spongy to the touch. From this vantage point he could see the extent of the cavern zone easier. Above, the roughly circular cap of dark brown tannic water provided a muted source of dim amber light.

He could make out more details as his eyes were now fully adjusted to the darkness. The jagged limestone white walls of the cavern initially matched the size of the sink hole on the surface but as the depth increased the walls spread out and away evenly until they disappeared at the edge of his light's penetration. It was like diving in a wine bottle; the deeper they went the wider the cavern zone grew.

Josh looked at his depth gauge – sixty feet – and began reeling out the cavern line from the tree, heading towards the closest wall, some hundred feet away. The other two followed his lead, their lights dancing from side to side with the occasional beam pointing towards the bottom.

Josh realized that the bottom dipped down as they swam away from the tree in the center. The side of the mound transitioned from a smooth uniform pile of dirt to a field of stark white limestone fingers that thrust out from the floor of the cavern.

Soon they passed underneath the overhanging limestone ledge and into the true overhead, their exhaust bubbles bouncing off the ceiling and rumbling up to the edge before disappearing into the tannic false ceiling.

Josh stopped when he reached the inner wall of the cavern.

Here the limestone was devoid of silt and stood pristine, projecting fantastical shapes sculpted by the hand of erosion over many years. He reached out and gently touched a curved piece of limestone and was surprised when it crumbled in his hands like aged cheese, tiny pieces of stone fluttering to the ground like butterflies.

This stuff is so ancient and untouched. I feel like we are the first ones ever to dive here.

Soon all three of them were at the wall, admiring the fossils of ancient sea creatures embedded within the limestone sculpture. Tiny beige sea urchin shells half buried in the limestone shared their ancient grave with partial scallop shells from primitive oysters.

Josh reached out carefully and noticed that the fossils felt rock hard and firmly attached into the limestone.

He found a stable limestone outcropping and wrapped the line around it, continuing their tour. They circled the interior perimeter of the cavern, following the corner where white vertical wall met the bumpy ground of silt, sand and limestone. Josh easily found tie-off points as he traversed the cavern. Above them the surface of the sink hole provided a dull ruby light, the reddish tint only eliminated by their dive lights.

Should be called Ruby Sink, not Emerald Sink.

Soon they were on the other side of the cavern. Josh turned and followed the line he had laid; satisfied that it was still secured. The line described a half circle around the edge of the inner perimeter. The water was so clear he could see the line of white as it went from the side back to the center tree and angled up through the tannic water.

This is the biggest cavern we've ever been in. Just majestic!

A light flashed repeatedly off to his right. He turned back and noticed Frank pointing forward and down. The floor dipped dramatically off into a black hole. An ancient yellowed line snaked down from the tree in the center of the cavern into the dark; clearly a cave connection. Josh's heart picked up a few beats at the sight.

He slowly played the beam of his brighter light over the ground and into the deep passage. He swam slowly, parallel to the floor and used sunken branches as tie off points.

He followed the bottom as it sank deeper and deeper, occasionally stealing a glance at his depth and pressure gauge. At one hundred feet he stopped and inflated his wing just enough so he could hover over a couch-sized boulder covered in a fine layer of silt. The silt puffed up slightly where his two fingers touched. Soon all three of them were side by side, facing down into the deep cave section, fascinated by the sight. The floor of the cavern zone continued its descent even deeper into the maw of a black-walled cave entrance, easily fifty feet high and twenty feet wide. Limestone rocks had tumbled haphazardly down the slope, intermixed with dead vegetation, branches and even an old metal newspaper vending machine laying on its side, the green paint darkened and flaked from years of being submerged. Josh could make out *Tallahassee Democrat* in faded white letters along the top.

Somebody must have thrown that in here. Too bad. We should pull it out of here some day.

Josh felt a tap on his left shoulder. He turned and saw Jon holding up his gauge, the "thumbs up" signal moving slowly up and down. Josh returned the signal reluctantly and watched as Frank also gave the end of dive signal. He knew they had to follow the cavern diving rules and had to respect the maximum depth and their turn pressures.

He waved his two buddies back towards the thin nylon line which guided the way back to the surface. Soon the team was moving back along the inner wall. Frank and Jon took turns pulling off the line from the objects he had attached them to, which made it easier on him.

All he had to do was keep reeling in the line as they fed it to him. He noticed that except for a small cloud of silt that still hovered over the boulder they had roosted on at one hundred feet that the cavern zone was free of any stirred up silt. He smiled with pride, a tiny bit of water creeping into his mask due to his facial muscle contractions breaking the mask seal. He used his left hand to quickly clear the water out of his mask and continued on.

Soon they were back to the tree. Josh unwrapped the line from the tree and started the slow ascent back to the surface, all three clearly reluctant to leave the magic beauty of the cavern. At twenty feet Frank stopped and signaled "safety stop". All three of them hovered at the edge of the clear water, glad that they could do their safety stop with great visibility.

Three minutes later Frank started his ascent, entering the rust-colored water zone, his right hand following the line. Jon grabbed Frank's left knee with his left hand and the line with his right and followed Frank up. Soon both disappeared, the dusky water roiling as their passage mixed up the clear and tannic water barrier.

Josh slowed down the reeling as he entered the tannic layer, careful not to run into Jon. The water temperature rose back up a few degrees as the visibility all but disappeared. Josh could see a lighter red ochre hue above him which soon resolved into the limestone ledge near the stairs.

Soon his head popped the surface, bright sunlight making him squint. He removed his regulator and mask. Jon and Frank were talking excitedly, their sentences running on top of each other.

"Man, I can't believe how clear it is down there! Absolutely beautiful!"

"Did you see all those fossils?"

"Best dive ever!"

"How about that deep cave connection? Awesome!"

Josh smiled.

"Guys, that was why we got cavern certified."

Jon grinned back. "Yeah, all this time this place was a short drive away but we didn't have the right stuff to dive it."

"The right training you mean," said Josh.

"Yeah, especially the training," agreed Jon.

"Did you notice how pristine that cavern looked?" asked Josh, "Lot fewer signs of divers having been in there and there's a lot more natural debris, like sticks, branches and stuff that's fallen into the sink over the years."

Frank laughed, "Yeah, that newspaper dispenser was a hoot."

"We should come back with lift bags and remove that someday," enthused Josh.

"We're definitely diving here again, that's for sure," replied Jon.

"Well, let's get out, warm up, eat and then swap tanks for another dive," suggested Frank.

Half an hour later the three of them sat on the tailgate of Josh's truck, legs dangling and swinging happily. They had all removed their wet suit tops and sat eating their sub sandwiches, the warm sun filtering through the pine and oak trees.

The wind had picked up slightly from the calm morning, providing a cool breeze that spread whispers throughout the gently swaying tree limbs. Their gear sat in the bed of the truck, dripping slightly brown water into the truck bed that gathered and streamed off the back and onto the sandy ground.

Josh watched as a sprig of lettuce covered with a dollop of mayonnaise slid out the lower half of his sub sandwich and plopped onto his wet suit leg. He flicked it off and wiped his hand on the damp neoprene and reached for his plastic bottle water and took a large swig, washing down the hearty bite he had just taken. He felt happy and deeply satisfied by the companionship, the food and the cavern dive.

Between bites he continued the discussion they had been having since surfacing.

"Yeah, I agree; the ceiling of that cavern zone must have fallen over many years of erosion. It created an inverted funnel where the sink hole is small but the cavern zone footprint is quite large." He drew a crude funnel shape in the sandy ground with his big toe.

"We saw at least one cave entrance here," his big toe stabbed at the sand, "and it headed that way." He swiped the sand with his toe, almost falling off the back of the truck with the effort.

Jon laughed, "Yeah, that's how I remember it. That deep cave section was amazing! The water was so clear and it just keeps going deeper and deeper. One day we might be able to dive that."

"Yeah, seems like the cavern card is just a teaser for cave diving," observed Frank, licking the last bit of mustard from his fingers, his sub sandwich gone. He polished off the rest of his bottled water and tossed it in the back of the truck, along with the crumpled wax paper from his sub. "I'd sure like to be able to go in deeper. I definitely want to save up and get a set of doubles like you, Josh. Hey, can I dive those sometime?"

Josh paused, considering the request.

"Well, technically they aren't mine but I don't see the harm if you try it in open water sometime, like at Jackson Blue. Believe me it does take some getting used to."

"Maybe for you; I'll probably take to them like a duck to water."

Josh knew Frank's case of hubris was mild; he would probably adapt to doubles just fine. It's just that he didn't want to go back to diving a single tank, especially in a cavern.

"I hope that we all have access to a set of doubles and canister lights one day so we can enjoy caverns even more, have a larger safety margin and take a cave class," said Josh, his tone slightly serious. He realized how much the underwater world of caverns and caves called to him and how important it was to share the experience with his best friends.

Frank pulled his dive computer from his pile of gear in the back and looked at it. "Yeah, well, for now let's get back in the water. My computer says we've been up long enough to do another dive to the same depth."

Josh pulled out a plastic trash bag from a plastic milk bin in the back and gathered up all of the plastic bottles and sandwich debris from their lunch. He squeezed out the air, spun the top and tied a knot in the top to secure its contents.

"OK, I'm ready," he announced, reaching for his wet suit top.

Thirty minutes later Josh placed his right hand on the line and descended, following Jon down through the tannic layer. Frank had already disappeared into the red gloom, reeling out the line as the team leader. A few minutes later Josh swam into the crystal clear water for the second time that day.

The sight was still awe inspiring, all the more so because of the anticipation of returning. He gave his "OK" as the team reformed and Frank headed for the submerged tree. Frank tied off near the same place that Josh had during the first dive and turned towards the deep section.

Might as well do the deep part of the dive first; that's supposed to be better anyway, thought Josh as he slowly frog kicked his descent, gliding within arm's length of the line.

Frank swam to the couch sized boulder, all previous traces of their brief visit gone except for three clumps of finger-sized lighter silt tracings on top of the boulder.

He wrapped the line around a tree limb jutting out from the side of the boulder and proceeded towards the deep cave entrance.

Josh kept a careful eye on his depth gauge. They shouldn't bust one hundred feet, at least not by too much. Frank was still breathing 34% Nitrox to ameliorate his penchant for narcosis and he needed to stay shallow due to the higher mix of Oxygen. His gauge read one hundred and two feet.

OK, not too bad, but Frank you better not go too deep.

Frank continued horizontally forward, maintaining a constant depth, his light swinging from side to side as he drank in the sight of the cave opening. Josh felt a shift in the light as the ambient light from the red curtain above dimmed and the artificial lights they carried became more dominant.

Hmm..getting close to the edge of the cavern zone. Gotta keep that natural light visible.

Josh looked down and saw the faded yellowed cave line as it wandered from the cavern zone deep into the cave zone. A blue triangular-shaped plastic line arrow attached to the line pointed back to the middle of the cavern zone and open water.

Interesting; somebody must have dove in this cave before and left that line and line marker. Wonder who it was and how long ago?

He looked up and saw Frank suddenly dip downward, sliding straight into the mouth of the cave. His hand-held light tumbled from his grasp and fell thirty feet to the bottom, creating a small mushroom cloud of silt. The cavern reel fell, hit the bottom and rolled, splaying line in a jumbled rat's nest before stopping against a small boulder. Frank's arms were waving wildly in front of him and his kicks became longer in stroke, his legs straightening in panic. Jon began to head towards Frank, clearly to help.

No! Frank! Don't!

Too late Josh watched as Frank disappeared behind a huge silt cloud created by his panicked fin kicks. Jon hesitated a second outside the cloud, looking back up at Josh, his hand on the now limp cavern line. The cloud grew until Jon was enveloped within it.

A large burst of bubbles erupted from the cloud where Frank had disappeared and rocketed towards the ceiling of the cave. The bubbles clawed their way up towards the dark red ceiling. Soon, small particles of limestone started to rain down on the scene in slow motion, lending a surreal effect to the events, like snow falling.

Damn! He's narc'd again…and going too deep!

Josh took in the situation and dove for the permanent yellowed cave line, which lead right to the cloud of silt that now emanated no light as both Frank's dropped light and Jon's light were overwhelmed by the density of the suspended particles.

Cavern line's too loose; can't rely on it for safe navigation in zero vis.

He OK'd the old cave line, the movement stirring up a fine line of silt that had settled on the nylon string over the years. He took a deep breath and tried to settle his mind and body.

Control your breathing first; it'll control your body and mind second.

He started forward and entered the cloud of silt, which by now had grown into an irregular shape twenty feet wide and ten feet high. He knew his friends were somewhere within.

Soon he was in total zero visibility. He twisted his right hand and shone his wrist mounted light into his face and only saw a dim orange glow; thick silt blocked most of the light. He moved forward slowly, one hand on the line and the other moving back and forth in a crude search pattern.

His search was rewarded when he came across the cavern line, draped loosely on top of the cave line. He knew this was the way back to the surface but first he had to secure the other end before it became more unspooled. He tugged the end of the cavern line that went back up towards the tree and once it snugged up he wrapped it around the cave line, touch tying a simple slip knot in the pitch black water.

Satisfied that one end was secure he started following the loose cavern line. He stopped breathing for a second and covered his light, listening and feeling for anything. He could hear the rapid inhalation and exhalation of a nearby diver and the cavern line in his hand twitched as if a fish was hooked on the other end of the line.

Encouraged he continued forward until he felt the moving hand of a diver. He followed the line and found the reel in the hands of the diver, slowly being reeled in. He squeezed the hand of the diver and touched his mask to the mask of the other.

"Ith Josh. Whoo-th thith?" he yelled through his regulator, the consonant sounds badly formed due to the mouthpiece. He knew, though, that you could carry on a limited conversation underwater while breathing through mouthpieces if you spoke loudly, carefully and closely.

"Ith Jon. Whereth Frank"?

He could barely make out the words but let out a sigh of relief that erupted as a burst of bubbles from his regulator. He reached back to Jon's hand, gently pried the reel from it, placed the line back in Jon's hand and locked the reel so no more line would spool out. He placed the reel on the ground and touched his forehead back on Jon's.

"Follow me."

He felt Jon's hand fumble towards his and an "OK" signal form in his palm.

He turned, line in hand and waited for Jon to connect with him in touch contact. Soon they were working their way back to the permanent cave line. By the time he reached the cave line the silt cloud had dispersed enough to see a foot in front of him. Jon's head soon moved in next to his as they looked at the cavern line, which looped around the cave line before heading off, upward, towards the open water and safety.

Josh gave Jon the "buddy" hand signal and pointed deeper down the cave line, where he suspected Frank had swam off to. Jon nodded and followed as Josh turned and went deeper into the cave. They worked slowly, mostly in touch contact but with occasional breaks in the silt cloud. At one point Josh stopped, covered his light, looked and listened. Jon caught on and did the same. Josh could make out a dim light off to the right and a surge of hope went through his mind.

Frank!

Josh inched forward, his light still covered so he could follow the other light. Within a few feet he came across Frank's hand held light, beam pointing upwards with Frank nowhere nearby. He pulled the light out of the silt, powered it off and clipped it to his left chest D-ring. The light jostled and bumped against his chest as he continued on the line, a trail of silt drifting downward from the light housing.

Josh knew Frank still had his backup lights but repeated covering of their lights revealed no telltale beacon.

A feeling of dread began to creep over Josh as they continued deeper. He recognized some of it was narcosis from the depth and the exertion from the past few minutes. He also feared the worse.

Jon tapped him and waved his pressure gauge in Josh's face. He was down to 500 PSI as a result of the depth and time spent looking for each other. Josh nodded, looking at his own gauge.

He still had 1,000 PSI in his double tanks which he figured should be more than enough for the both of them to surface if Jon went through this remaining air. His depth gauge said one hundred fifty feet and his dive computer indicated he had five more minutes of bottom time. He tapped his watch, held up five fingers and gave the thumbs up sign.

We'll look for Frank for five more minutes then leave.

Jon nodded and they continued downward. The visibility improved to two feet and just as Josh was about to call the dive he saw Frank's fins on the bottom, unmoving. He quickly swam up Frank's leg, past his torso and pulled his left shoulder towards him. Frank's open but unseeing eyes looked back, his mask half full of water, regulator no longer in his mouth.

"No!" Josh yelled through his regulator. Jon reached his side just as he shook Frank's left arm, which hung out in front of him, slightly bent as if in a ballet pose. He was in a kneeling position, shins on the ground, knees bent and hips straight.

Josh pulled the long hose out of his mouth and crammed it into Frank's mouth, hitting the purge button. Frank's cheeks filled with air that escaped from the sides of his mouth, the force of the air moving Frank's head obscenely. Josh, realizing he no longer had a regulator in his mouth, reached down and grabbed his backup regulator hanging around his neck. He pulled a long breath off of the regulator and purged the other regulator once more, hoping that Frank would start breathing.

Josh felt a grab on his shoulder and turned to see Jon. Despite the handicap of the scuba mask covering the majority of Jon's face Josh could see the despair, fear and sadness in Jon's eyes. Jon pointed to the two of them and gave the "we have to leave…now" sign slowly.

Josh held up a finger, exasperated, and reached over to Frank's BC. He hit the power inflator button until Frank's body started to slowly rise. He grabbed Frank's left elbow and motioned for Jon to follow the permanent cave line.

Jon proceeded to swim while Josh half towed and half pushed his dead companion back to the cavern reel. Despite the silt streaming off of Frank's wet suit and gear the visibility had now improved enough so that when they reached the cavern reel they could make out the pale white cavern line as it left the permanent cave line and pointed upwards towards clearer water.

Josh continued to pull Frank's body along until they had reached the tree at sixty feet when Jon signaled rapidly that he was out of air. Josh momentarily let go of Frank so he could give Jon his long hose regulator. Once they were set, both breathing regulators, he turned back to continue bringing Frank up but Frank had disappeared.

Frantic, he looked down and around until Jon tapped him on the glass of his mask and pointed up. Josh looked up and caught a glimpse of Frank's body moving rapidly up into the tannic layer.

One of his fins caught the cavern line which pulled the line taut back to the tree where it was wrapped. Josh could see the tips of Frank's fins poking out of the tannic layer, his upward motion arrested by the entanglement of their cavern line.

Josh looked back at Jon and both held each other's eyes for a few moments, trying to make sense of what had happened. Frank was positively buoyant and on his way to the surface except that his fin had caught the line and pinned him in place. Josh finally looked at his pressure gauge and dive computer and signaled for them to ascend to twenty feet to do their safety stop. They slowly made their way up the line to Frank's fins and hovered below them.

Josh started to shiver from the cold and shock and the thought of having to deal with Frank for the last twenty feet. He didn't want to lose him now. In broken scuba sign language he told Jon to unwrap Frank's fins after he had swam higher up to arrest Frank's continued ascent.

Safety stop finished, they both began their ascent into the tannic zone, where visibility reduced to six inches. Josh felt his way up Frank's legs and body until he found his left arm, still in that horrid ballet pose.

He dumped a bit of air from Frank's BC until Frank was only slightly buoyant and braced himself for the release of his leg. In a parody of life Frank's body moved downwards suddenly, jiggled up and down slightly and started a slow ascent.

Josh held one hand on Frank's power inflator and the other on the cavern line as he made his way through the dusky red water. His head surfaced at the same time as Frank's, who's head lolled to one side.

He added air to his wing and Frank's BC so they would both stay on the surface. Behind him he heard Jon surface and inflate his BC, the hissing sound reflecting off the water's surface.

"Oh my God, Josh. Frank's dead!"

Josh swallowed hard and reached out to Jon, embracing him. Tears started to build up inside his mask. For a few moments they bobbed on the surface, sharing the shock and pain. Frank's head fell forward into the water and his body drifted gently towards the side of the sink.

Josh pushed himself away from Jon. He pulled off his mask and threw it, hard, onto the side of the sink. The mask hit a sandy spot and tumbled down to the small stairs where it rested, halfway in the water.

"We need to get him out and call 911, Jon."

Chapter 41

Emergency lights flashed insistently but quietly on the tan sheriff's patrol car parked next to Josh's truck. Both front doors opened and officers emerged from each side. Josh and Jon stood at the back of the pickup truck. Behind them on the bed of the truck lay Frank's body, all gear still in place. Soon after surfacing they had towed Frank's body to the side of the sink, climbed back up the hill, removed their own gear and grunting, pulled Frank out of the water and placed him, face up, as carefully as possible in the truck bed. Jon had delicately wiped off the blood-tinged foaming froth oozing out of Frank's mouth and nose.

Jon had called 911 with his cell phone and they had sat, still in their damp wet suits, numb, waiting for somebody to arrive. Jon had had the presence of mind to pull his driver's license out of his wallet; Josh had done the same.

The tall muscular driver of the patrol car walked up and removed his dark sunglasses. He peered closely at Josh.

"I know you," he said as he scrutinized Josh.

Josh realized he was looking at Officer McDonald, who had given him a break not long ago.

"Officer McDonald. I'm sure glad to see you. We've had a horrible, horrible accident," sputtered Josh, "Our friend drowned."

The other officer, an African American with short hair and a thin but fit build stepped between Josh and Frank, removed his sunglasses and looked closely at Frank's body on the truck bed. He nodded to Officer McDonald knowingly.

"Hold up, son. Please step over here. Let's talk to each of you separately. Officer Campbell please talk to this young man."

Officer McDonald motioned to a nearby clearing alongside the sink and Josh followed. He watched as Jon was lead to the other side of the patrol car, out of earshot.

"Josh, isn't it?" asked Officer McDonald, pulling out a pen and a small notebook from a pocket. Josh handed over his driver's license which the officer clipped to the top of his notebook.

"Yes sir," answered Josh, surprised the officer remembered his name.

"Just tell me what happened. Start from the beginning. Don't leave anything out."

Josh started slow, explaining how well the first dive had gone and the events of the second. He realized part way into the conversation that he was being interrogated as if there had been foul play.

"What do you mean you saw him flounder?"

"Well, see, during our class last weekend he got a bad case of nitrogen narcosis,"

McDonald nodded. Josh remembered that he was on the Sheriff's dive team so he hoped that he understood all of the diving references.

"So he switched to diving Nitrox, which cleared it up just fine in class. He went back to one hundred feet and had no problems. But this time he got to one hundred feet and started acting weird again. I'm not sure why; I'm pretty sure he was still diving 34% Nitrox."

"Don't worry, we'll take all of his equipment, including his tank, and have it checked."

Josh felt a sinking feeling, as if he was guilty until proven innocent.

"Officer, I swear, we did the cavern dive by the book. Everything up to that point was within the rules we were taught in class. All I can guess is that he must have gotten a bad case of narcosis, or…"

Josh hesitated, unsure how much of Frank's nature he wanted to reveal.

"Or what?" McDonald leaned in closer, his curiosity tweaked.

"Well, Frank, he was, sort of, well, a bit of a maverick sometimes."

"Are you saying you think he purposely broke the rules and went deeper, knowing that he might get narc'd or tox out on his Nitrox?"

"I don't think so; I certainly don't want that to be his legacy. He was a great guy and a great dive buddy. I just can't say for sure what made him decide to dive deeper at that moment." Josh trailed off.

He looked over as an ambulance arrived, lights flashing and alarms silent. The ambulance was followed by a dark blue sedan labeled Medical Examiner on the side.

Two paramedics, one a thick bodied Hispanic woman with long dark hair pulled up in a large ponytail and the other a medium height freckle faced younger man with a shock of curly red hair, walked to the back of the ambulance, opened the door and slid out a collapsible gurney, the legs unfolding. The ME, a short slightly overweight older man with solid white medium-length unruly hair, strode over to the back of the truck and started to examine Frank's body, led there by Officer McDonald's pointing finger.

"Don't worry about them; they are just processing the scene. Tell me more about your efforts to find Frank and your rescue."

Josh repeated his recall of the attempted rescue but his attention was divided between answering questions and watching the paramedics and ME work with Frank's body. The ME photographed

Frank from a number of angles and removed his gear one piece at a time, carefully recording its condition.

They removed his mask and fins and placed them in black plastic bags with little tags. Frank's head, arms and legs flopped around as they removed the weight belt and BC until all that remained was his wet suit. It made Josh feel slightly queasy. Josh heard the explosive hiss of the second stage as they manipulated it, clearly testing whether or not it still worked. One paramedic checked the pressure gauge before turning off the tank valve and depressurizing Frank's regulators while the ME recorded information on a small notebook the same size as Officer McDonald's.

The scuba unit was disassembled, bagged and placed in the trunk of the ME's vehicle, along with the rest of Frank's gear. Finally the two paramedics unfolded a large black thick plastic body bag and slid Frank into it before pulling him onto the collapsible gurney.

Josh suddenly felt overwhelmed by the scene. He started to shiver and his knees felt weak, despite still being in the wet suit that by now should have him broiling in the early afternoon summer heat. A wave of nausea gripped him.

"Whoa, Josh, let's sit you down and get you out of that wet suit," said Officer McDonald, not unkindly. He started to lead him back to the tailgate of Josh's truck as the paramedics strong armed the gurney back to the ambulance, the rubber tires on the gurney hitting the occasional root and patch of sand.

Josh stopped, his head spinning, and placed his hand on a small pine tree for support. He vomited the remains of his sub sandwich onto the ground and stood, bent over, breathing heavily, partially digested food dripping from his mouth.

Officer McDonald retreated to the back of his patrol car and walked back to Josh, handing him an unopened plastic water bottle. Josh gratefully accepted the bottle, unscrewed the top and swished the initial gulp into his mouth, spitting out the remaining acrid taste.

"Feel better?"

Josh nodded and allowed himself to be lead back to his tailgate. He sat down on the truck bed, ignoring the space once occupied by Frank, and proceeded to remove his dive booties and wet suit pieces, slowly and mechanically. From this angle he could see Jon, still talking to the second officer, face earnest and hands waving in frantic explanatory gestures.

Jon had had the presence of mind to at least peel off his wet suit top and wasn't in danger of overheating. Their eyes met momentarily and a feeling of deep sadness rose in Josh at the shared loss of their friend.

The second officer, seeing the exchange, walked in front of Jon and continued scribbling his notes. Josh peeled off the lower half of his wet suit, arms shaking slightly as he bent his knees on his lap one after the other to pull off the remaining neoprene. The afternoon breeze felt cool on his damp skin and he took a deep drink from the water bottle.

"Thanks," he managed to croak, "I don't know what came over me."

"I'd guess it's a combination of stress at what just happened, maybe a touch of shock and definitely overheating in that wet suit," offered McDonald. Jon, escorted by the second officer, walked over to the truck and pulled himself up on the tailgate, a heavy "umph" escaping his lips.

Officer McDonald placed his hand out, palm up vertically in a command posture.

"You two stay here."

The two walked over to the ME's car, where the ME and the two paramedics stood talking. Soon all five people were deep in conversation, the hand gestures clearly indicating the topic of conversation as they pointed to the sink, Josh and Jon, and to the back of the ambulance, where Frank's body lay.

Jon, a miserable expression on his face, pulled off his wet suit bottom and threw it in the bed behind him. Josh handed him the half full water bottle, which Jon drank thirstily. He set the empty bottle down on the tailgate, staring at the water condensation on the side, his fingers rubbing the droplets absentmindedly.

"Guess they're comparing notes; seeing if we told the same story," said Jon, his expression transitioning from miserable to glum.

"It didn't occur to me until half way through my interrogation that they have to treat these sort of things like a crime first. It's not like they can get evidence from the 'crime scene', just us 'criminals'," fumed Josh.

"Yeah, good thing we didn't take off Frank's gear or they'd probably have us in handcuffs, sweating it out in the back of the patrol car."

"I just didn't have the heart or energy to remove his gear…that seemed so invasive," admitted Josh.

They lapsed into silence, momentarily lost in their own whirling thoughts. Near the ambulance the paramedics and officers were listening intently to the ME, his right index finger wagging professorially.

Probably figuring out the cause of death or something, thought Josh.

"Josh, what happened to Frank? Why did he drown?"

Josh looked at Jon, his lips pursed.

"You know, I am really not sure. You saw – we were all doing so great. I knew he wanted to check out that deep cave passage but up until he panicked he was doing everything right."

"Think he was narc'd?"

"Maybe, but he was diving Nitrox. I mixed it myself at *Wakulla Skuba*, analyzed it and then watched him analyze it again when he came to pick it up. It was 34% Nitrox. I'm 100% certain."

Josh was almost certain that he had gotten the Nitrox mix right. He'd done hundreds of Nitrox fills over the years and knew the technique. Still, a small nagging doubt remained. What if he had accidentally killed Frank by putting in too much or too little oxygen? Maybe the oxygen analyzer wasn't calibrated correctly? What if the air supply at the dive shop was contaminated with something like carbon monoxide? He knew he'd have to tell Kathy. They may have to have their gas checked for contaminants. He realized that he'd have to tell a lot of people about what happened today and his insides clenched with the thought.

"I suppose they'll do their own independent analysis of the mix."

"Yeah, they'll probably check all of the gear to see if it failed or not. I really don't think there's anything wrong with his gear, though."

"It could have been narcosis...he was acting fine and then just started swimming crazy. It's like he forgot he was in a cavern; he dropped his light and the cavern reel."

Jon frowned. "I wish we'd gotten to him sooner."

Josh clapped Jon on the shoulder and looked at his face.

"Listen, we did the best we could. Heck, we put ourselves in enough danger going that deep and risking getting lost in that silt. You saw how bad it was. Emerald is a beautiful place but that much silt can be deadly if you lose the line to the surface. We'd still be down there looking for the surface if we both hadn't taken the time to find the cavern reel first. You know that."

Jon muttered, eyes downcast, "I suppose..."

Josh continued his explanation, feeling oddly cathartic telling the same story to Jon compared to the way he felt telling it to Officer McDonald.

"I thought he was still alive and that we had time to try and find him safely. First, though, I had to make sure I knew where you were but before I dared go into the silt cloud I had to make sure I knew where the line was. I didn't know whether or not that cloud would grow to fill the entire cavern." Josh's words gushed forth in a mixture of pleading penance and logical analysis. He had to know what they had done was *right* or he would never forgive himself.

"Yeah, when I saw him drop the reel I went for that first then figured I would go get him in zero viz. You found me before I finished pulling up all the slack. I figured Frank was still alive, somewhere, nearby."

"Yeah, I think we did the right thing. Save ourselves first then save Frank."

"But we found him DEAD. He had to have drowned pretty damn quickly; I bet we were apart from him for no more than, say, five minutes, right? Why? He had air left. I know he was probably heavily narc'ed at that depth but STILL…"

"I don't know…maybe the equipment was faulty, maybe he had a heart attack or some other weird medical problem…maybe he was so narc'd he dropped his regulator and was too out of his mind to stick it back in his mouth. He sure did seem more erratic than that time in Orange Grove."

Jon nodded, his arms grasping the edge of the tailgate, head hung low, his dark curly hair still glistening from the dive.

Josh looked up as the two officers returned to the truck. Behind them the ME and ambulance backed up the dirt road slowly, lights still flashing. Josh felt another pang of sadness as he realized Frank lay still in the back, never to hang out with them again.

"OK, you two can leave. We have your statements and contact information," said Officer McDonald. He handed over both drivers' licenses to Josh and turned to leave with Officer Campbell. He paused when Josh spoke.

"Wait. What about Frank?"

"I'm sure you two are still pretty shook up. Don't worry, we'll take good care of Frank and his gear."

"How did he die?" inquired Jon, a little too loudly. McDonald took it in stride.

"Well, we don't know but the Medical Examiner is pretty experienced at figuring that sort of thing out."

Josh stuttered, "So, do…do you think we killed him?"

"Right now this looks like a terrible accident and I'm sorry for the loss of your friend."

Officer McDonald placed his sunglasses back on his face. Josh saw in them the reflection of himself and Jon, standing anxiously in their bathing suits, looking up at the tall officer. Officer Campbell had also placed his sunglasses back on his face, the shorter yet imposing figure providing two more mirrors.

"Just make sure you guys are reachable. More than likely you'll hear from a detective."

He turned to leave and stopped a second time, facing back to Josh.

"I think it's best if you let the authorities notify the next of kin. We have experience with that sort of thing."

Josh reached out his hand awkwardly and shook Officer McDonald's hand.

"Thanks, Officer, for everything. This is probably routine for you but we are pretty shaken."

"We don't have many scuba drownings and every one is a tragedy. It appears that you guys did all that you could have done. Getting his body out of the sink hole was a good thing, too. Talk to each other, talk to family and friends, maybe a counselor. Let yourselves work through the grieving process."

With that the two officers touched the tops of their flat brimmed Stetsons and walked back to their patrol car.

Chapter 42

Josh plopped onto his futon couch and dropped his keys on the carpeted floor, numb. He was tired and wanted to sleep but simply sat on the couch, allowing his mind to drift.

Somehow he and Jon had managed to load up their gear and drive out of Emerald and back to town. Both were too stunned and drained and spoke little during the drive.

Josh had helped Jon unload his gear at his apartment, made more difficult by the presence of Frank's stuff scattered all around the shared space. Neither had an appetite for dinner even though the sunset was almost complete when they finished unloading and storing equipment. Josh left Jon alone in his apartment, discarded the fleeting thought of trying to see Elise and drove back to Woodville.

He had parked his truck outside his apartment, walked up to the door in a zombie state and entered, leaving all of his gear still in the back of his truck.

He groaned and rolled off the couch, anxious to do something. He stripped off his bathing suit, still slightly damp from the day's events, and started a hot shower. The dive replayed in his mind while hot water pounded on his head and shoulders.

He relived the rescue attempt in his mind, trying to figure out if he could have done anything differently. He was the dive professional; the one that was supposed to take care of the team. The one they looked up to and respected. He couldn't shake the overhanging feeling of loss of control and guilt over Frank's death.

The cooling water from the shower head broke him from his reverie. He realized that he had been standing in the shower long enough for all of the hot water to be used up. He sighed deeply, turned off the water, pulled the nautical-themed shower curtain open and stepped out.

A few minutes later he sat back on his couch dressed in a comfortable threadbare t-shirt with "FSU Seminoles" barely legible on the front and a pair of dark blue and red plaid boxer shorts. He halfheartedly chewed on a Red Delicious apple while flipping channels with his remote, barely distinguishing one channel from the next.

The bulk of his addled mind was still processing the disaster. Some part of him knew the apple and channel surfing were automatic comfort behaviors that were doing very little to help the storm of emotions rolling through his brain.

He almost dropped the remote when his cordless phone started to chirp. He set down the remote and picked up the phone from the base unit on the side table.

"Hello?"

"Josh?" Josh didn't recognize the voice.

"Yes, this is Josh."

"This is Drew. I heard through the grapevine that Frank drowned at Emerald Sink today. Is that right?"

"Yes." Drew was the last person he wanted to rehash Frank's death with right now. Amazing how fast bad news travels.

"I'm sorry to call you so soon after the accident but I wanted to ask you some questions about it."

Josh allowed the phone silence to answer for him, his face slack and uncaring.

"Josh? You still there?"

"Listen, Drew, can we talk later? I really don't want to talk right now."

"I know, Josh, I know. Believe me I don't want to harass you so soon but since you guys just took and passed my class I have an imperative to learn as much as possible about the incident."

Josh noticed Drew had changed what happened from an 'accident' to an 'incident'.

"Why is it so important you ask me about it now? Besides, are the details supposed to be protected or something until the official report is released?"

Drew hesitated a few seconds before answering.

"The cave diving community has been tracking fatalities for more than thirty years. As you remember from your training we developed our curriculum around learning from the mistakes of others."

Josh grimaced. Did Drew think he killed Frank by making a mistake?

"It's also been true that the authorities usually don't have the proper cave diving background when they interview you for details of what happened. It's also important to tell what happened as soon as possible so the events are fresh and don't get poisoned by false truths that may develop in your mind as time goes on."

Josh admitted inwardly that Drew did have a point. He also thought Drew was digging for information to save his own ass. He was doing research in the off chance that Frank's family would decide to go after him legally for improper training.

That thought wormed its way into his brain and he wondered darkly if Frank's family would go after him as well. This situation just got worse and worse. He never had much patience for neither legal wranglings nor intrigue and decided to simply tell Drew the truth.

"OK, Drew, I'll answer your questions. Just don't expect a lot from me right now. I'm pretty tired."

Josh realized that he was fatigued but sleep still seemed impossible.

"OK, thanks. Just describe how the dive went. Don't leave any details out. I want to know everything; the dive order, the cavern configuration, how you ran the line, etc. Everything you can think of, no matter how important or not you think it is."

Josh began retelling the story slowly at first and picked up momentum, encouraged by the occasional nudging questions by Drew.

He replayed the dive as a story shared between two people that had both the knowledge and appreciation for the cavern environment.

He felt a desire to tell the story fully, with all the details. Maybe Drew could help him understand what he did wrong or if he and Jon had done the best that he could. His hunger returned and he polished off the apple during breaks in the conversation.

Josh finished the story at the point where they had carried Frank's body up the rough slope of Emerald and laid him gently in the bed of his truck, sides heaving from the heavy exertion.

"Who has Frank's tank now?"

"The sheriff took it and all of his dive gear. I suppose they want to test the gas."

"Are you pretty sure he was breathing 34%?"

"Yes, Drew, I swear that was the mix. I'll find out tomorrow if the oxygen analyzer at the shop is faulty but it calibrated just fine before I took the measurement. Frank analyzed the tank himself when he came to pick it up."

"OK, OK, just checking. Let's assume he was breathing that mix. He shouldn't have been narc'ed, like you said, at least not much. Hmm...not really sure what else would explain why he behaved like that. The only other thing I can think of is he just plain got scared and slipped into a true panic state. He wasn't thinking rationally anymore."

Josh's heart sank. He was afraid this was going to be Frank's legacy.

"But he's never been scared of anything...ANYTHING. We've done lots of crazy things over the years and he was always the one egging us on. He was the risk taker, damning the odds and charging ahead full steam."

Josh realized he had a large lump in his throat and tears made the TV screen swim.

"Damn, Drew, I really can't talk more about this right now," his voice quavered.

"Josh, I'm sorry. If it's any consolation I think you and Jon did as best as you could. I've been in Emerald, years ago, right at that spot and the silt is pretty heavy there. You HAD to protect yourselves first, just like I taught you. I'm proud that neither of you panicked. Think of it this way – you did save two lives, yours and Jon's."

Josh rubbed the lump in his throat and wiped his eyes. Drew's words helped a little bit.

"Well, I'll let you go. Thanks for answering my questions. Let me know when and where Frank's service is going to be held. I'd like to send flowers."

Josh realized with a start that there would be a funeral. Somehow he had lost the ability to think forward in time through the logical sequences that happened after a death. He dreaded showing up at Frank's funeral service but knew he had to.

"Josh, one more question before I go. I know it's too early to ask but will you go back in a cavern?"

Josh thought Drew was being awful callous and cruel. His ear canals still had residue from the tannic water of Emerald, where Frank had perished and Drew wanted to know if he was planning his next cavern dive.

"Gee, Drew, I haven't thought about it. I'm not sure I ever want to scuba dive anymore, much less go into a cavern."

The words flowing out of his mouth surprised him in its vehemence. Did he really want to stop diving, forever?

"I know it sounds mean and inappropriate. It's been my experience that you'll get through this sooner if you ask yourself that question early on. It gives you ammunition to put your life goals into a larger perspective instead of just allowing yourself to spin down into the emotions of a horrible loss.

"David's death in Mexico made me think twice about whether or not I wanted to continue cave diving. I think I continued first fueled by the anger towards his surviving team. Later on, though, I continued diving and eventually became a cave instructor because I love it and my tribute to David is to make sure others can enjoy the sport as safely as possible."

Drew paused.

"Sometimes, though, things just go wrong. Accidents happen. People die. I've lost other close friends over the years, sometimes due to scuba accidents, but more than likely from more mundane things like traffic accidents and cancer. You process these events and decide for yourself how you want them to affect you going forward."

Josh listened numbly. His mind stirred with conflicting emotions of loss over Frank, guilt over Frank, desire to continue diving and the pain of conflict over them all.

"Well, goodnight Josh. Thanks for talking to me."

"Goodnight, Drew."

Josh hung up the phone and stifled a huge yawn. He tossed his apple core into the nearby kitchen trash can and was treated to the thunk of a well-placed shot. He clicked off the TV and stretched out on the couch in the dark. Exhaustion closed his eyes.

The "ding dong" of the mechanical doorbell attached to his apartment door woke him up after only a few minutes. Momentarily disoriented he sat up on the couch in the dark. For a split second he thought he was back at the bottom of Emerald, searching desperately for Frank. The second tinny chime of the doorbell brought him fully awake. He reached over and snapped on the lamp next to the couch and walked to the front door, weaving slightly from fatigue. He looked through the embedded door viewer and was greeted with a fish eye view of his parents staring back at him, smiles on their faces.

He opened the door and stared at his parents.

"Hi Josh," started his mother, "We brought you dinner."

He could see a ceramic dish in his mother's hands, covered with a clean dish towel. Her purse swung underneath the dish. The smell of her famous meatloaf drifted to his nose.

"What's the matter, son? Don't you remember we planned this dinner a week ago?" asked his father as he stepped back to let them in. His mother placed the covered dish on his kitchen counter and flicked on the kitchen light.

Josh was dumbfounded. He had totally forgotten about dinner with his parents and didn't know what to do. He looked down, saw he was only wearing boxers and croaked out a "one minute". He walked back to his small bedroom, rummaged through his lower dresser drawers and returned to the small table positioned in the combination living room and dining room wearing a pair of jean shorts.

His mother had already laid out plates and utensils for the three of them and was dishing out meatloaf onto the plates. Josh could see the white sprinkles of feta cheese on top. It was her meatloaf signature that normally would have him craving for some.

"Beer, Josh?" asked his father from inside the opened refrigerator door.

"Um, sure Dad," said Josh. He sat down at the table almost out of instinct as his parents went through the typical pre dinner duties. They had been to his apartment many times. Both had helped to find the place and decorate it.

He was oddly comforted by their routine and familiarity with his apartment yet felt detached from the scene around him.

Soon they were all seated, frosty beer bottles in front of each plate of steaming meatloaf. He sat there, unable to do anything but watch as his parents began to eat their meals.

"Eat," said his father.

His mother finally looked at Josh closely for the first time since entering his apartment.

"Josh, what's wrong?" she said, a slight frown on her face.

Josh felt his face collapse with emotions. Tears started to stream down his face. He hated to show weakness in front of his father but couldn't help himself.

"Oh, everything. I'm so sorry, I just can't eat..."

"Josh, tell us what's really wrong. What happened?" His father's tone was stern but caring.

"I don't know where to start," sputtered Josh, "Frank's dead."

"Frank? Your friend?" asked his mother.

"Yes. He drowned while we were doing a dive today."

"What? Where were you diving?" asked his father, his tone now more stern than caring. Both parents placed their forks down.

"Wwwe were at Emerald Sink; myself, Jon and Frank. Just diving like normal and then Frank must have panicked and we couldn't reach him in time and..."

"Isn't Emerald Sink a cave? What were you doing in a cave?" His father was almost bellowing now.

"Dad, yes, we were doing a cavern dive. That's the advanced class you gave me the loan for -"

"Even I know cavern diving isn't necessary to become a scuba instructor, Josh. Why did you lie to us about what you really wanted the money for?"

"I...I...I didn't really lie; I just sort of stretched the truth a bit. It WAS a great class and it DID make me a better diver."

"Bill, Josh is in pain and shock. Take it easy on him," offered his mother.

He looked at her. "Jacki, our son lied to us! And now we find out he's involved in a diving fatality! He may be in legal trouble if he caused Frank's death. What am I going to say to Frank's father? He's a long-time customer of mine."

Josh glared at his father, seething with rage. He stood and leaned over the table, shaking.

"I did NOT kill Frank! You don't understand, Dad!"

His father stood in response, faces only a foot apart. His father's face was a mask of anger, held in check.

"Josh, you are in big trouble. This isn't the time to be mad at me and your mom. You'll need our help getting out of this mess."

"Mom and Dad, I love you dearly but right now I don't need your help. Please just leave. Now. Please."

A few seconds passed while father and son faced each other in impasse, mother's hand to her face. Finally his mother shoved back her chair and stood, grabbing her purse.

"Yes, Bill, we should leave now. Let's give Josh time to work this out. If he needs our help he'll reach out to us." She pulled back his chair and led her husband to the door.

Josh stared at his plate as the door to his apartment closed slowly and clicked shut. He took a long look at the three plates of food still steaming; his untouched and his parents' plates of half-eaten food. He put his elbows on the table and buried his face into his hands.

Chapter 43

The next morning he opened the door to *Wakulla Skuba* and was greeted by Bear, the black Chihuahua, who licked his hand profusely when offered. Josh scooped him up in his arms and nuzzled his face into the short soft shiny black fur, enjoying the mild scent of clean canine. Bear wiggled happily in his arms. He tucked Bear into his right arm like a football and walked towards Kathy's office. He still felt out of sorts from yesterday and did not look forward to talking to Kathy about it but knew it had to be done.

Kathy walked out of her office and headed towards the workshop, the smell of freshly-brewed coffee wafting from the mug in her hand. She wore a short sleeve button down loose shirt with a loud Hawaiian print, baggy beige shorts and dark brown flat sandals.

"Hi Josh. How was your weekend?"

She looked at his eyes and stopped. They were in the doorway of the workshop.

"Josh, what happened?"

Josh suddenly felt weak in his knees and plopped down into one of the work stools near the bench built into the wall.

He propped Bear on his lap and gently stroked his fur, drawing a canine calmness from the small dog. Bear looked up anxiously at his face, ears in full alert mode. Kathy pulled up another stool, placing her coffee mug on the bench.

"Jon, Frank and I dove in Emerald Sink yesterday. Frank had some sort of problem and…well, he drowned."

Kathy's eyes widened and her mouth formed an "O".

"Frank drowned? In Emerald?"

He could see that she was shocked and braced himself for the barrage of questions that he knew would follow. He wasn't sure how well he could hold up under her scrutiny, no matter how much he trusted and respected her.

He opened his mouth to respond and was suddenly overwhelmed by a strong sense of loss, despair and guilt. He looked down, ashamed, and tried to discreetly staunch the tears that had sprung from the sides of his eyes. Bear licked the salty solution off of his hand as he made multiple swipes.

Kathy stood, reached over and pulled him into a hug as Bear leaped to the ground and started to lick his ankle. Uncharacteristically she didn't say a word, just held him for a few minutes as he fought the onrush of emotions with loud sniffles and choked grunts of bottled outcries.

She murmured wordlessly, continuing the hug, until he felt the full force of his grief ebb and a tentative feeling of respite from the raw emotions flowed from her into him.

Sensing he was back from the brink she pulled away, patted his shoulder and sat back in her stool.

"OK. Tell me what happened." Her voice was very calm and quiet.

Josh took a deep wobbly breath and scooped Bear back into his lap before settling back on his stool. Bear, his ears partially bent down, resumed licking his hand in a successful attempt to calm him even further. He absentmindedly rubbed between the small dog's ears with his other hand.

As with Drew the night before he told the story as one diver to another. He found his mind wanted to regroove the events to help find meaning in Frank's death, even if it had yet to be found. Retelling the story, with occasional prompts from Kathy, soothed the open raw sore of his loss.

"So you are pretty sure it wasn't a result of the Nitrox mix?" she asked, eyebrows furrowed.

Josh nodded.

"One moment."

Kathy walked briskly out of the shop. He heard the back screen door rattle closed twice as she exited and returned to the inside of the shop, a minute gap between the sounds. She walked in with the oxygen analyzer they kept next to the fill station and held it out. The analyzer was a small grey box with a knob, a switch, a small LCD screen and a wire that connected the side of the box to a small cylinder embedded into the side of a six inch hollow plastic tube.

Josh knew the embedded cylinder contained the actual oxygen sensor that "read" the oxygen level in any gas supply fed into the tube.

One of his duties was to regularly test the internal battery inside the grey box, check the expiration date on the oxygen sensor and calibrate the device.

"Is this the one you and Frank used?"

Josh nodded again. Kathy turned on the analyzer and inspected the display. She placed the tube next to a scuba tank sitting by the work table and carefully turned on the tank valve, allowing a small amount of gas to escape. Bear perked up at the sound and watched the tank but did not flee. She stuck one end of the tube over the tank valve and watched the reading on the small LCD display. She turned off the tank.

"Well, it's reading 21%, like it should be. I just checked the maintenance log and it's up to date. I also checked the Nitrox fill log and saw the entry for both you and Frank for his two tanks, verifying that they contained Nitrox 34%. Hmm."

She pulled open one of the myriad of plastic drawers mounted on the wall above the work table and pulled out an identical oxygen analyzer. She performed the same ritual of power up, tank turn, tube placement and LCD reading.

"This one reads the same."

She turned off the tank and set down the second analyzer, clearly thinking about her next step.

"I'll call the Sheriff and talk to him about this right away."

She looked at him.

"Josh, are you OK to work?"

He nodded a third time and managed a weak smile.

"OK, then go ahead and open the shop for business. We have an open water class later this week and I expect folks to wander in throughout the day looking to buy snorkeling gear and pick up their scuba equipment for the pool. Think you can manage that?"

"Yes," he croaked. He cleared his throat.

"OK."

Kathy stowed the second analyzer back in the plastic drawer, stood, gave him a tight smile and squeezed his shoulder.

"Don't worry, Josh. I know this is a tragedy but we'll figure out what happened. I'll help you get through this." She strode back towards her office.

Josh placed Bear back on the ground and snatched up the first oxygen analyzer. He walked back to the fill station on the porch, Bear trotting alongside him and placed it back in its sealed plastic box.

He opened up the green plastic cover notebook stored underneath the analyzer box and thumbed to the middle, where the filled-out Nitrox forms ended and the blanks began.

He ran his fingers over the sections completed by himself and Frank, confirming the mix. 34%.

He paused gently over Frank's signature, a blend of bold strokes and oversized flourishes, remembering the excitement they had shared as they prepared to do their first cavern dive after passing the class. Frank had seemed so confident and positive about the dives.

No way he panicked, Josh thought for the umpteenth time.

On his way back through the central hallway of the store, he noticed Kathy's office door was closed and could hear her side of a conversation, too low in volume to pick out words.

A dark part of him wondered if Kathy was in cahoots with the Sheriff to pin Frank's death on him and distance any liability from herself or *Wakulla Skuba*.

Bear nudged his ankle and he shook the thought from his head, continuing towards the front of the shop.

Kathy burst out of her office, a mixture of triumph and excitement on her face.

"Josh. I just got off the phone with Officer McDonald. They know how Frank died."

Josh stopped, his heart beating faster. Was he about to be arrested? Fired for killing a customer?

Kathy grabbed his arm, her face inches from his. He felt a momentary pang of fear and started to pull back.

"He choked to death. He had a laryngospasm as a result of a foreign object, which would have been serious but survivable if he'd been on the surface."

Josh slumped, relief coupled with shock flooding him. A small part of him realized Kathy had grabbed him for support, anticipating his reaction. He was grateful.

"Oh my God!" he managed to get out. Bear uttered a rare bark and ran to the door, misreading the emotional state of his humans.

"Yes, Josh, he died from inhaling a small object that got stuck in his throat. It wasn't your fault. It wasn't Jon's fault. There really was nothing you could have done. You couldn't have anticipated such an event."

"What was the object?"

"Apparently some small piece of plastic. They're not sure how it got in his mouth, though."

A thought struck Josh, hard. He sucked in a large breath and pulled away from Kathy, running towards the front door.

"Josh, wait! It's OK! You're not at fault!"

He pushed open the front door, bolted down the stairs and reached the back of his truck. He grabbed the worn army surplus canvas bag stored in his truck bed and raced back to the shop, meeting Kathy at the door.

"Follow me."

Kathy followed as he half walked; half ran back to the workshop. He pushed aside a half-assembled customer regulator sitting on the work bench and dumped the contents of the green bag onto the surface. Kathy sat on a stool; Bear perched on her lap, watching intently.

"Look. Allen gave me these along with the doubles. *BreathMaster 250s*. Same as Frank!"

Josh held up the regulators as if they were deadly water moccasins freshly scooped from the Wakulla River. He grabbed one of the shiny silver chrome plated second stages.

He looked up at the wall and selected a small screwdriver from the sorted set arranged by size in tiny metal loops mounted onto the peg board. A quick twist and the outer casing of the second stage fell off, revealing the internal parts of the second stage. He looked closely at the bottom half of the regulator, where the mouthpiece was attached, and saw a small oval piece of black plastic partially covering the air exit port.

"Look, see?" He held up the second stage, parts dangling to Kathy's face. She pulled a set of reading glasses out of her shirt pocket and balanced them on the tip of her nose.

"I noticed that piece of plastic before, when I cleaned the regs after Allen gave them to me. I just figured it was some sort of air disperser that helped making breathing easier. See how it's worn there, where the black plastic has lightened? The plastic must have bent multiple times over the years. It must have finally given way on Frank's, snapped off and he just sucked it in without knowing."

He shuddered at what Frank must have gone through in his last moments. At first a normal breath, just like the thousands he's taken before on scuba, the trusty regulator delivering yet another blast of life sustaining air. But this breath was different; it was his last.

The piece of plastic must have hit his larynx, causing the involuntary spasm that shut down breathing and protected the lungs. He would have tried to inhale deeper and must have been terrified when he couldn't take any more air in. Frank would have fought it, hard, until succumbing to the lack of enough oxygen to keep him awake.

Kathy murmured, "That does agree with the coroner's report, at least as much as Officer McDonald was able to tell me. They found a small piece of worn black plastic lodged in his throat."

"Tell them to check the second stage! See how it's attached?"

Josh pointed with the screwdriver to a small metal pin attached to the side of the regulator that held the plastic valve in place.

"I bet it broke off right there, where the constant flutter of breathing over many dives finally stressed the plastic to the breaking point. There should be a piece of plastic still in the regulator on that pin that matches."

Kathy nodded and picked up the extension phone mounted on the wall next to the door. She dialed a number and after a few transfers was talking again to Officer McDonald.

"Hi. Yes, it's Kathy. There's something I want you to check on

Frank's gear. Do you have it?"

Pause.

"Good. Disassemble the second stage. The outer ring comes off with a small Phillips screwdriver."

Pause.

"Yes, now pull it apart like a scallop."

Pause.

"Look at the part below where the mouthpiece mates into the metal housing. You should see a metal pin with a piece of black plastic on it."

Longer pause.

"Yes, that's it. Does it look torn?"

Short pause.

"OK, does the piece of plastic removed from Frank's throat match it?"

Medium length pause.

Kathy covered the mouthpiece of the phone.

"He has to get it from the evidence file for the case."

The air thrummed with excitement as they waited. Josh opened up the second stage on his second regulator and confirmed that it also had a plastic valve between the mouthpiece and the air exit port. He frowned. This particular plastic valve showed stress lines near the metal pin and wobbled loosely when he touched it.

Geez, I was only a few breaths away from death myself!

"It fits? Are you sure?" Kathy's voice was taut.

"Yes, we actually have more of these regulators in the shop. We're looking at two of them now. They were very popular ten years ago but newer designs that breathed easier and were cheaper to make pretty much took them off the market."

Josh could make out the upward lilt of a question being asked by McDonald.

"No, I'm not aware of any other cases of valve failures with this particular design."

Kathy's eyes grew large and she dropped the phone, her gaze fixed on the half-assembled regulator in his hands. He could hear McDonald's 'hellos?' drifting tinnily from the handset speaker. Bear sniffed the handset as it spun from its cord, slowly wobbling.

"Josh. Oh."

Josh reached out and touched her shoulder.

"Kathy, what?"

"Don't you see? David!"

"What? David who?"

"Delaney! In Mexico! He was diving *BreathMaster 250s!*"

Josh connected the dots in one rapid 'ah ha' moment.

"So you think David died from the same defect? It wasn't bad gas or the incorrect mix?"

"Maybe. We could have analyzed the wrong tank. Or got the reanalysis wrong. Maybe he did breathe the correct mix at that depth."

"Did the autopsy find a piece of plastic in his throat, like Frank?"

"I don't know; the body was handled by Mexican authorities before being released back to the United States. No telling if they even bothered to determine the cause of death. I mean it was clear he drowned. I don't think the family did an autopsy since the cause of death was so obvious, at least at the time."

"So you, Allen and Drew have been estranged all these years for the wrong reasons?"

Kathy looked at Josh.

"How did you know about Drew's involvement in this?"

"We had a conversation once after class. He asked me where I'd gotten those doubles. When I mentioned it was from Allen you'd thought I'd said the Devil gave them to me. He blames you and Allen for David's death."

Kathy sighed.

"Yeah, I know he was upset originally but figured after all this time he'd come to terms with it. Maybe this will help."

Kathy pulled the phone handset up by the coiled cord.

"Sorry; I accidentally dropped the phone."

Slight pause as she listened to the other side of the conversation.

"OK, yes, no problem. We'll bring by the other two regs we have here so you can take a look for yourself. Thank you, Officer. Good bye."

She hung up the handset on the wall mounted cradle.

Josh's head was spinning with the recent discoveries. He thought furiously, making more connections about the faulty regulators.

"I wonder who has David's gear? We should take a look inside his regulators and see if any of them are also missing a piece of that black flap."

Kathy thought momentarily.

"I'm pretty sure that Drew got all of David's gear when it was all over with and we went our separate ways."

She grabbed his regulators and started dumping them back into his worn green canvas bag.

"What are you doing?" asked Josh.

"Let's go to Fort White Cave Diving now and show this to Drew.

It's about time I faced the past head on."

"Can Jon come along too? I know he's suffering and this would help him."

"Of course, give him a call and we can pick him up in Tallahassee if he can get off work."

Chapter 44

An hour later the three of them were traveling eastward on US 27 in Kathy's Cherokee. Kathy was at the wheel, Josh occupied shotgun and Jon sat in the middle of the back seat, leaning forward.

Bear sat on Josh's lap, his pointy ears vibrating from the wind and head jerking back and forth as he tried to focus on fast-moving objects as they passed by. Josh, surprised and pleased at Kathy's insistence, had put up the CLOSED sign on the shop and called Jon.

Jon had been more than happy to leave work and join the journey. He wasn't really at work mentally anyway and probably should have taken the day off. He still had his work clothes on – beige slacks, blue rugby shirt and light brown loafers.

His short black hair stayed still despite the air streaming into the Jeep from the open windows. The midmorning sun struck the vehicle at an angle just above the upper edge of the windshield. The bright blue day held warm still air; the promise of clouds from afternoon thermal buildup still hours away.

Josh and Kathy were bringing Jon up to date on the latest findings surrounding Frank's death.

"So the regulator killed him?" asked Jon incredulously.

Josh looked back at his friend and answered, "Yes, a small piece of his reg must have broken off while he was at depth and he basically choked on it. He was breathing the same types of regs as I got from Allen. Take a look in my reg bag. Be careful, though, they are still in pieces."

Jon pulled the dingy green bag on his lap, unzipped the opening and rummaged around. He carefully pulled out one of the partially disassembled second stages and held it up. Josh pointed to the black plastic flap exposed between the clam shells of the regulator.

"See there? That piece of black plastic is designed to be between the air source and the mouthpiece. It looks like it normally acts like some sort of device to spread out the air more evenly across the entrance to the mouthpiece. They say that the one in Frank's reg is broken and the piece that is missing was found lodged in his throat."

Jon whistled.

"Gee, Josh, that's horrible. He must have really suffered."

Josh grimaced, looking into Jon's eyes and seeing the pain of the shared experience.

"Yes, he must have. But at least we now know it was just an accident, a terrible unfortunate accident."

Kathy leaned to her right, her eyes still on the road and spoke.

"Not only that but if we are right this could bring peace to some folks that have been grieving over another death that might be attributed to this defect."

"Not to mention anybody else who may still have these regs and might not know," said Josh, "Like me, for example."

Josh could see Jon's eyes widen as he realized that Josh had been breathing the very same regs through the class and during the same tragic dive.

"Damn."

Two hours later, after a brief lunch at a fast food joint in Branford, they pulled into the parking lot of FWCD. Josh looked over at Kathy, wondering what was going through her mind.

He figured she had to be somewhat nervous being here. Outwardly she looked calm as she parked the Jeep in front of the classroom building and switched off the ignition.

To their left at the drive up fill station two trucks were parked with their fronts pointing outward, their truck beds open. Fill whips of high pressure air snaked from the complex maze of gauges and dials and connected into tanks sitting in the backs of the trucks.

A lone attendant, a skinny thirty-something scruffy man in flip flops, dirty yellow bathing suit and a bright green tank top with the FWCD logo rotated one of the knobs controlling the air flow as he looked back at Josh. The cloying humidity and heat of late summer dampened the hiss of air from the fill whips.

Josh could barely make out the soft liquid sound of the river as it drifted past behind the buildings. In the distance the sound of a small gas powered boat motor faded through the line of trees along the river bank as the unseen vessel moved farther away.

"This place has really grown since I was here last. Used to be just that first building over on the far left," said Kathy as she unbuckled her seat belt. Bear's eyes sparkled as he realized he'd soon be released from the vehicle.

"Drew could be in the dive shop, classroom or even in his trailer," mentioned Josh, motioning to his right towards the white and green-trimmed trailer marked "Private Residence" in the ubiquitous yellow-on-green sign design.

"Let's try the classroom. Jon, grab the reg bag please."

They emptied out of the Jeep Cherokee in unison, Bear jumping to the ground alongside Kathy, and began to walk towards the classroom entrance when a loud southern accent stopped them.

"Well, I'll be damned! Is that you, Kathy?"

The trio turned and Josh looked down to see Allen in his wheelchair, dressed in the usual uniform - grubby oversized t-shirt, grey shorts and dark sandals. His hair looked longer and more unkempt than before.

Kathy walked over to Allen, leaned over and gave him a hug.

"Allen! I haven't seen you since…, well, for quite a long time."

"Since David's funeral. I know, a long time," noted Allen. Josh noticed both of their voices had acquired a wistful tone.

Kathy pulled back up, a sad smile on her face.

"Yes, that was the last time we saw each other."

Bear jumped up into Allen's lap and curled up as if Allen was his long-lost owner. Allen grinned and stroked Bear's back.

Josh could sense a friendship reawakening that had been put on hold years ago. Neither had bothered to reach out to the other after all this time, despite being inseparable before their trip to Mexico. It must have been too painful.

"So, what brings you and your diving protégés to cave country?" asked Allen, leaning back in his wheelchair to look up at them.

"We're here to talk to Drew," Josh interjected before Kathy could reply. He sensed that she was a bit off kilter from seeing Allen.

"Yes, Josh is right," Kathy said, "I think you should come with us, too."

"Why? I try to avoid Drew as much as possible. I only hang out here because I figure I have as much of a right to be here as he or anybody else," said Allen. He looked up at Josh.

"Besides, now and then I meet somebody who reminds me of why I fell in love with cave diving. Josh, you taking good care of that gear I gave you? Diving the hell out of it, I hope."

Josh shifted his weight from one leg to the other.

"Um, well, sort of…"

It was Kathy's turn to move the conversation forward.

"Just come with us. I know you and Drew are like oil and water but you are going to want to hear this."

Allen nodded, a mischievous smile on his face. Josh sensed both were happy to see the other after so many years. He rubbed between Bear's ears.

"Fine. I think he's in the classroom."

The four of them walked over to the door of the classroom, temporary awkward silence falling over the group. Next door, a quick hiss announced the end of a tank being filled as the attendant disconnected the fill whip and coiled it up.

They reached the door of the classroom and opened it. Josh noticed that Allen frowned and looked down at the threshold, which was too steep to traverse in a wheelchair.

"Yep; that's Drew. The ADA hasn't quite reached everywhere in the US yet. I think he hasn't bothered to make his buildings ADA compliant just to piss me off," muttered Allen.

"We gotcha," said Josh, motioning to Jon to get behind Allen. Kathy held open the door as Josh and Jon, grunting, lifted up Allen's wheelchair from the front and back and wrestled it through the door. Bear, still in Allen's lap, shook as the cold air from the classroom poured over the group. Finally Jon closed the door behind them.

At the front of the classroom Drew was lecturing intently, his back turned as he drew a diagram on the white board with a dry erase marker. He was dressed in jean shorts and his usual FWCD green polo shirt. At the front table sat two young men watching the diagramming intently. Josh could make out Drew's lecture.

"So, let's say this is the main line. If we want to jump off the main line into this side passage then here's where we place our jump reel."

Drew X'd a location on the map and turned to his students. His eyes flicked up to the group at the back of the classroom and he dropped the marker.

"What is going on? What the hell are you doing here?"

The two students heads swiveled towards the back of the class. Kathy took a step towards Drew.

"Drew, it's Kathy. We need to talk to you. Now."

Josh could see Drew getting angrier by the second. The atmosphere felt electric; as if all of the humidity from outside had been compressed and pumped into the room via giant fill whips.

"How dare you interrupt my class? Leave now!"

"No," Kathy's tone sharpened, "We need to talk about David. Now. It's important."

Drew scooped up the dropped marker and slammed it on the front table, startling his students.

"Damn it to hell!"

The four approached the front of the class, Allen wheeling in the front. Bear growled softly and Allen hushed him with a gentle stroke.

Drew had recomposed himself slightly by the time they reached the front table.

"Sorry for the rude interruption guys. Take a break; it's lunchtime anyway. See you in, oh, two hours. You can leave your stuff here."

The two students stood and shuffled past Josh and his group, clearly anxious to get away. They all stood there, as if in a tableau, until the back door softly snicked closed.

Kathy pulled one of the chairs away from the table and motioned to the remaining empty chairs.

"Everybody sit."

She, Josh and Jon sat down in the seats and Allen wheeled up to the empty spot at the end. Drew stood, arms crossed and expression fixed in tight anger. He glared at Kathy.

"OK, so why are you here? Come to apologize for killing David? Bit late for that."

"We didn't kill David, you asshole," retorted Allen. Bear jumped off his lap and hid under the table.

"Well, it was never proven but I am certain of it. Why else would you hide in Tallahassee like Kathy or waste away like you, Allen?"

Allen placed both hands on the sides of his wheelchair and struggled to lift himself out of it. Drew started towards Allen, the threat of violence building.

Kathy pushed Allen back into his wheelchair.

"STOP!"

Both looked at her, Allen's chest heaving from the sudden exertion and Drew's face flushed with anger.

"Just. Sit. Down. Both of you. Hear me out!"

Allen and Drew looked at her, glaring, and each slowly settled back, Allen in his chair and Drew on the edge of the table.

"Listen to us. This is important," Kathy began.

"Drew, you know Frank died this weekend, right?"

Drew nodded. Allen's eyebrows shot up.

"What? Who?"

Josh answered, "Allen, Frank was one of my dive buddies that I was taking the cavern class with. Him and Jon here," he motioned to Jon who gave Allen a flat smile and a nod.

Heck of a way to get introduced, thought Josh.

"We went diving last weekend in a cavern near Tallahassee and Frank died during the dive," Josh explained. It still hurt to tell the facts of the story.

"What's this have to do with bringing Kathy and Allen here, dredging up all those old memories? You and I talked on the phone, Josh, and pretty much decided he must have panicked, right?" demanded Drew.

Kathy picked up the thread.

"No, he didn't panic, at least not initially. We know what killed him. Jon, show them the regulators."

Jon slid the army surplus green canvas bag onto the table and slowly dumped out its contents. Josh took one of the disassembled regs and handed it to Kathy. She held it out to show Allen and Drew, who leaned in to take a closer look.

"This is what killed him. See? Here, behind the mouthpiece in the second stage? That flap, the little piece of black plastic. On this reg it's whole, one piece. On the one that Frank was diving half of its missing. It was found lodged inside Frank's throat," she said.

Josh watched as the two men processed the information. First disbelief, then dawning comprehension followed by realization.

Allen found his voice first, his southern accent thicker with emotion.

"It's my old *BreathMaster 250s*…"

Drew continued, "Must have been a component failure. A design defect." He looked at Allen, all anger forgotten.

"David."

Allen nodded.

"I have his old regs; I'll be right back," said Drew quietly.

Drew exited the classroom via the back door. Josh felt a slight pressure change as the door opened and closed.

Allen picked up the regulator, fingering the plastic flap.

"Damn, Josh, I could have killed you. Geez, I have thousands of dives on these regs."

"Don't worry about it, Allen. You didn't know. Heck, we didn't know otherwise Frank would still be alive," offered Josh, leaning over the table. Bear poked his head out from under the table and looked up at Josh. Josh picked him up and set him in his lap. Bear shook his head rapidly as if to dispel the negative energy in the room and curled up.

"Yeah, David would probably still be alive too, if you guys are right," responded Allen. The conversation paused, almost as if in silent tribute to the two lives lost by a common cause.

The back door opened and Drew brusquely walked back in, carrying a large plastic container. The edges were sealed with strapping tape, peeling and brittle with age.

"Here's all David's regs. I just boxed 'em up and stored them after his funeral. Just wanted to put that business behind me."

He slid his finger along the edge of the box and the tape gave way easily. Flakes of tape material floated to the floor. He looked inside the box and reached, pulling out a tangled set of regulator hoses, first stages and second stages.

Like an aging human corpse the hoses had lost their suppleness and were stiff, cracking slightly as he awkwardly unfolded them, pulling apart the pieces. Eventually he separated out four second stage regulators, all marked with the *BreathMaster 250* etching within the flaking chrome plating. He picked up one of the regulators and looked around for a tool to take it apart.

Allen reached down into one of the side pockets of his wheelchair and pulled out a small Phillips screwdriver. Drew accepted the tool with a quick grateful nod. Josh noticed how both Drew and Allen were focused on the task at hand, their rift set aside, at least temporarily. He noticed the rest of the room watching Drew anxiously, waiting to see what he would find.

Drew took screwdriver to screw, repeatedly until announcing, "Damn thing's rusted shut."

"Here," said Allen, holding out a small can of Liquid Wrench. Drew gave him a questioning glance.

"I have lots of things tucked away in my side pockets. Being disabled does have some advantages," explained Allen with a crooked smile.

Drew raised an eyebrow and squirted the stubborn screw, waiting a few seconds and tried the screwdriver again. The screw gave way with a tiny screech. He pried apart the two halves and looked at the black plastic tab behind the mouthpiece.

He frowned, shook his head and turned the insides so the rest could get a view. Josh could see a whole plastic tab attached to the metal pin.

Drew continued disassembling regs with a squirt and a grunt and on the third one he cried out, "Ah ha!"

This time Josh could see only one half of the plastic tab. A jagged whitened edge indicated where the other half had been attached and had come loose due to plastic stress. He rummaged through the pieces of his regs and held up the second stage that had the badly-worn plastic tab that looked about to break and held it up for the others to see. The stress line on his complete tab matched the break line on David's reg.

"Well, ain't that something," drawled Allen, looking back and forth between the two opened regs.

Allen continued, "I'm pretty sure this is one of David's regs. See the 'DD' scrawled on the side?"

Josh looked, noted the location and turned his reg to find its owner's initials. The letters 'AW' were hand etched in the same place on both his regs.

"What's your initials, Allen?"

"AW – Allen Walborsky. We had so much gear on that trip we thought it best to label our own stuff."

Jon looked at Kathy and asked, "Did you dive those regs too,

Kathy?"

She looked up at Jon and answered, "No, these were considered the top of the line back in those days. I couldn't afford them. I dove a different brand. Sold them years ago."

Drew cracked open the fourth and final reg to discover an intact but about to split plastic tab beneath its mouthpiece port.

"I'd say that's pretty much a smoking gun," Drew admitted slowly. He slumped down, the need to be angry drained away. He looked back and forth to Allen and Kathy, his face sagging with emotions.

"I owe you two an apology. I've spent all these years blaming you for David's death when all along it was a piece of faulty gear, a fluke event."

Josh could see moisture on the edges of Drew's eyes. Kathy walked around the table and gave Drew a huge hug.

"It's OK, Drew, it's OK...we've all felt guilty about David's death. We've all hidden away from the pain in one way or another," she murmured. She pulled away and smiled, tears streaming down both their faces. Even Allen's face looked a bit puffier than usual as he tried to bottle in his emotions. Kathy reached over and grabbed his hand, squeezing it gently.

Allen's voice quavered, "I'm sorry too. Drew, for holding such a long grudge and Kathy for ignoring you all these years."

Drew squeezed Allen's shoulder in a reassuring gesture and for the first time in years they all smiled at the same time and place.

"What do we do about these regulators?" Josh asked quietly. It was satisfying to watch friendship reunited after many years of being split but the pain of losing Frank and his own team's angst was still fresh and raw. He wasn't ready to smile.

Drew wiped the sides of his face with his hand, pulled a chair around his side of the table and sat. Kathy returned to her seat as well.

"He's right. We need to get the word out about these regulators so nobody else has to die," drawled Allen.

"I have a former diving student who's a lawyer," commented Drew, "We should preserve all of this evidence, tell him about these incidents and see if there's a case to be made against the equipment manufacturer. We must make them pay for their bad design."

A flicker of anger returned to his voice. Josh felt his own touch of anger as he absorbed Drew's words. He hadn't thought that far ahead. Sure they needed to prevent any future deaths but suing for money? Part of him wanted the pain and constant reminders of Frank's death to go away but a larger part of him wanted revenge and restitution. Heck, his parents could be the ones fighting for him if he'd been the one that had sucked in one of those dangerous pieces of plastic at depth.

"Yes," said Kathy, her ringing tone picking up the note of justice, "We do need to get Josh's regs, Frank's regs if his parents will allow it and of course David's regs. Do you know of anybody else who has these regs?"

Drew thought a moment.

"Yes, I think I've seen a few others in the shop for servicing, mostly old-timers who see no reason to buy newer regs. I can go through the service records and contact them right away to tell them to stop diving them and see if they want in on the lawsuit."

Allen blanched.

"Yeah, in fact I'm one of those old-timers. My side mount bottles are rigged with *BreathMaster 250s* as well."

The group paused for a moment, thinking of yet another near miss.

"Well, then, let's get all of this equipment together, write up a statement of our experience with them and our belief that they are dangerous and see if your legal friend thinks there's enough for a case," said Kathy.

"We should get him to contact the company, too. They are still in business and need to issue an immediate recall," Drew offered. He looked at Allen.

"Allen, I'll loan you some brand new regs from a different company so you can keep diving. No cost; it's the least I can do."

Allen cracked a large crooked smile.

"Thanks, Drew, I'd like that."

"And Josh, you can borrow anything from the shop so you can continue your cavern diving as well," said Kathy, patting Josh on the shoulder.

"But I thought you didn't like me cavern diving," blurted Josh.

Kathy laughed, a sweet girlish tone.

"Yes, it's true; I wasn't thrilled with the decision you guys made to pursue overhead training. My mind was still clouded with the loss of David and the feeling that no matter how hard we trained he still died. I purposely turned my back to cave diving since I blamed it on David's death. Now, though, we know what killed him and Frank. I don't blame the environment. I blame that particular piece of gear."

She looked back and forth to Josh and Jon.

"Only you guys can decide whether or not you want to continue to dive. I know; heck, we ALL know what it's like to lose a buddy."

Drew and Allen nodded.

"So you learn from it, you deal with the loss, you somehow find a way to go on with your life. All three of us didn't quit diving totally. Drew is now one of the most respected cave instructors in the area. I'm making a living off of diving and even Allen has found a way to keep diving. Whatever you do, know that the three of us understand your loss and the impact it has on you and your future."

She reached up and grabbed Allen and Drew's hands.

"Whether you decide to dive again or not, we'll support you."

The three of them looked at Josh and Jon with a round of supportive nods and small smiles. Kathy dropped her hands back to the table.

Josh felt a lump in his throat. Now it was his turn to wrestle with emotional turmoil. He looked at Jon and could see the same whirl of conflicting thoughts on his face.

He nodded at Jon, who nodded back. He still didn't know whether or not he wanted to go diving anymore, much less cavern diving but felt grateful for Jon, Kathy and her rediscovered friends.

"Well, there. We have a plan," Drew said. He turned to Allen.

"So, this side mount thing? I've heard rumors that you've been developing some way to keep diving despite your disability. Tell me more about it."

Allen reached into his side pocket again.

"I'll do you one better. I've been working on coming up with a standard way to configure equipment for side mounting and even have a recommended curriculum I've been toying with to teach side mounting. I think side mounting can be mastered by any cave diver, not just those who can't handle the weight of double tanks. Haven't shown it to anybody until now."

He handed over a thick plastic covered notebook to Drew, who proceeded to thumb through the material. Josh caught glimpses of hand drawn diagrams of gear layout interspersed with typewritten pages of outlines and paragraphs.

Drew looked back at Allen, eyebrows raised.

"Wow, you have been busy. This is amazing work. Side mounting may become the next big thing in cave diving. Looks like there's an opportunity to design and sell new gear, too. I'm honored that you chose me to share this with."

Allen smiled.

"Well, with my brains and your teaching skills I think we can do great things with this."

"You know, I've been thinking," started Kathy, "There's lots of caverns and caves in the Tallahassee region but no real cave diving shop or training nearby. I'd like your help to get me back into cave diving, work my way towards the instructor rating and start carrying cave diving gear at *Wakulla Skuba*."

Drew spoke in a good natured tone, "You trying to steal my students?"

She grinned.

"I'd be honored to reintroduce you back to cave diving and help you get your cave instructor rating. I have contacts with the cave diving equipment companies and can help you get started there, too. We need strong advocates in all areas of the state that have caves to prevent deaths and protect the caves."

"Deal."

Kathy and Drew shook hands while Allen smiled triumphantly.

"Hey, lunch is on me!" said Drew.

Chapter 45

Josh stood with Jon, watching the line of cars wind their way into the cemetery. He scratched underneath the collar of his white dress shirt and loosened the dark blue tie that matched his dark blue suit. He wiggled his toes in the cramped-feeling shiny black oxford dress shoes. He felt awkward and uncomfortable with so many clothes on, unlike his normal work attire of flip flops, bathing suit and t-shirt.

Jon's clothes looked crisper. He wore his smartly pressed brown outfit – brown shoes, brown pants, white shirt, brown coat and dark brown tie with ease. His color scheme blended well with this dark hair and complexion.

The Oakview Cemetery, north of Tallahassee, sat on gently rolling hills of carefully maintained grass with old growth live oak trees gracing the eternal rest of its occupants. Spanish moss draped in the branches of the large oak trees, swaying gently in the morning breeze. The sun flickered between the oak tree branches and the summer day promised to turn hot, bright and humid. Josh could feel trickles of sweat building between his shoulder blades.

In front of them stood a crowd of darkly-dressed people that surrounded a green-tinted canvas funeral tent on top of a brighter green fake plastic grass carpet placed in front of the burial plot. The name of the funeral home was stitched in white across the edge of the tent covering. Josh always thought that was an odd way to advertise.

Above the rectangular hole the casket containing Frank was held above ground by the casket lowering device, decorated in black heavy drapes. Just outside the tent a podium held a funeral guest book with a slow moving well-dressed line of mourners waiting their turn in the warm summer air.

"I haven't seen Frank's parents in months," said Jon quietly, leaning towards Josh.

"Yeah, me neither. I just didn't have the heart to go to the viewing at the funeral home," Josh replied in an equally quiet voice, "Still not sure how his family feels about us."

He thought momentarily about his own parents and felt a pang of remorse. He hadn't contacted him since kicking them out of his apartment the day of Frank's death and they hadn't reached out to him.

"They may blame us for his death. Didn't somebody talk to them about the actual cause?"

"Kathy said that Drew's lawyer had contacted both the Sheriff's office holding Frank's gear and his parents. They agreed to be a part of the lawsuit and allowed his gear to be picked up for testing, along with your regs."

"Well, that's good. I hope it helps them, somewhat. So, what about you, Josh? Think you'll ever go diving again? Even in a cavern?"

Josh paused a moment, watching the crowd grow around Frank's casket.

"You know, I'm just not sure. Sometimes I feel the familiar urge to go diving but then I think about all that happened and I just deflate and the feeling goes away."

"Yeah, that's sort of how it is for me, too. I think I just need more time to figure things out."

Jon looked away momentarily as they both reflected on thoughts of ever diving again.

"Hey, isn't that your parents?" said Jon, pointing to his left. Sure enough, Josh could see his parents walking stately towards the funeral. His mother looked elegant yet somber in her full length grey dress with a black lightweight sweater.

His father looked every inch the respectful banker in a black dress suit with white dress shirt and somber dark green tie. He motioned for Jon to stay put and walked towards them.

"Hello Mom and Dad. Glad you could make it out to Frank's funeral. I know his family will appreciate it," he said in greeting.

Josh's father looked straight into his eyes. It was always like looking into a mirror that aged one twenty years in the reflection. His father's face was expressionless and blank with no trace of the animosity of their last meeting.

His mother gave him a hug and said, "It's so good to see you again, Josh. I'm so sorry about Frank. I know you were close." Josh returned the hug gratefully.

"Thanks, Mom. I'm sorry I got mad at you guys."

Josh's father gave him a wry smile.

"No, son, I owe you an apology."

Josh looked at his father questioningly and waited for him to continue.

"We called up Kathy a few days later to find out what really happened. She explained everything, your training, that fateful dive, the faulty regulator," said his father, placing an arm on his shoulder.

"Josh, I'm very proud of you. You have been tested more than many men and have survived. I'm sorry that I got angry at you. I have more respect for your career choice and we'll support you no matter what you do. We love you, son."

Josh felt a sudden lump in his throat. He swallowed it and

managed an "I love you guys, too."

"We'll talk more later, OK, Josh. Dinner Sunday night?" said his mother, beaming with pride for the two most important men in her life.

"Sure, Mom, I'll be there," answered Josh.

His father reached out with his hand and Josh took it, being sure to squeeze early and hard since he knew a strong handshake was his father's style. They smiled at each other and nodded. He watched them walk towards Frank's parents to pay their respects while Jon returned to his side after the private family moment.

Josh looked over at the line of cars parked alongside the black and grey weathered asphalt single lane road. His heart lurched as he watched Elise's garnet Camry pull over and park.

She exited the car and walked slowly towards them dressed in an ankle length short sleeved black dress. She looked stunning, even in this setting, her short black hair done up in Patrick Nagel style, complete with long pointed sideburns and swept up bangs. Jon looked at Elise and back at Josh, gauging his reaction.

"Uh oh...," Jon muttered.

Josh straightened up and held out both hands to Elise as she walked up to them. She placed her hands on his in greeting, face impassive.

"Elise," he said stiffly, leaning forward to kiss her cheek.

"Josh. Jon," she returned the greeting and pecked the side of his cheek, a whiff of her familiar perfume swirling into his nose. She repeated the ritual with Jon.

"I'm surprised to see you two here, considering." Her tone was flat and distant. The three of them looked over at the funeral scene, avoiding each other's eyes. Josh could see that the service was about to start.

"He was our friend," explained Josh, matching the same tone.

"Word is that he died because of faulty equipment."

"Yes," offered Jon, "It was a faulty regulator piece. There's nothing we could have done to save him."

"Well, that sounds convenient. Guess you sleep easier at night."

Josh felt a flare of anger. Jon's eyes squinted with suppressed anger.

"Elise, really? You have to dig at this here? Now?"

"I always knew your cavern diving would turn out bad," she stated.

"You don't understand now and you never will," said Josh tightly, seething, "Let's go, Jon."

They walked towards the funeral tent, staying a few feet ahead of Elise. Josh fumed with anger. How could she so mean at Frank's funeral? Her brother's death must have scarred her deeply to hang onto her anger for so long. Oddly he felt sorry for her and even missed her to some degree. They had broken up, though, and their differences were too great.

Josh and Jon signed the funeral guest book and stood at the back of the crowd as a minister started speaking to the group from a position near the casket.

Josh could see Frank's mother and father next to the minister. It was easy to see where Frank had gotten his features. His father was an older version of Frank – tall, blonde and in still good shape despite middle age. He filled out a smart all-black suit. His wife, also blonde and in good shape, had neither hair nor swipe of makeup out of place to match her expensive black dress. Both wore tired expressions of sadness and grief.

The minister finished his words of comfort and a family member spoke next, retelling fond memories of Frank's childhood. Josh caught movement of a car out of the corner of his eye and saw a white sedan park on the side of the road. Asrid emerged from the driver's side.

She was dressed in a black shiny knee length shift dress with short sleeves and a black cord at her waist. Unlike Elise her short blonde hair was straight, with simple bangs.

He nudged Jon and motioned with his head to Asrid. Jon's eyebrows raised. They both returned their sight towards the next speaker, an old high school chum of Frank's.

Asrid walked up behind the two of them and softly touched Josh's shoulder. He turned, gave her a brief hug and a quick smile. Jon did the same. They respectfully turned their heads back to the proceedings.

"Would anybody else like to say any words about Frank?"

Josh, surprising himself, hesitantly raised his hand and walked up beside the minister. This close to the casket he could see tags and cards on the flower arrangements lining the ground around the burial plot. He noticed Drew's name on a small arrangement almost hidden among larger bouquets.

He nodded to Frank's parents. The father gave a curt nod back but the mother gave no indication that Josh even existed.

Josh paused and began speaking in a clear voice that carried well.

"Frank was one of my closest friends. He was a dive buddy of mine, a person that I trusted my life with under any conditions."

He could see some family members looking at each other and shifting their weight uncomfortably. Clearly they knew who he was and what his part was in Franks' death, at least what they thought it was.

"Frank was always the guy in our group pushing the limits, taking the risks. He was the one prodding us to try the next big thing and he'd good naturedly rib us if we showed any signs of hesitation or weakness."

Josh cleared his throat to cover his nervousness, not really sure where he was going with this but he knew he was speaking from the heart.

"I'll miss Frank and I'll miss his style. We always admired his ability to pick up a new skill and thrive at it, much sooner than any of the rest of us. He was a natural athlete. He was a proud person and rightfully so."

Frank's father nodded with a tight smile of sad pride. His mother touched her husband's arm, face downcast.

"We loved him as a buddy, a friend and a great team diver," he nodded towards Jon and Asrid.

"Frank's death will not go unnoticed. His tragic ending is a beginning for others. His passing will save lives and make the world a safer place. I will sorely miss him pushing me, making me a better and stronger person. I am deeply honored to have known Frank."

Josh stopped and bowed his head towards Frank's casket. He felt a touch on his shoulder and turned to see Frank's mother looking at him, tears streaming down her face. She smiled a tiny quavering smile and mouthed a "thanks". He nodded and walked slowly back to Jon and Asrid. Frank's father hugged his wife as she dabbed delicately at her face.

Later, after the parents had endured an endless line of well wishers in the receiving line the three of them stood next to Frank's grave. The crowd started to thin as people, having paid their respect, slowly drove away.

"Asrid, great to see you," said Josh, "How did you hear about Frank?"

Asrid smiled and responded, "I went by FWCD and talked to Drew. He told me the whole story about Frank so I called Kathy at *Wakulla Skuba* and she said you and Jon were at this service. I drove over from Fort White to say goodbye to Frank."

She looked at the casket still perched on the top of the lowering device. Josh figured they didn't actually lower the casket into the ground until after everybody left, perhaps to not upset the family should something go wrong.

He shivered momentarily at the memory of having to drag Frank's body from the bottom of the sinkhole to the back of his truck and knew he'd seen enough of dead bodies.

"So, this is Asrid?"

Elise's voice cut through the air, breaking the contemplative moment. She walked up to the three of them, hands on hips.

"Asrid, this is Elise...," started Josh, motioning towards his ex-girlfriend.

Asrid held out her hand in greeting, which Elise ignored. She crossed her arms.

"You spent time with *her*? Learning *cavern diving*?"

Asrid withdrew her hand, slightly confused and looked at Josh.

Josh grabbed Elise's elbow and pulled her away from the casket.

"Look, Elise, please don't make a scene, not here, not at Frank's funeral," he spoke in an urgent whisper in her ear.

"Now I can see why you wanted to keep cavern diving. To be with *her*."

"It's not what you think; she's just a dive buddy. Besides, you and I aren't a couple anymore, remember?"

She glared at him, eyes glistening.

"Josh, I loved you. We would still be together if you hadn't continued with cavern diving. You really can't blame me after seeing how beautiful she is," Elise sputtered.

Josh looked back. Jon and Elise were facing Frank's casket, attempting to look like they weren't in the least interested in his conversation with Elise.

"I know you've been insecure about her but I have remained faithful to you, even after you split us up."

"Oh, so now it's my fault. You're the one who strayed, the one who was there when Frank died and I get the blame?"

Josh dropped her elbow and turned, looking her straight in the eye.

"Elise just stop. Now. Frank was my friend. Jon and I were the last ones to see him alive. We tried to save him but couldn't. We thought he had panicked or something but it turned out later on that he died from a piece of faulty scuba gear. You can't blame me, you can't blame Asrid and you can't bring your brother back after all these years or take it out on the people who loved you."

Elise's face turned red, she spun on her heels and marched back to her Camry.

Asrid and Jon walked up to Josh and they all watched as she

drove away, slightly too fast for the sedate speed required by the ambiance of the cemetery. She ended up waiting at the end of a long line of cars as they crept back onto the highway.

"So, that's Elise?" asked Asrid, a crooked smile on her face.

"Yeah, that's her. Sorry you had to witness that. She just has to work through some tough issues. I wish her the best but I can't waste any more emotional energy on her. It's been tough enough dealing with Frank's death."

Josh looked at Jon and Asrid.

"Hey, why don't we go grab a bite to eat and catch up?"

They nodded.

"OK, just follow us back to the *Watering Hole*. It's a bit of a drive from here but Asrid I'd like to show you my little piece of heaven on the Wakulla River," said Josh.

Chapter 46

Two hours later Sue served their lunch at the *Hole*. Kathy had joined them for a late lunch after a tour of the dive shop and *River Art*. Asrid had even picked up a small piece of art, a small framed watercolor of a particularly picturesque bend in the river.

"Something to remember the beauty of North Florida when I go back home," she had explained at the time.

Bear, perched on Kathy's lap, watched intently as Sue placed plates of steaming smoked mullet in front of each of them. The dusky smell of the mullet combined with the fresh fried scent of the hush puppies to start their mouths watering. Plastic glasses of ice tea sweated from the collision of the humid outside air and the cold ice in the glasses.

Sue put the last plate in front of Asrid.

"I'm so sorry to hear about Frank, guys," she offered.

"Thanks," said Josh.

"He'll be missed, that's for sure." Sue frowned, pausing for a moment, and quietly walked away.

"This is a small community," said Asrid, "Everybody knows and supports everybody."

"We like our little piece of the universe," said Kathy, "including the food. Dig in."

They all started in on their lunches. Josh was grateful for the food after a stressful morning. The porch around them was half full of early afternoon diners. The ceiling fans lowered the heat of the day and in the clear water of the river the occasional mullet leaped, as if to see and avoid what fate awaited them on the plates of the diners. The group contented themselves with small talk while they enjoyed their repast.

Sue returned to scoop up their lunch plates and replace them with smaller plates of yellow key lime pie. Josh enjoyed the tart taste of the initial bite of the pie.

"So how was the funeral?" asked Kathy as she forked a piece of pie.

"I haven't been to many funerals so some parts of it were weird. But it was good to see so much support for Frank. I was a bit worried how they'd receive us. Josh said some nice words about Frank that helped, I think," said Jon.

"That's nice, Josh. What did you say?" asked Kathy.

"Oh, nothing really; just that we all missed him." Josh didn't feel his impromptu memorial to Frank carried all that much weight.

"Oh, you did more than that, Josh," said Asrid, "You honored his name and gave his family some hope that his life had meaning."

"Yeah, he sort of mentioned the whole thing about the regulator defect and Frank's death having meaning. I thought it was going to go over like a lead balloon but Josh mentioned it in vague terms, without any details that might upset people," said Jon.

"So, guys, I'm in Florida for another week. I'd love to get in a cavern dive before I fly back to Sweden. Are you interested?"

Astrid looked directly at Josh, an inviting smile on her face. Josh looked at Jon and thought he saw a tentative flicker of interest.

A diminishing part of him felt almost ashamed at wanting to dive again, with Frank's body cooling in the ground. A growing part, though, wanted to return to the thrill and satisfaction of diving. He wanted to use his gear and skills to safely maneuver in a cavern, enjoying the sites and sharing the experience with people he liked and trusted.

He knew if Frank were here he'd insist on going diving as well. His gear was safe now so there was no reason to fear dying as Frank had died. Somehow their crazy journey into the underwater underworld had also brought together Kathy and her dive team after years of estrangement. Even his parents were now supportive of his career choice.

There it was. He wanted to dive again and badly. He wanted not only to be with Jon and Asrid as a member of the team but wanted to dive out of respect to Frank and his memory. Josh's love of the sport need not die with Frank. If anything it inspired him to flourish and continue on, learning how to make it even safer for those few who would inevitably feel the pull of the cavern.

Josh returned Asrid's smile and said, "I know just the place. Let's go dive in Jackson Blue."

Now available:

The sequel to *The Cavern Kings*

Join Josh and his friends as they embark into new diving adventures.

Josh Jensen dreams of becoming a member of the most elite cave diving team in the world. His biggest hurdle is that the head of the team hates his guts and doesn't believe he has what it takes to dive with the best of the best. Josh discovers amazing underwater finds that should ensure his rightful place in cave diving history but his loyalties, loves and bad luck continually get in his way.

Chapter 1 – The Age of *Aquarius*

The cloud of silt enveloped Josh, robbing him of vision and dousing his wrist-mounted light. He calmly swept his right arm along the wall of the underwater cave and felt the thin, strong nylon line catch in his fingers. He formed an 'OK' around the line with his thumb and forefinger, trapping the small string in his grasp. Exhaust from his scuba regulator rumbled across his cheeks and ears as he slowly exhaled. He began to work his way forward on the line.

A few seconds later he felt the hand of his dive buddy, also 'OK'ing the line.

Must be Asrid, he thought. A thrill of excitement shot down his spine. In the total darkness he conjured up a perky image of the petite and beautiful blonde Swedish woman.

He felt her hand touching his, tentative at first and then stronger, more insistent. He could tell something was wrong. Usually a silt out during a cave dive was a minor inconvenience, a justification for always going through all of the trouble of running cave line to the surface. He could tell she was scared of something, but what?

He felt her hand leave the line and follow his arm up to his face. She touched the outer round housing of the regulator in his mouth and quickly pulled it away, leaving him with nothing to breathe. He felt the slight pull of the water near his face and heard a sharp intake of air from the hose that ran next to his right ear. She was breathing heavily on his regulator.

Josh calmly reached his left hand to his neck, felt his backup regulator hanging on a necklace of rubber shock cord and popped the reg in his mouth. Breathing restored, he glided his right hand farther up the line. This time Asrid's touch was firm but stable as she acknowledged him with a squeeze. It felt like a gentle caress. Soon the two of them were moving along slowly in the pitch blackness, the silt cloud stubbornly refusing to evaporate.

...

Thirty minutes later they surfaced in the private blue-green pool surrounded by tall live oak trees. Both removed their regulators and masks, floating gently together in the mild spring current.

Asrid's brilliant blue eyes locked onto his. She drifted closer, the sun painting golden light on the side of her face. He thought she looked stunning, even in the dive hood that reduced her visible face to less than a nun's veil.

"Oh, Josh, you saved my life," Asrid murmured. She floated near, her face only six inches away. Josh leaned over and kissed her gently. The two spun slowly in the center of the spring while dandelion seed heads twirled by, urged onward by the gentle breeze.

Josh closed his eyes and pulled her closer, their kiss deepening. He felt the water dripping from the side of her dive hood splatter on his cheek, tasted the salt…salt?

"Jensen! Wake up!"

Josh awoke from his nap on the boat just as another round of salt water struck his face. He coughed, shook his head and cleared his stinging eyes with a swipe of his forearm. He scrambled up from the boat deck and looked at who had destroyed his dream at the best part. Lachlan Brown hovered over him, a dark ominous outline against the strong offshore sunshine. Lachlan was average height with a grey-brown crew cut, intense grey eyes and a well-tanned body builder's physique wearing only a tight brief-style swimsuit. He held a plastic cup in his hand, ready to splash him again.

"Quit dozing off. Get up, we're here. Time to get to work," Lachan ordered. His tone was harsh, as usual. Josh sighed inwardly and jumped to his feet.

ABOUT THE AUTHOR

Jeff Bauer is a cave diver and scuba instructor living in Tallahassee, Florida with his wife, adult children, and an alarming number of rescued Chihuahuas.

If you enjoyed this book and think others would enjoy it too please consider posting a review or commenting at the following places:

- Amazon.com
- Facebook.com/jeff.t.bauer
- Smashwords.com
- Apple iBookstore

Made in the USA
Charleston, SC
15 February 2014